RIDE OF THE VALKYRIES

Stuart Slade

Dedication

This book is respectfully dedicated to the memory of Marshal of the Royal Air Force Sir Arthur Harris

Acknowledgements

The Ride of the Valkyries could not have been written without the very generous help of a large number of people who contributed their time, input and efforts into confirming the technical details of the story. Some of these generous souls I know personally and we discussed the conduct and probable results of the actions described in this novel in depth. Others I know only via the internet as the collective membership of the History, Politics and Current Affairs Forum yet their communal wisdom and vast store of knowledge, freely contributed, has been truly irreplaceable.

I must also express a particular debt of gratitude to my wife Josefa for without her kind forbearance, patient support and unstintingly generous assistance, this novel would have remained nothing more than a vague idea floating in the back of my mind.

Caveat

The Ride of the Valkyries is a work of fiction, set in an alternate universe. All the characters appearing in this book are fictional and any resemblance to any person, living or dead is purely coincidental. Although some names of historical characters appear, they do not necessarily represent the same people we know in our reality.

Copyright Notice

Contents

Previous Books In This Series
Available From Lulu Press

The Big One	(1947)
Anvil of Necessity	(1948)
The Great Game	(1959)
Crusade	(1965)
Ride of The Valkyries	(1972)

Coming Shortly

Winter Warriors	(1945)

CHAPTER ONE
REVEILLE

Three miles short of Exit 15, Interstate 90, Massachusetts, USA

"What the blazes is going on?" The traffic on the Interstate highway was slowing down. It had been thin before but now it was congealing quickly as the vehicles' red brake lights came on and they started to stop. Up ahead, flashing blue and red lights told of an incident or something. "Damn, I hope nobody's blocked the road with an accident."

"I think you mean you hope nobody's been hurt in an accident."

"Errr, yes." That hadn't been what Colin Dole had meant at all and his wife knew it. "I can see now, there are two state police cars up there, across the road. That's odd, they've blocked both carriageways. Whatever it is must be big. Perhaps a truck's jack-knifed." The traffic had come to a complete stop now, forming up on all three lanes. *Strange*, Dole thought, *the police cars had stopped the traffic just where the road widened out, the two carriageways splitting apart for the long straight run up to the exit ramps*.

"There's somebody coming." Fran Dole had seen a group of men moving through the stopped cars, pausing briefly to speak with the occupants in each. Men in light blue, not the darker uniforms of the State Police. Air Force? A suspicion about what was going on started to form in her mind.

"Sir, Ma'am. Lieutenant Jones, Air Force Police. We have an emergency deployment exercise using this section of highway and it will be closed for the next 45 minutes or so. We have portable comfort stations set up down by the state police cars if you need them. On behalf of Strategic Aerospace Command, I would like to apologize for any inconvenience or delays. Please accept a small gift from SAC in partial compensation." It was a routine speech, learned by heart and recited almost on autopilot. The young lieutenant reached into a bag slung over his shoulder and handed in a small pouch containing a box of mints with the SAC logo on the cover and a few other items, a courtesy pack familiar to anybody who'd traveled on an airliner.

"Sir, which bombers are coming in?" Mikey Dole's voice piped up from the back seat of the car.

"*Sigrun* and *Skalma,* Sir. 100th Bomb Group out of Kozlowski." There was no trace of sarcasm in the officer's use of 'sir' speaking to an eight year old. Training for Air Force Police on this duty was strict; everybody gets treated with courtesy and respect. Especially children.

"I know *Sigrun,* Sir. I have her nose-art card."

Jones smiled. "Well, sir, how would you like this to go with it?" He dug into the bag and brought out a box containing a small die-cast model of a B-70 Valkyrie.

"Ohhhhhh. Thank you Sir."

"Don't think they should give the bombers German names." Dole's voice was grumpy, not least because he had a hunch he knew what was coming as soon as the officer left.

“We don't, sir. The names are the old Norse names for the Valkyries. The 100th names most of its bombers that way. The 35th uses English translations of the same names. The other groups forming up on the B-70s have their own traditions.” Jones smiled, saluted and moved on to the next car to repeat the performance.

“See Colin. An emergency deployment exercise. They announce those in advance on Radio AM-1560. That’s why all those cars were peeling off at the last exit. There must have been a diversion set up. I said we should have listened to the highway news service.” It was as Dole had feared; he was in the doghouse.

“But I wanted to listen to some music.” It sounded even more petulant than the words suggested.

“Well, now you can, undisturbed for 45 minutes. While we get to be late for my mother’s birthday party.” Fran Dole leaned back with the distinct message ‘If you thought you’d be getting some tonight, you’re wrong.’

Colin Dole leaned back in the driving seat. Then, he saw two long streamers of black smoke in his driving mirror and knew that on one point at least his wife was mistaken. He wasn’t going to get to listen to the music undisturbed.

Cockpit, B-70C Sigrun *Final Approach to Emergency Deployment Strip Zebra"*

“Altitude 400 feet, power nominal, all temperatures in safe range. Automated Landing Signal pathway active. We are in the groove, centered for both horizontal and vertical. Outer wing surfaces raised for slow-speed flight. Nose ramp retracted.”

“Flaps, fifteen degrees, lower main and nose wheels. Drop power ten.”

“Elevons down fifteen degrees. Main and nosewheels down and locked. All lights green. Control van confirms elevons down, wheels down, all down, cleared for landing. Still centered on landing path.”

"Electronics Pit. How's the new equipment behaving? Any problems back there?" *Sigrun* had been one of the original B-70As and had all the electronic problems associated with the new aircraft. Problems that had taken almost three years to fix. Finally they'd been sorted out and the new production B-70Bs had worked much better. *Sigrun* had spent three months over at the North American Aviation plant at Palmdale being modified to the new B-70C standard, one that marked some advances even on the B-70B. Perhaps the most important of them was that the B-70C had the full implementation of the Defensive Anti-Missile System.

"No, Seejay. Everything's fine. New gear just hums."

"Stand by. On finals now. Flaps twenty." The traffic parked on the interstate was racing beneath them now and Major C.J O'Seven imagined himself seeing the cars being pushed down as the shock wave from the aircraft hit them. It was the driver's fault, there'd been warnings all morning that the exercise was taking place but some people just never listened. Apparently the National Transportation Board was discussing an emergency message system using lighted signs but that would take years to design and build.

"Speed 225 Seejay. Altitude 350 feet. Still in the groove. *Skalma* twenty seconds behind us reports minor turbulence."

"That'll change when she hits our wake. She's above it now." *Skalma* was Major Daniel Ben's bird, a new-build B-70C.

"220, altitude 300, 750 feet short of touchdown point. Nose up, speed 215, altitude 250. Still in the groove."

"Whoa, *Skalma* reports a hell of a bump back there. Must have hit our wake at last." That was one characteristic of the B-70, its huge size and the close grouping of the six J-93 engines gave it a wake effect that was akin to a solid battering ram. One XB-70 had been lost that way, near Palmdale. An F-104 got too close and the wake flipped it out of control, causing a mid-air collision.

"Speed 190, altitude 100 feet, 250 short of touchdown. Start flapping the wings!" There was a burst of laughter on the flight deck. It was a standing Valkyrie pilot's joke that they flapped the downward-folding outer sections of the wings as the aircraft landed. A surprising number of people believed it.

"Speed 175 altitude.." There was a thump and a squeal as the tires hit the runway. "Zero, distance to touchdown zero. Full reverse thrust on all engines, bang the chutes!." As *Sigrun* raced down the Interstate carriageway, three braking parachutes erupted behind her while the engines roared in reverse thrust. In front of her, the interstate exit flyover appeared to be rising and falling as the nose porpoised up and down. Another B-70 quirk; the cockpit was so far in front of the nosewheel that the movement caused by landing was greatly exaggerated. It made a lot of people ill. "Speed 160, 140, 120. OK guys we're legal, no need to watch for the state troopers."

"That's a relief. Turn around coming up." The flyover was approaching fast. O'Seven could see the two trucks on top, one the flight control van, the other the ALS cabin. The rest of the Emergency Deployment Convoy would be waiting under the bridge. Coming up fast was a large sweeping turn, one that the State Police found very useful for speed traps and emergency service turns. Its real purpose was to allow B-70s - and B-52s before them - to turn around in front of the bridge. That bridge doubled as an emergency shelter in a number of ways, not all of which were public knowledge. It was not for nothing that the full name of this road system was the Curtis E. LeMay Interstate Highway System.

Sigrun turned elegantly onto the taxiway then stopped on the other carriageway, facing the way she had come. There was a dull thump from the rear as the parachutes were dropped off, collected by one of the jeeps. Already six fuel bowsers and two pump trucks were racing out from under the bridge towards her, ready to pour the vital JP-6 fuel into her tanks. O'Seven and his crew felt *Sigrun* lurch as the high-pressure pumps blasted fuel into her. Another truck came up from behind as soon as the blast from her engines had died down and was installing a new set of braking chutes while another part of the same vehicle pumped water into the aft tanks. Two more jeeps roared up under the nose, towing liquid nitrogen trailers that would be hooked up to that part of the aircraft's systems.

There were more whines and thumps as *Sigrun's* bomb bay doors opened so the two big munitions trucks could position their loads in her belly. She could lift 65,000 pounds of weapons in that bay and she was being loaded to the max. Two 550 kiloton nuclear gravity bombs, a battery of AGM-76 anti-radar missiles and the B-70Cs new weapon, the Pyewacket multirole air defense missile. Or, as the less reverential crews called it, the Frisbee. The 100th Bomb Group had spent almost twenty years at Nellis AFB in Nevada before returning to Kozlowski and they still had some west coast ways about them.

More trucks joined the circle surrounding *Sigrun.* The scramble around her only looked like chaos. In fact, this was a well-honed drill to get the bomber airborne again with the minimum possible delay. Twenty minutes to fully arm and fuel the aircraft was the formal target and fifteen earned the ground crews a commendation. Taking twenty five would earn them something that was only mentioned in fearful whispers but was a fate in which the Aleutian Islands featured prominently. Behind *Sigrun*, *Skalma* was sitting on the turn-around, surrounded by her own circle of courtiers, also working frantically.

One last job to be done. A heavily-sealed brown envelope was passed up to the flight deck. The terms of the exercise were that Kozlowski was under nuclear attack and her bombers had dispersed to emergency landing strips like this so they could be armed and fueled then sent to their targets. The crews wouldn't know where they were going until they opened that brown envelope.

"Ready for engine start!" There was another thump from the rear of the aircraft as the Ground Support Equipment Alert Pod was craned into place. That pod could get the whole aircraft's systems up and running in three minutes, according to the manufacturer at any rate. They were right; three minutes later *Sigrun* was running down the Interstate carriageway, her nose lifting as her engines roared. Then, she rotated and was back where she belonged.

"Where we going Seejay?"

"Moscow. Russians have asked us to do a profile mission against the city. They want to see how their new MiG-25s can perform against us. We'll be touching down at Sheremetevo as soon as we've finished. If its anything like our last visit, it should be a real good party."

Three miles short of Exit 15, Interstate 90, Massachusetts, USA

"WHOOOOO, look at them GO!" Mikey's voice was an excited squeak as the two Valkyries swept a thousand feet over their heads, the car shaking with the power of their engines as they climbed skywards.

"Thank heavens for that." His father almost snarled as he reached down to restart the car engine.

"Don't do that Dad. They'll have to move the trucks off the road and clean up any fuel they've spilled. It'll be some time yet."

"Huh? And you know so much about it?" His father scoffed at the advice. "What are you, SAC's advisor?"

There was a tap on the window. "I'd turn your engine off sir. We have to shift the trucks off the road and clean up any fuel and lubricant spills. You don't want that stuff on your tires. Be another 20 minutes at least."

There was a long, hostile silence in the car. Eventually, Fran Dole turned around to speak to her son. "Don't worry Mikey, one day your dad will be as smart as you. If he ever grows up."

Admiral's Quarters, INS Mysore, *First Division, The Flying Squadron, Trincomalee, India.*

She was only ten years old yet already she was obsolescent. It was a depressing realization but the truth was that she'd been built at just the wrong time. Her construction had taken place just before the anti-aircraft missile had changed the whole definition of air defense. *Mysore* had been built with a very heavy battery of Sagarika surface-to-surface missiles but her air defenses were weak.

Originally she'd had just her eight 4.5 inch guns and four 37mm quads. She'd just rejoined the Flying Squadron after a refit that had replaced the 37mms with four quadruple MOG missile launchers and four 35mm BOER guns but that left her still equipped only for point defense. Her successor, the *Karnataka* had already been launched; when she was completed, *Mysore* would go back to the shipyard to lose her heavy quadruple Sagarika launchers and be equipped with classrooms and living accommodation for cadets.

Until then, *Mysore* was the flagship of First Division, The Flying Squadron. Air defense of the squadron was provided by a pair of Project 21 destroyers, the *Ghurka* and the *Ghauri.* The force was rounded out by the three surviving Project 18 class destroyers, *Rana*, *Ranjit* and *Rajput*.

Admiral Kanali Dahm tapped his pencil on those names. Those three made the First Division the fastest of the three that made up the Flying Squadron. The other two divisions each had a trio of the slower Project 19 ships. The catch was that the Project 18 class were structurally suspect, the fourth ship of the class had broken up in a storm shortly after her commissioning. The shipyard management, whose corruption had been responsible for the disaster, had been hanged but a cloud of suspicion still hung over the Project 18s. The truth was, none of the Indian ships were that well built. Quality control was a serious problem, they just weren't as solidly constructed as their Australian or American equivalents.

The Flying Squadron was primarily a surface action group, heavily optimized for anti-ship work with a secondary land-attack mission. In that, they showed the Squadron's descent from the old British battlecruisers, inherited as part of the Imperial Gift. They, like the rest of those ships were long gone now but their heritage was carried on by the new battlecruisers. Dahm had seen the preliminary design of those 27,500 ton monsters; they were already being called the "Splendid Cats". Eventually each division of the Flying Squadron would have one of the new battlecruisers, two cruisers and six destroyers. But, for now, they had one cruiser and five destroyers each. That would have to do.

The Indian Navy had two carriers, old American Essex class ships that were worn out, far past the end of their effective lives and spent more time in the dockyard than out of it. There were new carriers on the drawing boards as well but who knew when they would appear, if they ever did. *Vikrant* and *Viraat* would have to do, deficiencies and weaknesses notwithstanding.

First Division had its orders, to sail for the Paracel Islands. The documents on Admiral Dahm's desk gave a quick background to the problem. The Paracels were one of those areas which everybody seemed to have a claim to. It hadn't mattered too much; for years the only people who had gone there were fishermen and they'd made their own arrangements. The problem was that times had changed. The islands now had strategic value; they were perfectly placed anchorages and fueling stations to cover the South China Sea, a function made necessary by the steady increase of piracy in those waters. They had tactical value, they controlled some of the key shipping routes in the area. Above all, they had economic value; they sat on top of what promised to be some interesting oil and gas reserves while their very existence gave economic sea exploitation rights over a vast area.

Most international legal authorities agreed that the strongest claims to the islands had been held by Vietnam and China with the claims of Cambodia, Indonesia and the Philippines being weaker. However, Vietnam and China had been forcibly conquered by Japan and their rights hadn't, or rather shouldn't, transfer with that conquest. Japan of course disagreed with that opinion and claimed that it had a double-barreled claim to the island that trumped everybody else's. They'd even suggested that the geography of the seabed meant that the Paracel Islands were just the southern extension of the underwater ridge that started with the Pescadores. That was why the Japanese now adamantly referred to the Paracels as the "Southern Pescadores".

Thailand had occupied Cambodia in 1940, but in their case they had the justification that the parts of Cambodia they'd occupied had been Thai territory 30 odd years earlier. A convincing case had been made that the Cambodian claim had devolved to Thailand. India had a weak claim, one based on the use of the Islands as a traditional fishing ground by deep-sea fishermen. Even the most devout Indian nationalists had to admit that was a pretty feeble pretext. Even Australia had a stronger claim than that, one based on Royal Navy exploration of the islands. However, Thailand, the Philippines and Australia had ceded their claims in favor of the Indians; Indonesia hadn't formally ceded its claim but had asked India to act for it. So numbers made up for strength and the consensus was that India had a reasonably supportable claim.

Just to add a final ingredient to the witch's brew, the Caliphate also had a claim to the islands. A very weak one, but enough. One of the stranger parts of maritime history was that the Sultanate of Oman had once been a significant force. Its power had extended to Zanzibar, other parts of the eastern coast of Africa, and portions of the southern Arabian Peninsula; the Omanis had operated a small fleet of ships of the line and a worldwide trading fleet. Oman had been absorbed by the Caliphate almost a decade before but some traces of that heritage remained.

One was an area of the coast called Gwadar. Now the seat of the Omani Government in exile, it was a thorn in the Caliphate's side that the Indian Government twisted with grim relish. The other was that Omani trading ships had used the Paracel Islands as an anchorage and trading post. The Omani Government in exile had ceded its claim to the Paracels to India as well, but the Caliphate had simply stated that they owned the islands and there was no more to be said upon the matter. Anybody who said differently could expect a string of terrorist attacks on their cities.

The Indian Government had decided to resolve the matter. In cases like this, possession was, in the final analysis, ten points of the law. They had decided to set up a weather station and a naval anchorage along with a landing strip and a garrison on the largest of the islands. Two regiments of Indian Army troops would land on the islands and secure them for construction to start. The First Division of the Flying Squadron would provide cover against potential interference.

It was a high risk operation, nobody doubted that. The Indian Government's assessment was that the Chipanese Navy had neither the capability to interfere nor the desire to exert naval force over any distance. Chipan, they said, was totally involved with land operations and the Chipanese Army dominated planning to such an extent that no significant naval operations could be mounted.

Dahm had heard assessments like that before. They all boiled down to one primary assumption. That the other side would cooperate by doing exactly what they were supposed to do. There was only one small, insignificant problem.

They never had.

Defensive Area Simone, French Algeria/Caliphate Border

When somebody discovered they had cancer, they had three courses of action open to them. They could ignore it and hope it would go away, they could scream insults and blame the doctors who'd discovered the condition or they could get surgery to cut out as much as possible and then try to burn out what was left.

General Marcel Bigeard believed France had cancer.

He hadn't realized it when he'd been a youth, growing up "between the wars." The worship of the past, the presumption that past glories guaranteed future power and influence, all seemed so normal, so accepted. That had been his first reaction to the cancer that had been eating away at France's national spirit. He'd ignored it, pretended it wasn't there, disregarded the nagging uncertainty in the back of his mind. He'd hoped that it would go away.

Then, the Second World War had started, the army had been beaten and France lay prostrate. He'd been sent to prison camps where the doubts echoing in the back of his mind had been reinforced by the sound of other prisoners justifying the surrender on the grounds that the 'rosbifs' had collapsed too. He'd been moved from prison camps in Germany to some in Czechoslovakia and there, one day, he'd heard the war was over. Germany had been destroyed; blasted off the map by a vast fleet of huge American bombers. He'd been able to go home after seven years as a prisoner of war.

His first response to France's cancer had ended the day he'd stood in the shattered wreckage of the Champes Elysee, looking at the road plowed to ruins, the destroyed buildings either side and the rubble of the Arc de Triomph at the end. Looking at them with tears streaming down his face and a treacherous wish in his heart that he was still a prisoner so he wouldn't have to look at such things. He'd raged and screamed at the Americans, the vandals, the barbarians who had so contemptuously cut the heart out of Paris. That had been his second response to France's cancer. He'd added his voice to the barrage of contempt and mockery that had poured out of the French establishment, echoed their claims and accusations. Today, he looked back on that time and cringed within himself; for now he knew the truth.

After two years in Paris he'd been sent to join one of the new parachute regiments training in the countryside. That's where his second response had ended. The first night in the mess, he'd repeated the party line about the criminal American acts that had defaced France and insulted its honor. The other officers had all started playing imaginary violins, their voices imitating the sobbing strains of a bitterly ironical 'hearts and flowers.' He'd been mocked; derided as an apologist for all those whose failures had doomed France to humiliation.

When the other officers had torn him down, reduced him to nothing, they'd built him up again. They'd shown him that France's failures were all due to worship of the past, that the memories of France's glories had become a substitute for achievement in the modern world. They'd filled the void in his soul with their own mission, to recreate France, to build a new French Army that took its pride in the achievements of the present. When visitors from one of the traditional cavalry regiments had spoken of their achievements at Austerlitz and Marengo, the paratroopers had chorused "Good. But what did you achieve *today?*" And then burst out into jeers and cat-calls.

They'd won the battle and the French army had been reborn in their image. The complacent, self-satisfied 'poilu,' the conscript who served his term doing as little as possible and then thankfully returned to civilian life had been replaced by the hard-bitten long-term professional 'paras' whose lizard-camouflage uniforms and caps had become the symbols of a different kind of Army. When the poilus had voiced "we are betrayed," their cry of defeat when things went wrong, the paras had replied "So what? We'll win anyway. Or die trying."

The new army had gone to war here, in Algeria. In 1960, Algerian nationalists, the FLN, had started a campaign to eject the French and regain independence. The war was a classic insurgency, combining military action in the countryside with terrorist attacks in Algiers itself. The paras fought them on their own terms in a brutal campaign that answered fire with fire. Only, it wasn't enough for the French settlers. They'd formed their own group, the OAS, to answer terror with terror and a two-cornered war had become a three-cornered one. Bigeard had commanded a regiment in the Battle of Algiers and had made his name there. What sort of name, well, that depended on who one spoke to.

The war had ended in an unexpected way. Throughout the 1960s, the rising power of the Caliphate had washed ever-closer to Algeria. Italy had pulled out of its North African colonies in 1966/67, granting them "independence" and seen them absorbed into the Caliphate shortly afterwards. That had brought the green tide of Caliphate fundamentalism to the borders of Algeria and what had happened next was strictly by the playbook. In 1968, Caliphate agitators had slipped into Algiers and fomented religious riots intended to bring the country into the Caliphate's grasp. It should have been easy, shouldn't it? Algeria was already racked by civil war, it was a plum ripe for the picking wasn't it?

As it had turned out, it wasn't. The FLN had been a creation of French left-bank "intellectualism", nationalist certainly, socialist certainly, Islamic certainly, but in that order. Their leaders, for all their Algerian nationalism had attended French universities and their political outlook had been formed there. They wanted an independent, socialist Algeria, not to become a province in a fundamentalist, feudalist Islamic Empire. They realized that if Algeria fell to the Caliphate, any hope of its independence would be gone forever. The OAS wanted Algeria to remain French of course; that meant fighting off the Caliphate. The FLN realized that their only hope of independence lay in fighting off the Caliphate.

So, the OAS and the FLN had buried their differences and started work burying the Caliphate agitators. The FLN and OAS had been hardened by years fighting against each other; when they combined to turn their guns on the Caliphate's rabble-rousers, the results were terrifying. In the Second Battle of Algiers, riots were answered by car-bombs, arson by murder, incitement to riot by disappearance without trace. The mosques taken over by Caliphate supporters were burned to the ground, frequently with their congregations still inside. The Second Battle of Algiers became known as "the Savage War of Peace" and its atrocities filled European newspapers with tales of horror. It took months and over 150,000 dead but by 1969, the Caliphate offensive in Algiers crumpled and collapsed.

Out in the Algerian countryside, the paras had mounted campaigns of their own. For all their hardness and cynicism, their officers were the intellectuals of the French Army. They read Thai manuals and counter-insurgency doctrines from the Burma and Isaan Campaigns and Australian descriptions of the Mindanao fighting against an enemy very much like the Caliphate. They'd read, with grimly ironic enjoyment, of the way the Viet Minh were running rings around the Chipanese forces in what had once been French Indochina.

Bigeard had moved on from commanding a regiment; he now commanded a full division and was deployed along the Algerian border. Already he had published eight books on military thought and philosophy, two of which had achieved the rather remarkable distinction of heading the best-seller lists. Between defensive blocking operations and offensive sweeps into hostile territory, Bigeard was writing another one. A book that described exactly how the tactics that had spread the Caliphate across the Middle East could be accommodated, countered and then defeated.

Compared to the highly publicized horror of the Savage War of Peace, the paras fought their war in silence and in secret and that was the way they wanted it. When the Caliphate tried to infiltrate the country, their formations were ambushed and sliced up by the paras.

Then the remnants were pursued across the border and harried for days inside their own countryside. Something Bigeard had noted was that the fighting quality of the Caliphate's troops had plummeted as the surviving troops trained by Model's Janissaries were killed off and replaced by barely-educated tribal levies. They had the equipment certainly, Chipanese for the most part, but the skills to use it were rudimentary at best. They were no match for the paras.

Something else had been achieved in the four years since the Caliphate had launched its assault on Algeria. Defeated inside the country by terrorists more skilled and ruthless than their own and defeated on the borders by the paras, the Caliphate's aura of invincibility had gone. It had very publicly vanished.

It wasn't over of course. At best, the civil war would start again once the Caliphate threat had gone, everybody knew that. Even now, victory against the Caliphate wasn't certain. Algeria was small, the Caliphate was huge. What was certain was that Algeria and the paras wouldn't surrender. At the meetings between the FLN, OAS and the para commanders, meetings that everybody denied had ever happened, the toast was to the "Last Man Standing". Algeria might fall to the Caliphate but if it did, it would only be after the last man went down.

"Infiltrators in the wire." The lieutenant spoke as much for his own information as for that of the general who stood behind him. That was another difference between the new paras and the old poilus. In the past, French generals had lived in chateaus far behind the lines, worn immaculately-tailored uniforms and discussed the virtues of rival fine vintage wines. The para generals wore the same baggy lizard-suits as the lowliest private, preferred the rough red wine ration issued to their men and ate the same food. And they lead from the front.

There was a series of coughs as the light mortars went off, then starshells exploded over the section of wire in question. The men struggling with the wire froze, their positions starkly revealed by the glaring white magnesium light. Then, the claymores went off; directional anti-personnel mines that spewed thousands of metal cubes at their targets. The infiltrators in the wire didn't collapse so much as dissolve in the fury of the light and fire. The machine guns in the French defense position started raking them with short vicious staccato bursts. They would be providing cover the for the pursuit group who would harry the enemy. Also, they would collect the weapons from the enemy dead and bring them in, weapons that would find their way to the OAS and FLN. Listening to the machine guns do their deadly work, Bigeard grinned from ear to ear as he recognized the cadence of the bursts.

Brrrp-Brrrp-Brrrp - pause - Brrrp-Brrrp.

Brrrp-Brrrp-Brrrp - pause - Brrrp-Brrrp.

Brrrp-Brrrp-Brrrp - pause - Brrrp-Brrrp.

Al-ge-rie, Fran-cais

Al-ge-rie, Fran-cais

Al-ge-rie, Fran-cais

Main Conference Room, National Security Council Building, Washington D.C.

"Good morning, President Johnson, President-elect Nixon. Welcome to the National Security Council."

"Pleasure to be here, Seer. I'm going to miss the Friday Follies." President-elect Nixon looked confused. "Richard, the Friday Follies are the classified briefing on what is going on in the world, as assembled by the NSC. As National Security Advisor, The Seer presents it personally, with his staff available to provide any additional data required."

"Don't I get to appoint my own NSA? I should have my own people in here."

"The whole purpose of the NSC is to provide an outside, independent viewpoint, one that is free of any perceived institutional bias, if you like. Believe me Richard, when I got this job I thought the same way you did and wanted my own people everywhere. It took time but I learned just how dangerous that is. You end up seeing the world though a very narrow tube. You need to have NSC looking at things with different eyes. Even if you don't agree with what they say, the fact that they say it is valuable in its own right."

"How do I know I can trust them? Same for my 'executive assistant,' Naomi? I'd rather have somebody I know I can trust in that position."

"Mister President-elect, it's Naamah. And you can trust me because I'm paid to be trustworthy. If I held this position because I agreed with you, I could change my mind. Since I'm paid staff, I can't do that; the only thing I can do is resign and this job pays far too well for that. Its the same for NSC, Sir. The organization is paid to be trustworthy."

"Suppose somebody offered you a better deal?"

"Sir, if we reneged on a contract, nobody would ever hire us again. So its in our interest to be loyal to our employers."

Nixon frowned somewhat resentfully. "Very well, I suppose I can live with that. I think." He didn't sound convinced.

Johnson laughed at his demeanor. "Richard, another thing about these contractors is that they tell you things that aren't what you expect to hear. I think you've had an example of that. It gets to be refreshing after a while and, believe me, you'll get to treasure the times they tell you things you don't want to hear. Naamah, I'm really going to miss you."

"And I you, Mister President. Here's your copy of the briefing book. If you could just sign in the usual place. Mister President-elect, please sign here, at the bottom of the front cover. This book is for your eyes only, when you've finished with it, return it to me and I'll bring it back here for filing."

"Gentlemen. You'll be pleased to know the world has been relatively peaceful this week. The major conflicts in progress include continued Triple Alliance activity against Islamic terrorists in Mindanao and more border fighting in Algeria. The Viet Minh insurgency continues to expand in Chipanese Indo-China and Chipanese forces in Tibet continue to run into heavy resistance. South African forces have launched some of what they call punitive raids into the areas to the north of their borders. In South America, we're picking up signs of tension between Argentina and Chile over the Beagle Channel dispute - again. Another potential dispute is in the South China Sea; both India and Chipan claim the Paracel Islands and they are both getting assertive over who actually owns that bit of real estate."

"What is our position on that issue, Seer?" Nixon's voice cut into the flow of the presentation.

"The policy of the present administration, Sir, is that the United States doesn't have a policy on it. The United States doesn't have a claim itself and its a matter of disinterest to the U.S. who occupies those islands. There's reputed to be oil and gas down there but U.S. supplies from domestic drilling and from Siberia are firm and abundant. We're studiously not getting involved and the current administration has decided not to take sides. The position taken by your administration is for you to decide. Now, looking at these hot-spots in more detail …. "

The Seer spoke for almost an hour, running over the various international complications and the issues that threatened the peace. Listening to the fluent presentation, Johnson felt pangs at the knowledge of how few such briefings remained open to him. In a few weeks, he would be out of office and this wealth of insight would be denied to him. "Seer, what are the problems likely to hit the new Administration?" Johnson decided to give Richard Milhous Nixon a helping hand. The Friday Follies were new to him and he didn't know which questions to ask.

The Seer thought for a few moments. "At the moment, French Algeria is the most dangerous situation we face. It shook everybody when the French held on there and even more so when they actually beat off the Caliphate assault. The Caliphate has cultivated an image of invincibility; that all they have to do is start the ball rolling and the rest follows naturally. It isn't true of course, in the early days the Turks slapped them stupid while Caliphate attempts to expand into the Russian southern provinces were a disaster. Since then, they've been picking off the low-hanging fruit; countries that were unstable anyway and likely to fall at a well-placed kick. Egypt was their most difficult target and once that fell, it opened up the Mediterranean littoral. Algeria is a blow to all that. Not just because it didn't fall at the first stroke but because its Moslem population are as anti-Caliphate as the French colonists and military. That's a second stinging blow; its a sign that the Caliphate isn't the unique voice of the Moslem world as it claims.

"The French have held there for four years so far. They've done much better than expected; in fact they've rebuilt their military power much more effectively than we thought. We can take some credit for that. When we took out the Champs Elysee, we intended it as a demonstration of what would happen if the French tried to continue their previous policy of assuming Europe was their own private back yard. We intended to show them that the days of Napoleon were gone.

"In fact, we did that better than we could have possibly hoped. There was a French Marshal, Purneaux his name was, who wrote a book saying exactly that. His thesis was that the bombing of the Champs Elysee had cut the heart out of French memories of glory and, to use his own delightful phrase 'turned a heady stew into packet soup.' He suggested that France could either try to rebuild what was and live forever with packet soup or build a new glory, a new set of traditions that were based on achievement in today's world. That book became the bible of the French military reformers and they've done a pretty good job of applying its lessons.

"So, Algeria is a reproach and an insult to the Caliphate and an example of resistance to the rest of the world. The Caliphate won't tolerate that. They'll try again. Their existing text-book strategy doesn't work so they're going to try and find something new. That might involve us; they've never forgiven us for Yaffo or Gaza or for any other part of that incident. Remember these people bear grudges that date back a thousand years or more. Something that took place seven years ago is like yesterday to them. If they can have a crack at us again and get away with it, they will.

"Any ideas on what they will try?"

"Nothing completely solid but we have picked up a couple of things with SR-71 overflights. The Caliphate has taken delivery of a significant number of Ki-127 Uncle bombers. They're based in Libya and Egypt. They're old, obsolete aircraft."

"Nuclear capable?"

"The older versions are not, the later ones are. We believe these aircraft are not nuclear delivery platforms although we can't exclude the possibility. They're a definite threat, to Italy especially. However, the same overflights picked up something much more worrying, here, and here, both newly-built Caliphate bases in Libya. The aircraft are Ki-115s, Slimes. They're specialized aircraft intended for the delivery of chemical weapons. The Chipanese have sold enough of them around the world as agricultural crop-dusters and, in fairness, a lot of them are used that way. They have tanks in the fuselage and spray gear under the wings so they're useful for that. However, it seems unlikely the Caliphate will be interested in dusting crops. We have to keep an eye on those birds."

"What's the threat to us?"

"Strategically? Mostly Chipanese. The Chipanese Army have long range ballistic missiles that can cover most of the western half of the USA. Their Navy has submarine-launched ballistic and cruise missiles and long-range cruise-missile carrying bombers. Our defenses can cope with an attack with a high degree of confidence. Our estimate is that the Chipanese may get eight or ten warheads through but that's it. That'll hurt us badly; in exchange, they'd be wiped from the map. Totally destroyed. The situation is swinging our way; once the first Manned Orbital Laboratories go up in two years time, we'll get much more and better warning of any attack.

"The Caliphate doesn't really have an ability to hit us at home, not yet. Their attempt to develop nuclear weapons is fairly feeble but we're keeping an eye on it with SR-71 and RB-58 overflights. There are a number of new installations at a selection of places in the Iraq and Iran Satrapies that we don't like the look of."

"Thank you Seer. There are some other issues I want to raise but they can wait. A very interesting presentation." Nixon got up and left, Naamah following behind him. Johnson remained behind.

"There's something worrying you about those Slimes, isn't there?"

The Seer nodded. "I don't like chemical and I don't like bio. Too unpredictable." Johnson nodded and followed the others out. As the door closed, The Seer added quietly to himself. "And I've seen what plague can do."

Top Floor, Bank de Commerce et Industrie, Geneva, Switzerland.

If a visitor was to go purely by appearance, Geneva was probably the most boring city in Europe. There was something about the stolid, dependable, cautious, reliable Swiss mentality that had transferred itself to the buildings they put up. They were unimaginative and dull but there was also absolutely no possibility of them falling down. Most other cities in Northern Europe were rebuilding themselves after the ravages of the Second World War. It had taken time, the war had been followed by the long, desperate poverty of the 1950s and the slow recovery of the 1960s. At last, though, the cities were coming back to life. In doing so, they were building new styles, introducing new concepts of architecture that showed the influence of the Italian architects to the south. But the Swiss had carried on in their time honored tradition, putting up buildings that just looked like those they'd built a century before.

Geneva had changed since its foundation. Then it had been a small village, its only distinction being that it was the first port of safety for the Knights Templar fleeing King Phillipe's efforts to destroy the Order. The survivors of the order had found refuge in Geneva; the Genevoise had sheltered them and then sent them to refuges further into the mountains. In exchange, the Knights had trained the mountaineers in the arts of war, turning a rabble of shepherds into a fighting force that had eventually been feared across Europe. Even The Seer, was impressed by their military achievements Thinking of The Seer, Loki's stomach knotted in anger at the image of the face with the mocking grin that always seemed to be plastered across it.

Because that image reminded Loki of something else. The day that the ground had shaken and thunder rolled across the sky. The day when the horizon in the direction of Germany had erupted with strange red-glowing mushroom clouds. The day of The Big One. So many things angered Loki about that day, most of all that he'd never been told it was coming, that he'd never had a chance to get his people out. He still had agonized memories of the long stream of messages sent out, each one more desperate than the last and none of them ever answered. None, until even Loki had been forced to accept the inevitable and realize all those people were dead.

That wasn't the only thing that irritated him; although it was the only one he'd admit to. Another was how the targeteers and SAC's bombers had got the credit for ending the war and the contributions of others had been forgotten. Especially his, Loki's. How his Red Orchestra had been the most effective spy ring of the Second World War, infiltrating Nazi Germany at the highest level and funneling back political, strategic and technical data. He'd got the details of the Type XXI U-boats out, warnings about the German jets, their new tanks. He'd warned of German plans, of where they'd strike next and how. All forgotten now, overshadowed by the one day in which SAC had destroyed Germany.

"I brought some lunch up Loki." Branwen opened the door with her hip, maneuvered the tray through and put it on Loki's desk. On paper, this was a corporate headquarters, the operating center of one of Switzerland's notoriously secretive transnational banks. In fact, it was nothing of the sort although most of the building was taken up by other banks. That too was a legacy of the Knights Templar. At the peak of their power, they had virtually invented modern banking practices and dominated European finances as a result. Their prominence and the fabulous fortunes they'd made had also been responsible for their downfall. The dangers of having a powerful king deeply indebted to them was a consequence they hadn't foreseen and that misjudgment had caused disaster. Still, the Templars had re-established their banking enterprises in Switzerland and they'd prospered. Most of the Swiss banks could trace their lineage back to the Knights Templar. If they wanted to, which most of them didn't. At least, not in public.

"Thank you Branwen. Oh my, smoked herring. Where did we get that from?" The radioactive pollution from The Big One had destroyed the North Sea and Baltic herring fisheries and turned smoked herring from a working man's staple to a fabulously expensive luxury.

"It's slowly coming back and I thought we deserved a treat. They had some in the gourmet place down the street so I grabbed it before they sold out. Those who were a little slower off the mark will have to make do with smoked salmon. Anything interesting come in this morning?"

Loki thought carefully. Most of his circle, his greatly extended family, was supported by commodity trading, something at which he was very good. Unless, of course, somebody had been making a conscious effort to plunder the market. Once again, Loki's mind knotted with anger. The words 'South Sea Bubble' echoed around his mind, then he forced himself to calm down. No point in spoiling the rare treat of smoked herring. After all, The Seer hadn't meant to nearly ruin him. "Something is worrying me. I've been looking into Swedish chemical and machine tool trading. I fear they're making under the counter deals with the Caliphate. If they're not careful, that could blow up in their faces."

Branwen nodded, her mouth full of herring and salad. After she'd savored it, she drank some of the beer she'd brought up and rotated the information in her mind. "Well, there isn't technically a trade embargo on selling goods to the Caliphate. Nobody tries that sort of thing, everybody knows embargoes are a complete waste of time. Mind you, it could hurt their standing with the Mediterranean Confederation countries. They're the front line where the Caliphate is concerned. They might not be too happy with a country selling stuff to their likely enemies."

"I know, that's what surprises me. I'd have thought there was much more money to be made dealing with Italy and the rest."

"By the way, Loki, we got a message from Washington."

"Oh what does he and his harem want now." Loki's voice was exasperated. Branwen swallowed her irritation, the feud between the Seer and Loki was sometimes hard on their associates. Several of The Seer's circle were friends of hers and she found the gibe about them being part of a harem insulting. The Seer's circle was his extended family, just like the circle here in Geneva was Loki's. And if anybody ran the anarchistic American circle, it was Nefertiti, not The Seer.

"He suggested we make contingency plans about moving out of here in case the Caliphate starts something." She was prevented from going further by the telephone ringing. She picked it up and listened for a moment, a grin spreading over her face. Like most inveterate practical jokers, most of Loki's efforts were a little tiresome; but every so often he came up with a classic. This was one of them. She put a hand over the mouthpiece.

"It's that British farmer. He needs to know, how big do you want him to make the crop circles."

HIJMS Aoba, *Flagship, South China Sea Squadron, Haiphong, Japanese Indochina.*

"Here it is. 'Tsuji is a venomous pimple that is bursting with septic corruption and spreading his purulent waste over the nauseating bed of putrefaction in which he and his running dogs wallow.' That's what the Viet Minh's latest propaganda sheet says."

"The Viet Minh are fools. Haven't they realized by now that flattery will get them nowhere?" Admiral Kurita was careful not to raise his voice too high. He and the Captain of *Aoba* were alone on the Admiral's bridge and the area was routinely swept for listening equipment but who knew whether the people who did the sweeping could be trusted? "Still they're the Army's problem not ours. We have challenges of our own."

Not least of which was keeping the fleet running at all Kurita thought. Once the Japanese Navy had been the pride of the country, arguably the most powerful in the world and it had ruled the Pacific. Those days were long past and the fleet's decline was obvious. The ships were old and wearing out. Every year, more became so decrepit that they couldn't be kept running any longer and would have to be towed off to the scrapyard with no replacements in sight. Only six carriers were left now, all more than twenty years old, some nearer thirty.

The South China Squadron was a good example of how the fleet was being run down. The centerpiece was strong enough, two rocket cruisers, the *Yashima* and the *Asahi* with 32 nuclear tipped long-range anti-ship missiles between them. It was their screen that was old and weak. Two heavy cruisers, *Asama* and *Aoba*, with 15.5 centimeter anti-aircraft guns, eight Kawari class multirole destroyers converted to missile ships and four of the old Type B destroyers.

That was the obvious state of affairs. It took an experienced eye to see what lay below the surface. That experienced eye would see a broader than usual strip of red along the ships' waterlines and know that they were running light. Their fuel tanks were more than half empty and there was precious little in the shore storage tanks to top them off. Chipan faced its standard, traditional problem; lack of oil. There were fields in China, but they were hard to exploit and the oil extraction companies didn't have access to the all-weather deep-drilling technology that had turned the Siberian oilfields into a treasure house. The Indonesian oil and gas reserves were cut off by the Triple Alliance that purchased every drop they produced.

Most of Chipan's oil came from the Middle East, from the Caliphate, and was paid for with military equipment. Another reason why the Navy was short of new ships and new weapons, why it was an aging anachronism. The Army in China got first call on new equipment, fuel, resources, everything it needed. Then, the Caliphate came second. Its demands had to be satisfied if the supply of vital fuel was to remain unrestricted. The Navy came a very poor third. *In fact*, Kurita thought, *if it hadn't been for the cruise- and ballistic missile submarines off America's west coast and the long-range missile-carrying bombers, I doubt if the Japanese Navy would even exist.*

It wasn't as if the Navy was trusted. Not after Soriva had taken *Kawachi* out to Formosa and made it the base of a new state. Not that it ever admitted that it was a new state of course. Chipan claimed that Formosa was a renegade province that had to be reclaimed someday. Formosa claimed that the rest of Chipan was a set of renegade provinces that had to be reclaimed someday. Still, it had been the Navy forces fleeing from the Showa Restoration Coup that had provided Formosa with the initial tranche of weapons needed to maintain its ambiguous position. And, for that, the entire Navy was the subject of grave suspicion.

"We have a mission, Captain. The Squadron is to sortie as soon as preparations are complete."

There was a silence. Neither the Admiral nor the Captain would admit it but the same questions were running through their minds. Just how fit were the ships for sea? They were old, in poor repair. The Type B destroyers were the worst, more than 30 years old, worn out and ready to fall apart. Would the ships be ready for sea? Or would engine failures and other defects cut into the squadron's strength before it even passed through the harbor entrance?

"We are to provide naval cover for a naval landing in the Southern Pescadores. A regiment of the Special Naval Landing Force is to be put ashore on Pattle Island. They will build a forward naval base where we can deploy fast attack craft to control those waters and interdict the naval supply line used by the Viet Minh."

There was a cynical grin from both officers at this point. Everybody knew that the Viet Minh drew its supplies overland, from the Triple Alliance in general and from Thailand in particular. And also that the whole supply operation was controlled through networks centered in the Free City of Saigon. The problem was that the majority of Chipan's hard currency earnings also came from Saigon. If there was trouble over that city, that supply of life-giving dollars and sovereigns would be cut off.

"The SNLF will be transported by an amphibious assault group. They will be accompanied by the seaplane carriers *Mizuho* and *Nisshin*. They will support the landing operations and establish a seaplane fighter base in the Pattle Island Atoll."

That made sense, Kurita thought, the excuse about interdicting Viet Minh supply lines was just that, an excuse. It allowed Chipan to claim it was acting against Viet Minh supplies, established that the Viet Minh were an externally-supplied force and not an internal resistance movement to Chipanese rule but did not move against the sacred cash-cow of Saigon. Much more importantly, the operation would establish Chipanese control over the Southern Pescadores and secure the rich fishing grounds there. Finally, it was believed there was oil under those waters and oil next to a major Chipanese naval base could solve a lot of problems.

"The Indians won't like it, Admiral."

"What can they do? Its a long way from their home waters. They're out of range of land-based air support, even the TSR-2s in Thailand can't cover them. Their carriers are even older and more decrepit than ours and the aircraft they carry are no better than ours. If it came to a fight, they're outgunned and without air cover. But they won't fight. They'll make angry statements and promise violent action but they'll eventually quieten down and accept it. They're scared of us, they remember what happened in '54 and '55 and they'll back down. And if they do decide to fight. . ."

Kurita turned around and looked out of his bridge, across to where the *Yashima* and the *Asahi* lay at anchor. The missile cruisers had been designed as replacements for both aircraft carriers and conventional gun cruisers. Their lack of armor made them relatively simple to build. Their small crews made them economical to run and their nuclear missiles gave them the firepower of a carrier. For one shot anyway. With nuclear weapons, the first shot was the only one that mattered.

The original plan had been to rebuild the Navy around missile cruisers then screen them with missile- and helicopter-carrying destroyers. The design books had been full of new cruisers and destroyers that would revitalize the Navy and give it back the striking power it had once had. It would even have had the ability to strike at the Americans and their aircraft carriers that now ruled the Pacific. But the Showa Restoration Coup had ended those plans. The missile cruiser program had been cut short at eight, two of those had already been lost. The destroyers had never been built. With the ships planned for the future aborted on the drawing boards, the Navy had started its long slide downwards.

Another part of the plan had been that the policing and patrol functions of the fleet were to be carried out by the Hayabusa class of fast attack boats. Gun-armed versions for coastal patrol and maritime security, torpedo boats for attack and missile-armed craft in case they needed to fight against major surface ships. Only the Hayabusas had never been built in the numbers planned. Despite the urgent need for them in Japanese waters, too many had been sold to the Caliphate, Djinns they called them, and the Caliphate had lost all too many in its futile attempts to face the Americans. Lost them stupidly, commiting them to battle without cover and without the support of major fleet units.

Kurita remained impassive, but inwardly he was sighing with despair. So many plans, so much had needed to be done and it had all been left on the shelf. Still, he had to put on a brave face before his junior officers and extol the virtues of the Navy and its missile cruisers. "And if they do fight, we have our missiles. We outrange and outshoot them and, in the final analysis, that's all that matters."

CHAPTER TWO
CALL TO ARMS

Senatorial Administration Building, Washington D.C.

"Tough day darling?" Henry McCarty's voice was concerned. Naamah was looking tired and that was rare enough to be worthy of comment.

"Very. This one's going to be difficult. He spent most of the afternoon complaining about his television coverage. He says the cameramen deliberately chose angles that make him look like a toad."

"Well, he doesn't come over well on television. That's probably why he lost to Johnson in '68. Cameramen can make people appear quite different. Look at some of my early pictures. They can't even print some of those the right way around."

"Yeah, but this is different. It isn't camerawork, its genetics. He really does look like a toad. That's not why he comes over badly though. Its because he isn't smart enough to carry a presence. He's OK when he sticks to his script but he will keep wandering off and trying to fly by himself and he just doesn't have the knowledge to do it. If his IQ was any lower, we'd have to water him."

Henry McCarty had very good reason to know that part of the art of surviving as a gunfighter was to know when trouble was about to break. A good street gunfighter could look at a peaceful town scene and know that an ambush was out there. He could even sense where the gunmen would be hiding and where the danger ground lay. Suddenly, quite without any forewarning, McCarty knew an ambush was coming and he and Naamah were standing right in the middle of the danger zone.

"GET DOWN!" His voice was still booming around the steps as he hurled himself at Naamah, bringing her to the ground and spreading himself over her. One of the Secret Service guards saw what was happening and started to run over, probably thinking that the President's Executive Assistant was being attacked.

He'd barely started to move when a car shot out from the other side of the street, swerving across the road while a tongue of flame erupted from the back window. The burst hosed the steps of the building, bullets screamed off the stone steps, others whined as they ricocheted off the statues or made dull thuds as they hit parked cars. There were other, duller, thuds as well, ones that Henry McCarty recognized all too well.

The Secret Service man drew his pistol when the car started to move but it was too late to be of any use. He'd gone down, the pistol thrown from his hand. It landed only a couple of feet from McCarty and he rolled over to grab it. He fumbled the grab; the pistol was a semi-automatic and he was only familiar with revolvers. By the time he'd got his hand around it, the car was racing away. It was tens of yards and moving fast but he got off his six shots.

Behind him, two more Secret Service men were running down the steps. McCarty swung around; as he did so, the pistol in his hand discharged again, the bullet glanced off the steps and whined away into who knew where. He'd forgotten that semi-automatics held more than six rounds. The sound attracted the Secret Service men. One of them started to head for McCarty; the older man, obviously his senior stopped him and whispered something. The younger man stopped briefly and stared at McCarty wide-eyed, then changed direction, towards where people were down. McCarty followed him, then stopped also. Naamah was still where he had left her, eyes closed, motionless on the ground. His stomach churning, he took the few steps back to her. Then, relief surged through him for one of her eyes had opened.

"My husband always said that when somebody responsible for my safety tells me to lie down, get down and stay down until I get permission to stand up." Naamah grinned impishly. "Works in the bedroom as well."

"Good advice. You're not hit." To McCarty's intense relief, it was a statement, not a question. "It's over, you can get up now." His voice had a tinge of reserve in it; when Naamah mentioned her husband, there was only one person she meant and it wasn't him. Naamah gave his hand a quick squeeze then headed for the casualties. A young man, on his back, surrounded by a splattered pool. Naamah wasted barely a glance on him. He'd only been hit once but the bullet had torn the inside of his thigh and severed the great artery that ran though there. He'd been dead within seconds.

A young couple, the man was bleeding from the shoulder, but he cradled a young woman. For a second Naamah thought her blouse was red but it wasn't. Or, rather, it hadn't been. It had been white before she'd been hit. There were others as well but they were the nearest. She knelt quickly beside them.

"She'd breathing but its bad. Press here, try to stop the bleeding. That's what'll save her." The man put his hands where he was told. The woman had a chance, not a great one but a chance. If she got proper help fast. The man's shoulder was a crease. He'd probably tried to do what McCarty had done for her but hadn't been fast enough or skilled enough. Then Naamah was aware of another man kneeling with them. The young Secret Service man. "Naamah Sammale. Executive Assistant to the President. Help on the way?"

The agent nodded. "Everybody you can imagine."

"Good." Naamah thought for a second. "Get a toxins unit sent over as well. If this was Caliphate, these bullets could be poisoned. Ricin for example." If that was the case, then there was no point in sending medical units at all. Ricin was a killer. "How's your man over there?"

"Dead." The Secret Service man's voice was neutral. It wouldn't matter anyway. Protocol in these things was strict, the Secret Service agents were the last to be treated. Principles first, civilians second, agents last. In the background, sirens started to shaft through the eerie quiet of the scene on the steps. The woman on the steps was going into shock. It would be a near run thing indeed for her, even with normal bullets.

Naamah got up and rejoined McCarty. He was standing, watching the road, his eyes hard and professional. "Henry, I wonder who they were shooting at?"

Cockpit, B-70C Sigrun *Altitude 85,000 feet, approaching Moscow Air Defense Zone*

"This just doesn't feel right. It never does."

"What's the matter *Sigrun*?" Major C.J O'Seven was slightly amused. They'd established a good rapport with *Sigrun* as soon as they'd collected her from the Palmsdale assembly plant four years ago. Some crews never managed it. For some reason, perhaps their own lack of empathy or something beyond human understanding, they'd never made the connection with their aircraft. It had taken weeks with his previous aircraft, *Honey Pot*, he and his crew had fixed her up and repainted her crew compartments but it had still taken time. *Sigrun* had been different. When he and his crew had boarded her for the first time and introduced themselves, she'd replied by the time they'd reached the runway. Her 'voice' had been neutral at first but had quickly picked up a slight Swedish accent.

"Having MiGs attack me. They're my friends, they escort me. As long as they can keep up of course." *Sigrun's* voice had a touch of smug conceit in it; well-deserved because the Valkyrie was the fastest aircraft flying. Just how fast was strictly classified but there were indicators. It had taken them barely two and a half hours to get from the emergency deployment exercise in Maine to the approaches of Moscow, a vast change from the old days when a lumbering B-36 would take the better part of a day to make the same trip. Another indicator had been over the Nevada test range. One of SAC's vaunted SR-71 reconnaissance aircraft had tried to show off to the new bomber. *Sigrun* had used a little less than full throttle and left the Blackbird floundering along in her wake. That wasn't the only difference, even at full speed, *Sigrun* could twist and turn in ways the Blackbird pilots could only dream of.

"It's only an exercise. The Russians want to see how well some of their new equipment works against high-performance targets and we want to give DAMS a work-out. Nothing to worry about, all the weapons have safety offsets."

"No nukes? Nukes make my skin itch." There was a ripple of laughter around the flight deck.

"No, *Sigrun*, no nukes. Not even high explosive. This ride's mostly air-to-air anyway and the Russians don't use nuclear-tipped air-to-airs." That was a big difference between the MiGs and Sukhois flown by the Russian PVO Air Defense Force and the F-108s of SAC and the F-112s of NORAD. The Americans used nuclear-tipped air-to-air missiles, the Russians didn't. Both sides made their arguments, both sides had their points. Each was happy with what they had and each knew the other's equipment well enough to make a judgment.

"Coming up on the Moscow Air Defense Zone now Seejay." The defense systems station, below and behind the main flight deck, was dominated by a large color display. The B-70C was the first aircraft to have full color displays and they were controversial. Some said it made putting too much information on the screen too easy and would overload the operators. Perhaps, but it made the situation displays much clearer. Anyway, with color television rapidly supplanting black-and-white in the civilian world, the extra cost of color had almost vanished.

There was a bright green dot in the center of the tactical display, around it was a huge light green egg. It covered an area 120 miles ahead of *Sigrun* and 40 miles behind her. The ellipse extended 90 miles on either side of her projected flight path. If there was a missile launch detected, *Sigrun* could be anywhere within that ellipse by the time the missile finally climbed to their altitude. That huge area was *Sigrun's* first line of defense, the uncertainty of where she would be at any specific time gravely complicated the task of those trying to intercept her.

Suddenly, the map changed from simple to complex. A series of red circles appeared as the ground target acquisition radars lit up. Captain John Henty, the Defensive Systems Operator, hadn't bothered to plot the long-range surveillance radars. Everybody knew you could see a Valkyrie coming a long way off, the important point was you that there wasn't much you could do about it. That was, of course, a lesson all in itself. *We're coming, you can't stop us so you'd better fold while you still have the chance.*

If the targets didn't get the message and tried to put up a defense, speed and altitude were *Sigrun's* primary defenses; those and her superb electronic warfare suite mated to the Defensive Anti-Missile System. The target acquisition radars were important. It wasn't they were so essential in themselves but they marked the position of the surface-to-air missile batteries. And Russian surface-to-airs, like American, were nuclear-tipped. The red circles marked the space the missiles could reach by the time they'd reached *Sigrun's* altitude. Within each red circle was a bright red line that pointed from the circle's center to *Sigrun's* position. That was the projected course of any missile launched from that site. Measure a line from *Sigrun's* position to the tip of that line and that gave the distance separating the racing aircraft from the explosion as the missile warhead initiated. That was a detail; the truth was that as long as *Sigrun* and *Skalma* stayed out of those circles they were safe.

It wouldn't be hard. The area covered by the red circles was a tiny part of that covered by the green ellipse. If there were no other defenses, the two Valkyries could thread through the missile screen without any great effort. A few wriggles, no more. In a B-52, at a quarter of the B-70s speed and 30,000 feet lower, it was a different story. The green ellipse would have been much smaller and the red circles much larger, the red swallowing the green. There would have been no safe path through, the B-52 would have had to fight her way through the missiles. That meant they needed support; RB-58s to find the defenses and take them down with air-to-surface missiles, F-108s to screen the bombers from enemy fighters. The B-70 didn't need all that, not at the speed and altitudes she could use. That was why Palmdale was turning out every B-70 it could, triple shifts working the factory 24 hours a day,

It wasn't quite as easy as that, of course. Many of the Russian systems were mobile and could shift positions as needed. The problem they faced there was that any missile capable of reaching *Sigrun's* altitude had to be big and heavy; moving those wasn't easy. They required time to take down and set up and that limited the benefits from their mobility. Another complication was that the Russians had developed a datalink system so that the target acquisition radar could be removed from the firing battery. That meant the missiles could fire from an unexpected position.

Sigrun had been equipped to deal with that threat. She carried a thermal imager that could pick up the flare of a rocket engine being fired up and an electro-optical camera system that gave a crystal-clear, highly magnified picture of the ground ahead. *Sigrun's* co-pilot had his eyes riveted to that display, watching for any suspicious movement. At the moment, the EO camera was set to panorama but he could zoom in on anything that seemed curious. Radar, electronic surveillance, thermal imaging, electro-optical cameras and good, old-fashioned Mark One eyeball, all integrated to form *Sigrun's* second ring of defense: unequaled situational awareness.

"Thermal launch signature, ahead, 11 o'clock." The alert came up on the navigator's console and the big defense systems display aft.

"It's out of range, very low threat. Firing AGM-76 anti-radiation missile." The displays had highlighted the radar system most likely to be the control for the missile now 'soaring up' to meet them. Under them, there was a bump and a slight vibration as an AGM-76 left the bomb bay, 'fired' at the guilty radar. In fact both missiles were smokies, exercise missiles fitted with a live first stage but that was all. They'd launch, make a short arc in their intended direction, then go more or less harmlessly ballistic.

The targeted radar blinked off the screen; the Russians had determined it was a good shot and would have killed the radar long before the missile it was guiding reached its target. *Sigrun's* third ring of defenses: her wall of air-to-surface missiles, taking out whatever the RB-58s had missed. Nevertheless, *Sigrun* changed course by about five degrees to increase the miss distance.

"Bandits, bandits. Total count six aircraft, three loose pairs. Dead ahead, ten o'clock, two o'clock. Climbing very fast, tentative identification MiG-25 Pchelas. Trying for video contact now." Beneath its transparent screen, the electro-optical camera swung to the bearing of the leading inbound aircraft and swept to maximum magnification. A quick search and the image formed on the screen; grainy from the high magnification but there. There was no mistaking the brutal, boxy shape of the MiG-25. "Let's shake him up a bit?"

O'Seven nodded then flipped onto the shared radio channel. "Good to see you, Gray-531. Welcome to the party."

There was a stunned silence for a split second on the channel. "Borgemoi, your camera is THAT good *Sigrun?*" The range was still great, but two formations of aircraft closing at Mach 3 plus ate distance quickly.

O'Seven looked at the image again and frowned. "Gray-531, for real, you're trailing a little white smoke or vapor. We can't see well enough to be more precise."

Another slight pause. "Nothing showing here. Thank you for the heads-up, *Sigrun*."

"That missile launch, they were herding us into the fighters Seejay." O'Seven nodded. At Red Sun, the Russians had shown they were experts at that sort of thing. They used their missile batteries to shape the battle, setting up SAM traps and dead-end flak pockets, using missile launches to steer intruding aircraft away from lightly-defended zones, into ambushes from heavy concentrations of anti-aircraft assets. They had raised deception and misdirection to new heights, what appeared to be the layout of their defenses rarely was.

Most people thought Red Sun was an air-to-air exercise but that was far from the truth. It was an integrated air defense exercise and the Russians had shown their SAMs could carry their weight in the battles. When the Russian SAMs were guests at Red Sun, their American equivalents could only watch and learn.

Sigrun was turning, trying to put the climbing MiGs into an impossible tactical position. It was the basic bomber defense maneuver, one that the B-36s in The Big One had used against German rocket fighters and one that still worked well. *Sigrun* had a huge turning circle at these speeds, more than 20 miles across, but that was enough. Her sheer speed meant that only head-on attacks were practical and closing at speeds approaching 5,000 miles per hour, the fighters had only a single shot.

As *Sigrun* swung around, one of the fighter pairs was already falling behind her. They might fire but their missiles, even the big R-40Ts couldn't catch a B-70 in a tail chase. The chance of a beam shot working was so slight it could be neglected. By the time the MiGs were in range, one pair was hopelessly out of position, one was marginal and only one was in a good launch configuration. Already, *Sigrun's* radar and ESM systems were tracking both aircraft and feeding their course into the DAMS computer. DAMS was calculating the course any missile would have to follow in order to stand a chance of hitting *Sigrun*.

DAMS exploited the weakness that all missiles, even air-to-airs, had. They were predictable. Fired from a given point, tracking a given target, they would follow a projectable course - and that made them vulnerable. The trick was to respond quickly enough to make the prediction worthwhile. That was where *Sigrun's* fourth ring of defenses came in. DAMS predicted an intercepting missile's flight path and calculated when to launch a Pyewacket defense missile. Even better, the DAMS could predict when the intercepting fighter would launch its missiles so that inbound and Pyewacket would be sent on their way almost simultaneously.

"DAMS is launching, Seejay." Henty's voice was neutral. In this battle between air intercept radar and DAMS, he was barely more than a spectator. The two MiG-25s in a favorable attack aspect had launched four missiles ‘at’ *Sigrun* although the safety offset meant that they would miss their target. That actually made DAMS job a little harder. It didn’t matter though, there was a barely perceptible lurch as the Pyewacket launcher in *Sigrun’s* belly launched four Pyewackets.

The missiles were weird, they didn’t look like missiles at all. More like a discus thrown by athletes. Pyewacket was a perfectly circular disk, 70 inches across, 12 inches deep and weighing 550 pounds, powered by three 10,200 pound thrust rocket engines. Their weight was perfectly dispersed across the disk, giving the Pyewacket stunning maneuverability as it accelerated at over 320 g to reach its full speed, just over Mach 7.0. Their original course had been fed into them by the DAMS computer, but they had an infra-red guidance system to finish the job.

They screamed away from *Sigrun* ripping up the distance between themselves and the inbound R-40s. Four brilliant flashes as their high explosive warheads shredded the inbound missiles told *Sigrun’s* crew that her fifth ring of defenses wouldn’t be needed. *Sigrun’s* turn had already left the last two MiG-25s behind her; now O’Seven started to reverse the turn to take him around the intercepting fighters.

“What is happening to Gray-531?” *Sigrun’s* voice was wary, concerned.

“Good question.” Jim Hook used his electro-optical system to focus on the lead MiG-25. “Crazy Russian hasn’t given up, he’s still trying to catch us. He must have pulled a 9 plus G turn as soon as we started to, he’s turning inside us. He might make it too, I’ve never seen a Pchela pull a turn like that.” There was a brief pause. “Uh-oh, he’s got a problem.”

In the screen, the brilliant light from the MiG-25s afterburners suddenly vanished. “My God will you look at THAT!” The MiG-25 looked as if it had suddenly run into a wall in the sky and two enormous gouts of flame shot forward out of its air intakes. O’Seven flipped the microphone onto the shared channel.

"Gray-531, you appear to have had a triple-sonic compressor stall."

"You think, *Sigrun*?" the Russian pilot's voice was shaky. "Perhaps that might explain why I am flying the world's fastest glider?"

"How bad? I'm Seejay O'Seven by the way."

"Paul Lazaruski. Very bad. Both engines gone and will not restart. Powered controls gone, most of the aircraft systems are out. The explosion must have ripped up the systems in the engine bay."

"Recommend you get out of there Paul, she's gone."

"Negative, Seejay." One thing about the Russians attending Red Sun was that their pilots not only spoke reasonable English, they'd picked up SAC-speak as well. "If we lose my *Anya*, we will not know what went wrong. Then some other pilot must find out. No, I will try and bring her in."

"Ramenskoye?"

"Sheremetevo. I do not have the control authority to make the turn for Ramenskoye."

"You hang in there Paul, we'll escort you in." O'Seven flipped to the appropriate radio channel. "Mayday, Mayday, Mayday. This is SAC B-70 *Sigrun* calling a mayday for PVO MiG-25 Gray-531. Gray-531 has suffered double compressor stall and has both engines and many essential systems out. Aircraft will make an emergency landing at Sheremetevo. Please clear all other traffic out of the way. We will be escorting the casualty in. Air defense exercise is terminated. How you doing in there Paul?"

"Badly I think. I am dumping fuel now and we are slowing."

"Dumping fuel? Can I have some?" *Sigrun's* voice was concerned. Her fuel consumption was rising steeply as her speed dropped to keep station on the crippled MiG-25. Another little quirk of the B-70; her cruising speed was, in every essential, the same as her maximum speed. Anything less than maximum and fuel consumption rose. At Mach 3.4 she sipped fuel for every mile she traveled; at Mach 2.1 she was gulping it.

Outside, the stricken MiG was clearly visible. Its smooth blue-gray paint was seared and blackened around the engine bay and the air intakes. The Valkyrie slowly moved relative to the MiG as Hook used his electro-optics to survey for visible damage.

"Paul, there's no visible damage on . . . what's your aircraft's name?"

"*For Anya Petrovna, Anya* for short. My cousin, killed by the fascists."

"Thank you. *Anya* doesn't appear to be hurt, there's no external damage we can see and our camera's looked pretty close. Whatever's wrong is inside. You know you've still got your missiles on board?"

"Not any more Seejay. Six black objects tumbled from the MiG. "I've blown the underwing and underbelly missiles. What is our speed please?"

"We're down to Mach 1.3. You've lost instrumentation?"

"I do not think I can trust it. I have never seen so many red lights in a cockpit before."

Ahead of them, the two parallel runways of Sheremetevo were visible in the distance. Both were designed to take a B-52 landing without brakes: long and wide. *For Anya Petrovna* could take one, *Sigrun* would use the other. Speed was now subsonic and the runways were approaching fast. The problem was that the MiG-25 had all the gliding characteristics of a well-thrown brick.

"Sheremetevo Control here. Gray 531 and *Sigrun* you are cleared for landing. *Sigrun* please take the runway on the right and thank you for your assistance." The voice chuckled slightly, more with tension than real humor. "And welcome to Russia."

"Control, Gray-531 I have an additional problem, undercarriage will not lower." *Get out of there Paul,* O'Seven thought, *she can't be saved.* "I am going to skid in on my belly missile rails."

"Can he do that?"

"Nobody's ever said it can't be done. Keep reading out airspeed and altitude John. And watch him with your box of tricks."

The routine readout of landing data was started. Ahead of them, the left-hand runway was brilliant white. Foam was being sprayed on the surface, to help the wheel-less fighter slide and to cut down the risk of fire. Just as O'Seven felt *Sigrun's* undercarriage touch the runway surface, the MiG-25, a hundred yards or so away on the other runway, touched the foam layer, looking for all the world like a water-skier who lost his balance and made a belly-flop into the water. Two great arcs of foam hurled skywards and sparkled in the pale Moscow sun. *Sigrun* slowed quickly as her brakes and drag chute brought her to a halt; the MiG raced ahead of them, still plowing through the foam, the airport emergency vehicles racing alongside to keep up. Finally, *Anya* halted and the rescue crews in their silver heat-insulation suits swarmed over her. The cockpit opened and they saw the pilot hauled out of the cockpit and rushed to a stretcher. In the EO camera screen, Hook could see him waving to *Sigrun.*

"Would you believe it? He's made it. Looks OK too, I think the stretcher's routine. I thought he was going to blow on the runway."

"So did I. That little epic deserves beer. Lots and lots of beer."

"And vodka," added *Sigrun.*

Private Conference Room, National Security Council Building, Washington D.C.

The 13th floor conference room was filled to overflowing, something rare and unusual. A thin trickle of people were still coming in, mostly those who had arrived earlier, seen the crowd and had the initiative to go to an adjoining office and get a chair. The rest of the overflow were sitting on the floor. Another unusual point, the Seer noted. A few of those here weren't the usual inhabitants of this building or its equivalents scattered over Washington. It made a point that was easy to forget, wrapped up in the cocoon inside the beltway.

There were 6,000 of his people scattered across the United States, of whom only about twenty percent worked for the federal administration. A few more worked for the state or local governments, but the vast majority just lived in the community, pursuing whatever work it was that met their needs. They had never been famous, and never would be, but every one of them depended on the NSC for new identities when needed and as a security net to fall back on if trouble arrived. The "Witness Protection Program" might have been founded to protect people who wanted to testify in court against the Mob, but it had far more useful purposes.

When news of the attack had been broadcast, some of those people living in the suburbs of Washington, headed this way. Partly to express support for the people who'd helped them; more, the Seer suspected, from a desire to find out what was going on and take a look at the mysterious NSC building. Getting the strangers in had been an interesting challenge; most were now wearing "visitor" badges to satisfy the security hounds. At the moment everybody was milling around, introducing each other and vouching for others known personally to them. More security and this time deathly essential. Strangers, not known to the group, could be identified and their bona fides established. Nobody spoke of what would happen if such an infiltrator was found. Fortunately, the eventuality had never arisen.

"Hi Seer!" The voice cut across the room. It was Judith Peterson, a resident of Alexandria. She worked as a realtor there, her husband was a building contractor. Both their businesses were successes; to add extra income, every so often she used her real estate connections to find and buy a run-down property and her husband rebuilt it for sale at a fabulous profit. They did very well, all things considered; except for one small point. Judith Peterson's husband was from outside this group, a stranger. She'd been warned against it, Nefertiti had tried to argue her out of it but Judith had been adamant.

The Seer banged a gavel and the room quieted. "Are we all known to each other? Are there any here who need to be identified? No? Very well, I declare the lodge tyled.

"We've gathered here to discuss the implications of the attack this afternoon on the Senatorial Administration Building. First of all, does anybody here need to know what went down?"

There was some backing and filling at that; people not wanting to admit they were out of the loop. Eventually, one voice spoke out from the back of the room. "I heard there had been an attack on the building and that the Presidents Executive Assistant had been caught in the line of fire. That's all though."

"Fair enough. Quick recap. Sixteen-thirty this afternoon, a car did a drive-by on the Senatorial Admin Building. Used a machine gun to spray the steps. Killed five people." In the background Lillith held up six fingers. "Sorry six, the girl didn't make it honey?"

"Bled out on the operating table. Bullet winged her aorta. When it let go she went in seconds."

The Seer shook his head, the girl had been some junior typist or other, meeting her boyfriend on the steps so she could impress him with the importance of her new job. Waste. "About twenty wounded. Naamah and Henry were on the steps when the drive-by went down. Thanks to Henry's quick reactions, they both escaped unhurt. Henry got off six shots in reply. By the way, Henry, the Secret Service found the car, you put all six through the back window and there was blood inside. Looks like you got somebody. Superior shooting under the circumstances if I may say so."

“This from the man who can’t hit a barn standing inside it and still keeps going for head-shots.” Achillea’s voice was affectionate although her criticism had an edge to it. Beside the Seer, Nefertiti frowned slightly, then grinned. The interjection had solved a problem she’d been wrestling with.

The Seer stared at Achillea coldly. “Quite. I’ve got some information from the FBI and the Secret Service. Henry, what do you make of it?”

“The cops retrieved a total of 186 rounds fired at the steps. Allowing for the ones they haven’t found yet, we can be pretty sure it was 200. The rounds were .45 ACP, hollow-points. Straight hollow points, as if that isn’t bad enough, not poisoned. So, we’re looking at a Tommy gun with a hundred round drum magazine. My guess is two of them; their foregrips wedged in the car window, one rear grip held in each hand. That sound familiar Seer?”

“Vincent ‘Mad Dog’ Coll?

“Or Jack ‘Machine Gun’ McGurn.” Beside them, Nefertiti looked confused. McCarty smiled. “Chicago in the 1920s Neffie. They didn’t call them the Roaring Twenties for nothing. Can’t be those two though, they’re both dead. Worth remembering the style is similar, though. Car was waiting the other side of the road. It accelerated out, swung across the road, sprayed the steps and they headed off down thataway.”

“Which gives us three questions Henry. First one, who pulled this stunt? Second, were you and Naamah the targets or was this an attack on the Senate staff as a whole? Third, if you and Naamah were the targets, is it because of your - specifically her - position in the government or because of what we all are?”

“The style isn’t Caliphate Seer. They’d have doped the bullets with ricin or something. The whole idea of a drive-by like this, its . . . I don’t know . . . cars and machine guns, it’s American somehow. If it had been a suicide bomber on the steps or a car bomb I could have thought Caliphate. This smells of the Mob, or at least somebody trying to look like them. But why would the Mob machine-gun a Senate building? It's the one thing they wouldn't do, it would bring all kinds of heat down on them. Be very bad for business. If this was a couple of Mob people doing some freelance work for some reason, expect to find their bodies in the trunk of a burned-out car. And don't think they were dead when the car started to burn."

"So, question two. Were you and Naamah the targets?"

McCarty tapped his teeth with a pencil. Age and eating properly had eliminated the overbite so prominent in his early pictures. "I went through the stuff you got from the FBI and the USSS and drew this up." There was an easel in one corner of the room and he put a chart on it. A beautifully-drawn picture of the steps with the bullet hits marked individually and surrounded by a red oval. When The Seer had first met 'William' in Chicago's 'The Lagoon' club, he'd seen an old man in a menial job and fitted for little else. Still, he'd the feeling to go on and that told him 'William' was one of his people. It had taken a little effort to find him and bring him in but when he'd managed it, he'd been stunned to find who the old doorman really was.

He'd been doubly stunned when something else had happened to Henry McCarty. The incredible ability with a hand gun was still there but his mind opened up. Perhaps it was having time to learn. Perhaps it was simply that, for probably the first time in his life he'd been with people who'd accepted him for what he was, who didn't expect anything of him. Who'd made him part of something, gave him somewhere he belonged. Hidden underneath the old man in the menial job had been a brain, a fine and analytical one that only needed encouragement and information to blossom. Thinking about it, it had to have been there all the time, a man couldn't be a gunfighter without the ability to instantly analyze a situation and act accordingly. Now, Henry McCarty was using that gift and every time he used it, it developed just that little bit more.

"Look how the pattern of bullets swept across the steps. It's an s-shape. That's why I think the barrels of the guns were wedged in place. When the car swung out, the side facing the steps dipped slightly with the curve so the bullet stream went low. Then, as the car reversed the turn to head parallel to the steps, that side rose so the bullets went high. Then the car straightened out and the stream leveled out here. Finally, when the car swung away, the side facing the steps rose again and the last of the shots went high. Gunman were lucky by the way; those hundred round drums were bad for jamming. We were lucky too, Naamah, we were where the bullets went high. If we'd been further down, that burst would have cut us in half. Like poor old Vinnie Coll in New York."

"So the burst was aimed at you and Naamah?"

"Perhaps. If it was, the target was Naamah, not me. I only went to meet her on a whim, nobody could have guessed I would be there."

"Naamah, honey, you don't usually work out of that building, who knew you'd be there?"

"Most of the office staff. It's not a routine stop for me though. If somebody set this up, they'd have had less than an hour to do it and that doesn't ring right."

"I agree Seer, the method and timing are wrong for this to be a hit on us specifically. My guess is that this was aimed at the Senatorial staffers in general. If it was aimed at Naamah, her presence was a way of increasing the value of the target set. That mane of red hair you sport is pretty distinctive Naamah. I think they saw you and decided to go for it while you were in the killing ground."

Naamah shuddered slightly. It wasn't the first time somebody had planned - or tried - to kill her but it never ceased being an unpleasant sensation. The Seer grinned comfortingly at her and then looked around the room. "Right people, that's what appeared to happen. Anybody got any questions?"

Judith Peterson put her hand up "Are we sure it isn't the Mob after us?" She'd grown up in the era of the New York gang wars and Mafia violence was something she still feared.

"I think so. We're not sure what's happening here but I can't think why the Mob would take the risk of pulling a stunt like this just to get even with us for something. They're businessmen, the harm this is going to do to their income can't be offset by revenge. Anyway, revenge for what?"

"Perhaps they found out what happened to Jimmy Hoffa?" The voice came from the back of the room. The ex-Union boss had fallen on hard times when the Mob had decided to kill him. Hoffa had duly vanished and everybody assumed the Mob had succeeded. The law enforcement people were still looking for his body. In reality, he'd been spirited out the country and was now running a small transport company in Siberia - and knew that if he showed his face in America again, his life would be measured in hours.

"They might be peeved but it's not worth all this. Anyway, they probably regard living in Siberia as worse than death. The nearest approach to Italian food out there is Pizza-Dacha. While we're all together, anybody got any other issues they want to bring up? By the way, if anybody wants to look around the basement, ask Lillith and she'll take you down in groups."

Administrative Corridor, National Security Council Building, Washington D.C.

Naamah sighed and padded down the corridor. The last of their guests were gone, probably back to their homes to savor the memory of a brief trip to the NSC Building. It had been hard work, something of a risk to bring that many non-cleared people into the building but worth it. Lillith was sprawled out on a couch somewhere, resting her feet. Meetings were hard on her, even after all these years.

"Naamah, have you got a moment?" Nefertiti's rich gentle voice interrupted the reflections.

"Sure Neffie."

"If you could step into my office?" Nefertiti's office was dominated by a painting of the pyramids. Not as they were now, yellow with age and ragged but as they'd been when they were new. Coated with limestone and blinding white in the sun. "Would you like some tea?"

"Yes please. Meetings like that leave my mouth dry."

"Me too, I've just brewed a fresh pot." Nefertiti poured two cups out and put honey in hers, lemon in Naamah's. "Naamah, what did you think of Achillea's little dig at the Seers ability to shoot straight?"

Naamah didn't need to think. "It was uncalled-for and wrong for her to say that. As it happens it isn't true, he's a pretty good shot but even if it was true, she shouldn't have said so. Wrong time, wrong place."

"So why do you think she said it?"

"Achillea judges everybody by her own standards and they're very, very high. She's a natural with weapons, give her one and, whatever it is, she can use it like a veteran in 20 minutes. She's the only person I know who can stand up against Henry in a walk-down with a gun. And she has no empathy, no sense of what others feel. She judges by her own standards, appropriate or not and doesn't hide the verdict."

"So, Naamah, you say Achillea was wrong in judging others by too high a standard and making that judgment public. So why do you do the same about President-Elect Nixon?"

Naamah started and put her cup down carefully. "I wasn't aware I had."

"'If his IQ was any lower, we'd have to water him.' And a few other choice verdicts. Oh, they're all inside our circle and they'll never leak out. They're still not fair Naamah and you shouldn't say them - or even think them."

Nefertiti sighed. "Look, Naamah, you were incredibly lucky. Your first husband was a genius, a man far ahead of his time. A superb intellect, a charismatic manner and a character that was wholly admirable. He was a very hard act to follow and I don't think you've ever found his equal. But you're judging people by his standard and finding them wanting. You shouldn't be doing that.

"I said you were lucky, perhaps you weren't. My first husband was a congenital idiot, literally, not metaphorically. Physically, mentally, morally; he was the ultimate shallow end of the gene pool. After him, anything was an improvement. A camel would have been an improvement. So instinctively I don't look for any better and so it's a surprise when I get some progress over that dismal start.

"You're judging Nixon, and the other politicians we deal with, by the standards of your Sammael, just as Achillea judges the Seer's shooting by her own unequaled expertise. You can't do that. The way the American system works, they select their politicians from their population. We didn't grow up that way, but its the world we live in. Some of the people they select are good, some are bad, most are average. Most are a mixture of all three. Part of our job is to help them grow into their jobs. To curb, ever so gently, the parts that are bad, and encourage, ever so softly, the parts that are good. That's why we're working so hard to get ourselves where we are.

"Naamah, you may think what you say and think about Nixon are private and for our ears only but they're not. They come out in your bearing and how you act. Nixon will spot them, he won't know why but he'll spot them. He won't trust you and you won't be able to do your job."

"He doesn't trust me now. He doesn't trust anybody."

"I know. That makes your job harder, being sarcastic about him to others makes it harder still. He's your principal Naamah, it is up to you to work with him. And that means not harping on his limitations, and I agree there is enough there to keep you harping for his full term. Probably both if he gets re-elected. The Seer doesn't think he will by the way. It's your job to compensate for his limitations and exploit his skills. Make him grow into his office."

Naamah sipped her tea and thought carefully. The companionable silence grew as she reflected on Nefertiti's words and the truth of them slowly sank in. "You know Neffie, you would have been an expert psychiatrist."

Nefertiti snorted at the idea. "Naamah, give Nixon a chance. Everybody deserves that."

N5M3 Ohtori Seaplane Fighter "105", Final Approach, Ulithi Atoll

Carrier pilots liked to claim that landing on an aircraft carrier at night was the most stressful of all aviation feats. They'd obviously never tried landing a seaplane fighter under the same conditions. Lieutenant Toda Endo had learned from experience just how difficult "landing" his Ohtori at night could be. There was rarely a distinct horizon, the sea and sky blended into each other with a diffuse, ambiguous separation at best. Lights reflecting off the swell added to the illusions, creating shadows that suggested obstructions where none existed and hid those that lay in wait for the unwary.

The swell added problems. When landing, the fighter's hydroski had to make its first touch at the crest of a wave. That way, the aircraft would skip from wavetop to wavetop until its speed had dropped to the point where it could settle into the water. If the pilot mistimed it, if he put the hydroski into the trough between waves, the speed of his aircraft would drive the ski tip deep into next swell. That swell would then break over the ski and pull it and the aircraft down to destruction. Toda had seen that happen; a fighter cartwheeling across the sea as it broke up. No, Toda though, carrier pilots had it easy. Even on night landings.

Which was why, of course, the Japanese Navy had its seaplane fighter pilots practice night landings so often. Once Japan's seaplane fighters had been treated as a joke; slow, clumsy, quite outclassed by their land- and carrier-based opponents. The jet engine and the hydroski had changed all that. Now the seaplane fighters were the fastest and most effective air superiority aircraft the Japanese Navy had.

The N5M3 was 450 kph faster than the carrier-based A13M, could out-turn, out-climb and out-dive it. Most Japanese seaplane pilots reckoned their mount could hold its own against the American F8U Crusader; although they were careful not to add that the F8U was already considered obsolescent and quickly vanishing from American service. Its successor, the F9U Super-Crusader was a much more threatening opponent. Japan had its answer to that aircraft as well: the N6M Tsurugi. That fighter was taking a long time to reach the operational squadrons. Until it arrived, the Ohtori was the best fighter the Japanese Navy had. Or so its pilots claimed.

Toda completed his pre-landing circuit. All was well; the two brilliantly-lit seaplane tenders in the atoll were clearly visible. The landing zone was free of obstructions, although there were other Ohtoris docked by the tenders and more had been craned on board for maintenance. And there was an H8K6-L transport flying boat anchored to one side. An old, piston-engined Kawanishi, withdrawn from front-line service but still serving the Emperor as a transport and liaison aircraft. Probably had flown out with orders and new personnel, Toda thought.

The Japanese Navy didn't like using radio or telegraph for secret messages. The Australians were just too good at eavesdropping. Relying on people wasn't really much safer though. When it came to buying people's treachery, the damned Thais had less conscience than a drunken salaryman looking for a bedmate. They'd pay anybody for their services. No Japanese would sell the Emperor's secrets of course. Would the Chinese? Or the Koreans? They would. And the Vietnamese would give them away out of spite.

Final approach now. Toda dropped his eyes to his instruments, keeping his fighter level, wings parallel to the horizon, nose up just a touch. This was another place where pilots died. They placed their faith in their feelings; followed their instincts, not their instruments. They tried to fly 'by the seat of their pants.' Because feelings without external references were treacherous, they lost orientation, lost control of their aircraft and crashed. Toda did not intend to do that; he kept his eyes riveted on his instruments. The new Tsuragi had a head-up display; the readings of the key instruments projected on the windscreen. The Ohtori lacked that refinement.

Instead, the pilot had to look down, with just quick glances outside. If he did it right, he was rewarded by the first lurch and hiss as the hydroski touched the surface of the water. Toda was rewarded, he caught the swell perfectly, his ski just kissing the top of the wave. Almost without thinking he cut the power back to idle and popped his drag chute.

Now there were a serious of jolts, each one pounding his spine as his Ohtori skipped across the waves. He'd left his instruments now and was watching outside for something, anything, to go wrong. The slamming changed, the initial sharp blows being replaced by longer, deeper, softer ones as the fighter settled in the water. Then, the motion changed as the N5M3 settled down in the water and floated on its belly. It wallowed in the waves, not bouncing on top of them. Toda jettisoned his chute, knowing that one of the small service craft would already be heading out to pick it up and pulled up the lever that retracted his hydroski.

His Ohtori was floating with its wing leading edge just half a meter above the water, the trailing edge on the surface. All it needed was a touch of power and he was 'sailing' towards his tender. The *Chiyoda*, was one of two that provided the floating base for the 48 fighters of the Takao Kokutai. *Chitose* and *Chiyoda* were painfully old ships, more than 40 years of service behind them, but they still did their job. Of the 24 fighters based on *Chiyoda*, three were still on a night training mission, 16 were anchored by the tender and four were up on deck for maintenance. So his fighter would be parked in a pen by the tender's side.

His space was still waiting for him and he 'sailed' into it. A few meters short of his pen, he cut power completely and touched the 'brakes.' That caused his ailerons and flaps to drop, effectively acting as spoilers. Another tricky piece of judgment. The low-drag airframe of the N5M3 meant that it also had very low water resistance; it was quite possible to send the fighter crashing into the tender's side. On the other hand, too little power, too much brake and she would run out of energy just a little short of the dock. Pilots were earnestly encouraged to err on the side of caution. It was easy enough to send a boat out with a line.

Toda's Ohtori came to a halt just two meters out from the side of its pen. A rubber raft was already waiting. A dockline was attached to the nose, two more to the tail, and the fighter was warped in the rest of the way. Finally, a wooden gangplank with a float on the end was pushed out, bumping lightly against the fuselage side.

Toda opened his cockpit canopy and stepped out, stretching his back. Some pilots actually carried their swords when flying. Mitsubishi provided a pair of clips in the cockpit to secure the katanas of those who chose to do so. Toda was not one of them. His sword was a cheap stamped piece of mild steel, one that a genuine katana would cut in half without even noticing. When others displayed their family heirlooms, Toda quietly contented himself with the promise that one day he would challenge them to a duel; their swords versus his Ohtori.

"Sir, Lieutenant Toda Sir! The Group Commander wishes to see you immediately in the Kokutai Office."

Toda acknowledged the order and salute and set off at a fast walk, the gangway rocking under his feet. In the Japanese Navy, immediately meant just that. Along the brows that formed the fighter pens, up the companionway to the deck of *Chiyoda*, then along the open deck that formed the stern two thirds of the ship. Amidships was covered by a steel platform, raised on four sturdy pillars. Underneath was the lift that took aircraft down to the workshops within the ship, above had once been triple 25mm anti-aircraft guns. They were gone now, replaced by shoulder-fired missiles.

"Sir, Lieutenant Toda reporting as ordered Sir." He saluted as he entered the administrative office. His commander and the captain of the *Chiyoda* were there. *This,* he thought, *did not look good.* They returned his salute but instead of dropping his hand, *Chiyoda's* Captain kept it in position. That meant Toda had to do the same; he couldn't drop his hand until both the senior officers had done so. Then his group commander started reading from a message.

"A message from His Imperial Majesty. Aware of the dedication to duty, skill, courage and honor exhibited by our servant Lieutenant Toda Endo and trusting in his loyalty and patriotism, we hereby command that he be raised to the rank of Lieutenant Commander and will immediately enjoy all the privileges and benefits of his new rank."

Toda's face was expressionless; inside he felt a warm thrill spreading throughout his body. The words were standard. In truth he doubted if the Emperor had ever heard of him, but they sounded as if he had. Who knew? The Emperor might have stopped at his name and said "who is this one?"

"A message from Imperial Navy Headquarters. Lieutenant Commander Toda Endo will proceed immediately from his present assignment and take command of the Second Section of the Tainan Kokutai, based on the seaplane carrier *Nisshin* currently stationed in Kagoshima."

"Congratulations Lieutenant Commander Toda." *Chiyoda's* Captain finally dropped his hand and Toda followed suit. "There is a Seiku leaving for Kagoshima in two hours. You will take it to your new posting."

The group commander reached across the desk, handing Toda the insignia of a Lieutenant Commander. He quickly unpinned the ones that had marked his Lieutenancy and pinned on the new badges. Then he braced himself and waited. Sure enough, there was a terrific thump on each shoulder as his group commander 'tacked' the new insignia firmly in place. "Good luck, Toda-san. And may the gods fly with you."

28,000 feet over Defensive Area Simone, French Algeria/Caliphate Border

"Bandit is 500 meters above you, range 28 kilometers, bearing 330 degrees." The dispassionate voice from ground control gave the information clearly and concisely. That was why women were used as ground controllers. Their voices cut through cockpit noise more easily than the deeper pitch of men. The Germans had realized that first, much good that it had done them. It was all very well to have one's ground controllers speaking clearly when the targets were high out of reach. But, Lieutenant Charles Plaisant knew, that was not happening tonight. The Caliphate intruder was above and ahead of him but his Mirage IIIF had its measure. Probably; assuming the aircraft was what everybody thought it was.

Plaisant's eyes searched the darkness ahead, peering through the silky blackness for the dark shadow of the Caliphate aircraft. He could spot it in an instant if he turned his search radar on but that would also warn his prey that they had been spotted and were in danger. Then, the enemy would turn and run for the border and friendly airspace. That was why ground control were swinging him in from behind. He'd hit the enemy from below and behind, they would never even know he was there until his missiles tore into their engines.

"Bandit 200 meters above you, range 20 kilometers, target should be dead ahead now." Control's voice was still impassive, steering him to his target. Plaisant strained his eyes, seeking out the target. Then, there it was. As always, once he'd seen the dark shape against the stars he wondered how he could have missed it. Cigar shaped belly, longish wings with even taper on leading and trailing edges. Two jet engines, about a quarter way out on the wings. An Uncle. If it was the early model, and most of them were, it had 2,000 kilograms of thrust from each engine and a single 20mm cannon in nose and tail. Later models had 3,000 kilogram thrust engines, twin tail guns and a single gun in the nose. The Caliphate had the later versions but they hadn't been seen around here. Not yet anyway.

"Control, I have acquired target. Locking heatseekers now." The heat of the jet exhausts set against the cold of a desert night made for a good target. The radar-homing Matra under his belly had a bigger warhead but that meant he had to illuminate the target with his radar first. Why warn the prey? In his ears, the beeping sound turned into a growl as the infra-red sensors in his underwing missiles locked on the Uncle in front of him. "Range eight kilometers." It was only a question of time before the tail gunner on the Uncle saw him, even against the dark of the ground.

"Destroy the target." Control's voice was still impassive.

Plaisant squeezed the trigger on his missiles, the bright stream of fire leaped out as they hurtled off through the darkness. One passed above the Uncle's wings, just a hair too far for the proximity fuse to explode the warhead. The other looked like it might miss as well, then Plaisant realized it had locked on the engine furthest away for some peculiar reason. It crossed just below the Uncle's fuselage and the proximity fused warhead slashed the bomber's tail to shreds. It lurched and started to descend in a wide circle, a downwards spiral that was inexorably tightening and steepening. *What was going on in the flight deck*, Plaisant wondered? A French crew would be fighting the controls, trying to get some measure of authority back; to pull out of the dive or at least give the crew a chance to bail out. Were the Caliphate pilots doing that? Or were they just praying, leaving the decision up to their god?

"Target is destroyed." Plaisant's voice was as impassive as Control's as he watched the Uncle transition from a descending spiral into a spin and then tumble out of the sky, breaking up as it went. A brilliant flash and a ball of fire on the ground marked its grave. The crew hadn't bailed, which was probably wise. There were OAS and FLN down there who reckoned the Caliphate owed them a blood-debt. If they captured a Caliphate airman, they'd take a payment on that debt. A long, slow payment.

Plaisant checked his fuel gauges and started the flight home. Seven Uncles shot down in four days by his squadron; a higher rate of action than they'd seen for months. What on Earth were the Caffs up to now?

Briefing Room, INS Mysore, *First Division, The Flying Squadron, Trincomalee, India*

"Gentlemen, we set sail tomorrow. The first wave will be three Project 16C destroyer escorts converted to transports. They will be carrying a battalion landing team built around the First Battalion, the Punjab Rifles."

There was a stir of satisfaction at that; a Sikh battalion was in the lead. The spirit of the long-dead but never forgotten Khalsa still lived.

"They will be escorted by two Project 22 Nilgiri class frigates. We will be the covering force. Once the troops have landed, the APDs will withdraw while the Nilgiris will join us as reinforcements. The aircraft carrier *Vikrant* was to have provided air cover. But I have just learned that she stripped her main shaft bearings yesterday. She will be in drydock for at least seven months."

There was an ominous silence as the phrasing sank in. Those present started looking at each other uneasily, a problem this big, this early did not bode well for the operation. Admiral Dahm looked at them with well-disguised sympathy. The sudden unavailability of the carried pointed all too clearly to the basic weakness in the whole plan. It would only work if everything went exactly according to plan. As had just been vividly demonstrated, it wasn't happening that way. Soundlessly he sighed and concealed his own doubts.

"*Viraat* is on her way around from the west coast but she will not be here in time for the initial phases of the operation." That caused a sigh of relief, one that Dahm wished he could share.

"The main body of the landing force will consist of the Second Battalion the Punjab Rifles, Second Battalion, The Ghurka Brigade and Fifth Battalion, the Maharatta Engineers. There will also be a squadron of the Kolkata Heavy Horse with their Centurion tanks plus an anti-aircraft missile battery and an anti-ship missile battery.

"They are being brought in by large amphibious transports screened by three more Project 22 class frigates. However, the Main Body is being held up until *Viraat* can join the Second Division of the Flying Squadron and provide them with cover.

"Before anybody asks, we cannot delay this operation until *Viraat* joins us. The key to the mission is to get to the islands first and establish our presence first. We understand the Chipanese are moving as well and if they get there first, we might as well pack up and go home. We absolutely must get our spearhead force into place first."

"Do we have any air cover at all Sir?" It was Commander Ditrapa Dasgupta, Captain of the *Rana*.

"We will have distant air cover from Thailand if things go critical, Arrows for fighter cover and TSR-2s for strike but response times will be long and their ability to stay over the target area limited. History has shown us that these arrangements do not work. We should plan on not having air cover.

"The good news is that the Chipanese are most unlikely to have it either. They have no carriers in this area, they are down to six now and they're all accounted for. They have aircraft based in Vietnam that can get to us but they will have the same problems we do. Long response times, little time over target. It looks like aircraft will be a minor factor in this particular scenario until *Viraat* arrives."

The question and answer session went on as each captain clarified his roll in the operation. Admiral Dahm still couldn't shake off his sense of unease though. It was as if *Vikrant* stripping her shafts that way had been a message; a symbol from the Gods warning the Indian Navy that, this time, it was sticking its neck out too far. Still, *Viraat* with her Tigers and Skyhawks would only be a week or so behind them. It couldn't be that bad. Could it?

United States Secret Service Washington Office, Treasury Building, Washington DC.

"Come in, Mike. How did the meeting go?"

Special Agent Michael Delgado settled down in the seat in front of his boss's desk. Meeting top Mob figures in the wasteland of a New Jersey swamp wasn't exactly one of the least stressful jobs he'd done.

"Pretty well sir, we were right, they're desperate for us to know they had nothing to do with the attack."

"Who did they send? Castellano? Persico? Gigante?"

"No Sir." Delgado's voice took on a hint of awe. "It was The Little Man himself."

Delgado shook his head. He still couldn't quite believe it, even though he'd been there. He'd stood by the car, watched the doors on the stretched Lincoln opening and seeing the face within. A face that was very high on the FBI wanted list. Unfortunately for them, a face that now lived in Cuba and was out of reach.

"LANSKY! My God, if Meyer Lansky himself came in person, this must have gone to Commission level. He must have come all the way from Cuba specifically for your meeting."

"And is probably back there now. I don't know why though, he didn't say anything any of the other members of the Commission couldn't have said. Just that nobody in their organization had anything to do with the attack and we could count on them for help if we needed it."

"Right. As if a federal agency is going to ask the Mob for help. We could ask the Cuban Government of course."

"Is there a difference?"

The Station Chief thought for a second. "No. But Lansky coming personally is a message in itself. He's telling us that they really take this seriously. He should, did you know there were two 'persons of special interest' in the line of fire?"

"No. Were they hit? Which ones?"

"It was Gunman and Deadeyes. They're both OK. There was a rumor that The Champ was there as well but she wasn't."

Delgado heaved a small sigh of relief. Of all the 'persons of special interest', the young woman called Igrat, code-named 'The Champ' was the one whom the Secret Service agents were fondest. Quite apart from being the best courier in the business, her bed-hopping exploits were the subject of awed and ribald fascination.

The Station Chief smiled, he knew exactly what Delgado was thinking, "Lansky couldn't know that of course. As far as we know, we're the only people who have that particular group under surveillance. He didn't send any other message at all?"

"No Sir, only that Frank Sinatra's new show at the Havana Flamingo was really something. He brought you a tape of one of the numbers. He said your kids probably like Sinatra and the record won't be released for months."

"Right, thanks Mike. Get some rest. Write up a full contact report tomorrow."

The station chief leaned over and put the tape cassette into his player. His kids thought Sinatra was ancient and unworthy listening, but he liked hearing the man still. Then, as the band struck up he realized that Meyer Lansky had sent him a message after all. One that was confirmed when Sinatra started to sing.

"South of the border, down Mexico way........"

CHAPTER THREE
SADDLING UP

General Observation Ward, Moscow Military Hospital

"May I help you Gospodin?" The nurse was standing in front of the double doors leading into the observation ward, arms folded and exuding an air of massive immobility. She viewed the four airmen with profound suspicion. The hospital was situated almost in the middle of a ring of four airfields: the American forward bomber base at Sheremetevo, the Russian fighter bases at Dromodevo and Molino and the Russian Experimental Establishment and bomber base at Ramenskoye. As a result, she knew airmen well and was firmly convinced that no matter how innocent they looked, they were always up to something. True, these wore American blue, not Russian khaki; but she knew, without being told, that they were scheming at something that would disrupt the smooth running of her ward.

"Tovarish Nurse, we have come to visit one of your patients, Major Paul Lazaruski. We were on exercise together today and his aircraft developed problems. He pulled off an emergency landing with great skill and we wished to commend him and ensure that he is well. Our friend is well, isn't he?" O'Seven put just the right hint of concern in his voice.

"Lazaruski, Lazaruski. Here we are." The nurse pulled a file from the rack by the door. "We will be keeping him in for another day, in case complications develop. The doctors are also a little concerned about some of his blood work. Nothing to worry about they say, just some inconsequential anomalies. Anyway, you may see him if you wish." Suddenly her voice hardened with suspicion again. "You are bringing him flowers?"

"No, Tovarish Nurse. We know who really runs the hospital and looks after the patients. These are for you. For our friend we brought some magazines to read, some fruit to eat. Here."

The nurse looked at the magazines, some on guns, some on cars and one with a naked woman on the front. *Typical of pilots* she thought. But the fruit was good, grapes and oranges and some apples. Healthy food. She checked the basket to see if there was a bottle hidden in there. There wasn't and O'Seven looked a little hurt at the suggestion there might be. The nurse ignored it. These airmen were up to something, she knew it. Then she saw the box one of the Americans was carrying. "What is that, can I see inside please." It was not, of course, a request.

"Gospodin Nurse, I am sorry but that is impossible. Those are the activation codes for the nuclear weapons on our bomber. That box must go wherever we go and we can never leave it while we are on duty. See, it has a combination lock and even we do not know the combination. Only when we get a special message from the President himself do we get the combination and can open the box to arm our weapons. It is called a permissive action link. I am so sorry we cannot do as you ask."

The nurse looked at the box again, and saw for the first time that it was handcuffed to the wrist of the American carrying it. Very well then. "I see. Please go in. Third bed on the left. Visiting times are restricted to half an hour.

Sigrun's crew pushed through the doors, hearing them close behind their group. "A Permissive Action Link, Seejay? Where on earth did you get that nonsense from?"

"Don't knock it, worked didn't it? Read it in a book sometime, novel about a nuclear war between us and Chipan, how it started by accident. 'Red Alert' I think it was called. Author had obviously never been on a SAC base in his life. Third bed on the left..... Hi Paul, how's it going?" O'Seven was slightly surprised. The Russian was older than he'd expected, mid-forties at a guess. Flying fighters was a young man's game. Usually.

"I have pulled my back and the doctors say I have a mild concussion but nothing to be concerned about thank you. Ah, some fruit, and something to read." Lazaruski's eyes gleamed slightly. Henty put the box on the floor and flipped it open. The impressive 'combination lock' was a fake. The "permissive action link' was actually an insulated picnic box, hurriedly painted Air Force Blue and covered with meaningless stencilled codes. Immersed in the ice inside were two bottles of top-grade vodka. Lazaruski's eyes folded into a delighted smile. "Well done my friends! Some of my comrades tried earlier but the guardian angel outside caught them."

"We heard, so we stopped off at Ramenskoye on the way over. We had American vodka on our base but we guessed you'd prefer the real thing. One bottles from us, the other's from them. Some paper cups around here?"

There were. Quite a few in fact. Vodka was poured and knocked back in a series of toasts. To Lazaruski, to Seejay, the MiG-25 and the B-70, to the Russian and American Presidents. By the time the half hour was up, they were toasting the nurse outside and the world had developed a decidedly rosy hue. At that point, the Valkyrie crew had to leave and they walked, a trifle unsteadily, past the nurse who watched them disappear down the corridor.

"Permissive Action Link" she sniffed derisively and went in to confiscate what was left of the bottles. The timing was good, the nurses were having a party that evening and all alcoholic contributions were welcome.

The Presidential Suite, Tropicana Hotel, Havana, Cuba

Cuba was strictly honest, even in small things. The Presidential Suite that comprised the whole of the top floor of the Tropicana really was where the President of Cuba lived and worked. On the other hand, it wasn't particularly difficult for Cuba to avoid breaking the law, there was, after all, so little of it.

"The Cuban Legal Code: it shall be a capital offense to kill, assault, rob, swindle, harass, annoy or mildly inconvenience a tourist. Here ends the Cuban Legal Code." Meyer Lansky, President of Cuba, rolled the line around with enjoyment. Dean Martin had come up with it at the dinner cabaret after the Commission had spent a long day dividing out the fabulous profits generated by the Island's gaming and entertainment facilities. Lansky had once remarked that organized crime was bigger than US Steel and that had been the bragging of a gangster. It wasn't any more, The Mafia-run businesses on Cuba were bigger than US Steel, and a lot more profitable. It had proved what Lansky had always said, right from the early days with Luciano and Siegel; to be a successful criminal you had to be honest.

That was how he'd got to be in the position he was. He'd established a record of being unimpeachably honest with his subordinates. When a job was done, there were no "last minute expenses," nobody was told there was a "smaller take than expected." Those who were with him got what they were promised, if necessary out of Lansky's share of the proceeds.

The reputation had spread and soon other gangsters had come to him to divide up the take from a job or arbitrate a disagreement. Never had he been anything less that absolutely fair and ever the most suspicious of wiseguys recognized the fact. So, when the Commission was formed, he'd been appointed the Chairman. It had helped that he was Jewish and could never be a member of one of the Mob families. And when the Mob had taken over Cuba, he'd become President of Cuba as well. Even now, he was still technically only an associate, never a made man. That didn't make any difference, Charlie Luciano had summed it up: "When The Little Man talks, you listen." His successors had never disagreed with that observation.

When Lansky thought about it, he couldn't really see the difference between his associates and politicians. The big shots in Washington called it 'Corporate Taxation,' here in Havana, Lansky and his associates called it 'skimming the take.' Even the percentages were similar. The operation in Cuba could have gone horribly wrong, the families could have fought in the streets over the take. Lansky had been firm, persuasive and, above all, right. Chaos would bring others in to take over and all that fabulous income would be gone. To keep their hands on the cornucopia of goodies pouring out of the Cuban casinos, the country had to be stable and peaceful. No gang wars and people had to be happy. That was another part of the Cuban Legal Code; "Those who rock the boat shall sleep with the fishes."

In a way, Lansky reflected, he and his associates had turned American foreign policy back against itself. The American Government were very explicit, they didn't rule the world, they didn't want to. They just wanted it peaceful. If it wasn't they would make it peaceful. So The Commission had made Cuba peaceful. The whole country was organized the same way as the Mafia families back in the states. The people living on each block knew their button man, the lowest level member of the family who was responsible for just that block. If they had a beef, they knew where he had his morning coffee or ate his lunch and they would see him. And so it went, all the way up the family tree. It wasn't even an approximation of democracy, he knew that, but it worked. Lansky, who was far better read than even his friends suspected, had thought about writing a book '*Feudalism for a Modern Age*', but eventually decided it would cause too many people to cry.

Cuba was rich, stable, peaceful and secure and as long as it was that way, the American Government would leave it alone. The tourists were drawn in by the uncontrolled gambling, the luxurious hotels, the sheer beauty of the place and the frisson that came from associating with the underworld. As Dean Martin had also remarked, Americans knew the faces of the Cuban Government better than they did their own. That wasn't surprising since pictures the Cuban Government were prominently posted on the walls of every United States Post Office.

The wiseguys tolerated the tourist requests to be photographed with them as a necessary part of doing business. In fact, some of them entered into the spirit of the thing; more than one family of tourists went back to Nowheresville with a picture of their children sitting on the lap of a notorious wiseguy holding a Tommy gun.

Lansky sighed. Tommy guns. That was the root of the crisis that faced Cuba. Some idiots had sprayed a government building in Washington with Tommy guns. From a passing car no less, like something out of the 1920s. There was no doubt that it was intended to look like a mob hit and the news had caused near-panic in the Commission. One result was that Lansky had flown to Washington himself to see the authorities and frantically try to convince them that the mob were not involved - and if any members had got themselves caught up in it, they would suffer a fate considerably more horrible than anything the Federal Government could dream up.

He'd made that trip in his persona of President of Cuba; if he'd made it as Meyer Lansky, professional gambler, he would have been arrested on the spot. Fortunately, it looked like law enforcement had also written off mob involvement on the very sensible grounds that they had nothing to gain and vast amounts to lose by conducting the attack. The other result of the Commission meeting was to see Lansky now.

His secretary, Estrellita, knocked on the door. "Presidente, your 11 o'clock is here to see you."

"Thank you Estrellita. Send him in."

The man who was following close behind him was young, only recently a made man but one who had already made his mark in the Gambino family. When the Commission had been debating who should run Cuba's to-be-formed security service, most of the Dons had proposed old friends, well known to the group. Fine, but they were all old friends and stuck in the ways of the past. Their names had been proposed to the Commission more out of loyalty than anything else.

Carlo Gambino had proposed John "Dapper John" Gotti as a new man, one who understood the new world that was growing around them, one whose decisions were not affected by the old, outworn traditions of the 1930s. A man who was known for his skill and intelligence in planning jobs and his daring in carrying them out. Gambino made his points and as he'd done so, the other Dons had nodded. Gotti was the man.

Looking at him, Lansky could see where he'd got his name. The suit was silk; Italian styled and very expensive. Shirt and tie were the same, expensive but in perfect taste. Lansky was well aware that when wiseguys started to make money, their clothes were dictated more by obvious cost than good taste. Gotti had avoided that trap. Looking down, Lansky saw that his shoes were also Italian-made and perfectly shined to a mirror finish.

"Welcome to Havana, John. I see you've patronized Fidel downstairs."

Gotti's face was confused. "Fidel?"

"The shoeshine guy in the reception area. The one with the beard?"

"Right, yes, I was told he gave the best shoeshine in Havana. Who is he?"

"Some old guy who used to run one of the revolutionary groups around here. You weren't around then but the middle 1950s were a mess here. Government that didn't know its ass from its elbow. A clutch of bandit groups who were worse, all killing each other as fast as they could. We've got a lot to thank them for. They destroyed this place as a functioning entity. We already had a few casinos and hotels in here so we imported our own security. The local goombahs tried to move in on them but the boys took their leader, some cluck named Guevara, out into the bay and dropped him off wearing a pair of concrete boots. So, when everything fell apart and the government finally disintegrated, we were the only stable area of Cuba and the only people with any real authority." Lansky shrugged. "You know all this of course, just allow an old man a few fond reminiscences. Fidel's one of the few survivors of those days so we keep him around as a souvenir. To business John, take a seat."

"Thank you Meyer." If it had been Gambino or Pescati or Colombo or any of the other Dons, Gotti would have kissed Lansky's ring. Meyer Lansky wasn't a Don and, anyway, he preferred real authority to an outward show of it. "And thank you for inviting me to Havana."

Lansky nodded. "You've heard about the attack in Washington?"

"Can't help it, all over the news. That wasn't us was it?"

"Of course not." Lansky's voice was irritated; for a moment he wondered if this young made man was as bright as supposed.

"Just asking."

"Right. No it wasn't us. And, thank God, the Feds know it. Or believe it. It's our job to prove their belief is right. That's where you come in. The Commission have decided that Cuba's too open. We don't have a police force, we don't have any armed forces, we don't have a security service. The families handle law and order in their own areas and that's it. If we got invaded, all we can do is send the boys to the beach with limousines and invite the invaders to go for a ride. Unfortunately, their mothers told most of them not to get into cars with strange men." Lansky and Gotti both erupted into laughter at the thought of wiseguys trying to take invading marines for the traditional mob 'last ride.'

"So, the Commission had decided we need some sort of island-wide investigating service. We talked it over and we decided that you were the guy best qualified to handle the job. You'll report directly to the Commission, you can recruit from the boys, your discretion who though I advise you balance the numbers out between the families. Ask you a question. John, you're a Gambino man, what happens if you find Carlo was involved?"

"I'd warn him then tell the Commission. Give him a head start. Honor demands it."

"It does, I wouldn't have believed any other answer." For a brief second Lansky's affable, friendly exterior vanished and the eyes were those of a hardened wiseguy who'd killed his first victim decades before. The question had been a trap and Gotti had escaped it. Perhaps Gambino had been right after all. Lansky hoped so.

This situation was something neither he nor the Commission had foreseen; when the families had taken over in Cuba, they'd become the government of a country. That meant they had to behave like a country and they were exposed to the same risks as a country. Being a national entity wasn't the same as just being a very large family cutting up a bigger take. Now, ironies of ironies, they were being forced to form a police force.

"Have we any clues where to look?" Gotti was thoughtful, his mind chewing over the problem. Somebody wanted to take out the present government of Cuba and didn't have the overt power to do it. So they'd tried to provoke the Americans into doing it for them. That had to be it. But who?

"Not much. You know we have a drugs problem here?" Gotti's eyebrows went skywards. Drugs were simply not mentioned in Cuba's brief official code of laws or its more extensive 'customs.' Like most things, the guiding principles were that something should not cause trouble and not annoy the tourists. If somebody wanted to sell drugs, fine, as long as he kicked back part of the take to the family controlling his patch. If he caused trouble, say by attacking somebody else on the same patch or annoying tourists with over-enthusiastic sales pitches - especially to children - then he vanished.

"The South Americans. They don't like selling though us or us keeping the drug problem low key. And prices aren't good because we don't get in the way of sales. Plentiful supply, price goes down. They want their own distribution that doesn't have us skimming the take and they want restricted supply, probably illegal, to send the price up. If the Feds in Washington take over here, they get both those. So, that's a good place to start looking."

Desert on the Mexico-Arizona border.

The truck was grinding along a poor-quality dirt road. It was a standard windowless van-body truck, the type used by most businesses for local deliveries. Two wheel drive put it at an instant disadvantage on the dreadful road surface. It would have been struggling anyway but the situation was made worse by two other factors. One was that neither the driver nor his assistant really knew what they were doing. Competent drivers would have slowed down and avoided the worst bumps and potholes. These men were coyotes, smugglers of illegal immigrants to America, and they did neither.

The other was that the truck was badly overloaded. The van body at the rear was packed tight with illegal immigrants. The driver could hear them in the back, groaning with the bumps and lurches but that didn't worry him. The van body was separate from the driving cab and there was only one way out of the back. Through the double doors at the rear of the truck.

His assistant offered him a cigarette and the driver leaned over to take it, his eyes leaving the road as he did so. He simply didn't see the boulder sticking through the road surface or the pit the other side. The first he knew was when the truck rode the boulder up, swing dangerously far over, almost toppling with the motion. Then, as the driver swung the wheel to try and correct it, the front went into the pit and the boulder made violent contact with the underbelly of the truck. It dipped and stopped, the truck nose in the sand.

The two coyotes got out and looked at the damage. The old truck was finished, there was no doubt about that. One wheel was almost parallel with the ground, the other scarcely any better. The front axle and steering had obviously been broken beyond redemption. There was a spreading pool of black oil and engine coolant as well, the sump had cracked wide open. This truck wouldn't be going any further. Without a word, the two coyotes got their hats and their supply of water from the cab. It was at least 20 kilometers back to the nearest Mexico-side habitation and that was a long, long walk in the heat of the day. But, they had water and they had the track to follow. They'd make it. They started their walk past the truck.

"What about them?" The driver's assistant gestured at the back of the truck and the voices coming from within the metal box. The driver looked at it. The rear doors were secured by a standard door lock, enough to hold them closed under normal circumstances but if desperate people started a determined effort to get out, the lock would burst. He took a crowbar form the tool kit and rammed it through the door handles, sealing the doors firmly and irrevocably closed.

"That's their problem."

Pilot's Briefing Room, HIJMS Nisshin, *Kagoshima Bay*

"Idiots." Lieutenant Commander Toda Endo looked around the briefing room. The seaplane fighter squadrons had an unusual structure, one unique to them and dictated by their unconventional operations. The Kokutai had 48 aircraft and two tenders, 24 fighters based on each. Those 24 fighters, divided into eight sections of three aircraft each, formed the two squadrons of the Kokutai. He commanded the second, the junior, of those two squadrons. Including himself, there should be 24 pilots in the room. This morning, there were 23. One was represented by an empty seat, the deceased pilot's hat and gloves placed respectfully on it. Endo looked around again and decided to reinforce the point. "Bloody fools."

That got a reaction at last. The pilots, stunned by the incident the night before were goaded to anger by the insult. They were kept in control by one thing only; a small thing but one that had implications far outside its size. It was a small ribbon on Toda's uniform, one placed above all the others. A white bar of silk with the Rising Sun in its middle. And in the middle of the Rising Sun was a small gold cherry blossom. It was the insignia awarded to those who flew the Ohka attack missiles, the pilots who, if the American bombers came to destroy Japan, would fly against American cities to exact their last, posthumous, revenge.

There were thousands of volunteers for the Ohka units, both the ones based on the Navy's Fugaku-Kai intercontinental bombers and on the missile-carrying submarines that cruised off America's coast. Thousands of volunteers and only a few were accepted. The selection process was rigorous, even brutal; all but the best pilots were quickly weeded out.

There was more required of an Ohka pilot than mere technical excellence in flying. The Ohka pilots had to represent the true spirit of the Samurai, the ultimate expression of the warrior spirit. They were being asked to fly alone, against enormous odds facing certain, inevitable death to deliver Japan's ultimate weapon. They were selected for their moral strength as well as their skills. In words that had become old-fashioned in the days of nuclear weapons and missiles, they were selected for nobility of character as well as flying ability.

That was why there was such suppressed rage in the briefing room. Every man there knew that Toda had been accepted as an Ohka pilot, had flown at least one operational tour as a Ohka pilot. How many tours he had flown didn't matter; once a man was accepted into the Ohka community, he never had anything else to prove.

The pilots knew the measure of the man standing in front of them, knew he was judging them by his own, exalted standards; knew that he believed they had failed to meet those standards and condemned them for it. Worse, they knew they deserved condemnation; that knowledge fed their guilt and anger at being exposed. Even worse, they knew their guilt was deserved; the events of the previous night had shown it.

Observation Platform, Bridge, HIJMS Nisshin*, Kagoshima Bay. Six hours earlier.*

There was something critically wrong with the Second Section of the Tainan Kokutai. Toda had got a hint of that earlier in the day. The Tainan Kokutai was equipped with the N5M4 version of the Ohtori. Four of the N5Ms six Tanto-Kai missiles were carried in a pair of internal bays. The lower doors were pneumatically sealed against water ingress so the bays were loaded through access hatches in the top of the fuselage. Somebody had realized that the same bays could also hold 100 kilogram bombs, the dimensions of bomb and missile were almost identical. That had been introduced with the

N5M4, giving the aircraft a limited strike capability. Toda hadn't seen the M4 version of the Ohtori before so, when he'd first arrived on *Nisshin,* he'd stood on the deck aft, looking at the four aircraft on the catapults, more on the deck and in the hangar being maintained while the rest floated alongside.

"Good aircraft these." The maintenance chief had remarked when asked. "Only a few hours on them." The gulf between enlisted ranks and officers in the Japanese forces was wide but when experienced NCOs spoke, wise officers listened. And there was much to listen to in those six simple words.

He'd scheduled a day flight for one element of the section and a night mission for the second. The day mission had been disappointing, station keeping was sloppy and the aircraft were flown clumsily. Both betrayed a lack of practice that stood ill against the Tainan Kokutai's reputation and the records of training missions flown. A slack commander, one who didn't push his crews to improve themselves, could easily explain that. What was happening as the night mission was landing had no such charitable explanation.

The first fighter came in too fast; instead of skipping across the waves to settle elegantly at the end of its run, it had hit the first, bounced high and then dropped bodily on to the water in a shroud of spray. It had, eventually, finished its run and been towed in but the aircraft would need a major inspection for structural damage caused by the heavy landing.

The second aircraft had less spectacular but potentially even more serious problems . The pilot had completely misjudged his docking and nearly put his Ohtori into *Nisshin's* unyielding steel side. Only the quick and deft attention of the boat crews had stopped the accident. Even worse, the pilot showed no sign that he knew how close his aircraft had come to disaster.

It was the third landing that topped off the disastrous mission. As Toda watched he knew what was happening. The pilot was flying by the seat of his pants, without watching his instruments. The nose-high attitude of the aircraft gave him wrong clues; the lack of an easily-discernible horizon prevented him checking on them. His instincts told him that the nose-high attitude meant he was climbing; in fact, he was already sinking slowly towards the sea surface. To correct the imaginary climb, the pilot was cutting back on power, causing his sink rate to increase still further.

The situation was already past critical; Toda saw the pilot realize his error and ram the throttles forward to try and regain flying speed. It was too late, far too late. The Ohtori's delta wing bled off speed and energy too fast for any recovery and too fast for the added power of the jet to compensate. A few feet above the sea surface the Ohtori stalled, its nose snapped down so that the aircraft was dead level when it hit the sea. The front tip of the ski dug into a wave, flipping the aircraft over in a perfect cartwheel. At the end of the first somersault, the tail hit the surface of the sea; the impact breaking it clean off. Then, the aircraft disintegrated in a ball of spray and flying wreckage that quickly vanished inside the fireball explosion of the remaining fuel. For a brief second, Toda believed he saw the dark shape of the pilot being thrown out of the cockpit but then it was too late and all that was left was fire.

Pilot's Briefing Room, HIJMS Nisshin*, Kagoshima Bay*

"You think we will meet our lost comrade in Yasukuni? I tell you now we will not. Yasukuni is the shrine for our fallen dead, those who died in honorable combat. Not for a fool who made simple, elementary mistakes that even the youngest of cadets, with their pilot's wings still shining and new, knows how to avoid. You!" Endo pointed at the leader of one of the elements. He'd picked the man because his eyes were bulging with anger but there was also fear there. "How many night landings have you made since you came to this group?"

It was a deadly question. The regulations said that each pilot should fly three missions per week; at least one had to be at night with total flight time not to exceed two hours. It was obvious from the previous day's performance that none of these pilots had even come close.

The chosen victim flushed red and shuffled his feet. "One." He admitted the fact as if drawing it from him caused personal agony.

Which it probably did. “One in the last year. And twenty in daytime.”

Toda nodded. The pilot’s log said he’d flown the correct number of fifty training flights at night and one hundred in daytime. “Is there anybody in this room who has flown the number of missions indicated in your logs?” There was a dead silence. “I thought not. What will happen if you go up against the Tripehounds tomorrow? Will you even see the fighter that kills you? You know no more of combat flying than the rawest recruits. So that is how you will be treated.

“I have ordered that your logs be taken to the incinerators and burned. They do not exist any more. Today, you all joined this formation and your training will start again. We have little time. Already, the South China Sea Squadron is preparing to sortie to secure our hold on our possessions in the area. The Tainan Kokutai is to transfer to the area after that has been done. So we must accelerate our flying schedule, make up for all the time that has been lost. We will be flying every day while we have the time to do so.”

“Sir, what will we do for fuel Sir?”

“Leave that to me.”

Captain’s Bridge, HIJMS Nisshin, *Kagoshima Bay.*

“So what did happen to all the fuel?”

“I have no idea. Your predecessor told me that the number of flying hours had been cut back due to the fuel shortage. I had no cause to disbelieve him and the amount of fuel being delivered was appropriate to the number of missions being flown.” It was true enough, the whole Japanese Navy was suffering from a fuel shortage. The seaplane units were lucky, they were being issued enough fuel for 100 hours flying per aircraft per year. The carrier and land based squadrons got enough for fifty. “I should have checked with *Mizuho* down at Ehime but it never occurred to me that it was not as I had been told.”

Toda looked at the Captain. Technically, the captain commanded the ship and he commanded the airgroup; that meant the captain was his superior. Only, on aviation ships, it was much more a match of equals than theory said. The captain's words rang true; he had to run his ship, why should he assume his air group commander was lying to him. "There was no reason why you should Sir. But, fuel will be arriving soon, a lot of it. We will be burning it off fast but the storage might be a problem. You have good, strong seamen in your engine rooms?"

"The best. As tough as they come."

"Excellent, may I borrow six of the strongest?"

Oil Fuel Storage and Distribution Facility, Kagoshima Bay.

"Yowurg shrugwap ghluff bawaayr!"

It didn't make much sense but coherent language was a bit difficult for the manager of the distribution facility. He knew what he wanted to say; the presence of the barrel belonging to an Argentine Star .38 Super pistol in his mouth made enunciating quite difficult.

"Let me clarify the issue." Toda spoke in a friendly and cooperative manner. As a concession to the dignity of the manager, hadn't taken the slack off the trigger of his pistol . . . yet. "According to your records, over the last year your facility has issued sufficient jet fuel for 2,400 flying hours to the seaplane carrier *Nisshin*. The problem is, *Nisshin* only received enough jet fuel for 370 flying hours. What, I wonder, happened to all the rest?" Endo's face was thoughtful as he contemplated this serious problem. Then, he had the solution and his face brightened. "I know, I shall hand this whole problem over to the Kempeitai and ask them to find my fuel."

"NOOOOOO." Terror of Japan's notorious "thought police" made the manager get the words out, even around the pistol barrel. Many believed it was better to be guilty when arrested by the Kempeitai; that way they would kill their prisoner, eventually. If their prisoner turned out to be innocent, they would leave them alive.

After a few hours in the hands of the Kempeitai, the living envied the dead.

"So where is my fuel?" Toda pulled the barrel out of the manager's mouth and looked with disgust at the mess on the end. That pistol was his prized possession, bought in Saigon. Tonight, it would be cleaned with loving attention and the use of fine white silk rags.

"I will tell you where it is. You have sold it to the Black Dragon Society. Now, I want it back. How you get it is your problem, not mine. But I want four hundred flying hours worth of fuel at the dockside tomorrow by 0900. Be assured, at 0901 I will be calling the Kempeitai unless I am too busy checking my fuel delivery. Then you will deliver an equal amount of fuel every time I call until the deficit is made up. Five deliveries in all; 2,000 flying hours. You may keep the other 30 for your trouble. Do we understand each other?"

The manager nodded, his eyes glued on the strip of white silk with its Imperial sunrise and golden cherry blossom. That simple ribbon meant that when this officer asked, even the Kempeitai would jump in response. Mentally, he did some quick calculations. He had enough fuel on hand to fulfill the first delivery and if he scraped around, called in a few old debts, he would have enough for the second. The rest? He would have to work the system for that. Perhaps he could short change two of the carriers? There were two here, both near derelict and their groups were virtually ghosts. He could take their fuel and reassign it, that would make up the third delivery - perhaps.

Toda walked away, much happier than he'd been all day. Behind him six burly members of *Nisshin's* black gang walked, filled with admiration for the young officer who'd set that corrupt clerk by his heels. Truly, the Ohka pilots were indeed proper examples of the true warrior spirit that made Japan great. Toda was aware of their admiration and his back straightened just a little as a result. He was, of course, only doing his duty but duty well-done brought its own rewards. Now, he had enough fuel to train his group now, they could squeeze a year's worth of flying into three or four weeks. He just hoped he had that long.

Eastern Airlines Boeing 747 Spirit of Atlanta, *Dillinger International Airport, Havana, Cuba.*

"Ladies and gentlemen. Welcome to Dillinger International, gateway to the island paradise of Cuba. Please remain seated until the aircraft comes to a halt and the accessway has been secured. When the floor light by each row of seats turns white, the passengers in that row will please go down to the lower deck of the aircraft, collect your luggage and proceed out of the aircraft towards the immigration area. Those who are disabled, have young children or need help with their luggage, just ask one of 'the boys' downstairs for help."

Outside, the eight engines on the 747 were running down as the "people hauler" started to unload its cargo of tourists. The short-haul, high capacity version of the 747 could carry almost a thousand people fully loaded, and handling that many passengers was an art form. The old-style pattern of check-in was long gone. Now, passengers took their tickets and were awarded their seat assignment on the upper deck of the aircraft and a locker on the lower deck. They carried their own bags onto the aircraft, stored them in their assigned locker, then collected them themselves on the way out.

"*Dillinger International*?" David Peterson's voice was awed. "They named their airport after *John Dillinger!*"

Judith Peterson chuckled at his shock. "They were giving the finger to Washington. Savannah named its airport after J Edgar Hoover so the mob here named theirs after John Dillinger. Get ready; the row in front is moving."

They were sitting in the two aisle-side seats of the left-hand bank of four. There was another bank of six in the middle of the aircraft then another aisle and another bank of four. Fourteen abreast and their cabin had 15 rows of seats. Two hundred passengers per cabin and five cabins per aircraft. Each cabin had its own galley, its own cinema screen and its own access way to the luggage/cargo deck beneath.

The Petersons had paid a premium and got seats in the foremost cabin. That meant they were first on and first off. The cheapest seats were in the middle of the aircraft, there the headroom was restricted by the wing that ran over the top of the fuselage and noise from the eight engines was a nuisance.

Out, down the steps and to their luggage locker. Their bags were there, safe of course, and they towed them out of the aircraft. That was one advantage of the people-haulers, the high wing and double decks meant that passengers unloaded relatively close to the ground. Around them, young men in gray suits watched the passengers move out of the aircraft. One of them spotted an old woman and her husband struggling with a case and moved in to help. The staff here were the lowest rung on the ladder of the Colombo family that ran the airport, a rung so low it didn't even have a name. Yet every one of them knew that good work was the key to the long trek up through the ranks of the family. In a weird, distorted way, mob-run Cuba was a meritocracy

"LOOK at all these advertisements. Are any of them legal back in ole Virginny?" The passenger accessway to 'immigration' was crowded with posters, publicizing the attractions of Cuba's various resorts. Judith Peterson guessed that the casino advertisements were illegal on the mainland; some of the floorshows certainly were. Then she realized that her husband's eyes were glued to a poster featuring an exceptionally buxom Latina woman posing seductively over a slogan that offered escorts for hire by the hour, day or week. She kicked him hard on the ankle.

"Nice dress she's almost wearing." Her voice was sweetly demure.

"Uhhh, just looking. They got male escorts too you know." That got him another kick on the ankle. "Glad you came honeybun?"

"Oh yes, we need a break. I was frightened when the shooting happened but it seems to have died down a bit now. I guess this must be immigration."

It was, and the speed with which the formalities were completed reduced other airports to envious despair. A passport was taken, stamped, and returned within a few seconds, the 'immigrant" barely had a chance to stop walking before it was back in his or her hands. After all, the whole point of the Cuban economy was to get people in, not keep them out.

"Excuse me, sir, how do we get to our hotel?" David Peterson was speaking to one of "the boys" who was lazing around by the immigration desks. Judith looked at the man more closely, he was subtly different from the kids who had been helping passengers and waving them through immigration. The eyes were harder and there was a bulge under his jacket. Tourists called all the Mob employees "the boys" but this man really was one; a Mob gunman, probably one of the airport security people.

"Which one are you going to, sir."

"The Imperial, On the Golden Boulevard."

"Limos are out through those doors. Take the ones with the green doors for the Genovese places. Need help with them bags?"

"No thanks. We need the exercise or will soon with all the good eating."

"Ain't that the truth." The wiseguy made the tip Peterson gave him vanish, then touched his fedora to Judith. "Welcome to Cuba Ma'am."

CHAPTER FOUR
SCOUTING

Desert on the Mexico-Arizona border.

"That doesn't look right." First Sergeant Esteban Tomas waved at the column of buzzards circling in the sky. "There's something dead down there."

The Force Recon Detachment was spread out along the hillside, looking across at the scene below. A wrecked truck on an ill-defined path in the desert was the center of the bird's interest. It might be meaningless buzzards had been known to mistake a truck for a dying animal and circle it, waiting patiently for it to fall over and die. But this didn't smell like that. There was something different about the situation, something Tomas couldn't quite put his finger on. His instincts were telling him this was a bad situation and instincts were there for a reason.

Force Recon units learned to trust their instincts early or they never made the grade. Popularly, Force Recon were lost in the glare of legend about the SEALs and assumed to be their Marine equivalent. In the real world, their roles were quite different. The SEALs went into heavily-defended areas and extracted things or people with as little fuss as possible. Notoriously, the first jailers time learned that their American prisoner had been rescued by a SEAL team was when they opened the cell in the morning to find it empty except for the traditional cartoon of a seal balancing a ball on its nose pinned to the wall.

Force Recon's job was to be equally invisible but to watch, to learn and to inform. The SEALs got in and out without being seen, Force Recon got in and stayed in - without being seen.

Now, they were watching the border, from the Mexican side. They'd been assigned the job shortly after the machine gun attack on the Senate building. Somehow, the law enforcement authorities had got the idea that the threat had been planned in Latin America, perhaps in Mexico itself, perhaps further south. There were probably other Force Recon teams down there watching, learning, reporting. And probably SEAL teams as well, picking up the people involved and spiriting them away.

Tomas had been in Force Recon for three years, after three more spent with the Ordnance Proving Ground helping to develop and test the Corps' new machine-gun. After the disastrous Battle of the Rock Pile, the Marines had insisted on a proper machine gun: a version of the MG-42 chambered for the .27-59 cartridge. That's how the project had started. Consulting with the Russians had come up with a better solution; the German MG-45. A roller-locked weapon capable of firing 1,800 rounds a minute, it chewed up ammunition fast but its firepower was devastating. Coupled with the high-velocity .27-59, it was a formidable weapon and was now the M-81 in American use. This Force Recon team had one although if they ever had to fire it, it would mean they had failed.

"Let's take a look. Alpha Section, come with me, Beta and Charlie Sections, stay up here on overwatch."

Tomas wasn't technically in command of the unit but the officer who was had gone sick a couple of days earlier. The four men in Alpha Section rose and jog-trotted down the slope towards the wrecked truck. It was obvious what had happened. Driven too fast down the track, it had hit a rock, wrecked its suspension and cracked the cylinder block wide open. Getting closer also revealed what was attracting the buzzards, the stench of decay was sickening. Tomas had a grim sense of certainty what he was going to find.

The rear doors of the truck were sealed shut by a crowbar forced between the two door handles. The door metal bulged out around the bar, creased where it had been forced against the unyielding steel. “Knock that bar out.” Tomas’s voice was quiet, almost afraid at the horror he knew was within the back of the truck. A quick swing of an M-14 rifle butt achieving what the people trapped inside could never have done, knocking the bar clear.

Without its reinforcement, the rear doors flew open, propelled by the weight of the pile of people stacked against them. They’d died trying to force their way out, or perhaps the doors had opened enough to allow a thin draft of cool air from outside. Even the 120 degree desert heat was cool compared to the inside of a sealed metal box, standing unprotected in the full glare of the sun. It took very little imagination to visualize the scene inside the back of the truck as those inside had fought for that tiny breath of cool air.

The Marines vomited at the foul stench that filled their world, a sickening draft of decay, corruption and despair. It was one that seemed to have absorbed the terror of the nightmare that had taken place in the back of the truck. A thick liquid ran out, staining the ground around the back of the truck. The two Marines closest jumped clear, trying to get away from the vile ooze. An arm flopped out and as it did so, some of the flesh fell away from the bones.

“Perfectly cooked. The temperature in there must have hit 160 at least. Poor bastards never stood a chance.”

The Marine stopped and looked at Tomas. The First Sergeant had never made a secret of his Mexican ancestry - or that he’d been a bandit before ‘seeing the light’ as he’d put it. The fact of his salvation and a suitably sanitized version of how it had happened was one of the standard sermons when he gave the homily at his local Catholic church. The Marine was afraid his words might have given offense and no Marine ever knowingly gave offense to a man who wore the pale blue ribbon.

“At least that high, they tried to batter their way out but they had nothing to do it with. They probably lasted a day or so, perhaps two, but the survivors would have been insane by then." Tomas's voice shook with rage and anger.

As if to contradict his words, there was a terrible racking groan from inside the truck body. Tomas's lips went dead white, his tanned skin turning to a sickening shade of gray. "Oh dear God, there's people still alive in there."

Main Conference Room, National Security Council Building, Washington D.C.

"There were *survivors*?" LBJ's voice was incredulous. "In that heat, without water for three days, that's little short of a miracle. That desert is a killer."

"It would be hard to call them survivors, Mister President. They were dead, they just hadn't stopped breathing yet. Their bodies were cooked through; their brains destroyed by the heat. They were displaying basic autonomic functions that hadn't quite run down. There was no consciousness there, no soul." The Seer looked slightly uncomfortable using that last word, it didn't fit in with the aseptic, clinical world of the NSC.

"Those functions ceased before they could be taken to hospital. The medical opinion verdict was DOD, dead on discovery. That's a kindness to the Marines more than anything else. What they found out there shook those men to their core. They needed to know that there was nothing they, or anybody else, could have done."

"Shook Marines to their core." Johnson's voice was almost disbelieving but his words belied that. "I can see how they might be."

"Shocking as this might be," Nixon sounded impatient, "we're missing the basic point of this incident. Why were these people trying to cross the border illegally? It's not as if getting from Mexico to here is difficult. The border is wide open. Too open some might say."

"That is a mystery. We've deliberately made crossing the border relatively easy for just this reason. It's better to have people come over legally than illegally. All a young man has to do to get entry to the United States is to join the armed forces. If they make the grade, five years service and they're eligible for citizenship. Most take it and re-up. Statistically, once in, they re-enlist once on average for a service of 10 years. Some a lot more than that."

"I'm not happy about so many foreigners in our forces."

"It's worked, Mister President-elect. So far anyway. We have, on average, 40,000 such immigrants earning their citizenship that way at any one time. By the way. 20 percent of those awarded The Medal were first-generation immigrants, some fresh off the boats or over the border."

"What medal? Citizens good conduct?"

Sitting behind Nixon, Secretary of Defense-Designate Melvin Laird winced perceptibly. Clark Clifford was less reticent. After all, his tenure of office was measured in days now. "Mister President-Elect. When somebody in this building mentions 'The Medal', they only mean one. The Congressional Medal of Honor."

Nixon's face took on a sulking expression. The Seer decided it was time to rescue him and move on. "Other than those who choose military service, all somebody needs to get in is an employer. If they have a job to go to, they come in as guest workers. Takes a bit longer to qualify for citizenship that way but it happens. There are agencies down south that act as recruiters for the appropriate companies up here.

"Companies that want to employ cheap, unskilled labor, for that's what most of these immigrants are, let those agencies know who and what they need. The agencies have the people who want to come and they match them up. It's a big industry in Mexico in particular. All quite legal and relatively easy. When the immigrants cross over, Immigration gives them a health check, makes sure their employment sponsor is genuine and then waves them through. Oh, Immigration checks on them once in a while, to make sure they are where they are supposed to be. If they change jobs they have to tell the INS but that's about it."

"So, since it's that easy, my question stands. Why were these people trying to cross the border illegally? And how many of them are there? Have we found other incidents like this?"

"So far, we have found the primary reasons why people attempt illegal crossings are associated with crime. Either workers are being imported for criminal activities, usually women for the sex trade, or criminals themselves going over the border in an attempt to find richer pickings up here. The latter don't usually last long, they make a couple of big scores by their standards, throw the money around and shoot their mouths off down there. Then, one night, they vanish and turn up in a courtroom here. The courts don't care how they got there, just that they did.

"SEALs?" LBJ's voice was amused, he could guess what was coming and wasn't disappointed.

The Seer threw his hands up in shock and rolled his eyes theatrically. "Us? Heaven forfend. We believe that they simply had a crisis of conscience and turned themselves in." There was a brief chuckle around the room.

"You know, Seer, looking back over the last eight years, we show remarkably little regard for other nations sovereignty."

"Sir, if other nations don't bother us, we don't bother them. If they respect our citizens and interests, we respect theirs. If they don't involve us in something, we don't get involved. We respect other nations sovereignty exactly as much as they respect ours." LBJ nodded, he knew that The Seer was speaking to Nixon, not him - and that he'd made the comment to get exactly that response.

"So what are the other reasons we get illegal immigrants over the border?"

"Mostly, its a racket run by people called coyotes. They offer transit over the border and tell their victims there are jobs waiting over the other side for them. They charge about half of what the regular employment agencies do. Mostly they just dump the illegals over our side of the border; then we pick them up and deport them.

Sometimes they just take the would-be illegals out into the desert and kill them. We find such massacres now and then but this one is unusual in its brutality."

The Seer stopped and stared into space for a few seconds. There were other reasons why people tried illegal crossings of course but none were very significant. He had the uneasy feeling he'd mentioned the significant one but couldn't put his finger on exactly which one it was.

"Seer, I know I'm not President until January 19th, but this whole situation makes me uneasy. There's somebody planning something down there and I don't like it. I suggest we step up border surveillance and put a stop to these coyotes." Sitting behind him, quietly taking notes for her principal, Naamah found herself agreeing with him. The old saying ran through her mind, '*just because somebody is paranoid doesn't mean other people are not out to get them.'* She could see why Nixon was worried. So could the Seer.

"I think that is a very timely precaution. Mister President?"

LBJ nodded. "First that gun attack, now this. Richard, nothing personal, no offense meant but this is the time when the whole government is weakest. I'm a lame duck and you're not sworn in yet. I don't like this happening now. Increasing border security is a good step. We'll do two steps, I'll order one, you order the second after the 19th. That way we both end up looking good."

The Elysium Fields Restaurant, Imperial Hotel, Havana, Cuba.

Sometimes, not often but sometimes, tropical nights live up to their reputation. This was one such night. Overhead, the stars shone with a brilliance only dimmed by the light pollution of Havana's Golden Boulevard. The scent of tropical flowers filled the night, mingling with the smell of fine cooking and accented by the chirping of the night lizards and crickets. A gentle rippling noise underlay that serenade, the signature of water flowing through the grounds of the restaurant. The place was laid out in a series of small islands, each with its own table, screened by bushes and flowers, joined by delicate wooden bridges. The islands had a dim, discrete light but not all were lit. A light that had been turned off didn't mean the table was unoccupied; it was a signal that the occupants did not want to be disturbed.

Judith and David Peterson picked their way through the maze of bridges towards an empty island, carefully avoiding the ones shrouded in tactful darkness. They'd already picked their table out. Their Floor Captain had done them proud, reserving one that was quietly tucked away yet easy to serve. They were about halfway there when another figure stepped out from a side island, a furtive figure, something that seemed incongruous in a society where everybody was either a wiseguy, employed by them or one of their clients. Where behavior that almost anywhere else would constitute brazen criminality was the norm, it was furtiveness that was abnormal.

"Hey, you want some party favors?" The man's voice was accented, not Cuban but from somewhere further south.

"No thank you." David Peterson's voice was polite but final.

"You try these. Its the best quality stuff. Better than anything else you can get here."

That really was suspicious. The Peterson's hadn't been on Cuba long but they'd already got a firm grasp on the fundamental rule of the society. *DON'T* annoy the tourists. Hard and soft drugs were openly on sale, the travel shop in the hotel stocked them alongside the magazines, on the same shelf as the aspirin, Tylenol and Alka-Seltzer. They were there, but if a guest wasn't interested, nobody pushed them. This man was pushing. The Petersons tried to step around him but he moved to block their path. That was another mistake; it attracted the attention of a waitress who apologized to the guests she was serving, picked up their table telephone and called Hotel Security.

"I give you coke best quality. Half the price the people here charge." Judith Peterson stopped suddenly. She'd grown up in Gangland New York, had lived there and knew the rules. Nobody, but nobody, undercut a crew on their own turf. What was going on here wasn't part of the local scene.

"Hey David, perhaps we ought to listen to him." Her husband started. Using his full name was a pre-arranged danger signal between them. If he was 'David' or she was 'Judith', it meant the speaker had spotted something wrong.

"You really think so, Judith?" She relaxed slightly. Message received and understood.

"Perhaps some party favors might be good. Got anything zippy?"

"Whatever you want lady. Just name it."

"Ma'am, this man troubling you?" Judith relaxed the rest of the way. Two men in the traditional light gray suits and fedora hats had arrived from behind. The bigger one grabbed the dealer from behind, pinning his arms to his sides. His partner looked inquisitively at the Petersons; hard, brown eyes glittering in the lights.

"He's trying to push favors on us. We stalled him until you got here. Says he charges half the price of the hotel concessions."

"He did, did he? Not a good thing. Mister Genovese thanks you for your help and apologizes for youse being inconvenienced." The wiseguy scribbled quickly on a card. "Give this to the waiter after your meal, Mister Genovese would like you to eat as his guests tonight. And he'll be offended if youse don't do yourselves proud."

The Petersons took off to their table, their annoyance at the interruption to an evening forgotten in the slightly guilty thrill of eating at the expense of the infamous Don Vito Genovese. Behind them, two more men in the familiar light gray suits had joined the "boys" from Hotel Security.

"No offense to Don Vito, Bomp, but the Commission needs to know what this guy thinks he was playing at. He wasn't one of yours gone bad, was he?"

Frank "The Bomp" Bompensiero looked at the terrified figure held firmly in the hands of his large assistant. Jack "The Horse" Licavoli lifted his prisoner up, turned him around and looked into his face, all without any apparent effort. The Bomp and The Horse exchanged glances and shook their heads. "Ain't one of ours, Dapper John. Youse welcome to him. With Mister Genovese's compliments." The Bomp was a made man and that gave him the right to speak for his Don.

If the Petersons had looked the right way as they were seated at their table, they would have seen their erstwhile "dealer" being unceremoniously sapped then stuffed in the trunk of a brand-new black Packard limousine. But they didn't, and their extravagant dinner was unspoiled by curiosity as to his fate.

INS Mysore, *Off Pattle Island, Paracel Group, South China Sea*

"*Nilgiri* reports that *Sukanya* is starting to unload now Sir." Admiral Kanali Dahm paced his bridge impatiently while his doggie made his report. The three Project 16C APDs had landed the landing force, First Battalion, the Punjab Rifles, smoothly and efficiently. As far as that part of the plan had been concerned, everything was well enough. The trouble was that the plans had been changed again. At the last minute, it had been decided to include an engineer unit in the initial wave so an early start could be made on building the runway on Pattle Island.

Like all small last-minute decisions, this one had started a chain of ramifications. The engineers equipment couldn't be accommodated on the old APDs so a small freighter had to be added to the group. Unfortunately, the vehicle transports in the Indian Navy were all 12 knot designs and the APD group would be running at 24. So, a civilian fast freighter had to be chartered at short notice. Civilian freighters didn't carry landing craft so the ones on the APDs had to do the job - and they could handle only one vehicle at a time. So an unloading process that was supposed to take one hour had already taken six and there was no end in sight.

"They won't be finished before dusk." Dahm's staff officer had anticipated the next question. "Nowhere even close. They'll have the light equipment ashore but the heavy stuff will have to wait until morning. We've looked at working under floodlights but the tides will be wrong and we don't have the equipment here anyway."

More problems. This initial landing was supposed to be an in and out job. That's why they'd used the APDs to bring the first group. Now they would be stuck here for at least 24 hours while they got the engineering kit ashore. Dahm stared at the situation chart and the strategic displays.

"Radio the commander of TG2.1. Tell him to get the *Sukanya* and the APDs inside the atoll by nineteen hundred. Order *Nilgiri* and *Udagiri* to take up positions three miles east and west of Pattle respectively. They're the goalkeepers if anything happens."

Dahm looked at the map, there were Chipanese bases to the north, northeast, northwest and west of them. The ones due west were Army tactical airfields and out of range. Army pilots didn't fly much over water anyway. The threat was northwest, the big airfield complexes around Hanoi and Haiphong. Some of those were Navy and they were close enough to be a threat. Chipanese bombers based there were in range of Pattle Island; only just, but they were in range.

"We'll position ourselves here." Dahm tapped the operational display. "Northwest of Pattle, on the direct route from the bases at Hanoi. That way we can spring a missile trap on any Chipanese friends that are up there. Do we have a list of what's at Hanoi?"

"Genzan Kokutai Sir. Orace bombers and Irene fighters. The bombers can only just make it down here, the fighters don't have a chance. Anyway, Orace is a nuclear delivery bird; it has no other function. It's bombload is pretty light so if it came in conventional, well, its a lot of effort to put a few bombs on target. There's some Quills at Haiphong, but they're Army now. Took them over from the Navy after the Showa Restoration Coup. I doubt if we'll see those."

"This won't go nuclear. Not yet at any rate. The Septics won't stand for it. They've made that very clear, toss a nuke and they'll throw a whole SAC-load right back. That's why we offloaded the nuke warheads for our Sagarikas. My guess is their fleet will do the same. Nobody wants to take the chance of having them on board." Dahm sighed. *The plan had been to get his ships clear of here by dusk. Now I'm chained here by the need to defend the shipping at Pattle Island.* He felt like he was trying to fight with one leg tied to a stake. "The threat'll come from Hanoi. Has to. We'll get between as a blocking force. If the Chimps do launch an air raid we can chew it up out there."

The staff officer stared at the display and punched in the coordinates for the indicated position. "If we set sail at nineteen hundred and make 20 knots, we can be there by midnight. Chimps won't be operating before then. If they're going to hit Pattle, they'll want to make the run at oh-three hundred or thereabouts."

"Agreed. Make it so."

B10N-1 Shuka Mi-121, *100 miles north east of Pattle Island*

"Niitakayama Nobore!" Captain Genda Minoru gave the order with triumph soaring in his heart His hands pushed the throttles forward, cutting in the afterburners and sending the two Ne-90 engines up to their full 11,000 kilograms of thrust. Sitting beside him in the cockpit, his weapons systems operator reached for the variable sweep controls, and pulled the wings back from their semi-swept position to the fully-swept setting. The combination greatly increased thrust and the low-drag swept position of the wings sent his speed soaring. The slam in the small of his back told him that his Shuka had come alive, that she was running at Mach 1.3 barely 50 meters above the surface of the sea. Alongside, the other five B10N bombers in the formation were keeping pace as the attack formation went from cruising to battle speed.

Shoulder-fired anti-aircraft missiles had made the low-level rampages of fighter bombers a long-dead tactic. In a world where any respectable army gave out such missiles to every platoon, every squad, every vehicle, flying low over a battlefield was suicide. Genda had read of the slaughter low-flying fighter-bombers had inflicted on ground troops, the stories of Sturmoviks and Ostriches, of

Thunderbolts and Grizzlies and heard his father tell of such things. Those stories were history; their tactics as obsolete as the phalanx, the longbow and the samurai.

Today, safety lay in speed and altitude, fly over the defenses the way the cursed Americans did. Only not here, not tonight, not with these aircraft, for the B10N-1 was a revolution in aircraft design. Its Ne-90 turbofan engines were economical yet powerful, but that didn't make the aircraft so different. It was its wings; wings that could swing backwards and forwards as the crew wished. Stretched out in the mid-forward position for high altitude, the B10N-1 could make Mach 2.6 and climb to 22,000 meters. Wings further forward still, the aircraft could take off and land on small airstrips, not the huge concrete plains the Americans used. With the wings retracted right aft, it could make Mach 1.3 only a few meters above the sea surface to skim under the enemy radar coverage.

The sea, that made the difference. There were no shoulder-fired anti-aircraft missiles at sea. There was no terrain either; the ground avoidance radar kept the aircraft skimming at a set distance over the surface. It would do that over land as well, but the natural contours of the ground made the aircraft bounce and lurch in ways that played hell with the pilot's back. Over the sea, the aircraft vibrated and shook but that was all. Down low, the enemy would only see them coming when they crossed the radar horizon, less than 90 seconds from their target. Flying faster than sound, there would be nothing to warn the Tripehounds that the Shukas were coming to punish them for their impertinence of landing on Japanese territory.

Fast, low-flying and more sophisticated than any other aircraft in the Japanese Navy or Army, the Shuka had had its problems. Severe development problems had made it more than four years late in entering service. Even now they hadn't been fully solved. During the test program, the navy had lost aircraft after aircraft as one problem had followed another. The Mihoro Kokutai only had 24 B10N-1s on strength; the six aircraft flying tonight were all that were serviceable.

Still, it was the first combat mission of the new aircraft. As the six had taxied out, their wings stretched forward, their cockpit canopies opened, the centrally-hinged panels looking strangely like seagulls in the dark of the night, everybody in the Hainan Island airbase had turned out to watch. Each of the twelve men in the Shukas had a white headband wrapped around the helmet of his flight suit, given to them by the ground crews to protect them on this mission. As the aircraft had taken off, their engine exhausts scoring long lines in the darkness, the entire airbase had cheered and saluted. Even the Admiral had been there to watch them leave. It had felt good.

"Running close to Pattle Island now. Enemy radar signal strength picking up." The WSO was using the aircraft's ESM receiver to measure the strength of the enemy radar. According to the satellite photographs they'd seen just before take-off, there were two frigates by the island. They had Jabiru anti-aircraft missiles and were the primary threat. They were defenses though, and they weren't primary targets. Each crew, on each aircraft, knew where they had to put their bombs to do the most damage.

The key was the radar on the frigates. If those could be disabled for just three minutes, their presence wouldn't matter. At the moment the six racing Shukas were below the radar horizon so the only energy they were picking up was that ducted along the sea surface. It would be below the threshold strength for a firm contact. As they crossed the radar horizon that would change suddenly, the signal strength soaring as ducted emissions gave way to direct paints. Just like it was doing now. . . . "East wind, hail!" The code words. East wind meant radar contact, hail meant hit the enemy radars with jamming. All six Shukas were running their jammers at full power as they tried to blind the search and fire control radars on the two frigates.

Operation Room, INS Udagiri*, three miles west of Pattle Island.*

Sub-lieutenant Gitta yawned and looked again at the scope of his Shiva air search radar. The big set was scanning constantly, surveying the sea far out to the west. Nothing there; why should there be? It was oh-three thirty, that dreadful time of night known across the world's militaries as oh-dark-thirty, when the whole world seemed asleep and those who were not would like to join them. Then,

Gitta saw a quick flash of a contact to the North East before his whole scanning system dissolved into a mass of pinwheels and rotating clouds. Jamming and that meant. . . . . .

"AIR RAID WARNING RED, RED RED. Say again, *AIR RAID WARNING RED, RED, RED"*

Even as he raised his voice to give the alarm, his hands were flying over the controls of his radar. He was trying to burn through the jamming and give *Udagiri's* Jabiru missiles a target. He recognized the patterns, this was barrage jamming, raw energy poured into the sky to blind the searching radars. Well, there were ways to deal with that. He flipped over a switch, shifted frequencies and narrowed the transmission. Now, he was pouring all his radar energy down a single, tightly-defined frequency band. *Udagiri's* radar burned through the hostile jamming energy; the enemy transmissions that were spread over a wide range of frequencies and could not match the power of a set operating on a single narrow band.

For a second the display cleared. Gitta could see six hostile tracks spreading out as the aircraft went for individual targets, climbing to get clearance for their bombs. Then, another display of electronic mayhem as the bombers identified the frequency he was transmitting on and went to spot jamming. This time they were concentrating their jamming energy on the frequency *Udagiri* was using, blotting out the returns again. Well, there were ways of dealing with that as well. Another flip of the switch and the radar went to frequency-agile; hopping around from one frequency to the next in an attempt to find bands that weren't jammed. The screen cleared again but the picture was jerky, half-obscured sometimes, the track indistinct.

One thing was clear though, in the time taken to get a track, the bombers had moved far and fast. Nearly 1,800 kilometers per hour, at a guess, and they were already nearing Pattle Island.

B10N-1 Shuka Mi-121, *Approaching Pattle Island*

There was a strange symbol on the head-up display, a long green bar terminating in a circle. The bar was the aircraft's projected course, the circle where its bombs would land if the release was pressed now. Ahead, Genda could see the large freighter in the island lagoon that was his assigned target. Behind it was one of the small frigates that was a secondary. The green line was right across the center of the freighter and it would only take a tiny change of course to put it across the small frigate as well. But primaries first.

Genda was silent, his lips pressed shut as the green circle marched with frightening speed towards the freighter. Silent because his WSO was fighting his battle with the enemy frigate radar and missile controls and didn't need to know about anything else. Survival depended on him winning that electronic war.

Chartered Freighter Sukanya, *Pattle Island.*

Captain Pradesh had always guessed that his urgent desire to earn money would eventually do him in. Now it looked as if he was right. The radio was blasting out warnings. The warships around him were frantically coming to action stations. He couldn't see what the threat was, not yet.

But, what was that? His binoculars to his eyes, he saw something terrifying. A dragon, surrounded by a ghastly glow of green light, coming straight for him. He shook himself. Dragons didn't exist; he knew that. The trouble was, it wasn't comforting to tell himself that something that didn't exist was demonstrably doing its best to kill him.

Then he understood. The thing hurtling towards him was an aircraft, flying very low and blindingly fast, the glow surrounding it was the spray thrown up by the concussion wave of its passage. Yet it was silent. The words 'speed of sound' swept through his mind. He started to shake, for there was no doubt. The dragon was coming straight for him

B10N-1 Shuka Mi-203, *Approaching Pattle Island*

Lieutenant Hara was lined up on his target, the tent encampment right in the center of Pattle Island. His aircraft carried eight cluster bombs, four under the wings, four in the belly bomb bay.

Dropped across the encampment they would shred anything underneath them. Seven years earlier, the Americans had shown what cluster bombs could do to a target. Since then, Japan had concentrated on developing its own. Like the Shuka itself, tonight was the first night the new weapon was to be used in anger.

Off to his left, fire erupted from the bow of one of the Indian frigates. For a second Hara thought somebody had mistaken her for a primary target and dropped his bombload on her. Then the fire faded and was replaced by another a second later. Fire from the 4.5 inch gun turret forward, probably on local control because his WSO hadn't reported a radar lock on him.

Then, more flashes below and behind him. He was moving too fast for the traverse of the turret to keep up. If he'd been going for the frigate, he'd have been in danger but he wasn't. That made him a crossing target, an order of magnitude more difficult to hit. The green line on his head-up display had already crossed the coast and the tent encampment was directly ahead. There was a twinkle down there, like fireflies in the dark. Rifle fire, and machine guns.

Encampment, First Company and HQ Company, First Battalion, the Punjab Rifles

The flash of *Udagiri's* guns briefly, very briefly, silhouetted the dark, arrow-like shape hurtling silently through the night. Around Second Lieutenant Lal, the men of his platoon were boiling out of their tents, snatching rifles. Already, a few men were firing into the sky. Not at the approaching shape but at the area of sky it had to fly through. Without even thinking, Lal had drawn his pistol and was firing also.

Over to his left, his platoon missileer had his Kris missile up and in the 'aim' position. Trying to lock the seeker onto the approaching aircraft, was a vain hope. The Kris was really suited to rear-sector engagements. Using it on a head-on target like this was a slender chance at best. Even that, though, was better than nothing. Once the bomber passed, nothing was all that would be left. Lal knew what would be coming down any second. Submunitions. Anti-personnel submunitions.

B10N-1 Shuka Mi-233*, Approaching Pattle Island*

The target was the big fuel and munitions dump. The weapon, 1,000 kilogram bombs fitted with fuze extenders. Mi-233 carried eight of them. Lieutenant Sakai reflected that the B10N could carry an impressive warload, he had no doubt about that. Once, he had wanted to fly fighters but they were a dying breed in the Japanese Navy. Only the seaplane fighters held a future and there were few enough of those. So he ended up in a bomber group and fell in love with the shark-like Shuka. Now, they were making their target run.

"LOCK! We have a lock." His WSO's voice was urgent, not panicky.

There was nothing Sakai could do. He had to keep his aircraft running straight. Already, the green bar on his head-up display was crossing the site of the supply dump. It was down to the WSO to deflect the incoming Jabiru. He was taking the pulses from the fire control system of the inbound missile and retransmitting them, the strength little changed, a little delayed. Done right, the missile would interpret them as showing a slightly different course from the real thing. They would be interpreted as a curve that would take the missile away from the racing Shuka, to where it could do no harm. Deception jamming wasn't the only tool he had. He thumped a switch and silver clouds separated from the rear of the aircraft, chaff that would envelop the aircraft and hide it from the approaching missile.

Bridge, INS Nilgiri, *three miles east of Pattle Island.*

The roar and vibration shook the bridge of *Nilgiri,* two great streaks of fire headed into the sky towards the bombers racing over Pattle Island. It was too late, Commander Simons knew it. The bombers had come in too fast. Their electronic warfare equipment had delayed the anti-aircraft fire just long enough.

The two Jabiru missiles were curving away, chasing after the nearest Japanese bomber. That was the problem, they were chasing the aircraft, there was no way they could catch it before it dropped its payload on its target. Even after that, it was a slender chance. Once the bomber was over the radar horizon, it couldn't be illuminated and the Jabirus would go ballistic.

Beneath Simons' bridge, the arms on the twin-rail launcher rotated and stood erect. Two new missiles slid from the magazine underneath to re-arm the launcher. They'd be waiting for the next wave of bombers, if there was another wave of bombers. Because this one had got in, free and clear.

B10N-1 Shuka Mi-331, *Approaching Pattle Island*

The thermal imager built into Lieutenant Sayona's bomb-nav system was projecting a heat picture of the enemy vehicle park on his screen. Unfortunately, the image was green and the green bar of his bombsight picture was almost drowned out by it. That was a problem nobody had foreseen and now it was making his life almost impossible, Sayona was slightly amazed nobody had discovered it during the B10Ns extensive test program. Still, if he strained his eyes, he could see it, just. The green circle at the end was quickly approaching the blaze of color that represented the still-warm vehicle engines. His aircraft was loaded with 500 kilogram bombs, 16 of them, all fitted with fuze extenders. He planned to salvo the lot, right into the center of the vehicle park. Dispersion would to do the rest of the work for him.

Project 16C APD INS Prabal, *Pattle Island.*

The Japanese aircraft was coming straight at the old destroyer escort. She was coming to action stations but her single five inch 38 caliber and four twin 40mm guns defense were a pitifully weak defense. The best she could hope for was that her gunfire would cause the Japanese pilot to flinch, to disrupt his bomb run and, just possibly, miss. The midships 40mm twin had already opened up. Its tracers were flashing though the darkness towards the dim shape of the bomber hurtling towards them. For a brief second, Commander Ghopal thought he'd scored a miracle because the target seemed to explode in light. The elation didn't last, he realized it was just the Chipanese aircraft dropping clutches of flares and chaff clouds. It banked slightly, telling Ghopal that he was its next target.

B10N-1 Shuka Mi-121*, Over Pattle Island*

The green circle touched the side of the freighter. Genda salvoed the four 1,000 kilogram bombs hanging under his wings. Then a quick touch of the controls, a slight change of course, the bang underneath as the snap-action bomb-bay doors opened and four 1,000 kilogram weapons dropped clear, heading for the small frigate in front of him. As the bombs left, Genda heard the doors snap closed. He pushed the nose of his B10N down slightly, running for the horizon.

Chartered Freighter Sukanya*, Pattle Island.*

Captain Pradesh saw the dark gray shape streak overhead, saw the objects detach from its wings. He even saw the tails on the retarded bombs snap out to form airbrakes. They would slow the bombs down so the aircraft that had dropped them had time to get away from their blast. He saw that was in the middle of the pattern and was mournfully aware that he was not going to make a profit on this particular charter. Then, he felt the ship heave up under his feet. The first bomb had been short, it had exploded in the water beside him and the shock wave was shaking his freighter like a rat. Then, the whole front of the bridge caved in, sending showers of glass fragments across the deck. The helmsman, standing right at the front just vanished, slashed to ribbons by the waves of splinters driven by the fury of the bomb.

It was hot, unbearably hot. Pradesh survived because the first shock had thrown him off his feet. He'd landed behind the navigation radar console and it had shielded him from the worst of the blast. Through the gaping hole that had once been the front of his bridge, he could see his ship looked like an old, tired boxer who had been punched in the face far too often. Her bow was crushed, bent to one side, torn and flooding. That didn't explain the heat though, nor why the night was suddenly so bright.

The explanation for that was aft. Another bomb had crashed into the serried ranks of engineering vehicles on the aft deck. They were burning, the pyre spreading even as he watched. It was no use. Pradesh knew his ship was gone. No merchant ship could fight a fire like that. No civilian freighter could take hits the way his *Sukanya* had been pounded. It was over. "I'm sorry old girl." The words were brief and quiet. Then he grabbed the megaphone; he knew there was not one chance in ten thousand thousand that the internal communications were working. "Abandon Ship!"

Project 16C APD INS Prabal, *Pattle Island.*

"Away Fire and Rescue parties!" Ghopal's cry was echoing around the bridge within seconds of the crash of the bombs striking home. There was a chance. A slim one only but a chance. The bomber pilot had misjudged his turn slightly and the line of thousand kilogram bombs had walked across the ship at an angle. One had exploded close alongside, Ghopal had felt the terrible hammer blow through his feet. Another had gone into the troop accommodation and LCVP davits aft, both now thankfully empty. The other two had gone way aft. For a second, he'd thought there had been a fifth bomb, an air burst. But it had been the supersonic boom a few feet over his head as the Chipanese bomber had flashed past. One hit, one near miss. *There was a chance, wasn't there? The fires aft didn't look too bad did they?*

"Damage Control here Sir. There's no hope of saving her."

What was that? There had to be. "Get hold of yourself man!" The captain snarled down the speaking tube. "Where's your backbone? Get firefighting teams aft, before the fires take hold. Check for leaks and get damage control timbers in place. Seal all watertight doors. Some of them will have sprung with the blast."

"It's no good Sir. Its not the topside damage, we can cope with that. Its the near miss that's done for us. It's sprung all the plates portside. The welds have all gone. We're taking in water along our whole length. There's not much coming through at one any point but its coming in everywhere. We've got an hour or two, no more. Then we'll roll over and go down."

"We have diesel power?"

"Yes, Sir."

"Then we'll run her aground. The shallows are only a few hundred yards away. We'll put her aground while she's still level. That way we can still use her guns. If we can't be a ship any more, we can at least be a flak battery. Engine room? Give me all the power you've got. Then get out of there."

Encampment, First Company and HQ Company, First Battalion, the Punjab Rifles

Lal was dead, he knew it. It was silent around him. The cluster bombs must have gone off and he was dead. The rows of tents set up only a few hours earlier were ripped to tiny shreds, fragmented by the deadly blasts of the little bomblets that had rained down on them. His men, they were gone. They'd still been firing as a last act of defiance. They had been ripped apart as thoroughly as the tents. Objectively, Lal knew that he was there as well; some of the unrecognizable fragments strewn around the ground. *So this was what it was like to be dead. Hell didn't seem to bad compared with the blasts of the cluster bombs. Interesting.*

He turned around, expecting to see the spirits closing to take him away. Instead he saw one of the light vehicles, a Tata jeep, starting to burn. *Petrol tank probably punctured and pouring over a hot exhaust. And one of my riflemen is trapped inside, fighting to get out.* Lal didn't think. He ran over and grabbed the handle, already too hot from the fire underneath. It was pointless, of course. He was already dead, what could he do to help a man who was still alive? But the door was moving. Instinctively, he and the rifleman coordinated their movements and the distorted door burst open. The man rolled out, his clothes already starting to burn. Lal was waiting and beat out the flames before they could take hold. The man was singed but safe. His mouth worked but Lal could hear nothing. Then it began to dawn on him, he wasn't dead, he was deaf. The supersonic boom of the bomber going over had damaged his ears.

"I'm not dead? I'm not dead!" The rifleman shook his head. Somehow, in the hell of fragments from the anti-personnel bomblets, Lal had survived. Well, most of him. His ears, only time would tell. His hands, he could feel the burns from the hot metal starting to hurt. But he wasn't dead!

Fuel Dump, Pattle Island

Nobody had ever expected to see it. 55 gallon fuel drums exploding and shooting into the air like rockets. The line of bombs had walked right across the dump. Their fragments had slashed into the fuel drums, spraying their cargo around the dump site. Blast and explosions had set the petrol and diesel on fire, causing pools of blazing liquid to flow around and under the ranks of drums and crates of munitions. The crackle of ammunition cooking off in the inferno added a surreal sound of applause to the more spectacular drum flights. But, expectations were right. Nobody could see the unexpected aerial exploits of the fuel drum because the people inside the dump were dead. Turned into blazing torches by the bombs and fuel, they'd run around, and screamed and died. The fuel and ammunition stockpile blazed unattended, the fires out of control as the carefully-unloaded cargoes exploded in their final eye-tearing inferno.

Vehicle Park, Pattle Island

"Get the dozer moved, and shift that backhoe!" The vehicle park was on fire as well but the situation was more contained that the dreadful sight of the blazing fuel dump at the other end of the island. The bombs had destroyed most of the vehicles. The survivors were damaged by the deadly fragments, but some could be saved. The two heavy vehicles were the key. With a dozer and a backhoe, positions could be built, holes dug and embankments built. Ground could be smoothed to make a runway.

Out to sea, there was another fire. The freighter than had brought the heavy vehicles was ablaze from bow to stern, her shattered structure outlined in orange fire. The vehicles she'd brought, the ones still on board, they were gone. This one dozer, this one backhoe, they were all that was left. Keeping Pattle Island Indian depended on saving two vehicles.

The engine on the dozer roared into life. "Get that vehicle out of here, get it clear." The sergeant yelled the orders but they weren't necessary. The dozer was already moving, on its way to safety. The survivors of the motor pool unit were still struggling with the backhoe, it didn't want to start but they were determined and they would not give up. Soon, it too was moving.

Operation Room, INS Udagiri*, three miles west of Pattle Island.*

Sublieutenant Gitta broke through the jamming at last when heshifted to war-only operating mode. This combination of jitter factors and prf variations was designed to give each radar pulse its own distinct fingerprint, one that the track extraction software would recognize and use. The fire control radars had locked on and he'd felt the vibration, the roar, as the two Jabirus had left the rails and chased after the vanishing bombers. It was too late, he knew that. They would be over the radar horizon any second. But it was better to take a shot than to let the bombers go unchallenged.

He quickly stepped out onto the bridge. The sight was a nightmare. Pattle Island seemed to be a mass of burning wreckage. The bombers had taken out everything. One of the ships in the lagoon was a mass of fire. She was already down by the bows and only had minutes to live.

One of the APD destroyer-transports was limping slowly to the shore. The fires aft were dying down but the ship visibly settling as she plugged grimly for the shallows. *Beaching her,* Gitta thought, *only thing to do*. Miraculously, the other two APDs seemed to have escaped. Then he became aware that *Udagiri's* bridge was black and . . . . . smoking?

"Number One, are we hit?"

Lieutenant Murray looked at his ops officer with grim humor. "Despite your best efforts, no." Gitta looked confused. "That pair of Jabirus you squeezed off cleared the bridge by less than two feet. If we'd had an open bridge, you would have roasted us all. You know, you are due for promotion, you don't have to create the vacancies."

B10N-1 Shuka Mi-121*, Over South China Sea, West of Pattle Island*

Genda eased back on the throttles and swept the wings forward into the subsonic cruise position as he climbed away from the sea surface. Something had changed in the wild ride over the Indian fleet. They'd started as three; a pilot, his WSO and their aircraft. Somehow, they'd become fused together into a single working entity. He glanced at his WSO and knew the bomb-nav operator was feeling the same.

Behind them, they could still see the angry red glow on the horizon that marked Pattle Island. It looked like sunrise; the evil sunrise that told of a thunderstorm coming. Beside them, the remaining five aircraft were closing in, resuming the loose formation they'd held on the way out. Six had come out; six were going back.

"Any damage?"

The radio negatives came in. They weren't quite true. All the aircraft had minor damage, some of it self inflicted, but the distinction was academic. They were going home and the Shuka had proved itself as deadly as its designers had promised. At last. Not only that, the Navy had scored a victory. At last.

"Well done, Ken-san."

The formal, polite, words, in the shared intimacy of the side-by-side seating sounded good. Suddenly a name popped into Genda's mind and he thought of the third member of the team. He reached forward and patted the instrument panel. "And well done *Kiku-San.*"

"Proud to have been of service."

The words, quiet and deferential, sounded in the crew's earphones. Pilot and WSO looked at each other in amazement. So the legends were true!

Dawn, INS Mysore, *Off Pattle Island, Paracel Group, South China Sea*

"Dear God what a mess." Admiral Kanali Dahm looked at the smoking ruin of the base. Two ships sunk in the lagoon. Huge black pyres of smoke rising from the island. Two frigates sitting outside, one with its bridge blackened. Ashore he could see the ever-growing lines of white patches. The dead in their shrouds. Hundreds of them. His ships had got the message as the raid had struck and returned at 32 knots. Too late to help but, hopefully, early enough to stop a follow-up raid. Or a full-scale attack. He'd also radioed the report back to India.

"Message Sir. From Command." The Sparks brought the flimsy in. Dahm read the orders. *Well, that made sense.*

"Captain, we're to remain here, render assistance ashore and also land reinforcements from our ship's guard. The Main Body has been ordered to make all speed here, not to wait for the *Viraat* or the other division of the Flying Squadron. They have three more frigates with them. Above all, we're to hold on here and repel any further attacks."

"Any air cover coming Sir? Without *Viraat*?"

"None. We're too far out. The message says the raid was by Harry bombers. We didn't think they were operational yet. It was the sort of raid one can pull off once, when somebody isn't on guard, but we'll be ready next time. They won't try it again. If they do, they won't get in clear like they did this time. Tell *Ghurka* to get her AEW bird up dusk to dawn though. Just in case."

Hainan Airfield, Hainan.

The roosters crowed first, then the dogs started barking. The sky, ever so slowly, was lightening in the east. The stars were still bright glowing through the pre-dawn. Then, without warning, a new star appeared, one lined up with the end of the runway. The new star quickly grew a shadow behind it and became a B10N on its final approach, nose up, wings outstretched, wheels and flaps down. It sank quickly towards the runway, a tired bird, one that had seen a rough night.

"ICHI!" The chorused number, the cheer went up from the airbase personnel who had been waiting all night for their aircraft to return. The first B10N was on the runway, slowing down, its parachute streaming behind it.

"NI!" The second Shuka was down, following the first along the painted runway to the hangars at the end.

"SAN!" The third was down, also rolling past the crowd whose numbers swelled as duty personnel ran out to see the bombers return.

"YON!" Number four safe. By this time the lead B10N had turned off the runway onto the taxiway and was heading for its pen.

"GO!" Number five down and safe and the cheering men also saw the last making its approach. If nothing went wrong now, then all would be well.

"ROKU!" Number six was down and safe.

The cheering went wild as the skies around Hainan lightened. The roar of the taxiing jets competed with the wild outbursts of cheering from the base, drowning out the sounds of the countryside coming to life. Most of the men were running alongside the runway, trying to keep pace with the bombers as they moved down the taxiway in a stately procession. Then, they turned off, into their designated revetments and the engine noise died down.

On Mi-121, now privately named *Kiku-san*, the two halves of the cockpit canopy pivoted upwards like a bird lifting off. A set of steps was already being pushed up and the tired aircrew tried to release their harnesses, fending off the over-zealous help of the ground personnel. Then the steps were cleared for an Admiral had come up. Genda tried to salute but the Admiral grabbed his arm and stopped him. To the stunned disbelief of the crowd of onlookers, the Admiral raised his hand in the traditional salute and held it. Beaming down with pride and respect at the two pilots in the Shuka, he passed across two small glasses filled with steaming sake and lifted his own in a toast. At last, after years of obscurity, the Imperial Japanese Navy was back in business.

Seer's Office, NSC Building, Washington D.C.

"Boss, Anne's arrived from the Pentagon with the pictures. She's got Brigadier General Kozlowski with her." Lillith released the button on her intercom phone and smiled at the visitors. "Please step right in Anne. General, how's *Xiomara* liking Washington?"

"She's a bit bored, Lillith. She sits down at Andrews most of the time, we only get to fly often enough to keep my hours up. We'll be glad to get back to the 305th." Kozlowski thought that was indeed the truth. Every officer knew that tours of duty in the Pentagon were required for an ambitious officer but the job of a pilot was to fly and the job of an RB-58F was to find things and break them. Flying a desk just didn't compare.

"Seer, I've got the pictures from last night's raid. Boy, the Chipanese really did a number on Pattle. Used the B10Ns based out of Hainan." Anne Bonney put the file she was carrying down on the table top.

"That was fast, how did we get them. Oh, welcome to The Building Mike. You haven't been here before, have you?"

"No Sir. In answer to your question, we put an SR-71 over them first thing. Chuck Larry's boy flew the mission. He wanted bombers, his old man wanted fighters so they compromised on SR-71s. Good pictures."

Kozlowski spread the pictures of the shattered base over The Seer's desk. The Seer looked them over and whistled quietly. "What's your opinion Mike? Professionally."

"Damned fine job Sir. You can see how they did the runs over the island, each aircraft knew exactly where it was going and why. I'll bet if we check orbits, we'll find there was a photorecon satellite over Pattle just before dusk. They were lucky though, nothing moved after nightfall. If they'd been Russians, they'd have shifted everything around out of force of habit." Kozlowski looked thoughtful. "I wonder if Harry can download data directly from a satellite. We're playing with that. Look, you can see how they plotted their course in. . ."

Kozlowski spoke for ten minutes, carefully analyzing the raid and the havoc it had caused. When he finished, he sat down and Lillith quietly put a cup of coffee into his hands. "Black, no sugar isn't it?"

"That's right ma'am. And thank you."

Meeting over, Lillith closed the doors. "Well Boss, what do you think."

"Before you answer that Boss, you should read this." Anne Bonney passed over a message flimsy. "Statement from the Japanese high command. They state that due to ongoing military operations, they are declaring a maritime warning zone 200 miles wide around the Paracels. Neutral shipping is warned to keep clear of that area in case they get attacked by accident."

The Seer nodded. "That's a message to us. They're telling us they want to keep this whole business confined to the area they've just defined. Smart of them. That only leaves one question, how long before Snake starts trying to persuade us to help the Triple Alliance out? Lillith, organize an office pool on it. Ten bucks entry fee, winner gets, ohhh I don't know, think of an interesting prize. Take the extra out of petty cash if you need to."

"Will you help them, Boss?" Anne's voice was curious.

"Can anybody think of a single interest of the United States at risk here? As long as the incident stays confined to the area the Chipanese have defined and doesn't interfere with maritime movements or start to spread, I can't. Anyway, the Indians stuck their neck out here. They're on their own."

"Snake won't like that."

"Snake will have to learn to live with it. She knows the rules. Our country's interests come first and we just don't have a dog in this fight. Anyway, we've got other problems.

17,000 feet over Defensive Area Annaliese, French Algeria/Caliphate Border

The Ki-115 was following a flight plan that had been carefully and expensively worked out. For weeks, martyrs flying Ki-127 bombers had flown into the airspace claimed by unbelievers. They had flown on steady courses, at varying times, speeds and altitudes. Watched on radar, they had all been intercepted and shot down. On each occasion, the time taken for the unbelievers to respond, where their fighters had come from, the type of aircraft they had used, how they had conducted the shoot-down, all had been watched and noted. As a result the Caliphate observers knew where the weak points in the defense screen were and when was the best time to exploit them.

This was one such weak spot. On the border between two defensive areas, where the fighter ground control should overlap but sometimes didn't. An area where the defending fighters were the older Super-Mysteres, not radar-equipped Mirages. In daylight that made little difference since the piston-engined Ki-115 was just as vulnerable to one as to the other. In fact, a case could be made that the older, cannon-armed Super-Mystere was better suited to a daylight destruction of a Ki-115 than the all-missile Mirage IIIF. At night the radar on a Mirage made a lot of difference.

The Ki-115 made its scheduled turn and started flying parallel to the border, towards the sea. This was where the weak point in the unbeliever's air defenses ended. As soon as the turn was made, alarms would be ringing all over the defense system and the Super-Mysteres would be scrambling to take off. Inshallah, by the time they made it and were able to intercept the Ki-115, it's tanks would be empty, its deadly cargo unleashed on the faithless ones down below. The ones who'd rejected the leadership of the Caliphate and spurned its teachings of the True Faith. There were apostates down there who'd thrown their hand in with the unbelievers and so they could share the same fate.

In fact, the Ki-115 pilot was wrong. He'd been spotted several minutes earlier since the weak point in the French screen was indeed weak, but it was not a gaping void. The Ki-115 Slime had been spotted later than it should have been and it had taken the defense a little longer to respond but that was all. A Super-Mystere was already closing on the Slime when the Caliphate aircraft started spraying its cargo. It was closing fast with clearance to open fire already in the French pilot's hands.

As usual, the Super-Mystere was steered in so that it came up on the Slime from below and behind. The pilot of the Slime simply didn't see the French fighter until the glowing tracers whipped past the Slime's cockpit. The French pilot had made a slight mistake; he'd over-estimated the speed of the Slime slightly and most of his first burst missed. Two did not. One ripped into the port wing, disrupting the chemical spray system built into the wing structure. The other hit squarely on the fuselage aft, ripping open the large tank behind the Slime's cockpit. The damage caused the contents of that tank to pour out in a dense cascade. The result was that what was supposed to be a fine mist covering a large area was, instead, a dense mass.

The two hits threw the Slime out of control. Never an easy aircraft to fly at the best of time, the sudden damage caused the aircraft to rear upwards, stall and then lurch into a spin. A competent or capable pilot would have averted that. He would have brought the aircraft under control quickly and started his evasive maneuvers. The Caliphate pilot was neither skilled nor well-trained. In fact, he had fewer than ten hours flying the Ki-115. In a strange way, that aided him. An untrained pilot should have panicked and made desperate attempts to correct the spin, each of which would have made the situation worse. The Caliphate pilot simply took his hands off the controls and started to pray. Without him making any mistakes to make matters worse, the Slime automatically stabilized and was now diving steeply downwards. His faith vindicated, the Slime pilot resumed his grip on the controls and pulled out of the dive, heading north for the sea.

The French Super-Mystere pilot was stunned by the evasive maneuver and assumed he was facing one of the Caliphate's few veteran pilots. From his seat, the Slime's maneuver looked like a wingover followed by a dive to extend range. His jet was closing on the enemy aircraft's position too fast to copy the maneuver directly, his turning circle and response times were just too great. He performed a steep climbing turn to bleed off speed, then brought the nose sharply around and dived after the Slime. By now, the Caliphate aircraft was flying low over the sea, heading for home. More significantly, it was now lost in the sea clutter and the ground control radars could no longer coach the Super-Mystere in on its target. The French pilot searched visually for his enemy but the piston-engined aircraft was lost in the darkness. With his fuel running low, he decided to head for home, while the Caliphate pilot made for his base.

It never occurred to either pilot that, in their maneuvers, both aircraft had flown through the cloud released from the Ki-115s tanks.

The Presidential Suite, Tropicana Hotel, Havana, Cuba

"Senor Presidente, your 3 o'clock is here to see you."

"Thank you Estrellita. Send him in."

Meyer Lansky took his seat behind his desk. He'd had reports of Gotti's investigations and had been pleasantly surprised. The young man had done quite well; he'd picked up on some unusual affairs and developed the leads further while avoiding confrontations with the Capos and Captains in the area. In fact, they'd spoken well of his tact and discretion. Interesting.

"Dapper John. You got news?"

"Meyer, sorry this is happening at short notice. You gotta see the scene of the latest incident. Gonna help make many things a lot clearer."

Lansky's face was impassive but he looked on the invitation with suspicion. Private meetings in the families all too often turned out to be terminal for one of the parties. This wouldn't be the case here though, could it? Anyway, he had his precautions in place.

"Another incident? Where?"

"Coffee shop downstairs. Not a real big thing but worth your attention."

Lansky relaxed. The busy coffee shop was a fully public place, noisy and crowded with tourists; it wasn't any place for a hit. "Sounds good. Estrellita, I'll be out of the office for a while. Field any calls for me." The middle-aged Cuban secretary nodded and flipped a switch that directed all of Lansky's calls to her own terminal.

"What have you found, John?" The two men were standing in the shop, leaning with their backs to the wall, eyes watching the door. This place wasn't just safe, the noise levels made eavesdropping impossible.

"We picked up a dealer last night. An unauthorized one. He was harassing a couple of tourists so a waitress called the boys and they handed him over to us. Smart tourists by the way. They stalled the heel until the boys got there. They got their meal free and I slipped the waitress a couple of hundred." Lansky grimaced slightly, those were details he didn't need to know. He took it for granted that the people who'd helped had been properly rewarded.

Gotti saw the expression and mentally kicked himself. He was too newly Made to be entirely confident in his actions but it was bad policy to let it show. "Sorry Meyer. Anyway, we reasoned with the guy and he spilled everything. He was dealing right enough. Heroin and cocaine , all of it smuggled in."

That made Lansky start. "Smuggling? H and Coke? In the name of God, why?" His amazement was genuine. Smuggling drugs into Cuba was absurd. If somebody wanted to import them, all they had to do was package them up and put them onto an aircraft for delivery. So much was being flown in, quite legally under 'Cuban Law,' that pilots of cargo aircraft from Colombia and Turkey had adopted the traditional SAC salutation 'Fly High!'.

It wasn't even a case of avoiding import duties, because Cuba didn't have any. Cuba's proud boast was that it was a tax-free society. The casino's fabulous profits saw to most things and, of course, the mob skimmed the take. Tax free wasn't quite true. *Is there any difference between property taxes and protection money/"* Lansky briefly reflected. *After all, a family paid their protection money to their button man and he looked after them. Fixed the roads and sidewalks, made sure the residents on his block were safe and helped them out if they were struck by misfortune.*

"But why smuggle the stuff in? I suppose if they really want to carry the stuff over a beach at midnight there's no reason why they shouldn't." Lansky snapped his fingers. "Its distribution, they have to be setting up their own distribution system and they don't want us to know about it."

"That's what our pigeon said, Meyer. He told us where his stash was and we collected it. Lot of prime-grade coke and H. Guess the coke comes from Colombia or further south, but the H? That's a question. Not the interesting bit though. The guy had a list; which hotels were doing what, who was selling what and where any shortages were. Very interesting list. Covered all the families."

Lansky's face was thoughtful. The families in Cuba had an agreement. Nobody wanted a tourist to be inconvenienced by having their hotel run out of their favorite party favors so if one hotel was running short, another would tide them over. At market rates of course, as Joe Profaci had said when the system was being set up "after all, we are not communists."

All the transfers were recorded and the families settled up at the end of each month when the skim was being divided up. That meant that there were records of who was having supply problems and who was in surplus. Those records were held in Lansky's personal office. If it had been a leak from just one family, then the records could be from that group. For all of them, it had to be Lansky's own office. Now, Lansky saw why Gotti had wanted this meeting away from his staff.

"We gotta rat. There has to be a leak. In my office. You done good John." Lansky's speech had slipped back into his early New York days. "Question is, who."

"Any ideas Meyer?"

"Could be any of a dozen people. We got another question. The coke we know about, the people down south will sell their grandmothers. But the H? The Turks aren't going to screw us over, so where is that H coming from?"

"You might not like this, but there is one group who can help." Lansky raised an eyebrow. "The Federation of Bungling Idiots back on the mainland. They give our people back there a real hard time, analyzing stuff and tracking sources. They could analyze the stuff we picked up and tell us where it came from. If they wanted to."

Lansky thought for a second. The families working here on Cuba had grown used to the environment where nothing was actually illegal. Most of them had forgotten what 'the life' was like back on the mainland. They'd forgotten what it was like to have law enforcement trying to make cases against them. That was why all the smart money had come to Cuba. The American end of family business was now a mixture of a training ground for wiseguys and a dumping ground for the fourth rate who didn't warrant a share in the financial wonderland of Cuba.

The FBI could help the mob on Cuba but why should they? It was reputed that the director of the FBI was one of the strongest voices urging that the United States invade and 'straighten the island out.' No danger of that of course, any administration that tried to do something to America's favorite playground would never get another vote.

"Won't go to them direct. I know a guy in the Secret Service, the one I met on my last trip. Good kid, his grandfather was one of Moran's boys back in the old days. He's investigating the Senate shooting and this ties in somehow. It's too neat to be coincidence. I'll take another 'Presidential' trip over and ask the Secret Service to get this done for us. Their job is Presidential Security, they'll do it. Dapper John, I want you to have a word with the Lucchese. One of his hotels is about to run short of H."

"The Lucchese family is having problems with supply Meyer."

"I know. That makes it credible. We'll make the records look like a different hotel in each case. Then see what flushes out."

"There's a hitch, Meyer, the lists don't give hotels by name; they each have a two or three-letter code. We'll have to identify which hotel corresponds to which code."

"That makes it harder, not impossible. John, you've done good so far, Brought a lot of credit on your Don. Think up a plan and get it underway. You can get more of those lists?"

"We can. The louse we picked up told us the how and when."

"Then do it." Lansky sighed. "You know, I never liked Washington."

Seer's Office, National Security Council Building, Washington D.C.

"Take my advice, stay out of this one."

"But we have a treaty, one we need more than our partners."

"I know, but it doesn't apply in this case. Look, Snake, back at the time of Jungle Hammer, we told you that your military co-operation arrangements were deficient. That's inevitable; the Triple Alliance is just what its name says, an alliance, and they're weak almost by definition. What you can do is the lowest common denominator that will be accepted by all three partners. At the same time, you're trapped by what they do. Why do you think we don't have alliances and don't get tangled up in multi-national agreements?"

"You have Russia.'

"Indeed we do and it's a weakness that worries me. However, the benefits we get from the Russian alliance outweigh the trouble it causes us.

"The Triple Alliance benefits us more than it costs. And the treaty is still there."

The Seer sighed quietly to himself. *That was the trouble with helping somebody out once, they kept expecting you to do it again.* "It doesn't apply. The Triple Alliance is a mutual defense treaty, if one member is attacked, the others come to its aid. Note the words **if one member is attacked**. It's quite arguable that India did the attacking here. Look, we built you a Permanent Military Council to stop this sort of thing happening. What went wrong?"

"It's not a joint operation. The Indians went ahead and did it by themselves."

"And what do they want you to do? As if I couldn't guess."

"They want us to use our TSR-2s to hit the Chipanese bases on Hainan. They're in range, that's no problem."

"And you know what the immediate response will be, don't you? The Chipanese will hit your airbases - and quite rightly so. Doesn't worry us, we'll watch and learn how the Chipanese plan such things. But you won't have an air force left."

"We have air defenses."

"Snake, you have fewer air defense assets in your whole country than we have around one of our major cities. If you don't believe me, I'll take you to see. You hit the Chipanese and they'll take your entire air force out. If you're lucky. If you're not, they won't stop there. You've got to stay out of this one."

It was The Ambassador's turn to sigh. "How? We have treaty obligations. It's not our fault; for years India was run by the Congress Party and they knew what was happening and why. Since the last elections, its being run by the Hindu Nationalists and they want to flex their muscles a bit. It's not a mistake Sir Martyn would ever have made and I'd guess Eric Haohoa is chewing his fingernails to the knuckles over there but its done. We've got to have help. If you send a carrier group or two into the South China Sea....."

"Why should we do that? There's no vital American interest at stake here. We're watching the situation and that's all. You've already been outmaneuvered on this one. The Chipanese have defined the area of conflict and publicly promised to confine the fighting to the disputed area. You spread it outside that area and its you who are in the wrong. If you want to bomb anything, find something in that area and pound that."

"There isn't anything."

"Right. Like I said, you've been outmaneuvered. Those B10N Harrys have changed the regional equation. We knew the Japanese Navy was playing with a theater-level medium bomber but we didn't know they were this close to putting it into full-scale operational service. By doing so they've pulled a very slick, very deft piece of political maneuvering. First they demonstrate that they can hit the Indians from outside the area of conflict, leaving the Triple Alliance with nothing you can do to retaliate. Then they piously send around a diplomatic message that limits both the scope of the conflict and sets out the geographical limitations of the combat zone. That keeps us out. We've made it clear we want a peaceful world and if nations want to get involved in a conflict, they'd better make very sure it is fought under exactly those limitations."

"You sound like you admire them."

"I do, I admire anybody who plays the game this deftly. They've left you holding the bag and without any options that won't leave you worse off than when you started. Anyway, you need to look at this situation from a different perspective. Your opposition here isn't Chipan, its India."

"Wha. . . a . . . at" The Ambassador was genuinely astonished.

"Who else's actions have put you into an impossible position? They've gone ahead and dropped you in it with a vengeance. You've woken up earlier because your closer but the Australians will look at a map soon and realize they've been dropped in it as well. So they're the opposition here that has to be thwarted.

"Now. Do you still want our help? And it will, I promise, cost you."

"I thought you said you wouldn't get involved."

"We won't. We can get you off the hook though. State is going to release the following statement: *The United States views with concern the outbreak of hostilities in the South China Sea and will take the most serious of views should any party to the dispute spread the conflict beyond its present confines. In the interests of international harmony, the United States offers its full support to any parties who act to bring about a peaceful solution to this situation.*

"That gives you the perfect excuse to refuse to join the conflict because you now have reason to believe that, if you try, the Chipanese won't take your Air Force out. We will. That's a risk that no government can reasonably be expected to take. But, this also gives you the opportunity of offering to act as a peaceful intermediary. That's as far as we're prepared to go."

"You wouldn't really bomb us would you?" The Ambassador was shaken by the concept.

"You don't want to know the answer to that question Snake. As long as you don't know, the threat hanging over you is very credible. All you need to do is to tell the Indians the Americans won't allow you to do what they ask and have threatened dire consequences if you ignore our 'advice.' Then tell them you can help them more by trying to act as an honest broker and make the Chipanese look bad. As for the Indians, they wanted to flex their muscles, now they have the chance. I hope they enjoy the experience. It can get very cold and lonely out on the sharp end."

"And what is this going to cost us?"

"A free run at your intelligence coming in on the political and military affairs in Chipan and everything you've got on Caliphate biological and chemical warfare programs. Also an intelligence run-down on what's happening in Indonesia. Snake, lessons in geopolitics are worth exactly what you pay for them. And I've just charged you top dollar."

Sitting outside the office, Lillith was typing up some memos and the results of the office sweepstake. She looked up as The Ambassador stopped by her desk on the way out. "Lillith, could you kindly contact The Cheesecake Factory and order me a 16 inch white chocolate and raspberry? To be delivered to my hotel? Thank you so much."

Lillith looked at the departing figure and picked up her telephone. "Naamah, is Tommy Blood in the Building? If you see him, tell him he won the sweepstake. And, boy, is she not happy."

CHAPTER FIVE
MEETING ENGAGEMENT

HIJMS Aoba, *Flagship, South China Sea Squadron, Haiphong, Japanese Indochina.*

The motion of the ship was quite different now she was heading out to sea. Trapped within the confines of the harbor for so long, she'd seemed idle and listless. Heading down the channel leading the squadron with a bone in her teeth and her twelve 6.1 inch guns elevated to 70 degrees, she seemed urgent, eager, glad to be free of the land at last. Two ship lengths behind her, the *Asama* was also picking up speed as she cleared the restricted lane and followed *Aoba* into cruising speed.

Behind them, long and low, sliding through the sea with the same stealthy menace as venomous snakes through grass, were the rocket cruisers, *Yashima* and *Asahi*. One of the things that had delayed the squadron's departure was that their nuclear tipped long-range anti-ship missiles had been off-loaded and replaced with conventionally-headed versions. There had been hard words spoken about that, hard and enraged, but the logic was indisputable. If somebody threw a nuclear-tipped weapon, the Americans would erase that country from the face of the earth. They'd made their position very clear. They weren't interested in this conflict, they didn't care who held a group of unimportant little islands in a sea in which they had equally little interest. As long as the fighting stayed contained to a small area where nobody else was involved or threatened, the Indians and the Japanese could kill each other as much as they liked.

Admiral Kurita stepped onto the bridge wing and stared through his binoculars at the rest of his fleet. Eight Kawari class missile destroyers were screening his cruisers. He'd decided to leave the four old Type Bs in port. Two of them had broken down while being readied for the sortie and the other pair were only being kept running by sheer force of habit. They could break down at any time and the oil in their tanks was better placed elsewhere. Oil had been the problem all along, the terrible shortage of oil. His ships had been pinned in port, unable to move while oil fuel trickled in and slowly filled his tanks. That had given the Indians time to dive in and grab Pattle Island and start building their base there.

Kurita left the open wing and looked around his bridge. The Indians had got to Pattle first, but they'd paid for their temerity. The B10Ns in Hainan had been pounding them for a week now and the Japanese Navy pilots were becoming heroes to a people and a fleet that had badly needed heroes to believe. Their first strike had got in clean and reports were that it had inflicted terrible damage on the Indians. The follow-ups hadn't done as well; the Indians had dispersed and dug in while two B10Ns had been shot down by the Indian Navy's missiles, but they'd succeeded in bringing the work on Pattle to a standstill.

Now it was time for the real punch, the heavy blow from the fleet. The two rocket cruisers would eliminate the Indian squadron defending the island. That would allow the two gun cruisers to pound the garrison into oblivion. Then, the SNLF could land and take what was left. Leaving the nuclear weapons behind was a wrench but Kurita recognized the brilliance of the move. By doing so, and by publicly limiting the battlezone to a small area, the Japanese had lured the Americans into effectively holding the ring for the Japanese Navy. The Japanese bases in Indochina and Hainan were safe. If the Japanese Navy couldn't use nuclear weapons, nor could the Indians.

At first, the Japanese Navy bases in Indochina had been on alert, waiting for the Thai TSR-2s to retaliate for the bombing of

Pattle Island but it hadn't happened. The Thais had stayed out, claiming that the Americans had warned them of the most serious consequences that would result if they'd launched the strikes. When American strategists spoke of "most serious consequences" they only meant one thing and nobody blamed the Thais when their TSR-2s stayed at home. Their Arrows were trying to provide some cover to the troops on Pattle but so far, without success. The range was too long, the response time too great and the time on station too short.

Overhead, Navy J12Ks orbited to provide cover, their weirdly-swept wings gleamed in the noon light. They were his air cover now, but they wouldn't be around for long. Their endurance was too short, they gulped too much fuel. Once out of sight of land, he would have to depend on his missiles for protection. Well, that wasn't too bad. He had ten quadruple mounts for Nodachi surface-to-air missiles on his ships. They would be enough to provide a good firepower defense against air attack. Not that his two gun cruisers were entirely helpless, their 15.5 centimeter twin turrets were dual purpose after all.

It wasn't as if he had a carrier to worry about. One of the two Indian carriers was in drydock with machinery problems and would be for months. The other was coming around from the East Coast but wouldn't be in for days. That set the time limit for this operation. The Indians had to be ejected from Pattle and a Japanese garrison put in place before that carrier arrived. The moment it did and the Indians had fighter aircraft on scene, it would be too late.

Behind the cruisers, the eight destroyers started to move forward. Soon, they would be in their proper place, four in a picket line out in front, one on each side of the cruiser column, two behind. Then, they would launch their helicopters to provide search and targeting for the Kabuto anti-ship missiles. It was time to reverse the humiliation of 1959 and the two rocket cruisers were just the ships to do it.

INS Mysore, *Off Pattle Island, Paracel Group, South China Sea*

The troopships had arrived at last and were unloading on an atoll ringed by Indian warships. The anti-aircraft missile units had landed first. Now that the batteries were fully set up, each of the six land-based Jabiru launchers was ringed by three point-defense MOG-2 launchers and three radar-controlled twin 35mm BOER guns. Their radars were in place as well; long-range surveillance sets as well as target acquisition systems and fire control. If the B10N Harry bombers came back, they wouldn't get the clear run they had been enjoying all week. If they came tonight, they'd have a reception waiting for them they would not forget in a hurry. Already, the radars were probing the gathering dusk, searching for the swing-wing bombers to appear.

That was just the start, it would take days to unload the fat-bellied transports. Artillery, tanks, engineering equipment, troops, supplies and more supplies to replace the ones destroyed by the bombing raids. There were no port facilities here on Pattle and the heavy equipment was being shipped off one at a time. Too many landing craft had been lost to make the process a fast one. The APDs had brought twelve but only three of them were left; the rest had been destroyed by bombs or fire. The main body had brought more, but not enough. There just weren't enough, not in the whole of India, to unload this fleet quickly. Quietly Admiral Kanali Dahm cursed the politicians who'd pushed this idea through without thinking of the resources that were needed to make it work. It wasn't the obvious ones that were the problem. It was the things nobody really saw, like port facilities on a deserted atoll.

Still, the warship screen had increased as well, reinforced by three more Project 22 frigates that had escorted the troop ships in. One of those, plus the two that had escorted the first wave, had been added to his division of the Flying Squadron. So he now had his cruiser, three gun destroyers, two anti-aircraft missile destroyers and three general-purpose frigates. More importantly, each of the frigates carried a Fairey Defender Mark 52B rotodyne, equipped as anti-submarine and anti-ship platforms. His two Project 21 destroyers had a Defender Rotodyne each as well, a Mark 52C equipped as an airborne early warning and surveillance system. They'd been offloaded to Pattle and now took turns watching out for the intruding Harry bombers.

"Admiral, Sir!" The Sparker barged on to the bridge without waiting for formalities. "Message just come in from base. On the secure channel. The Chipanese are at sea. Their fleet's out."

"Where? When? How many?" Dahm was irritated. Not by the lack of formality since the urgency of the message justified that, but by the lack of hard information.

"From Haiphong, Sir. Four cruisers, eight destroyers. Set sail at noon."

Six hours ago, the fleet could be 200 miles closer by now. The message had to come from the Viet Minh. The Thais were sitting out this confrontation, they had to, the Americans had seen to that, but that didn't mean they were supplying all the covert assistance they could. Intelligence from the Viet Minh was vital. Dahm gazed at the charts flattened out before him. The direct course from Haiphong to Pattle was already marked.

"They hold cruising speed, 18 knots, they'll be here by now." The pencil ticked the point. "That means they'll be here" another pencil tick "by dawn. 200 miles short of us. That means they'll be ready to hit Pattle by noon."

"Sir, if they go to battle speed, they could be right on top of us by dawn." *Mysore's* Captain was concerned. The Chipanese had already sprung one nasty surprise.

"They won't do that. They can't, they're measuring oil with an eyedropper out there. They'll hold cruising speed to save fuel. Anyway, they want us. They want to take this squadron out so they can flatten Pattle at their leisure. Come charging in and its a dawn dogfight around the Atoll and they must know we're landing anti-ship missiles. Or think they know. They'll assume we're landing Jabirus as well and they know that's got an anti-ship mode. So has MOG come to that. All at once, its a messy battle. The Chimps will want to take us out far north then deal with the Island later."

"But they may think we think that Sir and come straight in, assuming we'll be heading North. That way they can take the Island out behind us."

Dahm sighed. *We think, they think, we think they think, they think we think they think. And so on into infinity. The hall of mirrors.*

"I know, but I don't think they will. They want us first. These are Navy remember, Chipanese Navy, everything about their doctrine is to seek out a decisive battle with the enemy fleet. That's us. We set out now, we'll hold 28 knots. We'll take *Nilgiri, Himgiri* and *Udagiri* with us. *Dunagiri* and *Taragiri* will stay with the amphibs. They'll act as picket ships and extra anti-aircraft protection. Damn. If the Chimps had waited another day, the land-based SAMs would be operational. I don't know if the missileers have got the systems calibrated yet and we can't take the chance. One more day and we could take all five frigates.

"OK, we'll hold an intercept course. At midnight, we'll put a Defender up to spot for the incoming Chimps. When the fighting starts, all three frigates to get their Defenders up and out of the way. If this goes right, we'll intercept the Chimps at dawn. Range will be about 100, 150 miles. Perfect for our Sagarikas. Order *Ghurka* and *Ghauri* to get Jabiru-2s up on their rails. That gives us one long range shot at anything inbound before we switch over to Jabiru-1s"

The Sparker left to send the orders while Dahm drummed his fingers on the chart. Only his Project 21 destroyers had Jabiru 2s and they only had them for the first shot of the engagement. The problem was that the Indian ships all loaded their missiles vertically, the twin-rail launchers swinging up to 90 degrees elevation and the missiles sliding up from underneath. It was compact and it was fast. Vertical loading allowed the launchers to get three salvoes off per minute. The problem was that vertical loading couldn't handle Jabiru-2s, not easily at any rate. The -2 was too long with its booster fitted. The Jabiru-1 had to be loaded onto the rails, then the interstage manually installed, then the booster loaded up from underneath and fitted to the interstage. It took at least ten or 15 minutes and the whole launcher was out of action while it was being done. The Australian Wellington class destroyers loaded their launchers horizontally so they could have multiple salvoes of long-range missiles, but that solution was expensive in terms of ship length and weight. For the Indian Navy, the long-range Jabiru-2s were one-shot only, then it would be back to the medium range Jabiru-1s.

"Sir, the frigates are calling in." The Sparker was back. "Do you want them to load Jabiru-2s ready on their rails as well?"

"They don't have them." Dahm was irritated.

"No Sir, but their Weaps says he can make them up. They have the right interstage on board and they can take the boosters off Ikaras."

Dahm kicked himself. Jabiru had been designed as a modular system with a variety of upper stages and a common booster system. Jabiru 2 was simply a Jabiru 1 mounted on the booster used by Ikara using a special interstage.

"Tell them yes, immediately. And pass my commendation to the Weaps responsible.." It was easy to forget that the weapons could be reconfigured at will. Now, he had a really potent long-range anti-missile punch. Underneath his feet, he could feel the vibration as *Mysore* picked up speed.

HIJMS Aoba*, Flagship, South China Sea Squadron, Dawn, South China Sea*

"Enemy task force closing Sir, range 250 kilometers. Read nine contacts."

Kurita's face was impassive. Nine enemy ships to his twelve. He had the numbers and the quality. He had his two rocket cruisers ready to fire and eight missile destroyers. Three of the Indian ships were gun destroyers, obsolete in the age of missiles. Three were frigates, slow and lightly armed. The odds were good. He'd guessed the Indian navy would seek a decisive battle, that they would try and face down their enemy, the way the old battle-cruiser *Hood* had faced down her enemies fifteen years earlier. The Navy had never really recovered from that humiliation. Only, now they wouldn't get the chance. The rocket cruisers would see to that.

"*Yashima* and *Asahi* report they have locked their missiles onto the enemy positions, Sir. They're ready to open fire as soon as you give the word."

"Very well. Order *Yashima* and *Asahi* to open fire on the enemy formation. Full salvo."

The four cruisers were in a line abreast now, the two rocket cruisers in the center, the gun cruisers on either side. Six destroyers formed a line in front of them with one more on each side. Across from *Aoba*, *Yashima* suddenly erupted into flame forward, looking for all the world as if she had exploded. The roar of the Kabuto missiles leaving their tubes penetrated even the bridge of *Aoba*. Beyond *Yashima*, *Asahi's* bows were covered by the same ball of red flame as her forward bank of missiles discharged. Then, the fireball elongated as the second rank fired, the Kabutos screaming away through the dying flames of the first group's launch. The third rank fired, then the fourth, the fire spreading back along the ship's bows until it seemed the whole ship was in flames. Yet, the smoke and fire died away to leave the two rocket cruisers intact except for the blackening of their paint.

"Missiles away Sir. All 32 heading for the enemy formation."

Thirty two missiles Kurita thought, *about three and a half per enemy target. Enough to wipe out the Indian ships completely.* For a brief moment he wished that the Kabuto missiles had pilots like the strategic Ohkas. A pilot could look at the enemy formation, see which ships had been hit, which had not, and plan his attack accordingly. The Kabutos had a radar guidance system with a datalink back to the firing ship. That allowed the crew there to see which missiles had locked in on which ships and transmit go or reselect orders as needed. A substitute but no replacement for a pilot in the loop. But it would have to do.

INS Mysore*, Flagship, First Division, The Flying Squadron, Dawn, South China Sea.*

"Enemy have opened fire Sir. Raid count, 32 Vampires inbound. Closing high and fast."

Thirty two missiles Dahm thought to himself. *That made his own counter-salvo seem puny.* Still, Sagarika flew lower and faster than the Chimp Kabuto so its survival odds were better. Time to let fly.

"Open fire, all eight Sagarika's in the tubes. Aft mount, reload with four more long range Sagarikas and fire. Bow mount, reload with the four short-range Sagarikas and stand ready."

The two quadruple launchers were already trained and elevated. The aft mount fired first, its four tubes exploding onto a ball of flame as the missiles streaked out and away. As the bow mount fired, the aft mount quickly retracted into its hangar, the four additional long-range Sagarikas sliding out into the tubes, then the mount elevating once again and firing. It had taken less than a minute and the last of the twelve Indian long-range anti-ship missiles were on their way. That left *Mysore* with just her four remaining short-range missiles and her guns.

Dahm glanced at his display. Deep in the ship, the Combat Direction Center was well equipped to show what was happening. The positions of the two formations was shown on the big vertical situation display: long red fingers reached from the Chimp group towards his formation. Soon, his own green fingers would reach out in return. It would take seven minutes for the missiles to cover the distance between the ships but the battle would be over a long time before that. He paced the bridge, snapping his fingers with impatience as the clock ticked by. Soon, the enemy missiles would be within range of the Jabiru-2s.

"Air defense ships firing, Sir." *Mysore's* Ops officer spoke quietly.

The two missile destroyers and the three frigates had fired. The balls of flame were smaller and less impressive than the big anti-ship missiles but the white trails the Jabirus left behind them were oddly reassuring. What was less so was that two of them fell out of the sky within a second or two of launch. Malfunctions, two out of fourteen, leaving twelve on their way. The green tracks of the Jabirus ate up the space, making the anti-ship missiles seem lethargic in comparison. Dahm ground his fingers into the palms of his hands. In the Mediterranean, off Gaza, the American Terriers had an abysmal hit rate against anti-ship missiles. Would the Australian Jabirus do any better? He'd know soon enough, the tracks were converging.

A roar of cheers went up in the CDC. The tracks had converged and the Jabirus had vanished - but so had eight of the inbound Chimp missiles. Twenty four left. The air defense ships should have three salvoes, fourteen Jabiru-1 missiles in each. If they scored as many hits as they had with the Jabiru-2s, then the attack would fail. The rails on the air defense ships would already be vertical, the missiles sliding into place.

"Air defense ships firing again, Sir." That would be the Jabiru-1s going off. The destroyers and frigates would be firing as fast as they could now, to get as many missiles in the air as possible. The green lines of the outbound missiles were blurred into one mass, too many for the resolution of the screen.

"One hit, Sir." There was an appalled gasp around the compartment. One hit out of fourteen? What was going on? Why had the Jabiru-1s done so badly? That was as low a hit rate as the Terriers. The confidence that had been growing evaporated. There were still twenty three missiles inbound.

"Twelve hits Sir." Another cheer, an uneasy one but still there. Eleven missiles left and there was still the third salvo of Jabirus to score.

"Six hits, Sir." Another cheer, half-hearted. Five of the 32 enemy missiles had got through the Jabiru screen and it was down to the point defense systems to save the Indian ships.

Two of the Kabutos had selected *Mysore* as their target. Although their electronic brains could not take pride in the achievement, those two missiles had done well. They'd picked the most valuable ship in the formation and also the one with the weakest air defenses. Before her refit, *Mysore* would have been almost helpless. That refit had given her MOG short-range missiles and twin 35mm BOER guns. The midships MOG quadruple launcher started firing off its missiles, the first three missed the diving targets but the fourth exploded just underneath the leading Kabuto. The blast didn't destroy it but the big warhead flipped the anti-ship missile up, out of its dive path. The homing head lost acquisition and the missile made a ballistic arc, over *Mysore* to explode some five hundred yards away.

The other missile was confused. *Mysore* was firing chaff and the echoes from the strips of aluminum foil falling behind her seemed to make the ship grow longer. The missile shifted its aim aft, trying to keep the center of the ship in its sights. At the last second, it realized how it had been fooled and tried to correct, but the sudden change tumbled its gyros and the missile went out control. Yet, it almost made it. The Kabuto crashed into the sea about 30 yards short of its target and the explosion of its 2,200 pound warhead cracked open seams and sent white-hot splinters flying through *Mysore's* side. The cruiser lurched and black smoke poured upwards as the fire and damage control parties got to work, sealing compartments, plugging leaks and bringing the fires under control before they could take hold.

The two Kabutos that had selected *Ghauri* as a target had made a mistake. She was regarded as the best anti-aircraft ship in the fleet and her performance proved it. She got off two more Jabirus from her aft launcher as the attacking missiles started their dive and got one Kabuto with them. Her MOG crew amidships got the other, hitting it twice with their missiles. The 55 pound warheads reduced it to scrap in mid-air. That scrap showered down on the destroyer but did little damage.

The fifth missile scored big. It picked the frigate *Himgiri* as a target and its dive was precise. The frigate was designed as an escort for convoys and other support roles, not to take part in a fleet engagement. She'd already done more than her share, and this was just that bit too much. *Himgiri's* MOGs missed, not by much, but they missed and the ship's EW fit wasn't adequate to beat the Kabuto's homing head. The missile struck almost exactly amidships. The warhead blasted the engine rooms open and sent a fireball rolling through the ship's structure. Just aft of the point of impact were the MOG magazines and the fireball opened them up with little effort. The missiles exploded and initiated a chain of ammunition detonations that ripped through the heart of the frigate. When the smoke of the eruptions cleared, she just wasn't there any more.

It was over. Dahm looked up from the display, grief at the loss of *Himgiri* and the damage to his flagship mixed with relief that the rest of his squadron was intact. "What's happened to our missiles, then?"

HIJMS Aoba, *Flagship, South China Sea Squadron, Dawn, South China Sea*

The cheering echoed around the bridge; the officers ostentatious in their delight, the enlisted seamen restricting themselves to the satisfied smiles their status imposed. "Five enemy ships hit, Sir. They're heavily damaged at the very least. Five of our missiles got through to strike the enemy, and destroyers cannot take a hit from a Kabuto. Perhaps their cruiser survived, but four of the destroyers *must* be sinking. A great victory, Sir!"

Admiral Kurita looked unconvinced. The rocket cruisers were the pride of what was left of the Japanese Navy so their promoters, which included virtually everybody, assumed the best of them. Kurita wasn't so sure; he'd seen too many exaggerated claims, too many assumptions that had proved to be false. *Still, the radar trace showed that five of the Kabutos had got through. If they'd had their nuclear warheads, there would be nothing left of the Indian fleet. They didn't though, and the conventional warheads were hardly in the same league as ship killers. Five missiles though didn't mean five hits. One, perhaps.* Kurita was dispirited. *The salvo from the rocket cruisers was supposed to be the battle-winner, the devastating first punch that would leave the enemy shattered and the survivors ready to be mopped up. That wasn't happening.*

"Where are the enemy missiles? Did they launch a salvo?"

"Not yet, Sir.... Wait one.... Negate that, enemy anti-ship missiles, probably Sagarikas, crossing the radar horizon now, three groups of four...... destroyers opening fire."

'Negate that', Kurita ran the words around in his mind glumly. *The Americans might be too weak to turn their immense power into world dominance but SAC-speak was infecting the whole world. The delay in spotting the Indian missiles made sense though,* Kurita reflected as he watched the sterns of the six destroyers ahead of his cruisers erupt into flame. The Nodachi missiles leaped from their storage boxes towards the incoming weapons. The Japanese Kabuto flew a high, arcing trajectory intended to allow its radar homing system to detect its targets as early as possible. That increased their vulnerability but made them independent of outside aid. The Indian Sagarika flew much lower but was steered to its target by information from the airborne Fairey Defender Rotodynes. That made them less vulnerable but dependent on outside assistance. Now, the Indians would see if their concepts worked.

Ahead of *Aoba*, the six destroyers were firing rapidly, one full salvo at each group of four. *Another difference in style,* Kurita reflected. The Japanese had four missiles ready to go on each launcher but it took time to reload, the Nodachis had to be manually pulled from their reload hangar in the base of the superstructure and fitted to the rails. This gave a very heavy defense against a first strike but a long time before the launchers would be ready to engage a follow-up strike. The Indian, Australian really, Jabirus had a twin rail launcher that only took seconds to reload, suited to a prolonged engagement. That was why Kurita was holding the Nodachi launchers on his two remaining destroyers and the two rocket cruisers in reserve.

"First group, three hits!" Cheers on the bridge again as only a single Indian missile penetrated the first salvo of Nodachis.

"Second group, four hits!" The cheering redoubled as the second group of Indian missiles, only a split second behind the first group, vanished in a welter of explosions that stained the horizons black. "Sir, two of our missiles flew through the wreckage of Sagarikas that were hit a split second earlier!" The warfare officer broke off as the third group of missiles, a few seconds behind the first two groups, was intercepted.

"Third group, three hits!" Kurita saw the six destroyers fire again, three ships taking each of the missiles that had penetrated the screen. Both Sagarikas vanished as the missiles hit home. Across the bridge, the warfare officer ticked his pad. "Sir, that makes 24 missiles fired, two malfunctioned, 12 hit. And, Sir, several of the misses were only because their target had been destroyed already."

"Very Good. *Very Good.* Order the destroyers to reload." Kurita was thoughtful for a second. "We must make a note, we did this wrong. We should have held our fire for later, at shorter range, given the enemy less time to respond. And allowed us to follow up more quickly. Still, at least this way we have time to reload our Nodachi launchers."

"We need time Sir, between firing the long-range missiles and finishing up the enemy. Time to let the initial radiation and fallout subside, allow time for us to decontaminate and avoid poisoning ourselves."

"Yes, when firing nuclear weapons. But today we did not. And we should have held our fire."

INS Mysore, *Flagship, First Division, The Flying Squadron, Dawn, South China Sea.*

"They got them, Sir, all of them." Weaps' voice was crestfallen, almost ashamed. "All twelve, just blotted them out."

Admiral Kanali Dahm sighed. "We did it wrong, we should have held our fire. Somehow I do not think these long range missiles are quite all that their designers promised." That was the truth, with one Indian ship literally blown out of the water and his flagship lightly damaged, Dahm had to concede the first blood had been scored by the Chipanese. "How long to close quarters action?"

There was a split second delay. "Just over an hour Sir. We'll be in Jabiru and Ikara range then."

“Very well. Order the *Ghurka* and *Ghauri* to load Jabirus Is ready for surface-to-surface fire, the two remaining frigates to load Ikaras with their torpedoes set for surface targets. And we’ll throw in our own four short-range Sagarikas of course. We’ll give the Chimps a blast of missile fire then close the range as quickly as possible. The missile ships will keep up a sustained missile fire while they have shots in their magazines while they try and open the way for the gun destroyers to get at the cruisers with torpedoes.

“We’ve got to get a short-range engagement as quickly as we can. If we hang off at long range, those two six inch cruisers out there will shoot us to pieces. At close range, it’s our rapid-fire 4.5s that have the edge. As soon as the missile ships are hitting the enemy, all ships will close at maximum possible speed.”

“All missiles, Sir?”

“All of them. We’ll rely on our MOGs for anti-aircraft and anti-missile fire. Damage control, what’s happening down there?”

“Under control Sir. The fires are out, they never amounted to much anyway. We’ve stopped the flooding from the strained welds. A couple of the bulkheads weren’t as tight as they should have been but we’ve dealt with that. We’re dewatering the flooded areas now and sealing up. Thirty minutes and we’ll be back up to scratch.”

“Well done. Once your finished, get ready for emergency work as needed. We’re going to be going straight at the enemy. You won’t be short of work.”

“Very good Sir.” The damage control officer did not sound overjoyed at the prospects of his services being in urgent demand. In fact, although Dahm didn’t know it, he was wondering if there was still time for a quick transfer to the Air Force.

“Get the message out to the rest of the squadron, make all preparations for a full-scale action.” He thought for a second. “And tell the Ship’s Poisoners to be ready for casualties. A lot of casualties.

The Admiral's Doggie noted the order, nodding grimly while he did so, then tapped his pad. "This, Sir, is going to be bloody."

Dahm nodded. "In many ways we face the same situation Jim Ladone did back in '59 when he faced down *Yamato* and *Musashi*. There's an amphibious force back there, 15,000 soldiers, and we can't let them down. We can't let the Chimps through to hit them. We have to take them down out here. We don't have time to be clever or to nibble away at them. This has to be a sledgehammer job, we're going to have to do a ram raid on the Chimp fleet. Which reminds me, any Delhi underworld figures on board? We might need their skills."

A ripple of laughter ran around the bridge. Delhi was notorious for its ram raids on expensive stores. A couple of badmashs would steal a cheap car, a Tata or a Marati, ram it through the windows of a gold or jewelry shop, grab what they could and retreat in another car driven by a confederate. They would be gone by the time the police turned up. Or so the plan went.

"What do you plan to do, Sir?" Weaps was having to suppress his snorts of laughter. "Rob their pay office into the bargain?"

"Not a bad idea Weaps, not bad. Only hardly worthwhile the way the Chimps pay their sailors. I just thought, if we get close enough, perhaps our dacoits from down in the engine rooms could get me a samurai sword off one of their officers. Sort of grab it as we go past?" There was another ripple of laughter, the Admiral's jokes were always funny.

"So, we have our objectives. Order the squadron to make 28 knots, we'll open fire at 20 miles range. Weaps, work out a fire plan for the ships. Check the CBs, find out exactly which ships we're likely to be facing and target accordingly. Blast a hole through the middle of their destroyer screen. And may the Gods smile on our endeavors today. If we forget them, let us hope that they do not forget us."

Bridge, INS Rana, *First Division, The Flying Squadron, Dawn, South China Sea.*

"This, Sir, is going to be bloody." Captain Ditrapa Dasgupta's first officer was quite unconscious of the fact he was echoing the Admiral's comments an hour earlier. Dasgupta nodded, his eyes fixed on the radar repeater. The Japanese formation was now some 35,000 yards in front of them: two lines of six ships, smaller blips showing the destroyers in front of and beside the four larger echoes of the cruisers.

The same display showed the Indian formation beginning to spread out despite the orders to hold 28 knots. Oh, everybody was obeying orders but that didn't change basic physics. The three Project 18 class destroyers were capable of ten knots more than that speed so they'd pulled slowly ahead, their extra power helping them overcome any momentary losses. The two surviving frigates could barely hold 28 knots: if their speed dropped for a second or two, they couldn't make it up so they had fallen slowly to the rear. In the middle were the *Mysore* and the two Project 21 class missile destroyers. They were the keys to the next stage of the game.

Any second now, Dasgupta tapped his binoculars on the bridge rail for luck and went to the wings. Behind him the two Project 21s were plowing peacefully through the waves; even as he watched they suddenly picked up speed. He wished his *Rana* had those engines, the gas turbines in the Project 21s gave them terrific acceleration. Then, they seemed to lengthen and distort as they swung off course to unmask their stern rails. They held that position for a second, then they seemed to shudder and vanish as their missile launchers fired at almost zero elevation.

The Jabirus were off on their way, streaking across the sea towards the enemy destroyer line. Eight of them in all. Dasgupta heard their screams as they passed *Rana* on the way out. In his mind's eye he saw the launch rails elevate to vertical, the missile magazine hatches open and the next pair of Jabirus slide upwards into the arms of the launcher. The doors slammed shut, the rails dropped to horizontal and more missiles went screaming across the sea.

Only 20 seconds elapsed between salvoes, yet the first group were already more than 2/3 of the way to their targets by the time the second group of missiles were on their way. Over the Chipanese fleet, Dasgupta saw the sky turn black with explosions as the Jabirus met the enemy defense.

Almost at the same instant, the order came in: "All ships close on the enemy at maximum possible speed." The meaning of that had been made clear, get every scrap of power, every last ounce of steam pressure, every last small fraction of a revolution out of your machinery and close on the enemy fast. Dasgupta felt the vibration under his feet suddenly become almost painful as *Rana, Ranjit* and *Rajput* accelerated towards the enemy. On trials, they'd all exceeded 38 knots. Now, they would find out if speed trials actually meant anything.

HIJMS Aoba, *Flagship, South China Sea Squadron, Dawn, South China Sea*

"Missile fire Sir! Enemy formation firing missiles."

"Bring them down!" Almost as if the launchers had been waiting for the orders, the ten Nodachi missile ships opened fire. A full salvo of ten missiles streaked out to meet the eight inbound Indian missiles. It seemed almost instant; the two waves of missiles closing so fast that no time seemed to elapse between the roar of launch and the black clouds of the explosions.

"Eight hits! Enemy first wave of missiles gone!" That was a great success, it made the American bungling a few years earlier look amateurish in comparison. "Another wave inbound Sir, eight more! Closing fast."

The Indians had got their punch in first and they had the initiative. They were punching with their missiles and the Japanese were defending, trying to fend off the blows. Kurita realized he'd hit a great truth in this type of missile warfare; being first was everything. As long as one side was attacking, the other had to defend and that put them at a disadvantage.

“Four hits!” That meant four more were coming through. “And another enemy wave inbound.”

“Leave the leakers, hit the intact waves.” His order was being executed even while he spoke. Leave the leakers to electronic warfare and the guns. The missile’s jobs was to break up the mass attacks. Kurita felt *Aoba* shake under his feet as her forward 155mm guns opened up, reinforcing the 100mm guns on the destroyers, now pumping out 35 rounds a minute from each of their four guns. They weren’t shooting at the missiles, they were trying to lay down a wall of fragments in the area the missiles had to fly though. They wouldn’t hit the missiles, the missiles would hit the splinters of steel. Meanwhile, the EW crews would be repeating the Indian target designation pulses, the frequency and timing subtly changed so that the homing heads would steer for the wrong position.

As Kurita watched, one of the white trails from the Indian missiles went into the sea, its passing marked by an oily explosion. *Flown into the sea, probably a simple accident, but a fortunate one.* Another vanished in a ball of smoke, probably fragments penetrating its rocket motor and causing it to burn up. That left two. One was clearly going astray, angling gently away from its target as the seductive electronic signals mislead its simple brain. It shot aft of the destroyer it was targeted on, the *Aotaka*, and exploded in her wake. The fourth and last missile shot over *Aotaka,* the EW crew hadn’t deceived it in deflection but they had in range. The missile actually passed between their bridge and mast, exploding just a few seconds later. *Fragment damage and probably casualties, but nothing more. Aotaka had evaded the missiles as deftly as a geisha avoiding the probing hands of a drunken customer.*

“Third wave, four hits! Fourth wave inbound.” The intercept had happened while he had been watching the final runs of the leakers. Kurita didn’t need to repeat the orders. The Nodachi launchers were already training their last remaining ready-missile on the fourth wave. The leakers were again for the point defenses to handle. Once again, a delicate electronic fan-dance mixed with the brutalism of the heavy gunfire. Once again, the explosions in mid air as inbound missiles disintegrated or an elegant swing in their white trails as they were deflected by the modified signals.

A short, gray streak came from the target of this wave, the *Agano*. One of the original light cruisers that had given birth to the Kawari class, twice rebuilt now and an old ship, she'd fired a shoulder-mounted surface-to-air missile as a last defense. It failed, never came close, but Kurita saw one of the two missiles it had been aimed at streak past *Agano's* bows. For a second he thought the other had missed as well, the white trail of its motor vanished. For a millisecond that seemed like an age nothing happened. Then, there was a boiling mushroom of black smoke and flame from *Agano*. A hit, dead midships. His mind saw the scene on her now, the emergency sirens going, men running out with hoses and stretchers through the smoke and noise, through the wrecked structure, around the mangled men, seeing the flames, the ship burning at the point of impact. The Indians had drawn their first blood.

"Fourth wave, six hits!" Two more leakers, well evidence was showing that the point defenses could handle those, even with *Agano* out of the fight. "Fifth wave inbound."

That dispassionate comment was the crack of doom for the Nodachi launchers were empty. Oh, there were reload missiles available. Even now the launchers would be retracting into the decks, the crews running out, manhandling the missiles in their launch boxes from the hangars, rolling them along the deck tracks, sliding them onto the rails. But that took time. The Japanese system was built a round a short, sharp engagement; a decisive battle where everything was decided with the first salvoes. This was turning into a prolonged brawl.

Kurita watched the wave of eight missiles slashing towards his ships. Gunfire, more gunfire. It had taken down the two fourth wave leakers, now the point defenses faced a worse threat. The fifth wave was concentrated on the *Fubuki*, a destroyer already twisting and turning as the missile wave closed in on her. Some exploded, others were deflected, some simply missed but three did not. Two hit almost side by side, at the base of *Fubuki's* funnel. The third hit right aft, the fragments of its detonation scythed through the crews working to reload the missile launchers. Other fragments peppered the hangar, cutting fuel lines and ripping through electronic circuitry. *Fubuki* lurched under the hammer blows, her sirens sounded the ship's screams of pain and distress as her crew boiled out to put out the fires and stem the floods.

INS Mysore*, Flagship, First Division, The Flying Squadron, Dawn, South China Sea.*

It was like the siege of a castle. The walls stood and the battering ram slammed into them. The first blow did nothing, the second barely more than that. But, with each blow, the stones were a little weaker, the damage just that bit greater. One day, one final blow would be enough and the wall would come tumbling down.

"Admiral, fifth wave of missiles got through, at least three hits, perhaps five on one of their destroyers. No defensive missiles fired, we've run them out of ammunition."

And the walls came tumbling down, the words echoed again through Dahm's mind. The enemy were out of long-range anti-aircraft missiles and the range was dropping fast, down to around 25,000 yards. *Just about maximum gunnery range* he thought. *Wasn't the record for long range hits some German battlecruiser taking pot-shots at a British carrier back in 1940? That had been around 25,000 yards hadn't it. Long range for guns, short range indeed for Sagarika.*

"Hit the cruisers with the four remaining Sagarika, one at each. Then order the frigates to open fire with Ikaras on the cruiser line." Dahm looked at the score board. The two Project 21 class destroyers had stopped firing, their Jabirus gone. In exchange, three pyres of smoke could be seen on the horizon, burning ships. They hadn't paid the debt for *Himgiri* yet but it was a start.

HIJMS Aoba*, Flagship, South China Sea Squadron, Dawn, South China Sea*

"Report from *Agano* Sir. The missile hit the forward end of the superstructure, just aft of No.2 turret. Hull damage is superficial but they regret to report that No.2 turret and the forward missile fire control radars have been knocked out by splinters. The ship's armor deck has prevented more serious damage. *Agano* reports a fire in the area of impact, its limited and under control but its the very devil to put out."

Rocket fuel thought Kurita, *it burned hot and contained its own oxidizers.* Nothing would put it out until the original fuel was exhausted, all the crew could do would be to keep the surrounding area cool. The furnace-like rocket fuel fires would otherwise heat bulkheads to the point where they would ignite the contents of adjoining compartments by radiation.

"*Mutsuki*, Sir, the Gods are looking after her. She's taken four hits. Two hit the deck right aft and skidded clear, she's got minor fragmentation damage there, no more than that. Another did the same on the bows, hit just under the flare and went right through before exploding. The one bad one was aft, into the hull, just above the screws, only it failed to explode. *Mutsuki* reports a few injured, some dents and splinter holes, no fires, no flooding.

"But *Fubuki*, she's hurt. Two missiles took her amidships, one where the aft part of the funnel enters the deck, another where the forward part joins the superstructure. The fragmentation went right through her, her machinery spaces are flooding and the whole midships area is on fire. Third missile took her right aft in the hangar. Missile fire control is gone, the hangar's shredded and the fuel lines are pouring aviation fuel into the missile fire. Captain reports she's dead in the water, listing heavily, no power and pumps running on emergency. Damage control crews are trying to establish fire and flooding perimeters, they're reinforcing bulkheads with timbers and trying to seal off the fires but its the missile fragments, she's really torn up."

Missile fragments. Rocket fuel. Fires, splinter damage. Almost no mention of the explosions, as if the warheads on the Australian anti-aircraft missiles were of little account. If Japanese intelligence was to be believed (and it should be, since they'd got the information from the brochures given away at arms exhibitions although why they had then stamped those sales brochures "Top Secret" was a mystery to everybody), the Jabirus had a continuous rod warhead. A thick steel bar, notched at carefully chosen-intervals was wrapped around the explosive charge. Then the warhead went off, the rod burst in a corona of fragments concentrated in a narrow doughnut around the missile and spraying outwards.

It was supposed to slash through aircraft and break them up but it punctured bulkheads and cut wiring runs just as effectively. Worse yet, it worked with the rocket fuel fires, ensuring paths by which they could spread. The words of a song echoed in Kurita's mind. *It was a stupid song form one of the spineless, brainless, cowardly Americans. One of the ones who prattled on about love and peace. 'Fire, water, earth and air' it went, the four elements in 'nature's circle'. Well, those four elements are crippling my destroyers. Fire from the rocket fuel, air feeding the flames, steel fragments from earth, slashing holes in bulkheads and shell plating, and water seeping in to destroy buoyancy and stability. Fire, water, earth and air. Love had nothing to do with it.*

"Inbounds! Four more on the way!" The urgent cry broke into Kurita's reverie. Compared with the first salvoes that had torn the sky up as they'd raced towards the Japanese ships, these ones seemed to be almost leisurely. Yet, they were coming in fast, four tracks, one obviously targeted on each of his four cruisers. Closing at 2000 meters every three seconds, they were slow only by the standard of the anti-aircraft missiles. Kurita felt the deck rumble under his feet as *Aoba* opened fire with her forward 155mm dual-purpose guns.

Abreast of her, *Asama* was doing the same. For a brief moment, the big guns had the field to themselves and they were rewarded by the sight of the white streak of the Sagarika turning gray, then black-and-red as the missile was hit and turned into a tumbling mass of fragments. Then, the 100mm guns on the destroyers and the 76mm weapons on the two rocket cruisers cut in, once more staining the sky black with the flak bursts. Another inbound missile was hit, and then a third but the fourth made it through the anti-aircraft barrage. Helplessly, Kurita watched it slice in on *Asama*.

The short-range anti-ship Sagarika had a 4,400 pound warhead, the explosives packing the space consumed by fuel tanks and datalinks in the long-range versions. It wasn't the weight of the explosive charge that did it, crippling though that was. What did it was that the explosive warhead was designed as a shaped charge, one

34 inches across. Armor piercing capability of such warheads wasn't determined by weight of explosives or speed of impact, it was determined by that diameter. As a rule of thumb, the penetration of a normal shaped charge was at least six times its diameter.

The Sagarika warhead wasn't a sophisticated design and it barely managed the rule-of-thumb minimum. That still meant it could penetrate 204 inches of armor plate. It wouldn't have mattered if *Asama* had been the long-scrapped *Yamato.* For all the cries of those who wanted to see battleships back in the fleet, there was no practical thickness of armor that could stop that blast.

The missile slammed into the cruiser between No.1and No.2 turrets, angling aft as the cruiser turned to avoid the incoming weapon. It crashed through the outer plating and drove inboard for a few feet while its delayed action fuse started to work. Then it exploded, sending a jet of flame more than 40 feet long into the ship's heart. The six inches of armor on *Asama* at the point of impact vanished in the fury of the shaped charge blast as if it had never been there. The jet roared into the No.2 turret magazine, melting the brass cases of the serried ranks of six inch shells and spreading their contents out into the flame. A microsecond later, the propellant ignited. The magazine was a large space by ship standards but nowhere near large enough to contain the effects of all the shells in No.2 turret igniting. It wasn't, technically, an explosion, not immediately, but it might as well have been. Its effect on the shells in that magazine was to convert the massive over-contained fire into a real explosion.

It wasn't like *Himgiri*. That ship had simply vanished in a flash of light. Kurita saw the fireball of the explosion on *Asama's* bow and, a minute fraction of a second later, the eruption as No.2 turret magazine exploded. Then, the explosions seemed to roll along the ship's length, ripping her apart as they went.

The blast from No.2 turret magazine went two ways. One was forward, searing through the bulkhead separating it from No.1 turret magazine and starting the same cataclysmic process there. As No.1 turret magazine exploded, the whole bow section of *Asama*, from No.1 turret forward, detached and somersaulted across the sea.

The other component of the blast wave went aft, penetrating and detonating No.3 turret magazine. That reinforced the blast wave, sending it through the accommodation and command center under the bridge, into the boiler rooms. Those big spaces should have allowed the blast to expand and dissipate only beside the boiler rooms were the magazines that fed the forward four twin 100mm mounts. Those magazines had no protection against and explosion from inside the ship and they contributed to the blast wave that was gutting *Asama.*

Next to go were the machinery compartments, aft of the boiler rooms. Again, their size should have allowed the blast wave to expand and absorbed some of its fury but above the machinery spaces were *Asama's* torpedoes. She had two sets of five in the tubes and two sets of reloads. They added both explosion and fire from their oxygen cylinders to the cataclysm engulfing *Asama* and made the explosion of the aft 100mm magazines a formality. Reinforced by the latest additions, the blast wave still raced aft, into No.4 turret magazine and the cycle that had started in the bows was completed. No.5 turret magazine exploded a split second after No.4 turret and No.6 turret magazine followed them the same interval later. Finally, the blast wave exited via the ship's stern.

Kurita watched appalled as the cruiser vanished under the chain of explosions, her shape indistinguishable under the clouds of smoke and flame that had engulfed her. The spaces that had once housed her machinery collapsed and the ship mercifully broke in half. The two parts rolled apart as the explosions racked them. The bow portion, now open at both ends sank almost immediately. The stern took a little longer. Its shape seemed to rise upwards as it started its plunge downwards. The distinctive curve of the fantail highlighted against the sky, looking for all the world as if a giant sword was being shaken in a final act of defiance against the heavens that had failed to smile on *Asama*. Then, the 18,000 ton cruiser was gone.

"Target that cruiser. All guns, now!" Kurita looked at the scene outside the bridge. Three Indian destroyers had pulled right ahead of the rest of the squadron and were racing into the attack, spray piling over their bridges, spectacular bones in their teeth. Kurita was a traditional Navy man and he recognized a traditional destroyer torpedo attack when he saw one. "Destroyers to engage those three there! Get our torpedoes ready for launch."

"More missiles inbound!"

Kurita shuddered at the words. *Was this seemingly endless barrage of missiles never going to end?* Intellectually, Kurita knew what the Indians were doing, by keeping up this steady stream of missiles, they were keeping the Japanese squadron on the defensive. As long as they did that, Kurita would be trapped into reacting to their moves and that was a sure and certain way to lose a battle. *Still, their magazines had to be running low, didn't they? Missiles weren't like shells, missiles were costly and space consuming. Ships couldn't carry that many of them.*

Kurita watched the tracks of the latest salvoes. These were a lot slower than the previous waves, subsonic by a wide margin. Even as he watched, gunfire brought down the first wave of eight but the second wave got through with only two shot down. *Still,* Kurita realized, *they weren't a threat. They were targeted on the cruiser Asahi but were obviously going to pass astern of her.* Then, he realized his mistake. As the missiles glided past the stern of *Asahi*, they seemed to split in half, the bottom section falling away and growing a parachute as the top half went unstable and broke up. *Torpedoes!* The Australian Crocodile 16 inch torpedo was also dual-purpose, its passive homing system was capable of targeting surface ships as well as submarines. In his mind, Kurita could see the six torpedoes curving after the *Asahi*.

In point of fact, he was wrong. Two of the torpedoes had malfunctioned as they'd hit the water. The other four had overshot their target but picked up *Asahi's* screws and set off in dogged pursuit. *Asahi's* Captain had already spotted the threat and was turning into them, forcing the torpedoes to spend energy in a tight curve. The Australians liked to put big warheads on their weapons and they paid for those explosive charges with range and speed. The torpedoes were in a tail-chase, trying to catch the cruiser that had gone to emergency speed to avoid them. If they'd been capable of doing the maths, they would have given it up as being a bad job but they weren't and didn't. They continued the chase, and by doing so, forced *Asahi* to continue evading them. That put her on a reciprocal course to the rest of the Japanese squadron and meant she couldn't turn until the torpedoes ran out of fuel. That wouldn't be long but every second put her further out of the battle.

"More missiles inbound Sir."

'Tell me something surprising why don't you.' The sarcastic rejoinder rolled around Kurita's mind but he kept the thought to himself. Eight more of the torpedo-carrying missiles were on their way, clearly targeted on the already damaged *Agano*. The weakened gunfire of the Japanese squadron got five of them but the remaining three splashed into the water around *Agano's* stern. One picked up the rhythmic beat of the destroyer's propellers and set off to intercept them. It ignored, or not register, the explosions as the other two torpedoes exploded in the target's wake. The Crocodile had a large warhead but it was still small by torpedo standards. Even so, it did what it was supposed to do; the homing system took it into the destroyer's screws and the Crocodile blew one of the blades of the port screw off.

Suddenly, the prop was completely unbalanced and started to thresh around on the end of the shaft. With each revolution, the spiraling action of the screw got worse, forcing the shaft further and out of line. There was only so much stress the shaft could take and that limit passed so quickly nobody on the destroyer could have stopped what was about to happen even if they'd had a chance to realize what was coming. The shaft suddenly gave, its previous mathematically-precise straightness rupturing into a 30 degree bend about a quarter of the way back from the screw.

The racing shaft now proceeded to rip open the inside of the shaft tunnel, shattering the bearings and throwing an insupportable load onto the main gears. They blew under the strain, cutting the power to the starboard propeller. *Agano* lurched to port and came to a halt, dead in the water, her machinery plant damaged beyond any feasible repair, the whole of her aft half flooding form the ruptured shaft tunnel.

"More missiles coming in Sir."

Shut UP! Kurita wanted to scream the order at the Ops Officer but he forced himself to remain calm. "Open fire on the Indian cruiser, fire our torpedoes at those three destroyers."

"Target the center destroyer Sir?"

"Yea....." Kurita looked at the display again. "No, the one to starboard. That way, any overruns have a chance at the group of ships further back. And get that cruiser under fire."

"Yes Sir, Seven missiles down sir, the one survivor, it's gone wild. Either malfunctioned or didn't acquire."

INS Mysore, *Flagship, First Division, The Flying Squadron, South China Sea.*

"My God, look at her go! That evens things up for *Himgiri*!"

The rolling cloud of black smoke over the Chipanese fleet covered the death-agony of *Asama* but her fate had been obvious. She'd blown up, even more spectacularly that the Indian frigate an hour earlier. Admiral Kanali Dahm felt the twinge of sadness every sailor felt while watching a ship dying and then ruthlessly dismissed it. *War was war*. Then, he corrected himself. *An international incident was an international incident.*

"We're pounding the destroyers in the center of the Chipanese line Sir. Some of the missiles are getting through and hitting. Looks as if two destroyers are dead in the water and I think we scored well on another. I think we got another cruiser as well, she's dropped out of the line and is wandering off. We may have got her in the steering gear."

For a moment, Dahm thought his binoculars were telling him that the other Chipanese gun cruiser had exploded as well. A rolling shroud of orange flame appeared to cover her, but it cleared almost immediately and the dark shape of the cruiser was unchanged.

"Hard a-port, all emergency power from the engines!" *Mysore* started to swing as the shells erupted into the water around her, a full broadside of twelve. The salvo was short but not by much and almost perfect for line. *Radar fire control had a lot to answer for*, Dahm thought.

Mysore's Captain had already seen the danger. "Helm, steer port ten, head for the splashes." That was the trick, the Chipanese gunners would correct their aim so where the previous broadside had landed was the one place the next one wouldn't. Or so the theory went. "Engines, more power! I want every scrap of steam you've got."

"Sirra, I dinnae think she can take much more of this." The message from the engineering officer came over in a broad Scots brogue that echoed out of the bridge speakers.

Dahm's jaw dropped. "What's with the Scots accent? Engines is a Tamil from Trincomalee for Heaven's sake. He's about as Scottish as Masanobu Tsuji."

"Tradition Sir. All the engineers like to think they've just come from the backstreets of Glasgow. Starboard fifteen, executing NOW."

Mysore swerved again as another group of shells exploded around her. *Interesting* Dahm thought. *They're spot-on for range and bearing but their patterns are so loose, we can slide between the splashes*. There had been rumors for a long time that the Chipanese cruisers had shot dispersion problems. Something to do with their hulls being too long, thin and lightly built. "Two more minutes and we're in 4.5 inch range. We'll hold fire though, once we cut lose with them, we'll be out of ammunition damned fast." *Unless they hit us first of course*.

INS Rajput*, First Division, The Flying Squadron, South China Sea.*

As *Rajput's* screws rotated, each blade entered a thin film of turbulence that streamed aft from the ship's hull. No designers, no shipyard, could make the steel-water interface entirely smooth so every ship had a shell of turbulent water around it and left a trail behind. Every time that blade hit that shell, it caused a small pulse of vibration called "blade beat" to pass down the length of the blade to the hub. From there on in, it went into the shaft and radiated up through the shaft towards the machinery. From there, it passed into the ship's structure and radiated forward from her hull. In fact, blade beat was the only component of the ship's machinery that radiated noise forward. It wasn't loud, but it was there and it made a very precise ticking noise, a very easy-to-isolate sound signature.

Approaching *Rajput*, the Japanese torpedo was listening for just that precise ticking noise. It had made most of the run out with its homing system turned off, but at a preset range, it had turned on and started listening. Three of its fellows were doing the same but the fifth had failed and was running unguided. At this range, its chance of hitting anything was indeed slender. The homing torpedoes, they were different.

The homing head was a series of arrays wrapped around the torpedo nose and it picked up the signature it was looking for. The Japanese had had an advantage when it came to designing homing torpedoes, in the 1940s they'd had the world's best old-fashioned straight-runner and its 24 inch diameter gave them much more room to work in. As a result, their torpedoes were a long-range and very accurate anti-ship weapon.

As the homing head isolated the noise, it made a slight change to course, putting the target in the middle of its acquisition cone. It also sent a signal to the oxygen-powered engine to pour on full power. The torpedo responded and it surged through the water. It was alone in doing so, the target was out of the acquisition arc of the other three working torpedoes.

With the target coming in at 38 knots and the torpedo going out at 48, it took only a few seconds for the range to close. That was when another system on the torpedo kicked in. The fuse on the warhead picked up the approaching magnetic signature of the steel ship, picked it up and measured it. Then did so again. The signal was increasing in strength, the target was coming. The homing head continued to do its job, making minor course corrections, placing the target dead ahead of the torpedo. As the destroyer passed over the torpedo, its magnetic signature peaked. Then, with the heavy steel of the gun turrets past, it dropped slightly. That drop was the signal and the 500 kilogram warhead exploded directly under *Rajput's* bridge.

The explosion formed a huge, expanding bubble in the water that lifted the middle of the destroyer up but left its bow and stern behind. That was a strain no ship could take and *Rajput's* back broke. Then the bubble started to collapse, only it had been flattened into an ellipse by the weight of the destroyer on top of it. Yet, by the laws of physics, all the parts of the bubble collapsed at equal speed so the bottom of the ellipse formed a water jet that punched through the bottom of the destroyer. The under-the-keel hit was more than overkill for the destroyer but overkill was the motto of the day. Here, in the South China Sea, eggshells were fighting with sledgehammers.

Bridge, INS Rana, *First Division, The Flying Squadron, South China Sea.*

"Oh My God." Captain Ditrapa Dasgupta watched appalled as *Rajput* disintegrated under the hammer blow. She'd been lifted up, broken by the under-the-keel explosion then dropped back in the water a split second before the second great surge had smashed her. He'd even had a chance to see the puff of black smoke from the funnel, driven out by the jet of water that had crushed her from beneath. *Rajput* had broken in two and both parts were twisted and going down fast.

"Sir, Signal from Admiral Dahm. Signal reads. 'Engage the enemy more closely.' That's all, Sir."

Dasgupta shook his head slightly. "Right, he wants to trade quotations does he? Signal back......"

"Sir, Signal from *Ghurka*. Signal reads 'Ayooo Ghurkali.' Signal ends."

"Damn, they beat us. Send. 'I have not yet begun to fight.' Prepare to open fire, guns and torpedoes."

"Sir, Starboard!"

Dasgupta shot a glance out towards the threat. Three incoming destroyers, moving to cut off the two surviving Indian ships from their target. The geometry played quickly in his head, they couldn't quite cut them off, but they would snarl the *Rana* and *Ranjit* in a short-range gunfight and prevent them from getting to the cruisers. The countermove was obvious.

"Make to *Ranjit.* Attack gun cruiser with torpedoes then engage targets of opportunity with guns. We will hold off counter-attack developing from starboard. Message ends." Dasgupta briefly wondered if he actually had the authority to send that message. It really didn't matter, it was the only thing to do. "Break starboard now, intercept course for the enemy destroyers."

Rana swerved in the water. Her designers had made a bad mistake with the American Fletcher class, one that had made those destroyers less agile than an Iowa class battleship. When they'd designed *Rana*, they hadn't made that mistake again. In fact they'd gone overboard trying to avoid the error. Even at.... Dasgupta glanced at the readout.... 38.1 knots, she could turn on a pinhead. He felt her stern shooting out and the ship starting to skid in the water as the helm was put over.

"Center ship is *Yahagi* Sir. Two other Kawari class with her, I think one is *Kisaragi*, her mast's different from the rest."

"Target torpedoes on *Yahagi*." She was armored; *Rana's* 4.5 inch guns would be less effective against her. "Hold fire until the torpedoes hit, then A and B turrets engage port target, X and Y turrets the starboard."

Normally splitting fire was a mistake but not this time. *Rana's* 4.5s each threw 45 55 pound shells a minute and she had eight of them. Naval commentators had said she had the firepower of a WW2 Atlanta class cruiser but that wasn't true, she had at least twice that. The Chipanese 3.9 inch gun threw 35 28 pound shells per minute and each ship had only four. *Rana* outgunned both Chipanese Kawaris put together. Of course if *Yahagi* survived the torpedoes, that changed things.

Rana straightened out with a dull whine as the quintuple torpedo tubes swung to bear. Dasgupta felt the lurch as the torpedoes fired out in a spread. Hopefully, they'd get one of the Chipanese destroyers, perhaps even two. They were good torpedoes, technically still British Mark 8s but actually a hybrid of the Mark 8 and the American Mark 14. Very good torpedoes, but straight-runners, not homing torpedoes. Would they be good enough? Shooting at fast-moving destroyers, even with a ten-torpedo spread, was a notoriously chancy business

Her torpedoes gone, *Rana* was snaking, trying to chase the splashes from the Chipanese 3.9 inch guns. In this wild knife-fight, speed was the only thing that kept ships safe and he had to wait until he'd closed the range. The problem with his rapid-fire guns was that they ate ammunition terrifyingly fast. He had a huge supply of ammunition by destroyer standards, 365 rounds per gun. Enough to keep his guns firing for exactly eight minutes. Across the water, *Yahagi* had seen her peril and was frantically making a turn of her own to try and comb the inbound spread.

"Any second now....." Weaps voice was tense. "Any second......" And there they were! A column of white water erupted on *Yahagi* right forward, between the bow and No.1 turret. A second later, a second column erupted right aft, astern of the missile launcher. She'd almost made it, almost turned between the torpedoes but not quite. She'd been hit in the screws as well, no doubt about it. "GOT HER! Topped and tailed by God!"

The bridge crew cheered, the sound mixed with slightly forced laughter at the description of the damage. After all, the unsavory habits of Saigon's underworld were well known. Dasgupta swung his binoculars onto the Chipanese destroyer. She was going fast, no doubt about it, bows blown off right up to No.1 turret, stern a crushed wreck. She was already slowing and rolling over, only the fact she was flooding from both ends was stopping her doing a final dive. *Not many would get off her*, Dasgupta's mind told him grimly, *she and her crew were a goner*.

"Guns, designated targets, open fire." The bridge shook as the forward guns crashed, Weaps was firing in the forward guns in pairs, less than a second separating the salvoes. The first pair were short but the guns elevated slightly between each shot, the director correcting for elevation and range.

It was a perfect ladder, the last pair of bursts were obscured by the enemy ship, the *Kisaragi* Number One had said? The gun barrels dropped a tiny amount then both turrets went to full rate of fire, a two-gun salvo every three quarters of a second. An orange ball erupted from the *Kisaragi*, then two more revealing that the guns had the range. With that rate of fire, as long as the radar tracked the target, they wouldn't lose it. Dasgupta swung his binoculars onto the second destroyer. She hadn't been hit yet, the secondary fire control aft was taking longer to get the range. Then, another bright ball as the first 4.5 inch rounds struck home.

Suddenly *Rana* lurched, smoke eddying up from below the bridge. A shot had cracked home, just at the base of the foremast. The nav radar up there was probably gone but that was of little import. Another 3.9 inch shell struck home aft of the funnel, demolishing the useless 37mm quad mount there. Then, as Dasgupta was still looking, another shot slammed into the rear of the forward superstructure, sending the glass screens scything across the bridge. *Rana* wasn't the only ship that had got the range of her opponent.

INS Mysore*, Flagship, First Division, The Flying Squadron, South China Sea.*

If the torpedo was human, it would have lost hope. It has missed its enemy; the sound of screws had never appeared within its acquisition cone. It had run on, its acoustic sensors straining in the water for something to home in on. Then, when almost all chance had gone, the torpedo picked up the rhythmic beat of screws. Right on the edge of the cone, but there. Almost thankfully, the torpedo turned towards the sound and the faint, steady beat of the screws crept over into the center of the cone. Now, it was more distinct, easier to analyze. Screws, threshing wildly in the water, cavitating madly. The torpedo accelerated to maximum speed and set off into its attack.

"Sir, high speed revolutions to starboard! Inbound."

Dahm cursed. For their sonar to pick up high-revving screws at the speed *Mysore* was making, the source had to be very, very close. Once again, Mysore's Captain was ready. "Emergency turn NOW, full starboard rudder, starboard screw full reverse, port screw emergency ahead." *Mysore* started to skid in the water, her starboard side dipping deep, her portside lifting high.

It was that reaction to the forces working on her hull that saved the ship. Not from being hit for the inbound torpedo was far too close for that, but by turning a lethal under-the-keel shot into a side impact explosion. The torpedo itself helped matters in that. Faulty depth-keeping was an inherent fault in the design, and it was running shallow. The torpedo hit only a few feet below what would normally have been *Mysore's* waterline, directly under the aft funnel.

The explosion tore a hole almost 40 feet long in the ship's side, ripping open the aft boiler room. The lucky boiler-room crewmembers were killed by blast and fragments. The not so lucky drowned in the mass of water flooding into the compartment. The really unlucky were scalded to death as that water hit the boilers and filled the compartment with superheated steam.

Yet, for all that, *Mysore* was a lucky ship. The flash from the explosion went aft, into the Sagarika missile magazine. Now empty, it took the blast wave and sucked the life from it. Even more fortunately, the path aft was much more attractive to a blast wave than trying to force through the thick, unpierced bulkhead that separated the forward machinery space from the aft boiler room. The *Mysore* had her machinery arranged on the unit plan and that meant she could have movement again within a few minutes, if she lived that long. That was the rub. If she lived that long, because slowing down in this maelstrom of racing ships and the hammering of rapid-fire guns was death and *Mysore* hadn't just slowed down, she'd come to a complete halt, broadside on to the Chipanese formation.

INS Nilgiri, *First Division, The Flying Squadron, South China Sea.*

A few hundred yards away, Captain Simons on the *Nilgiri* watched his flagship surrounded by the white columns of six-inch shell splashes. White, not the ugly black and red of direct hits. The wide Chipanese salvo spreads had saved *Mysore* from the first salvo but her luck couldn't, and didn't, last. A few seconds later, another broadside tore in and this time, the twelve shots scored five direct hits. Simons watched helplessly as *Mysore's* bridge crumpled under the impacts and black smoke boiled up as fires took hold on the stricken cruiser.

"Weaps, fire our remaining Ikaras at that damned Chimp cruiser. If she's firing at them, it'll give *Mysore* a breathing space." *And bring in her fire on us,* Simons thought. In this wild, frantic battle, speed was life and his frigate just didn't have enough of it. Speed or life, take your pick. Didn't matter, *Nilgiri* didn't have enough of either. Barring a miracle of course.

HIJMS Aoba, *Flagship, South China Sea Squadron, South China Sea*

If there was a Yasukuni for dead warships, that Indian cruiser would soon be joining Asama there. It had been a gift from the Gods, a totally unexpected torpedo hit that had left the biggest ship in the Indian fleet stationary and helpless. A few second earlier, she had been twisting and tuning between the shells hurled at her. Now, she was disabled, listing, burning, and at *Aoba's* mercy. As if in contemptuous disregard of the concept, *Aoba's* twelve guns crashed again, sending more shells into the pyre of smoke that marked the position of the Indian flagship.

"Missiles inbound!" Kurita wanted to cry in despair. *Not again. How many of the wretched things did the Indian ships carry?* He had to swing his main guns to deal with that threat, still, the Indian cruiser was badly hurt and not going anywhere. Time for her later. The 155mm dual purpose guns blended their roar with the crackle of the 100mms and the two inbound Ikaras were blotted from the sky.

Then, there was a cry of alarm from one of the lookouts. Another Indian destroyer swept out of the smoke drifting across from where *Asama* had exploded. She was less than 5,000 yards meters away and the old, traditionalist naval officer in Kurita recognized a perfect torpedo attack. He'd been hoodwinked, his guns were pointing the wrong way, it would take precious seconds to bring them to bear on that destroyer and blast her from the water. Only, he didn't have those seconds and she was coming in far too fast. If there had been two destroyers, he'd have been caught in a hammerhead attack and his flagship would have joined *Asama* but there weren't. The other Indian destroyer had taken on three Japanese ships to buy this attack and the hammerhead had only one side. That gave *Aoba* a chance. The 18,000 ton cruiser started to swing but cruisers weren't destroyers. They didn't skid and swerve the way the destroyers did. Their movements were more stately and in this frantic engagement, stately didn't cut it.

Bridge, INS Ranjit, *First Division, The Flying Squadron, South China Sea.*

"Got them!" Captain Gill thumped the bridge rail in triumph. He'd used the smoke and chaos caused by the missile barrage to mask his move until the last minute. Then, he'd burst out of the thick, foul-smelling smoke and made his run, across the bows of the two Chipanese cruisers in the formation.

"Forward tubes, take the gun cruiser, aft tubes take the rocket cruiser."

His crew were expecting that. They had the tubes already trained and the black torpedoes left their launchers almost as the order was given "Guns, prepare to fire on that rocket cruiser. Maximum rate of fire, all eight guns. I want that ship raked." *Ranjit* could fire 360 rounds a minute, six rounds a second and at this range at least half of them, probably more, would hit. *The theorists would say that no unarmored ship could take that kind of punishment. Now was the time to see if they were right.*

A cheer on the bridge broke his concentration. Two columns of water had erupted on the Chipanese gun-cruiser's hull, the first directly under her torpedo tubes, the second under her aft 3.9 inch gun mounts. A second later, there was another explosion, a big one that mashed the superstructure aft of the funnel into a tangled mass of metal. *Aoba* had been reloading her torpedo tubes and the hit had exploded the reloads. Gill had always said those Chipanese oxygen-powered torpedoes were a liability not an asset; the Indian Navy had agreed with him. Across the sea, the gun cruiser was coming to a halt, listing heavily.

"And again Sir!" The rocket cruiser was hit, a single explosion right forward on the bows. That would slow her down, a bit, but it wasn't the crippling damage the gun cruiser had suffered. "Guns opening up now."

HIJMS Yashima, *South China Sea Squadron, South China Sea*

When he had been a young boy, Captain Fumai had made a wooden model of an American battleship. It hadn't been a very good model. It had been made of soft wood and it was crude; just a block for the hull, another for the superstructure and smaller ones for the turrets. It had been painted gray and had a crude stars-and-stripes painted on it. He'd taken it to school; to the cheers of his schoolmates, he'd pushed it bow-first into an electric fan. His teacher had praised his patriotism, then punished him for damaging the blades on the fan. Now, looking at his cruiser, Fumai remembered how the wood had splintered as the fan blades had chewed it apart.

The destroyer was barely 3,000 meters away and its gun turrets seemed a solid sheet of flame. The first few rounds had been short but the gunners were excellent and they'd walked the fire onto the hull of the cruiser. Now the shells were hitting so fast that there was no way to distinguish between the explosions or count how many had been scored. The old joke about Ainu counting, 'one, two, many,' ran though his mind as the hull of his cruiser disintegrated under the hammering. Steel was flying into the air, the forward rocket launchers had been mangled into scrap, hurled around by the sheer number of shells pouring into his ship. The damage was marching backwards, just as it had when he'd pushed his wooden battleship into the electric fan. Then, the explosions reached the bridge and Fumai's last thought was that he was being punished again.

HIJMS Aoba, *Flagship, South China Sea Squadron, South China Sea*

The sirens were going off all over the ship and Kurita could feel the thunder as the damage control crews ran to stem the water flooding in from the torpedo hits. They were insignificant though, beside the sight of what was happening to *Yashima.* The torpedo hit right forward had come as a disappointment rather than a surprise; any destroyer skipper who got in this close to two big cruisers would spread his salvo between the two, hoping to get both.

In a way, the Japanese cruisers had been lucky. Neither had been critically damaged, although the shambles of *Aoba's* midship section was a nightmare to look at. Then, he'd thought the Indian destroyer had exploded, the sheet of flame along her length looked that way at least. Only, she hadn't. It was her guns, firing at a phenomenal rate, faster than any main gun the Japanese Navy had. The first few rounds had missed, but the avalanche that followed them had not. *Yashima* had looked like a tree decorated with twinkling lights as the wave of explosions had washed along her, leaving nothing but tangled and devastated wreckage in its wake. Kurita's CBs gave the performance of the Indian 120mm gun. Simple mathematics told him that the unarmored rocket cruiser had been hit by the equivalent of a full broadside of 45.6 centimeter guns. Yet she was afloat, erect and obviously under power although at whose orders was an interesting question. With the ship's superstructure nothing but tangled wreckage, nobody could be around to con the ship. Not up there at any rate.

"Damage Control Reports Sir. First torpedo hit shallow and exploded our reloads. The damage is spectacular but superficial. Nothing below the armor belt. Second torpedo hit the side, the torpedo protection system almost coped with it. We've lost a boiler room portside and had to counterflood a starboard side boiler room to compensate. We'll be able to make 20 knots as soon as the boilers come back on line in the other rooms. Flooding is limited, the crews are shoring up bulkheads and sealing leaks now. We have a flooding perimeter."

That was a mercy. An established flooding perimeter meant that the ship was safe, the flooding was confined to the already-affected area. With an established perimeter, work could start on dewatering compartments and reclaiming them from the sea. Losing the boiler rooms was a problem, Kurita cursed the designers who'd put a midships longitudinal bulkhead in the engine rooms. It was a recipe for capsizing.

"We've lost our aft guns, Sir." The First Officer was still speaking. "Power failure, we might get them back soon. Forward guns are still operational under local control. Shall we hit that destroyer?"

Kurita shook his head. "She's heading right into our three right flank destroyers. They'll finish her. We'll start taking the two smaller ships out there, by the cruiser we've crippled. Before they can launch any more of those torpedo-missiles."

INS Nilgiri, *First Division, The Flying Squadron, South China Sea.*

Simons saw the cruiser being hit and lurching to a halt. Hit but not killed was his judgment. And that meant retribution for his pair of Ikaras was still impending. Sure enough, the forward guns on the cruiser fired, but the shell bursts were wild and scattered. Not surprising, considering the battering the cruiser had just taken. Even firing was a fine display of seamanship.

"Hard to starboard, full rudder, emergency speed!" *Nilgiri* swerved to starboard, her hard-worked engine crews squeezing just a little more power out of her gas turbines. *One thing about his gas turbine engines,* Simons thought, *they are much more responsive than steam.*

"We've got two Ikaras left Sir" Weaps was gently prodding his Captain.

"Very good, Weaps. I know how you hate to be left out of things. Shoot them at that damned cruiser before she rapes us."

"Firing now Sir."

The old expression ran though Simons' mind. *When rape is inevitable, the best thing is to lie back and enjoy it.* Once again, he reflected on just how stupid that saying was. There was no way anybody could enjoy being on the receiving end of six inch gunfire. All he could do was keep chasing splashes

Bridge, INS Ranjit, *First Division, The Flying Squadron, South China Sea.*

Ranjit cleared the Chipanese cruiser line, leaving behind a six inch cruiser fighting for her life and a rocket cruiser reduced to a floating wreck. *The experts had been right, the rapid-fire guns could devastate an opponent. Much more so than fewer bigger guns,* Gill thought to himself, *they distributed the destruction evenly over the ship, smashing everything and leaving the damage control crews no secure place to start. If everything needed repair immediately, what did one repair first? I doubt if, after today, any Indian ship will be built without its battery of 4.5 inch guns.*

"Sir dead ahead! Three enemy destroyers closing fast."

Gill looked and cursed, the three Chipanese destroyers on the far side of the formation were carving in fast to intercept him. He was in much the same position as *Rana* a few minutes earlier. *Come to think of it, what had happened to* Rana*?* He hadn't heard from her since she'd swerved to one side to keep the other three destroyers away from *Ranjit*. There were two important differences though. *Rana* had still her torpedoes on board and a full load of 4.5-inch ammunition. *Ranjit's* torpedoes were gone and that wild firing pass on the rocket cruiser had burned almost half her ammunition supply. This was going to be bloody.

"All guns, take the Chimp destroyer in the middle." Try to take her out first and that would even things out. His own guns crashed and for an insane second Gill thought that the shells had fallen over the side for as his guns fired, white columns erupted all around his ship. Then, he realized it was much simpler and much more dangerous than a mass misfire. The Chipanese destroyers had opened up as well and their first salvoes were deadly close. It really was going to be a good question whether *Ranjit* could survive her first major battle.

INS Nilgiri, *First Division, The Flying Squadron, South China Sea.*

Avoiding fire by chasing salvoes was a perilous game. It depended on the gunners the other side being so stuck in their routine that didn't realize what was going on. In theory, chasing salvoes was a master-stroke, one that allowed a ship to survive under the worst possible odds. In reality, it just bought the Captain a few minutes to think of something better. In *Nilgiri's* case, that hadn't been many minutes although the wide dispersion in the Chipanese salvoes had bought a couple more. The problem was, buying time meant that time ran out.

The 6.1 inch shells that slammed into her couldn't have been better placed. The first impacted between the 4.5 inch turret forward and the Jabiru launcher immediately behind it. Fortunately for *Nilgiri*, the missile magazine was empty and the brass-cased 4.5 inch shells weren't ignited by the blast. So, *Nilgiri* was saved from the earlier sudden demise of her sister. The second shell hit the navigation radar on top of the pilot house, passed through it and exploded in the CIC underneath. Fragments from the blast scythed through the bridge, killing Captain Simons, Weaps and the rest of the bridge watch. Another knocked out the missile guidance radar forward, cutting the waveguides and power supplies to the main search radar complex amidships. The last hit aft, wrecking the Rotodyne flight deck and jamming the hangar doors shut. That one salvo left *Nilgiri* blind, deaf, defenseless and brainless.

Nilgiri swerved to one side, reeling under the shock of the four 123 pound shells. Five seconds later, three more crashed on board. One landing right forward, its splinters finishing off the destruction of the frigate's 4.5 inch gun turret. The other two landed almost beside each other, tearing through the deck to explode in the ship's machinery spaces. Without her gas turbines, *Nilgiri* was powerless and defenseless. Even worse than the direct damage was the secondary effects of the shells. The two amidships hits had sent their fragments flying through the ship's sides. Flooding from those was already inundating the whole midships section. Between them, the six hits had also started three fires. One, the paint locker up forward was inconsequential and could be left to burn itself out. The other two were both in the machinery spaces and were fed by gas turbine fuel sprayed onto the flames by the severed piping there.

The Damage Control Officer was the only line-of-command officer left alive. Fortunately he was in the best place to assess the devastation wrought on the frigate. She wasn't intended for fleet actions; she was a convoy and amphibious group escort. She had neither the internal subdivision nor the fire-fighting capacities of her larger sisters. The ship rocked with another hit, this one into the hangar starting another major blaze. It was obvious she could neither fight nor be saved. The DCO used his new-found position of seniority to issue just one command as *Nilgiri's* skipper: "Abandon Ship!"

Fairey Defender Rotodyne Avashi-Two*, South China Sea.*

"They never told us it would be like this!" Lieutenant Lall looked up from his display scope, his face appalled at the carnage underneath. At the Naval Academy, battles had been described as stately processions, with divisions of ships maneuvering to perform specific actions. It was nothing like the wild chaos underneath. The two formations of ships had hit head on and splintered into a series of frantic duels that merged and separated as the Indian and Chipanese formations mixed. The Rotodyne's search radar was having problems distinguishing between the two sides. As damage had mounted, the ship's IFF systems had been knocked out. Without IFF, the radarscope had no way of telling which ship was which.

The three Defenders were orbiting clear of the battlezone. *Avashi-One* was the surveillance aircraft, carrying drop tanks to extend its range as it relayed formation data back to the ships beneath - although how much use that was to them now was an arguable question. *Avashi-Two* and *Avashi-Three* were acting as back-up and escorts. All three Defenders had AIM-9 Sidewinders on their wingtips and a full load of ammunition for their nose-mounted 30mm cannon. *Avashi-Two* and *Avashi-Three* also carried four air-launched MOG missiles on their underwing hardpoints. That gave them some anti-ship striking power. As its name Multi-role, Optically-Guided suggested, MOG was a multi-role system. Like all such systems, its proficiency in any one role was compromised by the requirements of the others.

Avashi-Two and *Avashi-Three* were tasked with defending *Avashi-One* in case the Chipanese tried to attack it. It was unlikely. The eight Kayaba helicopters were staying well out of the battlezone and, in any case, they had no known air-to-air capability. Even if they did, the Defender was more than 250 mph faster than the Kayaba; if the enemy helicopters started to approach, it could simply leave the area. Suddenly, Lall was seized by a frightening thought. "What are you thinking of doing?"

His pilot grinned a bit sheepishly. "Our ships are in trouble down there. They don't need battle information from us any more, they do need all the help they can get. *Avashi-One* isn't under threat and can take care of itself. We could always give our ships some support."

"What with? MOGs?"

"Why not? The Ozwalds say that a MOG has the hitting power of a 9.2 inch shell. That's a lot bigger than anything else down there."

Lall wasn't impressed, he never had been dazzled by MOG. He'd done his radar training in America where the emphasis was on building a specific system for a specific role. Multi-role meant too many compromises. It needed a lot of thought and careful consideration before adopting the idea. "You'll note they stopped saying that after we'd bought them. Still, if the MOGs fail to perturb the Chimps, we can always bare our buttocks and fart in their general direction."

The pilot snorted into his mask. "That's banned under the Hague Convention. I'll run the idea by the others and if they want to go, we'll clear it with *Avashi-One*."

"Shouldn't we ask the Admiral?"

"What Admiral?"

HIJMS Aoba, *Flagship, South China Sea Squadron, South China Sea*

"Enemy aircraft approaching, Sir, From the Southwest, range approximately 70 kilometers. Speed estimated at 650 kph. Raid count, small, two or four aircraft at most."

What NOW Kurita wanted to wail. *After the unending stream of missiles that had pounded my squadron, there was to be an air strike?* "Skyhawks, they have to be Skyhawks, and that means the Indian carrier is out there somewhere."

"Sir, we have no positive identification. We know there are three enemy Defenders out there, this could be them."

"No, they're Skyhawks, probably an armed reconnaissance mission. Trying to find us. They'll probably have a couple of Bullpups each, no more. But the rest of the air group will be behind them sooner or later.

"ESM reports air-to-surface radar emissions, Sir. Tentative identification Seaspray. That's consistent with a Defender Rotodyne.

"They're Skyhawks." Kurita's mouth set in determination. In any case, they'd know soon enough. Then, as he watched the display, he saw four tracks leap over the fleet towards the approaching aircraft. *Asahi* had finally shaken off the torpedoes chasing her and was running her machinery dangerously into the red in an attempt to catch up with the rest of the squadron. She'd also taken the opportunity of reloading her Nodachi launcher and had four SAMs ready to go. One malfunctioned shortly after launch, its gyros tumbling to send it spinning helplessly into the sea. Another simply missed its target. The other two worked perfectly, blotting both of the approaching aircraft from the sky.

Bridge, INS Ranjit*, First Division, The Flying Squadron, South China Sea.*

He'd made a mistake, a bad one. Now *Ranjit* was paying for it. He'd concentrated his gunfire onto a single destroyer instead of splitting it between two. His intent had been to finish his target as quickly as possible before switching to the others and he'd done that. The Chipanese destroyer he'd targeted had been torn apart by the intense gunfire. She was already on her beam ends and going down fast. Only, that had left two other Chipanese destroyers undisturbed. By the time he'd switched fire to them, they'd already hurt her badly. He'd returned the compliment and another of the Chipanese destroyers was suffering from *Ranjit's* remaining 4.5 inch guns but that didn't help too much.

"Captain Gill, Sir, Engines reports that we're losing power fast. Its not just the hits, its the fragments from the near misses. They're tearing up steam lines and causing floods. A couple of minutes more and the engines will be offline."

And that meant no power and *Ranjit's* guns were power-operated. They had an emergency manual cycle but that would sacrifice her main advantage, her immense rate of fire. Not probably too much to worry about though. Her magazines were running dry and two of her turrets were already out of action due to battle damage. As if to emphasize the point, *Ranjit* lurched again as more shells from the destroyer to starboard tore into her. The Chipanese were firing slowly and deliberately. *They must also be running short of ammunition, they'd probably burned most of theirs in the air defense effort.* Even so, a slow rate of fire just prolonged *Ranjit's* agony. *Still, as long as her guns kept firing. . . . .*

"Sir. To port, look!"

The second Chipanese destroyer *Ranjit* had savaged was surrounded by shell bursts, white columns, liberally mixed with the black and red of direct hits. Out of the smoke shrouding the sea erupted two long, low gray shapes. *Ghurka* and *Ghauri* had arrived. Their own 4.5 inch guns started to tear apart one of the destroyers tormenting *Ranjit*. Even as Gill watched, the two split apart. *Ghauri* closing on the already crippled destroyer while *Ghurka* poured on more power to engage the remaining Chipanese destroyer.

HIJMS Mutsuki*, South China Sea Squadron, South China Sea*

Mutsuki had lived a charmed life. Hit four times by missiles and twice by gunfire, she was still largely undamaged and her fighting power was intact. Even better, her missilemen had braved the storm of gunfire and reloaded her Nodachi launcher aft. She had four missiles ready to go when the Indian destroyer erupted out of the smoke and headed for her. The Nodachi had much less anti-ship capability than the Jabiru but that mattered little. The four shots would buy enough time to retarget the destroyer's main guns.

The four Nodachi missiles rippled down *Ghurka's* hull, almost evenly spaced along her length. The first hit just aft of the forward 4.5 inch gun turret, jamming the mount in train. The second scored a direct hit on one of the 37mm quadruple mounts. A third impacted just ahead of the aft Jabiru launcher but the empty magazine gave the explosion space to vent itself harmlessly. The last hit the empty rotodyne hangar. *Ghurka* twisted under the impacts, slowing down and turning into the shots from her attacker. Then, she was surrounded by 3.9 inch shell bursts as she replied with her aft 4.5 inch twin mount.

Bridge, INS Rana, *First Division, The Flying Squadron, South China Sea.*

There was a typical sequence from one of the hundreds of action films that poured out of Bollywood, the network of film studios that surrounded Bombay. It consisted of the two male leads fighting each other into helpless exhaustion over a woman while the heroine stood under a waterfall, singing that it did not matter who won the fight since she was going to run off with somebody else. Hanging on to the bridge rail for support, Captain Dasgupta saw that the three ships in this group were all in much the same state as the men had been after that fight.

The torpedoed *Yahagi* had already gone. She'd rolled over and sunk a few minutes after being torpedoed. The other three destroyers, *Rana*, *Kisaragi* and *Katsuragi* were exhausted and helpless. Firing had ceased simply because all three ships were dead in the water. Their engine room spaces had been opened up by direct hits and fragments from near misses. The turrets themselves were damaged, some destroyed by direct hits, others jammed in train by the shock of near misses.

In another way, the fight was still going on. The gunnery crews were working to get *Rana's* B turret operational again. They were splicing cables and trying to restore some semblance of supply for the shells. Other crews were working in the engine rooms, trying to bring the boilers and turbines back on line. The question now was whether they could manage it before the Chipanese crews could succeed in their repairs.

"Engine room here." Dagsupta grabbed the intercom system, still miraculously working, wincing in pain while he did so. He'd been badly cut by the flying glass when the bridge viewports shattered and hurt again by fragments from a near miss by the bridge. "Bridge. What's happening?"

"We've restored stream pressure on number one boiler Sir, and we've got number one turbine back on line. We can start picking up speed soon. I can give you five knots now, perhaps ten in twenty minutes. I wouldn't push it harder than that, things are held together with spit and Band-Aids down here."

"Very good engines, VERY good. Thank you." Dasgupta had only just put the microphone down when it buzzed again. The weapons officer was on the line.

"Weaps here, Sir. B turret is back on line. Manual loading and training only and we'll have to use the on-mount optical fire control but we've got both guns."

"Excellent work Weaps. Stand by to open fire. Number One, we're operational again."

"Make a course to get clear of this mess Sir? There's no point in doing more."

Dasgupta looked at his Number One in disbelief and fury. "Number One, **I'll have no man call me Langsdorff**. This ship is a warship, as long as we have steam to move with and guns to shoot, we fight. There is an amphibious group back there with 15,000 sailors and soldiers depending on us for protection. The more harm we do to the enemy now, the less they can do if they get past us. And, anyway, by the look of things, both sides here are so badly hurt, a few more blows might be decisive. Do you understand?"

"Yes Sir."

"Good, then bring us round behind the destroyer to port, *Kisaragi*. Take us into her blind zone aft and we'll start dropping shells into her from where she can't shoot back. I said we fight. I said nothing about fighting fair."

HIJMS Aoba*, Flagship, South China Sea Squadron, South China Sea*

Wherever he looked, there were shattered ships. Over to starboard, there was a group of five destroyers exchanging fire, three were dead in the water. One Japanese destroyer had already sunk and the Indian destroyer looked like she might slip under at any time. Another Japanese destroyer was sinking in front of him. *Yashima* was a riddled, floating wreck, her crew frantically trying to stop the flooding from spreading through her riven hull. All that was left of *Asama* was a stained patch of water covered with floating wreckage. Off to port was yet another group of destroyers; all three looked to be on the verge of sinking.

Half an hour ago, the sea had seen two groups of fine ships. Now there were just floating wrecks, each marked by a column of black smoke. *This couldn't go on. It just couldn't.*

Kurita swung his binoculars back to the group of destroyers to port. At first he didn't believe his eyes but he looked again and it was true. The Indian destroyer was moving. Even as he watched, she painfully, slowly, crawled around and headed for the *Kisaragi*. Her B turret flashed and a column of white water erupted, short of the target for certain, but the sight finally made up Kurita's mind. *The Indian destroyer was moving and fighting again. They just would not give up.*

"Signal all surviving ships. Make course North by North West, best available speed, destination Haiphong. We've finished here."

"Sir, we can't! *Aoba* can make twenty knots, *Asahi* is undamaged, so is *Mutsuki*. We've won here, the Indians are fought out, they can't stop us. Their amphibious fleet is at our mercy. We can't turn back now."

"Have you seen how the Indians fought? They came straight at us, they didn't care whether they lived or died." *Very Japanese* thought Kurita although he didn't say so. "Do you think they would have done that and left their amphibs uncovered? Of course not. The Second Division must have arrived overnight and brought the carrier with it. That means we are faced by another task group as powerful as the one we have just fought here, one with its magazines full and its ships undamaged. Our ships are wrecks and our magazines are empty.

"Remember those Skyhawks? Their naval aircraft are searching for us and they will find us soon if we do not head for home. We can't fight an air attack any more than another missile barrage. We go home. Anything else would be useless."

A ripple of disgust, not very well hidden, passed around the bridge of the *Aoba*. Kurita ignored it for he knew that his duty now was to save the ships that were left from destruction at the hands of the second Indian squadron that he was so sure had to be closing in on him. He felt the pattern of sea and waves change as *Aoba* began her turn to the north west. He'd won a great victory, the first to be scored by the Japanese Navy in many years. It was enough and to carry on would throw that victory away.

At the back of the bridge, the Navigation Officer turned to the two Midshipmen under his care.

"Tonight, you will be writing up today's battle in your journals. Do so with great care and in great detail for at some time in the future, people will read of this battle and of how we, at great and terrible cost, fought our way through an Indian fleet. And, having won the battle, we just turned around and went home. They will not believe it and they will ask you 'How was this so?' and you will consult your journals and say with great authority that, even though you were here, you do not know."

INS Dunagiri *Off Pattle Island, Paracel Group, South China Sea*

Captain Gandhi (no relation) was pacing his bridge. He was known throughout the Navy as Gandhi (no relation) from his insistence on making it clear that he had no known family connection with the controversial politician. It revealed him for what he was, a wise and cautious man. If he had claimed a relationship with Mahatma Gandhi, he would have been damned by those who despised the politician as a naive and foolish near-traitor while he would have been despised by Mahatma's supporters for trying to cash in on the memory of their revered hero. By denying any relationship he pleased both sides. Caution was bedeviling him now. There were thing he had to do to make preparations but what they were depended on what was happening far to the North West. He was about to take another circuit of the bridge when the quiet was interrupted by the noise of the secure communications unit.

The Ship's Sparker was behind the console in a second, acknowledging receipt and writing down the message as it was decoded. Slowly, he went white and his eyebrows raised until they met his hairline.

"Sir, message from Commander Dasgupta, captain of *Rana* and the senior surviving officer." Gandhi (no relation)'s face went white also at that piece of news.

"He reports a major fleet engagement started at dawn. *Mysore* has been torpedoed and hit by six inch gunfire. Admiral Kanali Dahm is dead, the ship is dead in the water, on fire and listing. It is unclear whether she can be saved. *Rajput* torpedoed and sunk with heavy loss of life. *Ranjit* is dead in the water after suffering heavy damage from 3.9 inch gunfire, *Udagiri* has superficial damage from splinters and is putting *Ranjit* under tow. *Rana* is severely damaged by 3.9 inch gunfire, she can make ten knots. *Ghurka* is heavily damaged by missiles and gunfire, she's burning. *Ghauri* has superficial damage from splinters and is alongside *Ghurka* helping to fight fires. *Himgiri* exploded and sank with no survivors after a direct hit from a Kabuto missile, *Nilgiri* sunk by six inch gunfire, a few survivors, not many.

"Sir, Commander Dasgupta reports that all ships are almost out of ammunition and the gas turbine ships are low on fuel. He is withdrawing to the south."

“The Chimps, what about the Chimps?” Ghandi (no relation)’s voice was anxious, the catastrophic toll of sinking and burning ships, of dead and wounded sailors had shaken him profoundly. He’d read about naval actions but nothing had prepared him for this scale of butchery.

“One cruiser sunk, two crippled. Four destroyers known sunk, three more dead in the water. Only one of the Chipanese destroyers remains capable of fighting.” Suddenly the Sparker’s voice rang with pride. “The Chimps have disengaged and are withdrawing to the northwest Sir. They’ve given up and are going home. We’ve won.”

Air Operations Center, Hainan Province.

“We can send Shukas out to finish off their survivors. Admiral. They’re in range.”

“No, we cannot. And we will not, Have you read how bravely the Indian sailors fought? Outnumbered, outclassed, they sailed their ships into the middle of our fleet and fought their ships to the end, firing their guns even while their destroyers were sinking under their feet. Such opponents do us honor and we should be proud that we have fought them, toe to toe, ship to ship. To send aircraft to slaughter them now when they are defenseless would be despicable. Cowardly and dishonorable. They are out of the fight, they have nothing left to defend themselves. To send our bombers against them now would be a craven act, the vindictive murder of gallant men. It would be the act of a vicious and treacherous butcher. We cannot do it; we will not do it.”

The Admiral smiled gently. “We will say of course that we let them escape out of respect for their bravery and that is not so far from the truth. The Americans are a sentimental people and the gesture will be of much importance to them. It will dissuade them from interfering and that is of critical importance to us. But never forget, the reason we let them go is a matter of respect for our own honor and our own character as virtuous warriors.”

CHAPTER SIX
REGROUPING

The Roof Garden, Imperial Hotel, Havana, Cuba.

"You're sure about this, Dapper John?" Meyer Lansky's voice showed that the question was just a formality. He already knew the answer, it made far too much sense. In the midst of the pain from trust betrayed, he felt a deep sense of relief. Better this, better this by far, than the rat being one of his protégés. Meyer Lansky, like all wiseguys, knew all too well that life was limited. The Grim Reaper waited for every person and that he was no exception to the rule. One day, soon in the cosmic scale of things, he would die, either by an assassin's bullet or by what was charmingly known as "natural causes." He knew that day was coming and also knew that disaster awaited Cuba when it did.

Meyer Lansky was a member of no Family, yet was trusted by them all. That was how he was able to make Cuba work. When he died, there would be the question of who took over from him. If it was any member of the Families, the power struggle would tear Cuba apart. Also, if the new President wasn't known and trusted by the Families, there would still be the same power struggle. Lansky was quietly proud of what Cuba was now and what it was becoming. He wanted to give it a chance to settle down, to mature, to become a real country.

With that end in mind, he had spent his years on the island watching for youngsters who reminded him of himself. He'd picked them, brought them up, trained them and indoctrinated them in his own philosophy. They were his aides and they spoke for him. Any that betrayed that trust were dropped from the program, sent back into the whirlpool that was Mob-run Cuba. The others, the ones that held to the code, they were slowly building the same level of trust with the Families that Lansky enjoyed. One day, the best of them would succeed Lansky as Chairman of the Commission, a member of no family, trusted by all. Just as Lansky was Jewish and could not be a made man, they were Cuban and could not be made. That meant that, with them, Cuba would be safe.

Thank God, the name he had been given was not one of them.

"Absolutely certain Meyer. I'm sorry, but there's no doubt about it. You can see why I wanted us to meet here, away from your pad. We leaked different information to all the suspects and, sure enough, we got a message back. MH was short of H. So we leaked more information with different details of each Hotel. MH was the Havana Metrodome. A Lucchese hotel but that doesn't matter. We tried a couple more just to nail it down, but it all came out the same. I'm sorry."

"No need for that John. Rats have always been a part of our Life. Look, I got news for you. We got word back from the USSS on that stuff we asked them to look at."

"The H? Anything interesting?"

"Kid called Delgado brought us the results. Good kid, his grandfather was in The Life, one of Moran's men back in the old days. Anyway, it went the way we hoped. The USSS pressured the FBI into running a trace on the H. It's from what used to be Afghanistan, now called the Afghan Satrapy. The Caliphate makes a big thing about suppressing opium growing but they're lying through their teeth. Oh sure, they whack an opium farmer now and then; but all the farmers have to do to get official protection is to swear not to sell to Moslems. The ones who break that oath are the ones who get whacked. The rest are cordially encouraged to sell as much opium to us infidels as we'll buy. It's Afghan heroin, John."

Lansky watched Gotti chewing the information over. "Its weird Meyer. To cover the costs of the operation, the people bringing this stuff in must be getting it virtually free. It doesn't make sense. If they're getting free H, they'd make more money by bringing it in and selling it openly. Their cut to the local crew would be less than the cost of smuggling it in."

"Bit more information John. We gave the Feds four samples picked up at different places. They're all from the same batch. Cut the same way, same profile. Its like a fingerprint and they're all the same."

"So they got a big batch." Something clicked in Gotti's mind. "Whoever it was got paid for services rendered with a huge batch of Afghan H. They're using it to try and infiltrate here, set up a shadow drug trade." Another light went on. "And they staged the Washington shooting to try and get the Feds to send Marines in here to clear us out. That way, drugs would become illegal, the price would skyrocket and they'd would have a ready-made supply line, smuggling route and distribution net."

"That's what the USSS thinks. We're off the hook for the Washington shooting. Even the Feds reluctantly admit that. As for who? I'm sure the rat will tell us that. Eventually."

Room 6212, Imperial Hotel, Havana, Cuba.

"Quick darling, its on. . ." Judith Peterson hurried from the bathroom and settled in front of the television. There was no way she was going to miss this. The staccato beat of the theme tune was already starting, played over a montage of 1930s automobiles and men carrying Tommy guns,

In the 1920s and 1930s, a group of dishonest hypocrites and sanctimonious killjoys teamed up with crooked politicians in a giant

conspiracy called Prohibition. The intent of this conspiracy was nothing less than to cheat the honest working man out of his right to a drink when his day's labors were through. Yet whenever tyranny raises its hand, a group of Americans will stand against it. A small group of brave young men fought the Prohibitionists by smuggling the working man's drink over borders, defying bad weather and Coastguard patrols to bring it across seas and lakes, and by building and operating secret breweries. As word of their skill in evading the treacherous traps and ambushes staged by Prohibition Deputies, Treasury Agents and FBI men spread, these young men became known as THE UNCATCHABLES. The music swelled triumphantly. This is their story. *Tonight's episode is First, Fight Thirst.*

The credits stopped and the program cut to an advertisement for some cigarettes whose active ingredient was quite definitely illegal on the mainland. Judith took the chance to settle herself more comfortably. "You know, Dave, I really wish they'd show this back home."

"A few of the independent channels do, very late at night. The Colombo family will sell the show to any network that wants to put it on. Don Joe Colombo was so annoyed at the way Italian-Americans were depicted on *The Untouchables*, he started a TV studio here in Cuba just to make his reply. You've got to admit, the way he depicts Elliot Ness is a real hoot."

Judith Peterson giggled. *The Uncatchables* showed Ness as a buffoon, always taking surreptitious swigs out of whisky bottles concealed around his office. "Hey, Dave, I don't suppose *Warpath* is on here this week is it?"

"Season premier is next week. I looked it up before we fixed the dates to come here. We'll be back home for the new season." David Peterson shook his head. The previous series of *Warpath* had ended in a cliff-hanger that had kept the whole country agog. Would the gallant Union Army scout Brave Eagle rescue the beautiful Mary-Lynne Chambers before she was ravished by the evil Captain Cartwright Towers of Quantrill's Raiders? Tune in next season folks. . . . .

The advertisements finished and the television cut back to the show. A street scene, reputedly a Chicago precinct.

An hour later, it was over. The Prohibitionists' evil plot to steal the precinct election had been foiled and the stuffed ballot boxes replaced by the originals. The anti-Prohibition candidate had won and his party was throwing a party to celebrate when The Uncatchables turned up with a truckload of beer for the celebrations. All was well with the world, until next week at least.

"Time for dinner. Fancy going to the Margarita?"

"Mmm sure. They do gorgeous tongue there." David Peterson laughed and took his wife's arm as they left their room. He'd never eaten tongue until she'd persuaded him to try it, now he was a firm convert. The lift bell rang and the doors slid open. They were about to step in when they saw the four people already inside.

"Ohh, I'm sorry Mister Lan. . . . I mean Mister Pres. . . . Your Hon...."

Lansky gave an affable grin. "Mister Lansky will do just fine. Step in, we're going down. And how are you two doing at our tables?"

Judith gulped a little. She'd heard that even the most powerful people on the island used public doors and elevators like everybody else but she hadn't quite believed it. Then, the reasoning came to her. Like everything else, the security situation in Cuba was a weirdly twisted version of everywhere else. The gangsters knew they were safe as long as they were surrounded by tourists. It was when they were on their own they were vulnerable. So they always mixed with people as much as possible. "Its been up and down Mister Lansky. We've lost more than we've won I'm afraid."

"You'll forgive me if I say I'm pleased to hear that Ma'am. It's not winners who pay the electricity bill for the Golden Boulevard." The six people in the lift laughed. "You going back to the tables now?"

"After we've eaten, we're going to the Margarita for dinner first. They do wonderful tongue there."

Lansky nodded. "Tongue sandwich, using a Kaiser roll. My favorite lunch. When you order, tell the waitress I said you were to get the middle cut of the tongue. No tip or end. Give her my card, she'll see to it."

"Why, thank you Mister Lansky." The lift stopped in the galleria and the doors slid open. The Petersons left, Judith clutching Lansky's business card in her hand.

"Nice couple." Gotti's voice was casual.

"And they'll remember Cuba fondly enough to come back John. And lose more money here."

The party crossed the lobby. Outside the hotel, Lansky's stretched Lincoln was waiting, two mob gunmen leaning against it. Lansky's party settled in and the car swept them out into the stream of traffic. A lot of Ambassadors on the road tonight; the shifts on the tables were changing. The little Indian Ambassador was a perfect car for Cuba, cheap enough for the Cubans to afford, tough enough to run without maintenance. Gotti looked around the car.

"You like the Lincoln Meyer? I prefer the Packard myself. Bigger trunk."

There was more laughter from the wiseguys. Lansky shook his head. "The Lincoln's got a better ride, especially with the weight of armor this thing carries. Caddy's been too clever for their own good with the Coup de Ville, too many gadgets. The Packard's good though. Nice engine."

The car pulled up at the Tropicana. Once again, the quick trip through the lobby, surrounded by tourists who couldn't quite believe that the President of Cuba used the lobby and the public elevators like everybody else. Then, up to the penthouse suite that served as Lansky's palace. In the anteroom, his secretary was putting the cover on her typewriter and packing up to go home.

"Estrellita?"

"Yes, Mister Presidente?"

"I'm sorry to keep you so late but there's one thing I have to ask you to do before you go home. Could you step in please?"

"But of course, Mister Presidente."

The doors closed behind them. Once inside his office, Lansky sat down behind his desk. "John?"

"Estrellita, I've been preparing a report on security here for Mister Lansky."

"And you would like it typed? I will be happy to do this for you."

"Thank you, but before I finish it, could I ask your advice on something? You see I don't speak Spanish. Could you tell me what the Cuban for a female rat is?"

"Why of course. Spanish for a female rat is. . . . . ." Suddenly the meaning of the question struck home and the woman's eyes opened wide in panic. She turned quickly, running for the door but two of Gotti's gunmen were already waiting. They grabbed her effortlessly by the arms, one carefully removing her bag in the process.

"Thanks boys. Take her down, we'll deal with her later. I'll be right with you."

"She should be able to tell you everything you need to know." Lansky's voice was neutral, then he looked up. The affable smile and gentlemanly nature had gone completely, leaving the New York gangster in sharp relief. Gotti was suddenly scared of Cuba's President and remembered another thing that Lucky Luciano had said about him. *Meyer Lansky is the hardest man I have ever known.* "And when you've got everything you need, I don't see any reason why a rat should die easy, do you?"

Seer's Office, National Security Council Building, Washington D.C.

"Good evening Snake. The boss is in a meeting I'm afraid. I'll tell him you're here though." Lillith smiled at The Ambassador and pressed a switch on her intercom, "Boss, Snake's here to see you."

"Oh. Probably a good thing, ask her to step right in please. And, Lillith honey, we're done here for the night if you want to go home. You can take Raven back with you if you like."

"Thank's boss, I'll hang on though." Lillith let the switch go. "Step right through Snake." This, she thought was going to be interesting.

The Ambassador stepped through the door into the Seer's office. He was behind his desk as usual but the person with him was a stranger, one she had never met before. A woman, long black hair, olive skin and a definitely Mongol cast to the eyes. Not Asian, Mongol. Russian perhaps? Not a beautiful face but a strong one with character. There was something disturbingly familiar about her, yet also something very strange.

It took The Ambassador a few moments to pin the strangeness part down. The woman's clothes were cheap. Oh, they were clean and neat but cheap. A simple white blouse and a dark skirt. Store bought, probably one of the chain stores that sold things at cut price. The blouse didn't fit quite right and that was what had seemed so strange. The Ambassador was aristocracy and had lived a very long time, all of it with people who were wealthy. She was so used to custom-made clothes and expensive fabrics that anything else looked strange. Especially here. Then she gave the woman a point in compensation. Her clothes were cheap but her necklace was beautiful; a sort of carved white ivory with purple overtones.

"Snake, I'd like you to meet an associate of ours." The Ambassadori picked her ears up at that phrasing. *So the woman was a friend but not part of The Seer's family.* "Snake, I'd like you to meet Raven of the Shoshone Nation. Raven, may I introduce the Princess Suriyothai, Ambassador-Plenipotentiary of the Throne of Thailand."

That was why her face was so familiar. The United States was introducing a dollar coin at last; the face chosen to decorate it had been an Amerindian heroine called Sacawagea. Something to do with an expedition a hundred years or so earlier. The picture used to make the coin engraving had been in the glossy magazines. This woman was obviously the model for the face on that coin, the strength of character and steadiness were apparent. She was standing up stretching out her hand.

"Your Highness, you too are one of us?"

The Ambassador did a slight double take at that. *How come she didn't know who I am?*

"And you, Raven? We must become better acquainted."

"That would be a good idea." The Seer's voice was even, perhaps slightly amused. "Raven, we're about done here. I'll talk to Bill and see how he's getting on. Lillith's still outside; she'll take you back to your hotel. Thank you for coming over."

The woman left. The Seer relaxed back into his seat. "Now Snake, what can I do for you?"

"You've heard about the firefight this morning?"

"Firefight? Full-scale naval slugging match is the version we heard. Sinking ships all over the place. That's why I don't like naval warfare, Snake. On land, if all else fails, one can always get out and walk. At sea, that can be tricky. As far as we can make out, both sides got badly hurt. The Chipanese communication links are glowing red-hot all over the place. Their high command and top-grade links must be glowing white hot and the suggestion is they are not best pleased."

The Ambassador looked embarrassed. "Seer, I hate to say this but I'm not sure we're getting an accurate picture of what happened from the Indians. They say they took out a dozen ships or more including cruisers and destroyers and only lost a couple of small ships. The Chimps say they lost a couple of destroyers but took out most of the Flying Squadron. The Ozwalds had one of their submarines not too far away and you know what their ELINT capability is like."

The Seer nodded. The Australian submarines were superbly equipped for intelligence gathering, second only to the U.S. Navy's nuclear boats - and the margin was very close.

"Well, they say it was a slaughterhouse. They put the losses in killed and crippled very high for both sides. Seer, I need to know how bad this was. You've got recon assets like nobody else, you must have satellite shots. What really happened out there?"

The Seer pulled a file off his desk and flipped through it. "I assume you need to know so you can help resolve this conflict peacefully?" The Ambassador nodded and wasn't lying. This stupid incident was getting to be very dangerous.

"Very well, we'll give you what we know. We've picked up one thing already that's a good pointer; a light cruiser and three destroyers left Hong Kong three hours ago and are heading for Haiphong. We've got pictures and some data for you, we'll get more. By the way, what do you know about Afghan Heroin?"

Suriyothai looked slightly confused. "There's too much of it. Doesn't worry us though, we have all we can do to cope with the Golden Triangle. Why?"

"Some of its turning up in unexpected places and in unexpected ways. There's something going on and we're missing an important piece of the puzzle. Anyway, let's go eat while the staff get your package together. I have a yearning for Italian."

"Me too, and while we eat, you can tell me who Raven of the Shoshone Nation is."

The Seer shook his head. "Very long story. All to do with setting up some casinos on Indian tribal land and, by the way, righting some old wrongs in the process. Raven will tell you about it if you ask."

Conference Room, Naval Headquarters, Tokyo, Chipan.

"All the advantages won by our bombers have been thrown away. In one act, the surface fleet has snatched defeat from the jaws of victory. I say this was a craven decision that betrays everything we stand for!"

The speaker's was standing at on one side of the long table, his small mustache bristling with anger. On hearing his last words, a buzz ran around the room. Some in agreement, some in anger at the insinuation, all in amazement that words of that kind had been said at all. The four surface fleet officers the other side of the table leapt to their feet, fists clenched, eyes blazing. Admiral Kurita, with great difficulty kept his voice even.

"You were not there. You have no authority to comment on my decisions."

"I do not need to be there to see the results of the surface fleet's action! It is obvious to even the youngest child. The Indians are left in possession of their base and we cannot do anything about it. Their reinforcements have arrived, a carrier and another division of their Flying Squadron. The carrier arrived today, not three days ago."

"Gentlemen. Resume your seats." Admiral Koga's voice echoed around the room. "The purpose of today's meeting is not to allocate blame for the regrettable decisions that lead to this debacle." There was another sharp intake of breath. Koga might have said blame was not being allocated but Kurita had just been tried, sentenced and the decision announced.

"It is to decide what we do next. If it is within our power, we cannot allow this situation to stand. The fact that the South China Sea Squadron has been defeated is not, as yet, public knowledge and we will keep that so. Fortunately, the film of the damaged Indian ships is very widely distributed while our own losses have been kept secret. Indeed, our announcement that we would allow their ships to withdraw unmolested by air strikes has won us much favorable comment. That was a wise decision. The question is, where do we go from here?"

There was a profound silence. It was indeed easy to cast blame and to second-guess decisions; making a constructive proposal was quite another matter. Both sides of the long table looked around, at each other or down at the papers in front of them. At the far end of the room, in serried ranks, sat junior officers, watching their seniors make decisions. For these were the picked men, the cream of the crop, the men whom their superiors had recognized as having great merit and being, possibly, worthy of high command. Given time, experience, and the good fortune to survive both.

Amongst them sat Lieutenant Commander Toda Endo, a man deeply shocked by what he was witnessing. He had imagined that such strategic planning meetings would be solemn affairs, each of the speakers providing the information their expertise gave them as contributions to a common pool, out of which a great scheme for achieving victory would arise. Instead, they were lesser men, each promoting their own factions, each scoring points off and denigrating their rivals. He had a mental picture of a flock of chickens in a farmyard, so engrossed in their own petty squabbles that they failed to see the foxes closing in.

"There is nothing the South China Sea Squadron can do. *Aoba* will require at least six months in dock. In terms of operational ships we have but the cruiser *Asahi* and the destroyer *Mutsuki*. Both have refueled and rearmed and can sortie at four hours notice."

"I have ordered the cruiser *Yubari* with a Sawari class missile destroyer and two Type C destroyers to join the South China Sea Squadron. This leaves the Hong Kong squadron with just sixteen Hayabusa missile craft but that is no great matter. We use them for coastal patrol only." Admiral Nashima, Commander of the Hong Kong Squadron, sat down. *That was more in the spirit of a Japanese warrior* thought Toda. *A man sacrificing part of his command and his own status for the common good.*

Koga obviously agreed. "A most generous gesture. That will strengthen the weakness of the South China Seas Squadron and guard the coast in that critical area." *And a gesture that has just made you Kurita's replacement* he added mentally. "But we are still left with the problem of the Indian occupation of the Southern Pescadores. How do we cope with that? Can our Shukas aid us now?"

Admiral Tanaka, commander of the Mihoro Kokutai stood; his expression was grave. "If ordered we will continue our attacks but I must advise that the cost of so doing will be high. The Indians have two more missile destroyers and two frigates already around the island and an anti-aircraft missile battalion on it. We can cope with that, although not without cost, but the carrier means that they also have fighter cover and together, that means we have too much opposition. We have few serviceable Shukas as it is.

"We have six diesel-electric submarines we can deploy to the area." It was the man who had spoken so scathingly to Kurita. A submarine force officer. "They may get lucky and take down that carrier."

Koga nodded, reluctantly. '*They may get lucky.' Was that what the Navy had fallen to? They had to depend on luck to take down the enemy carrier?* The chances of a diesel-electric submarine taking on a fast-moving naval task group were slim indeed. It was worse than depending on luck, they had to depend on the enemy making a mistake at a critical point as well as being just unlucky enough to stumble onto the diesel-electric. "The surface fleet? Can we send carriers of our own?"

This time the silence was embarrassed. "We have but six and three of those are in dockyard for prolonged repairs." Everybody present winced at the euphemism. Prolonged repairs meant rotting in a dockyard because no money was available to overhaul them. The carriers may be listed on the pages of world naval reference books but nowhere else were they considered operational. "At most we could deploy one, of equal force to the Indian carrier, but her aircraft are obsolete and of lesser power than those they would face. To lose a carrier..." The phrase didn't need to be repeated. The Navy could hide the loss of some surface ship, a carrier going down would be too much.

“And we cannot invade until we have air superiority, until the defenses are worn down.” Commander, Amphibious Forces, simply said what everybody knew. “Can we get cover from land bases?”

“Our fighters are short-range, point defense interceptors. We do not have long-range fighters any more. The Army have some but not many and they are mostly deployed on the Russian Border.”

“Must I record that we have run out of options? That the defeat of our surface fleet means we must accept this Indian occupation?” The silence that surrounded the table was eloquent. “There is nothing we can do?”

Suddenly the silence was broken. Toda couldn’t bear it any longer. “There is something we can do!”

“Shut up, you young fool!” Toda’s commander hissed the warning too late, far too late. All the eyes around the main table fixed on the source of the interruption. Eyebrows went in all directions, some up in astonishment at the unheard-of interjection, others down in rage that a lowly Lieutenant Commander would dare to speak in the presence of his betters. The submarine officer was about to bark in rage when Koga cut him off.

“I think one who wears the ribbon of the Falling Cherry Blossom has earned the right to be heard.” *And this had better be good* was the unspoken message directed at Toda.

“Sir, Honored Sirs, we can get fighters into range. The main Mihoro Kokutai airbase is well inland, on the mainland part of Hainan Province. But all along the southern coast of Hainan Island are bays, many, many sheltered bays. We can base seaplane fighters in any one of them, less than 300 kilometers from Pattle Island. The range is long, yes, but our Ohtoris can cover it easily and still have fuel reserves for air combat.”

“The Indians will track you back to base and their air strike will destroy you.” Koga’s voice was thoughtful. *There was an idea here.*

"Sir, we have our flying garrisons. The ones intended to fight any American offensive in the Pacific. They have infantry to guard the base, engineers to build it, surface-to-air and anti-ship missiles to defend it. All carried by flying boats. That is why we have them. Sir, we arrive at dawn and the Seiku-Kais can unload immediately. They carry everything we need. We can be flying fighter sweeps by noon.

"We can try and find the Indian naval fighters and pick them off, anything else we can locate. At night we can escort our comrades in the Shukas while our comrades in the Submarine force can provide a picket line out to sea to warn us of any attacks. Our tender, the *Nisshin* can follow us down, but there is no reason why we cannot be supplied by our flying boats. That is how the Flying Garrisons are supposed to operate."

"And if the enemy fighters attack our flying boats? They are helpless against fighters."

"We must hope that is what the Indians do - for then they will be throwing their handful of fighters into a battle where we have the edge. We won't sink their carrier, but what good is the carrier without aircraft? And the Indians have no replacement aircraft nearer than Trincomalee. Sir, this way, at least we will be attacking and while we attack, the Indians must defend."

A murmur of acknowledgment spread around the table. The submarine commander rose, his eyes shining. "Our young friend had shown true valor, not just in having his plan but in daring to speak it here. The submarines will be proud to assist this effort."

Koga nodded again. The seaplane fighters were orphans, not carriers, not surface fleet, not submarines. They tended to be forgotten, yet the part they could play here was decisive. This young Lieutenant Commander Toda Endo had done well to remind everybody of that. Now was the time to test his mettle further.

"Very well. The proposal is adopted. Lieutenant Commander Toda Endo, you will ready your command and pick your bay. A Flying Garrison will be alerted to take possession of your selected bay and establish a base there. You will move into that base and engage the enemy. Good luck, Toda-san."

Bone Airfield, Defensive Area Annaliese, French Algeria

Major-Doctor Pellatiere stared at the paper in front of him, almost as if he wished the words would appear by themselves. More than anything else, at this precise moment, he did not wish to put down the words that ran though his mind because putting them down would make them real. Words in the mind were insubstantial things, they came and went, leaving no trace. Once written down, they were tangible, real and could not be denied. Pellatiere desperately wanted to deny what the words would say because their meaning was horrible. Bone Airfield was closed down as effectively as if the Americans had dropped one of their atomic bombs on it. He almost wished they would, death by an atomic bomb would be merciful compared with what was happening here.

It had all started two weeks earlier with an outbreak of infection. He'd thought it was just influenza or a particularly bad outbreak of the common cold. The victims suffered from fever; they were coughing and sneezing, then they started to develop pains in their muscles and stomach. That had been the first danger sign. Was it cholera? Typhoid perhaps? Or something worse? Now he knew just how much worse; but he couldn't have known that back then. He'd even traced the outbreak back to Case Zero, the original source of infection. It had been the ground crew of one of the Super Mystere fighters. They were all the first cases and they'd all thought they had a cold, or something like that. So, they'd kept working bravely. Also stupidly because in doing so they'd infected almost everybody else on the base. That ground crew were the pathfinders, they were the ones who showed the rest the horrors that were to come. By the seventh day, the disease had spread to their stomachs and they'd started vomiting. That was when the pain and exhaustion had finally forced them to the sick bay. Too late, far too late.

Five days ago, the unseen attacker had finally unmasked himself. The earliest victims had found pimples erupting around their mouths, like little grains of rice embedded in the skin. Within hours, they had spread to the hands and arms and, by the end of the day, their whole bodies were covered. The pimples were called macules and they were the undeniable, absolute confirmation of what had struck. The unseen attacker was smallpox.

Major-Doctor Pellatiere had reacted fast and decisively,. He'd sealed the base off; all visitors were turned back at the gate. Not by contact but by signs and a burst of machine gun fire in front of those who ignored the written word. He'd called Algiers and told them the news, expecting to be reprimanded for his stupidity and foolishness in spreading groundless rumors. Instead, he'd been told that four border villages had also experienced smallpox outbreaks over the last few weeks. They, also, were quarantined.

The French Air Force had tied the location to a Slime that had been intercepted at roughly the right time. Pellatiere had taken less than a minute to confirm that the ground crew whose infection had started the outbreak at Bone were the ones who had serviced the Super Mystere when it had landed. As it was, Pellatiere had been told, the Center for Disease Control in America had been alerted. The Americans had responded with speed and their usual efficiency. A C-144 Superstream, the executive jet version of their B-58 Hustler bomber, had been loaded with the latest vaccines in an attempt to help treat the outbreak. They'd proved useless.

Pellatiere had been worried but the situation was still containable. After all, smallpox was a disease whose lethality was greatly overstated. In its most common form, *variola minoris*, its mortality was around one percent. It crippled, mutilated and blinded; but it did not, often, kill. Over the last three days, the first victims had continued to deteriorate, even as the later cases started to filter into the hangars that had been turned into emergency treatment centers. Their pimples had filled with pus, turning them first into blisters and then into pustules. This was the critical point, after three or four days, the pustules would slowly start to deflate and then they would begin to dry up. Eventually they would be completely dry and the skin covering them would start to flake off, leaving a deep pit that the patient would carry for the rest of their lives. At that point, the patient would be considered cured; if cured was the word for the ravages smallpox brought with it. One percent mortality, although mortality did not measure lives destroyed but not ended.

Only, it hadn't happened. Yesterday, he'd had an emergency call from the hangars. He'd hurried over and seen what was happening for himself. On the first patients who'd contracted the disease the blisters and pustules were starting merge together into super-pustules, large sheets of infection that covered the whole body. Even as Pellatiere had watched, the advancing edge of the lesions reached another pustule and the border between them had broken down, the individual pustule loosing its identity in the cloud that was covering the man's skin. That was when Pellatiere had finally known the true identity of his enemy, it was not *variola minoris,* it was *variola majoris.* Confluent Smallpox. A disease whose mortality was rarely less than 40 percent.

Overnight, the *variola majoris* had continued to flay its victims alive. The sheets of infection had started to detach the outer layers of skin from the underlying flesh, which itself was rotting and dying. The textbooks told of the fate of those who contracted this form of smallpox. Even if they survived, they would be hideously mutilated. The mercy was that *variola majoris* was not very infectious; only a tiny proportion of smallpox victims progressed to suffer from it. That had been Pellatiere's hope. It hadn't lasted long. By the end of the day, all the victims had progressed to the confluent smallpox stage. Now, he was writing that report up and had to put into words the grim conclusions.

He was saved from writing those words by the sound of his telephone. A message from the treatment hangars. It was the one he had been dreading; an urgent request to come down, right away. Overnight, the situation had become even worse.

When he got to the hangar, it took Pellatiere just one look to understand that there was no hope. There would be no cures, no survivors. If a person caught this disease they would certainly die. The areas between the sheets of confluent pustules had turned charred and black with internal bleeding. Already, one of the victims was showing the dreadful symptoms of hemorrhagic smallpox, the whites of his eyes were turning a deep red. Pellatiere knew that the same bleeding had already begun in the internal organs. For these victims, death was inevitable. It might occur from loss of blood or by other causes such as brain hemorrhage. It might occur by dehydration from loss of fluid. Probably it would occur from both, and from many other reasons as the disease lead to multi-organ failure. For this was hemorrhagic smallpox and its mortality was 96 percent.

Pellatiere knew what was wrong. All the textbooks said that Confluent Smallpox and Hemorrhagic Smallpox were mutually exclusive; the development of one automatically prohibited against the other. Just as in the old days, cowpox had provided immunity against smallpox. Yet these victims were developing both. Something that had never been noted before. Grimly, Pellatiere thought that the discovery should get him published in the most prestigious and noted medical journals. Quite an achievement for an obscure and inconsequential Air Force Doctor. It didn't matter though. Pellatiere knew that because he had a headache and his back ached. And, that morning, he had started to run a temperature.

As he left the hangar, one of the nurses stopped him. Her eyes were bright and her face flushed, she too had the disease. "Doctor, we've been talking, the nurses I mean. We all think, we don't want to die looking like that. Please, once its certain, can some arrangement be made? Something, please?"

Pellatiere nodded. The base had plenty of morphine and he would write the nurses a prescription for a 'pain killing' dose that would certainly end their suffering. He said nothing but bowed his head in agreement. Then he went back to his office to phone the news in.

Again, he hadn't been the first. All the affected areas were showing the same symptoms, all had the same prognosis. The good news was that the disease wasn't spreading that fast; it seemed to require personal contact for transmission. That was good. The base was isolated from the communities nearby and the long war against the Caliphate terrorists had cut down travel.

Pellatiere spoke for almost an hour, carefully relaying symptoms, observations, physical measurements, how the disease had spread across the body of its victims, the exact time it had taken them to develop each stage. He'd had blood, tissue, every sample he could think of prepared and packaged in a box. That container had gone through the most rigorous sterilization procedures he could think of. It was being left by the air base gate so that it could be collected by specialized hazardous materials teams. Pellatiere almost laughed, he could win a good deal of money by betting those who collected the box would be wearing isolation suits that made the American space suits look positively permeable. He didn't though. The thought of laughing brought on a fit of coughing.

The he thought of something else. At the end of his recital, he added one thought prompted by the conversation with the nurse. "I've seen the way these people are dying. It would be kinder if you asked the Americans to drop a bomb on us." There had been silence at the other end of the telephone. Then a voice had said very gently, very kindly. "That is not possible, my brave friend. But you must do what you must to ease the suffering of those afflicted."

A county road, Somewhere in the New Jersey swamps.

Agent Mike Delgado pulled his government-issue Studebaker alongside the Lincoln limousine. These meetings were getting to be quite routine now, although he'd never met Lansky again. Mostly, they were messengers with information from the Cuban "Government." This time, though, the limousine meant somebody more important. Delgado felt a flare of resentment. *The Studebaker was a mid-range sedan, not a cheap economy model like the Nash, but why should a bunch of gangsters drive around in luxury limousines while I get a family sedan? One of the penalties of being honest I guess.* He got out of the car. One thing, the Studebaker was front-wheel drive; an unusual feature in cars of its type. The police and FBI were sticking with their rear-wheel drive Fords and Chevvies. The Secret Service had decided to test Studebaker's claim that front wheel drive made the car a lot easier to handle in snow and wet. After all, the Secret Service followed people around, it didn't chase them. Not very often anyway.

There were two mob gunmen waiting for him. They patted him down, removing the Smith and Wesson Model 10 revolver with an only-slightly exaggerated expression of disgust. They carried fast-firing semi-automatic pistols, either M1911s or Czech Model 50s, depending on their opinions in the velocity versus bullet weight argument. The Czechs were moving fast in the small arms world. Their Tokarev 7.62 Magnum Skorpion machine pistol was a deadly piece of kit, almost as good, some said, as the Australian Robow. Then, relieved of his revolver, he got into the back of the limousine. John Gotti was waiting for him.

"Good evening Mister Gotti. I thought you preferred Packards to Lincolns?"

Gotti smiled at the gambit. 'See how good our files on you are' was the clear message. "Agent Delgado, thank you for coming. This is Decavalcante Family country so I advised them I was on their turf and they kindly loaned me this limo. Your grandfather must have told you about courtesy between Families from his time with Moran back in the old days." *And there's my trump* thought Gotti '*and we know all about you too'*.

Delgado smiled at the reference. "Gramps did tell us kids a lot, yes. Mostly when teaching us to shoot. He told us that if we made our living with guns, the best we could hope for was to end up like him. He took a bullet in the flipper in some shoot-out in a Chicago bar. Smashed his shoulder so badly his right arm never worked again. Just withered and he had to learn to do everything with his left."

Gotti smiled with remarkably little sympathy. "Tough break."

"Gramps didn't think so. See he was in hospital for five months while the docs took splinters of shoulder joint and bits of lead bullet out of him. During that time, Capone's boys caught Moran's men in a garage and machine-gunned the hell out of them. The Saint Valentines Day Massacre. If Gramps hadn't been in hospital, he'd have been in that garage too so he reckoned he'd paid for his life with his arm. He got religion after that, went the whole way, got ordained and everything." Delgado's voice softened at the memory of his much-loved grandfather. "Anyway, Mister Gotti, you have news for us?"

"We caught a rat. Never mind who but it had a lot of access to good information and stole all of it. Sent it to its cousin who's a coke supplier down in Colombia.

"Look, here's what we know. The cartel its cousin worked for was supplied with a huge amount of pretty much pure heroin, we're talking tons of the stuff. They planned to use it to set up an undercover drug ring in Cuba. See, the way they thought was this. There's no law against selling drugs in Cuba, no problem with supply. As long as the sellers kick back up the family chain, they can do what they want. That means the prices are pretty low. Now with prices being low in Cuba, that depresses the price here on the mainland. So, the Colombia Cartel wanted to take down Cuba, have the drug trade there made illegal like it is here and that would send the price of their H and Coke skywards. Hence spraying the Senate. That's confirmed now."

"So the Caliphate just gave a bunch of South American drug lords a few tons of heroin. All due respect Mister Gotti. . . . "

"John."

"Thank you, I'm Mike. All due respect John, that doesn't sound like them. There's more to this than that."

"Of course. But our rat didn't know what. Believe me, it would have told us if it had known. All it knew was that the heroin was payment in advance for services about to be rendered. What those services were the rat didn't know. If it had known, it would have told us, believe me on that."

"I suppose this rat is dead?" Delgado had mixed feelings about that. Anti-mob operations on the mainland depended heavily on informers and the FBI cultivated them, treated them as heroes. That was the FBI and Delgado was USSS. This informer, this rat, was part of a scheme that had caused an attack on the Senate, probably something much nastier than that. He was also aware that the Mob had very strong opinions on rats also; ones that caused them to be markedly unforgiving to the ones they caught.

"Nah, it's still alive, we got it on ice for a while." Gotti's grin was fearful to see. The last time he'd seen the rat, she had been hanging upside down in the cold storage unit of a meat processing plant. The treatment she had received had left her almost unrecognizable as the woman who had been Lanski's secretary but he didn't intend to tell Delgado that. The Secret Service had such tender susceptibilities concerning the rights of suspects.

"If you want to talk to it, you can come over to Cuba. Be our guest, take the chance to play the tables a little, bring your wife if you like. What we need from you is this. You and the Feds must have better files on the syndicates down in Colombia than we do. Our relations with them are strictly business. If you can link up the rat and its cousin with their boss, maybe you can pick him up and find out what he did to earn all that H."

Delgado thought it over. "We can probably do that, or at least the FBI can. They'll need the fingerprints of your rat though; that way if it's ever been printed over here we can make the links. Can you send them over?"

Gotti's grin grew even more fearsome. "Brought them with me Mike." He took out a box and handed it over. Delgado opened it, went white and gulped. Inside, packed in a plastic bag surrounded by ice, were eight neatly-severed fingers and two thumbs. All obviously female. Gotti shook his head sadly, Secret Service agents definitely had far too tender susceptibilities. "Fingerprints still attached to the fingers. Sorry about that Mike, but taking fingerprints makes us nervous. Bad associations and all that. There just ain't a fingerprint kit in all of Cuba."

Pilot's Mess. Dromodevo Fighter Base, Moscow, Russia.

"One! Two! Three! GO!"

The sled was made from the outer wing section of a Ta-152H, smoothed off and polished. The rider sat towards the back, holding two ropes attached to the wingtip end. The stairway in the mess had a long, straight down section, running from the third floor. Before it reached the end, it had a landing and a 90 degree bend. If the sled rider jerked his control ropes at exactly the right time, he could lift the nose of the sled enough to transfer from the stairs to the landing without disaster. Lift too late and the sled's nose would dig in, sending the rider cartwheeling across the floor. When they regained consciousness, they would be expected to stand drinks for the Mess. If they pulled the ropes unevenly, the sled would spin out of control. Then, the rider would have the choice of jumping off or staying with it. Either way would cost a round of drinks. However, if they did it just right, the sled would slide across the landing, off the other side, and land on the bar underneath. That got the rider free drinks from the Mess.

Major C.J. O'Seven couldn't help but feel it was a very Russian game somehow.

The sled rider, a MiG-21 pilot, had made a mistake. He'd jerked the nose of the sled too high and lost too much speed in the transition from stairs to landing. As a result, when he'd launched from the landing, he hadn't quite enough speed to make the bar and had hit the end of it, catapulting him onto the floor. He rose, dazed from the impact. A considerate comrade, O'Seven couldn't see whether he was American or Russian, dumped a pitcher of iced water over him. Then everybody closed in on the bar for their free drink. Behind them, the sled was being carried to back to the top of the stairs for the next rider.

"Our friends in the MiG-21s don't seem to be doing too well this time around."

"Hello Paul! I see the sawbones let you out at last. Clean bill of health I assume?"

"Indeed. They say apart from some minor abnormalities in my blood chemistry, perhaps due to growing up in the famine of the 1930s, I am remarkably fit for my age. Fit enough to continue flying fighters for a while anyway. How have things gone in my absence? Has the Rodina survived?"

"We've flown 96 profile missions against Moscow in the last fifteen days, 60 by us, 36 by the 35th out of McDill. Zero losses to the air defense missiles, the Tu-128s got close a couple of times and the MiG-25s scored twice. You're right about the 21s, they didn't even register. They're useful enough against aircraft in the B-52 class but against our B-70s? They're out of their league."

Lazaruski nodded thoughtfully. The single-engined MiG-21 had been designed with aircraft in the size and weight class of the Chipanese Frank in mind. It was a good point defense interceptor but its speed and performance were optimized for intercepting the turboprop powered Chipanese bomber. "I think we've seen the last of the single-engined fighters, they just don't have the power or the load capacity."

"I wouldn't be too sure Paul. We've got the F-116 coming down the pike. That's a souped-up F-104. The prototype won't be flying for years though."

"I have seen the drawings of the F-116 and there was a model shown here. It is much money to spend for such a limited aircraft."

"It's for the Air National Guard; part-time pilots flying for their own cities. So it has to be simple yet capable and that's a hard thing to achieve. But the threat might be changing a little. Have you read about the Harrys operating down in the South China Sea?"

"They have done well, I will give you that. The Chimps are behaving quite unusually; they are playing the political game as well as they have played the military one. I do not think, though, that their Harrys would last too long over land. Too many missiles, too many shoulders to fire them from."

O'Seven nodded in agreement. That was the problem. The low-flying rampages of fighter-bombers in the last years of the Second World War had focused everybody's eyes on the threat they posed. Which was fair since that threat was a devastating one. One result had been predictable. Every army now had radar-controlled anti-aircraft guns added to its order of battle and never went anywhere without them. The other had been less easily foreseen, the evolution of shoulder-fired anti-aircraft missiles that were simple enough and cheap enough to be handed out like rounds of ammunition. It was an exaggeration to say every solder carried one, but it wasn't that much of one.

Low level penetration had been tried post-war at Red Sun and it had been a catastrophe. Losses were simply too heavy to be contemplated. Not just losses from the defenses either. Flying low and fast through broken terrain was dangerous. More than enough aircraft had crashed to show that clearly. Shoulder-fired anti-aircraft missiles were effective up to 8,000 feet. The individual chance of a hit wasn't great but with enough being fired, the losses mounted up too fast. In the eyes of the USAF, the sky was closed below 8,000 feet over land. Their attention had turned to getting pinpoint accuracy for bombs dropped from above that level.

"Seejay, how did your DAMS system work out anyway?"

O'Seven thought carefully. "We're still exploring what it can do. On an individual aircraft basis, we can defend against any type of SAM coming up in our frontal arc and, of course, we really don't have to worry about them coming from behind. Of course, DAMS doesn't just work for the individual aircraft; the datalinks exchange information between all the time so there's a pooled operational picture to draw on. When we have RB-58s out front to help us out, that'll be even more so. We'll know what is where before we stick our head in."

"You hope." Lazaruski chuckled, thinking about the maze of dummy transmitters and decoys that surrounded every Russian surface-to-air missile battery. "Who's that doing the ride?"

O"Seven looked at the top of the stairs where a light blue suit was taking its place on the sled. "That's Captain Mike Yates, he flies *Shield Maiden* in the 35th. He pinched the best electronics crew chief I ever had, when the 35th switched from B-52s to B-70s we sent cadres of technicians down to help them over. We didn't get many of them back."

"And this surprised you?" Lazaruski was amused. There was constant competition between units to steal good technicians and maintenance staff from eachother. There were dark rumors that any particularly able American engineers or technicians who went on TDY to Russia found themselves surrounded by officially-encouraged Natashas who were well aware, as were the Russian armed forces, that an American man marrying a Russian woman would find his duty station in Russia made permanent. As in career-long. A dark rumor, much denied, but it caused American units to be very careful who they sent to Russia on TDY. Even now, almost thirty years after the end of World War Two, the gender gap in Russia was a serious social problem.

"One! Two! Three! GO!"

The sled sped off, crashing down the steps. The transition onto the landing was perfect; the old wing section slid across the floor without losing much speed, then it tipped off the edge to swoop down, hitting the bar with a crash that set all the bottles behind it rattling and chiming. Yates slid about half way down the bar and the spectators held their breath. Would he make it off the end of the bar and land on the floor, still on his sled? If he did, it would be free drinks for life. It was also a feat nobody had ever achieved. Alas for Captain Yates, though probably fortunately for his liver, it was a feat still unachieved. The sled came to a halt about two thirds of the way down the bar.

Behind the polished mahogany, the barmaid stepped forward to pour the first drink. "Ohh Captain, you are so strong and skillful. Your wife must be very proud."

Yates took the drink and lifted it in toast to the Regimental crest over the bar, a gesture that won a quick burst of applause. "I fear I am not yet married." The barmaid's eyes lit up in suddenly awakened hope. "But soon, my fiancée and I will indeed be joined in holy wedlock. Look, here is her picture." He pulled his wallet and showed the head-and-shoulders shot around to the appropriate collection of lascivious, suggestive and sometimes downright obscene remarks. The barmaid went through the motions of complimenting the American Captain but her heart really wasn't in it. After all, she had been sadly disappointed.

O'Seven wasn't very happy either. Even from several feet away he'd recognized the caramel skin and black corn-row woven hair. *So that was how Yates had stolen his electronics crew chief.* Briefly O'Seven contemplated strangling the young Captain but decided it would come under the heading of 'Conduct prejudicial to good order and discipline.' Then, he had a much better idea. "Paul, will you please get every Natasha on this base and throw them at Captain Yates, singly and in batches, until he succumbs to their charms. I want my crew chief back."

Lazaruski laughed, then stopped dead. An eerie quiet had fallen on the Mess for standing in the door was a Very Senior Officer. Very Senior Indeed, for even by Russian standards the gold braid was profuse. The General walked across the room towards the bar, then grabbed Yates in bear hug, swinging him around. "A good ride on the sled my American friend, and a perfect landing. Although I am not a member of this mess, may I be allowed to buy our friend from over the Atlantic his drink?"

There was a roaring cheer of approval. Lazaruski took the opportunity to speak quietly with O'Seven. "That is General Oleg Penkovsky, Commander of the Moscow Air Defense Region. It is against his fighters and missiles that you have been flying for the last two weeks. He is also a personal confidant of President Cherniakhovskii and one of the possible successors when the President decides to retire, as he will in the next few years. Many hope that General Penkovsky will indeed be the chosen heir. He is a forthright man, one of great patriotism and courage yet also one who is not afraid to speak out and take action when he believes something is wrong. The sort of leader Russia needs."

Lazaruski grimaced slightly. "Of course, forty years ago he would have been shot out of hand for such behavior." The comment surprised him slightly, he'd grown increasingly cautious about indicating to the people around him just how old he was. But then, good friends and good vodka would make men's guard drop and that too had resulted in them being shot out of hand back in the old days. "Come, I will introduce you."

Lazaruski waited until the General had finished exchanging jocularity's with the pilots around the bar, then cleared his throat.

"Tovarish General? May I introduce Major O'Seven of the B-70 *Sigrun?*"

Penkovsky turned around, his eyes lighting up at the sound of Lazaruski's voice. "It is my old friend Paul Lazaruski. It is good to see you still fly in the Rodina's defense. And Major O'Seven, your *Sigrun* has taught us much over the last two weeks. You have given our designers a great deal to think upon. Have you flown often at Red Sun?"

"A couple of times in *Honey Pot*, my old B-60, and for the last three years in *Sigrun*. Now that we have our defensive systems fully operational, we are giving the Nevada defenses a very hard time. DAMS allows us to take out SAMs and that throws everything onto the fighters. It's the old problem Sir. By the time a fighter gets up high enough and fast enough to intercept us, it has only a few minutes to do the necessary actions. Time just runs out on it. Even our F-112s are having problems and they have nuclear-tipped air-to-air missiles."

"And you think our fighters should have such weapons too?"

"Frankly, Sir, yes."

"There is much opposition to that, for very good reasons. Perhaps it needs to be discussed further. Gentlemen, I know you are fighter pilots but I have news of the air force for you. Today, we have ordered that the Sukhoi T-4MS experimental bomber will be placed in full production as the Sukhoi Su-28. In 1974, the first operational squadron will be going to Nevada to join the Red Sun Exercise there."

More cheering erupted it in the room, some a little muted from fighter pilots who would have preferred to hear of a new fighter type. Penkovsky's voice dropped out of public address mode and he clapped O'Seven on the shoulder, making the American stagger slightly. "And, Major O'Seven I hope our new bomber makes your missile crews cry as much as your *Sigrun* has made ours weep in despair."

Main Conference Room, National Security Council Building, Washington D.C.

"Good morning, President Nixon. Welcome to the National Security Council. Here's your copy of the briefing book. If you could just sign in the usual place?"

"Miss Naamah. In future I wish to arrive at the Friday Follies 30 minutes in advance of the start of the meeting so I can read the briefing book first. Please arrange that in future."

"Certainly, Mister President."

"No arguments or reasons why I shouldn't do that?"

"No Sir, I think its a very good idea. President Johnson liked to listen to the briefing first and then read the book at his leisure so he could present a list of written questions. Your way is the way it will be from now on. But, Sir, its just Naamah, not Miss Naamah. I really haven't missed very much in my life."

Nixon sniggered while Naamah carefully hid her grin. She was beginning to get the measure of this man now; he had a coarse, schoolboy's sense of humor, one that centered around sexual innuendo and foul language. He'd already sworn in front of her a couple of times, something that LBJ had never done. Johnson had an expert's command of foul and profane language which he had sometimes used to great effect but which he'd never employed it in front of women and he had not smiled on those who did. In contrast, Naamah suspected Nixon actually got a thrill out of shocking the women around him. She was also looking forward to telling The Seer that this President would have read the book before getting the briefing; she rather suspected he preferred not to have his audience fully informed on the subject under discussion.

"Mister President. Welcome to your first solo Friday Folly." The Seer had slipped in and was standing by the podium in a corner of the room. Nixon glanced at the wall behind him. A large map of the South China Sea. Well, that could be expected. He took the padded, high-backed seat traditionally reserved for the President and leaned forward slightly. "I am afraid, Sir, that you start your Presidency in a world that is very far from being at peace and there are a number of situations that demand our attention. The first is here, in the South China Sea."

"I saw some of that on television. The Indians got a bloody nose didn't they?"

"They did, only they broke a couple of Chipanese kneecaps in the process. Our satellite shots and a couple of SR-71 overflights have shown it must have been a desperate fight. We know the Indian losses, a destroyer and two frigates, with the rest of their ships badly chewed up. We've seen the film on television. From what we've been able to see, they took down a decent honor guard though. One cruiser sunk, another smashed up, probably beyond repair, a third hurt. Five destroyers down, two crippled. From what we can make of it, the Indians didn't do subtlety. They simply went for the Chipanese head-on and slugged it out - then kept slugging until the Chipanese broke off.

"Admiral Stanley is impressed and a bit perturbed. If the Indian Navy really intends to fight like that, he reckons we need to double up on the short-range armament of our ships and give the new designs splinter protection to their electronics and machinery."

"Do we need to budget that, Seer?"

The Seer thought for a second and shook his head. "We don't fight that way; in fact we try not to fight at all. If we were ever in the same position, we'd just drop nukes on them. They can be as brave as they like underneath the fireballs. Anyway, we use carriers for sea control not surface ships. One thing though, this shoot out is a godsend for us. Its the first real naval battle since Wild Bill Halsey took the German fleet out in 1945 and the first surface gunfight, ohh since the River Plate in 1939. We're learning a lot just by watching. Not least of which is the war-emergency modes for the radars both sides use."

"Suppose the enemy, whoever they are, manage to slide in close? Too close to use nukes. I don't know how, come in at night, pretend to be a merchant ship or hide in radar shadows or something. What would one of those Indian ships do if it got within gun range of a carrier?"

"With those rapid fire guns? They'd create holy hell on board. Rake the hangar with those and the ship would be an inferno. Like the old *Shiloh*." The Seer watched Nixon gave a satisfied nod and reminded himself not to underestimate this man. Oafish he may be, but his first question had put a finger on a very valid point.

"However, Sir, I don't think that upping close defense firepower on the ships will be useful, if they're that close, its already too late. The Indians proved they'll keep coming until somebody physically beats them under the water. It is a threat we should consider but I think the answer lies in improving surveillance so they can't get that close and pushing the outer defense ring a bit further away. Still, that's a matter for the Navy tacticians. From a strategic point of view, we have to recognize that the Indian Navy is now a regional player, worthy of note. That affects how we deploy to some extent. We're going to have to take the Indian Ocean a little more seriously from now on.

"The big question is, what do the Chipanese do now? Their original plan was obvious. Soften the island up with bombing; send the surface group in to wipe out the shipping and defenses, then follow up with a landing. Not a subtle plan but all the better for that. Only its gone now. They've moved ships from Hong Kong to strengthen what's left of the South China Sea Squadron, but those reinforcements don't even begin to cover their losses. The obvious move is for them to bring down a pair, or more, of their carriers but their Navy is stretched desperately thin.

"Also, they've played this one really carefully so far, I don't see why they should stop doing that. You know, the Indians are doing us a tremendous favor here although they don't know it. We're learning more about the Chipanese Navy and how it thinks than we've done for years. I'd almost be tempted to pay them to carry on the fight just to see what'll happen next."

“We didn’t bribe them to start this did we?” Nixon’s voice was suspicious.

“No, Sir, we did not. I wish we’d thought of doing just that a few years back, though. Anyway, the South China Sea isn’t a dangerous situation in that its controlled, confined and restricted. As such its none of our concern. We should watch it, of course; I’ve already said how much we’ve learned from it, but we can let that situation develop.”

“It’s dangerous for the people in it. Doesn’t that count for something?”

“For them, obviously yes. But that’s their problem; the situation does not threaten to spread or affect our interests. So, for us, it ends there.”

The Seer paused and drew breath for a second. Then he changed the map, to one of French Algeria. “On the other hand, this situation is spreading, is very dangerous and does directly threaten us. It is, therefore, our business.

“The French have experienced five outbreaks of smallpox in French Algeria. Four are villages located here, here, here and here.” At each point, the Seer’s pointer tapped a red circle on the map. “The fifth is the French Air Force airfield west of Bone, here.” Another tap. “As you can see the four villages hit are in the same locality and very close. In fact, they form what the French Army General Bigeard calls a ‘Communale.’ That’s a group of communities that have banded together for mutual support in economic and defensive matters.

“We don’t know if they were all infected or whether one was, and infected the others. That’s something that doesn’t matter now. What does matter is that all four are being decimated by this disease. The airfield at Bone is quite separate from that communal, but the link is there. About two weeks ago, a fighter from Bone attacked a Slime that crossed the border near those villages. It appears that, somehow, the Slime infected the fighter as well as the village or villages.”

"How do we know this isn't just a natural outbreak? For all our efforts, smallpox isn't wiped out in the wild yet."

"I'll come to that shortly. In passing, I'm not so sure that wiping feral smallpox out is a good idea, but again, we'll have to think on that one. Anyway, the French reported the outbreaks to the Center for Disease Control and we shipped them a planeload of vaccine in an attempt to contain the outbreaks. Ever since then, they've been shipping us all the data they can get and have sent us tissue, blood, all sorts of samples."

"I thought the French hated us."

"They do, sir. They always have, especially after the Champes Elysee. In passing, that seemed like a very good idea at the time but with a quarter century to look back, I'm not sure it was. Goes to show how useless hindsight really is. Anyway, the French don't want to be indebted to us, so they've gone over the odds in paying off for those vaccines. That's how we know this is a deliberate biowarfare attack. Sir, I've asked an expert from AMRIID to join this briefing to explain what appears to have happened."

The Seer pressed a button on his intercom and spoke quietly. A few seconds later Lillith opened the door and showed in a mild, inoffensive looking man whose nervous rubbing of his hands suggested he was inordinately concerned with preserving the health of his fingers. He stepped up to the podium, rubbing an eyebrow reflectively.

"Mr President, National Security Advisor, Ladies, My name is Doctor Stens, I am the director of biological weapons research at Fort Detrick."

"I wasn't aware we had a biological weapons program."

"We don't, Sir. Our efforts in that area are purely defensive. We identify new biowarfare agents and develop treatments against them. In this case, we were immensely aided by the samples and reports from the French. They have an Air Force doctor over at the

Bone Air Force Base, Doctor Arnold Pellatiere, who's been calling in every day to describe his symptoms and the course of the disease.

"He's refused treatment for himself so that he can give us the most accurate picture of how this disease progresses and what the various stages of its development are. He says he can keep going for another couple of days or so before the smallpox reaches a point where he won't be able to make further reports. He's reporting horrendous mortality.

"Sir, smallpox normally exhibits as a disease that has relatively low mortality. Those who die of it are the unfortunate souls who develop one of the more extreme forms: Confluent Smallpox where the pustules merge together or Hemorrhagic Smallpox where the disease progresses inwards and attacks the vital organs. The chance of either developing is very small and they are an either/or proposition. Get one, you don't get the other.

"Only here, all of that is gone. All the patients progress from normal smallpox to the confluent form and then to hemorrhagic form. And, as far as we can see, they all die eventually. This is nothing that's been seen in nature before and something that is most unlikely to occur naturally, a disease so virulent burns itself out quickly and evolves to a less lethal form. This has to be a deliberately-engineered virus."

"How does one 'engineer' a disease?" Nixon's voice was scornful but the scorn was the product of fear, not disbelief.

"There are quite a few ways of doing that. The simplest way in this case is to infect a large number of people with smallpox, allow the disease to progress unchecked and harvest the virus from those who develop the confluent form. Culture that virus, infect a new group of victims and repeat the process.

"Continue until development of the confluent form is the norm, not the exception. In other words, just as we selectively breed cattle for better meat or milk yields, they selectively breed smallpox virus for its tendency to develop into the confluent stage. Run a parallel program for hemorrhagic smallpox and eventually they would have two strains of smallpox, one of which went confluent as a matter of course, the other hemorrhagic.

"Then, this is the clever bit. They take cultures of both and mix them together. Viruses have a strange habit, mix them together and they start to exchange bits of their DNA. So mix our two strains together and they'll do the same. Keep infecting victims and soon, very soon, one will develop both confluent and hemorrhagic symptoms. Isolate that strain, breed from it and there you are. All done."

The room was silent, shocked by the implications of what they had just been told. Eventually, The Seer broke the appalled quiet. "How long would that take? Years? Decades?"

Stens thought for second. "Minimum of four years, more likely six to ten. Depends how ruthless they are; the more test subjects they have, the quicker they can move."

Nixon's voice was equally hushed. "Six years. How infectious is this disease? How is it spread?"

Stens thought again. "In its natural form, smallpox isn't very infectious. The great epidemics were more a response to poor and overcrowded housing and terrible sanitation than anything else. But, this disease isn't smallpox, its something new. My colleague in Bone calls it blackpox and that's as good a name as any.

"Remember how I said viruses exchange DNA? It applies to all viruses. Mix the blackpox virus with, for example, influenza and eventually there will be an influenza virus that exhibits the symptoms and mortality of blackpox. Yet it will be as infectious as influenza. Even so, the very high lethality and infectiousness won't last. There's a thing called progression.

"A very lethal virus kills its host so fast it can't spread so the ones that tend to spread are the less lethal variants. There's an evolutionary driver to lower mortality. Each generation will be less lethal than its predecessor so the epidemics tend to burn themselves out. In this case, I think we have seen all first-generation infectees, ones that had the grave misfortune to contact the original culture.

"Thanks to the French, we have samples of that culture and we can produce a vaccine that will guard against the current form of blackpox. My guess is that the original culture was sprayed and the subsequent infections were by close contact."

"Thank you Doctor. You have been most helpful." Nixon's voice was thoughtful, calculating. "Doctor Stens, you have a new infectious diseases unit at Detrick don't you. Completed last week I believe. It is to be named the Doctor Arnold Pellatiere Memorial Center. You'll be getting a Presidential order to that effect shortly." The Doctor left the room.

"Seer, are you thinking what I am?"

"Six years, Sir; right after Yaffo. This is their retaliation for the Yaffo attack and the associated incidents. This sudden epidemic is aimed right at us. I'd guess that the attack on Algeria was a test run, to make sure the virus and its distribution really are viable. This tends to fit the third topic I wished to bring to your attention today Sir: Cuba.

"We've been in contact with the Cuban authorities over some unfortunate developments."

"Authorities! Why do we deal with a bunch of gangsters. We should just clear them out." It was obviously still the horror of the disease that was speaking, not Nixon's thought processes.

"Sir, Cuba is America's playground; you do anything to upset that and I guarantee your party will never get another vote. I don't mean never win another election, I mean never get another person to vote for you. Anyway, they may be gangsters; well they are gangsters of course. But they're no worse than a lot of other governments I can think of. Also, they have been very helpful to us.

"Their investigation of the Senate Steps Shooting, intended to convince us not to invade, lead to some unexpected places. For both of us I might add. In passing, we owe the authorities in Cuba for this one; without their help we would still be floundering around."

"Helped by gangsters." Nixon shook his head; this was not an idea he liked. "We'd better find another way. Anyway, what did they find out for us?"

"In the case of Cuba, it lead them to discover a massive effort to smuggle large quantities of heroin into the island. That sounds weird and is actually even weirder. The simplest way to get heroin into Cuba is to send it by parcel delivery. The Cuban Authorities don't care who imports or sells what. As long as they get their kick-back from the sales and it doesn't scare the tourists away, they're happy. Smuggling drugs just isn't economic; why do it when nobody bothers to stop you importing the stuff legally?

"Anyway, it turns out that the Caliphate have paid off a Colombian drug cartel, the Medellin Syndicate, with a huge quantity of free heroin to perform some unspecified services for them. In short, there are two ends to this affair. One is the Medellin Syndicate's effort to try and get involved in Cuba's drug trade; the other is the same syndicate being hired to do something on behalf of the Caliphate.

"The two halves are related only by the fact that the second has effectively funded the first. My guess is that it's the second part, the one we haven't defined yet, that is crucial from the Caliphate's point of view.

"My guess also is, and Doctor Stens briefing has strengthened this feeling, that the second part of the plot is aimed directly at us. It is too much of a coincidence that this whole thing should blow up at the same time as the Algerian epidemic.

"I believe that the Medellin Syndicate were hired by the Caliphate to carry out a biological warfare attack on the United States. How, when and where, we don't as yet know. I would suggest that it is a matter of high national priority that we find out."

"What do you recommend?"

"Sir, from the Cuban authorities we have learned who is involved in the Medellin Syndicate. That person must have the full picture and know what is happening. By the way, they may well not be aware, in fact almost certainly are not, of the fact they are involved in a biological attack. They probably believe that this is something much less than that. Whatever it is we shall have to find out.

"I doubt very much that the Medellin Syndicate would knowingly do anything to bring our full fury down onto their heads. On the other hand, it is very much in line with Caliphate thinking that they would dupe the Syndicate into doing something that would have that effect. The Caliphate planners probably hope that this would and our attention from the real attacker. They're probably hoping that we'll drop the hammer on the Medellin Syndicate so thoroughly that we'll destroy any evidence of Caliphate involvement in the process.

"The problem is, of course, that the Algerian attack has really eliminated that possibility. My belief is that there was a kind of bandwagoning effect. What started as a very simple scheme has seen every faction within the Caliphate adding its own pet ideas into the pot. The result is an over-complex plan that's tripping up over its own feet. That's fairly typical of inexperienced planners. The first rule of any operation is to keep the whole thing simple and concentrate on the immediate objective. Diversifying away from that point or trying to cover multiple objectives is always a bad idea. General Phil Sheridan said it right. 'Combinations never work.'

"We need to attack this problem at the source, the point where all the threads come together. That's where the weakness of the whole scheme lies. So, I suggest we send a SEAL team down into Colombia immediately, pick up the people in question and bring them back here for interrogation. Find out what they think they are doing and put that together with what we know and discover what is really going on. Once they realize that they have been thrown in the deep end and left to drown, they might well be a lot more cooperative than the Caliphate planners expected."

Nixon thought about it and frowned. "Another expedition into South America, trampling all over the people down there. I don't like our apparent attitude that we can do this sort of thing at will. Even so, in view of the circumstances, I'm going to approve this. Make it so and give that operation top priority. Now, what else do we have to deal with today?"

CHAPTER SEVEN
SKIRMISHING

Sugu Bay, Southern Coast of Hainan Island, Hainan Province, China

The seagulls were annoyed. In fact, they were furious; in their eyes at least, quite justifiably so. This was their bay. They'd lived here for generations and it was their home, their fishing ground, their whole world. Then, just as the first light of dawn had touched the eastern horizon, just as the first sounds of a new day woke the seagull community, those sounds were drowned out by the whining roar of new birds, big, green and gray monsters that kissed the calm pre-dawn waters and invaded the once-calm, once-tranquil community.

The first of the big birds were H13K-3 Seiku-Kai flying boats, personnel transports that carried the Special Naval Landing Force troops and engineers. They, at least, had the courtesy to anchor out in the bay, well away from the shore where the seagulls sat on the rocks and screamed at them in impotent fury. The hatches on each side of the fuselage, directly under the high-mounted wing opened. Strange-looking cylinders slid out on rails built into the lower surface of that wing.

As the disbelieving seagulls watched, the cylinders opened and transformed into a rubber assault craft, hanging level with the lower edge. Men scrambled out; 12 per landing craft plus two more to drive the boats. *Humans*, the seagulls noted grimly. *That meant trouble*. Once loaded, the landing craft were winched down into the water, detached and headed for shore. The first wave of troops to form the Sugu Bay Naval Base were landing.

It took the four boats carried by each Seiku-Kai five trips to unload all the men on each of the six H13Ks. By the time they were making the last trip, the big flying boats were already turning around, heading back for their base in Japan. Their place was being taken by more than a dozen H13K-2s. These were similar to the personnel transports but optimized to transport heavy cargo and vehicles. The engineers were already moving along the shore, marking the areas on the beach where the approach was unfouled by rocks. The H13K-2s followed the beacons in, lowering their beaching gear as the taxied towards the beach. The wheels stayed underwater but when they touched the gravel, they lifted the nose of the flying boat to prevent damage. Then, the clamshell doors in the nose opened and vehicles started to unload down a ramp that extended towards the dry shale.

Some of the transports were carrying Lajatang launch batteries. There were four vehicles per transport, three missile carriers and a radar fire control unit. Each launch vehicle had three missiles and more reloads were carried on trailers towed ashore by the prime launch units. They headed quickly for the high ground. Another transport carried a complete radar station, mounted in three vehicles with a fourth carrying a telescoping radar tower. More carried anti-ship missile launchers: a single missile on the back of a heavy, sixteen-wheel truck. Only two of those per transport, they were the least economic of all the equipment being landed in space and weight terms.

As they drove ashore, the flying boat's unloading ramp creaking under the weight, their drivers picked out their assigned destination. About a quarter of a mile inland there was a gentle rise. It was not high, but the anti-ship missile launchers stationed behind it would be protected from direct fire. The other transports carried engineer vehicles, bulldozers, backhoes, graders, generator trucks, all the equipment needed to build a base, all specially designed to use the transport facilities of the flying boats to maximum capacity.

By the time the sun had cleared the horizon and the temperature had started to rise, the vehicles were ashore and at work. The radars were scanning the horizon waiting for any aircraft to appear. The anti-aircraft missile crews were checking their systems, calibrating radar guidance heads, getting the equipment at the peak of efficiency for this was the critical time. The new base was totally dependent on them for air defense, it wasn't ready to receive the seaplane fighters yet. If the enemy moved fast, the base was vulnerable. The only defense was to move faster, to build the base before the enemy could destroy it.

More H13Ks landed. These just carried supplies, food, fuel missiles and bombs for the aircraft. Four carried trucks, long low-loaders, with a strange dark-green roll on their backs. They disappeared behind the ridge as well. A few minutes later, huge snakes appeared from some of the Seiku-Kais and headed inland, dragged by their servants. Then, the snakes began to throb and the rolls behind the ridge unfolded and turned into fuel tanks. Flexible fuel tanks called blivets, holding enough fuel to keep the Ohtoris flying for hours. More fuel, more blivets would be ferried in later.

Yet more H13Ks touched down as the sun rose higher. Out in the bay the rubber boats scurried around, laying the beacons that marked the landing strip for the seaplane fighters. On the surfline, floating pontoons were quickly being assembled to make the quays that would provide the fighters with anchorage and protect them from swells. Portable buildings were being thrown up. It wasn't in the authorized plan, but the first one the engineers put up was for the fighter pilots. They knew the Ohtoris would be fighting against the odds; 24 of them against at least 36 and possibly twice that many Indian carrier aircraft. The Ohtoris would be flying around the clock, sweeping the skies by day and escorting the famous Shukas by night. The pilots would need all the rest they could get. So their quarters went up first. If the book said different, well it had just accidently been dropped in Sugu Bay.

At ten o'clock, the sound changed. The whining of turboprop flying boats gave way to the whistling of jets; the tearing sound that made the sky echo. The first twelve N5M4 Ohtoris had arrived. They swept over the bay before heading in to touch down on the newly-marked landing area. They threw spray up as they hit; ironically much more than the big flying boats had, but the landings were immaculate. As the fighters taxied in, the rubber boats met them and helped them dock.

Lieutenant Commander Toda Endo could barely stand erect. He'd been sitting in his cockpit for the long flight down and now his back felt as if it had permanently molded itself to the shape of his seat. Still, the sight of the seaplane base rapidly coming together around him was enough to overcome the cramps. Even as he walked down the jetty, there was a crash as the walls of another pre-fabricated building were lifted and locked into place. People might laugh at flimsy Japanese buildings but they were light and quick to assemble. And, after all, if somebody dropped an atomic bomb on them, strength didn't matter so much. It had taken less than five hours so far to throw this base together and the Flying Garrison could dismantle it just as quickly. That was the defense against nuclear weapons, don't be there when they go off. On dry land the base commander was waiting for him.

"Welcome to Naval Base Sugu Bay, Toda-san!"

"It is an honor to be stationed here. It is even more of an honor to see what a magnificent job you and your men have done. It will be an privilege to fly from this base. I have our first fighter sweep planned for 1130 and it is your efforts that have made this possible."

The base commander beamed on hearing the words of praise before turning to issue the fuelling and arming orders. Beside him Toda looked at the new base with pride and the seagulls stared back with impotent rage.

Villa Blanco, Medellin, Colombia.

It was a very nice stone. In fact, it was a fine stone, the sort of stone any wall could be proud of. Captain Jeff Thomas ran his hand along it, thinking affectionately of its surface, of what a wonderful wall had been built out of these fine stones. He had established a rapport with the stones. He felt he was being accepted by them, regarded as one of their own even. And for such fine, strong stones that had produced such an excellent wall, was it not a good thing to be accepted by them?

He didn't hide in the shadows, nor did he try to make himself inconspicuous. Those would be unnatural things, things that were put of place and they would catch the eye and hold it. Instead he just stood quietly by the wall, accepted by it, a part of it. It helped, of course, that the sentry was such a complete and total idiot. He was pacing around the walls of the Villa Blanco on a regular beat and that was bad enough. To make matters worse, he hadn't washed for several days and he had tried to hide the smell with a virulent cologne. Thomas didn't need to see him, the smell made his eyes water. Regular soap was bad enough, the scented soaps used by civilians could be smelled a long way away. But that cologne was extraordinary.

As was the noise. The man's equipment rattled and squeaked. His boots sounded as if they had never been polished. The nails hammered into the soles clacked on the stones and the man's ammunition belts clattered and rang with a melodic rhythm Thomas hadn't heard since he'd sat on a balcony underneath a set of wind chimes. Beneath it all was the man's breathing, coarse and ragged. Finally, there was his cigarette; a spot of bright red moving unevenly in the darkness. Idly, Thomas wondered if the sentry was tired of life and had decided to commit suicide.

The sentry continued to pace his beat along the path around the villa. He wasn't really thinking of what he was doing; he was thinking of drinking with the others, perhaps of going down to the village for a woman. He actually looked straight at Thomas and his eyes slid straight past the figure comfortably resting by the gray stones of the wall. The camoflage uniform, three shades of gray and off-white, rippling in deceptive, eye-soothing patterns, had helped but it was the attitude that made the difference. The sentry actually had an uneasy feeling that he had missed something but couldn't think what it might be. He never got to know. At the right second, Thomas flowed out of the wall, hooked one hand under the man's chin and squeezed the pressure point under the man's ear. He slipped down, never making a sound. Just as quietly, he slipped into unconsciousness that would last for hours.

Two more figures joined Thomas, each having dispatched a sentry with the same ruthless efficiency. They linked hand to form a step and boosted Thomas over the gate, allowing him to drop the other side, still soundless, still undetected. There were more men inside but they were blinded by the floodlights and the shadows to them were inky spots of total darkness. They didn't hear the bolts slipped or see the gate swing open just enough to allow the rest of the SEAL team to enter.

This would be the interesting bit, Thomas thought as the strike element of SEAL Team Two moved through the gate and started to spread out along the perimeter wall. *Four guards in the courtyard, two more by the front doors, two additional ones in a jeep off to one side.* They were the first ones to be taken out, the machine gun on the jeep was too dangerous to leave. They were plucked from their seats and left unconscious as unobtrusively as the sentries outside.

The SEALs had a back-up plan of course; by their standards it was crude and unsubtle. Amateurish even. They carried silenced semi-automatic pistols: highly modified M1911s whose mufflers meant the loudest noise they made was the click as the firing pins hit the primers. If necessary, they could simply shoot the guards but that was hardly the point. The SEALs synchronized their movements with the guards, flowing closer to them, quietly, undramatically. The first of the inner guards turned a corner and simply vanished, taken down with the same skill as all the others and added to the growing pile of unconscious "guards." The others went down just as fast, none aware of the silent specters that ruled the Villa Blanco compound that night.

Inside the villa, the guard sergeant by the hall desk was reading a comic book, one starring some strange super-hero or other. He even noticed the slight ripple in the air but it didn't register. Then, instinct took over and he looked up, to see Thomas sitting on his desk, smiling politely. The guard sergeant tried to grab a weapon but he didn't get very far. He too joined the pile of bodies sleeping peacefully in a corner. That more or less did it for the drug lord's "elite guard." Their "reinforcements" had been asleep in their guard room; now the application of a little sleeping gas meant they slept a lot more soundly than they had before.

Once again, the SEALs flowed quietly through the villa, seeking out the real target of the night's operation. The head of this particular gang and one of his lieutenants, an accomplice who was the cousin of a secretary in Cuba. A secretary who had made the ultimately fatal mistake of ratting out the Mob. Thomas himself found the drug lord, asleep in bed with two of his women. He produced a gray-white cylinder from his pocket and waved it gently under the nose of the trio. Their breathing grew deeper and slower as they slipped from sleep to unconsciousness. Then he hoisted his chosen prey up into a fireman's carry and left the two women to sleep off the gas they'd inhaled.

The rest was very, very easy. They exited the building as quietly and unobtrusively as they had entered and joined up with the cover team waiting outside. If everything had fallen apart, it was the job of the cover team to provide fire support as the strike group fought its way out but things had never got to that point. And never would, not if everybody did their job right. From there, it was a two mile trek through the jungle to the small, air-portable four-by-fours. Thomas dumped his burden into the carry section at the back and mounted up.

They had about an hour to drive the fifteen miles to the Medellin Airfield where a beat-up, tattered Air Colombia Rotodyne was waiting for them. It was the regular flight from one of the other small towns; it had arrived on schedule and would depart the same way having been "held up by engine trouble." Of course the real Air Colombia flight had been held at the previous destination and word hadn't got through. It would simply be a matter of driving to the airfield, up the tail ramps and into the aircraft and then the whole team would be out. Of course, their Rotodyne was tattered and damaged from the outside only. Inside, it was in excellent condition and its Kuznetsov turboprops gave it almost three times the power of the Darts on the real airliner.

And it really was just that easy. The SEAL team made their rendezvous with their transport and boarded it, running their little mules into the cargo hold. The Rotodyne took off just before dawn and headed for Cali. Until, that is, it was over the horizon; then it rapidly changed course and made for the sea. The deception wasn't even suspected until the real Rotodyne landed at Medellin two hours later, the pilot telling a strange story of engines that had suddenly stopped working and telephones that hadn't had a dialing tone.

Almost the same time, the "guards" at the Villa Blanco started waking up and found that their leader and his first lieutenant had mysteriously vanished in the night. That lead to much doubt and anxiety and a number of baseless accusations. Of course it was the feared SEALs who had done it, but they must have had help from inside, surely? In the end, the Second Lieutenant took over and became the new boss of the gang, one who would always have the cloud of suspicion hanging over him. Just why had he chosen that night to be away from the Villa? It was indeed a baseless and unjustifiable slur on his character, but fairness was never part of the human condition.

Far offshore, a U.S. Navy LPD was waiting. The Rotodyne swung in to land just as the drug lord woke up. He looked around in fury at the grinning SEALs who surrounded him.

"You will all pay for this. My men will kill you all." The threats were bombastic; their effect ruined by the tremor in his voice. The SEALs looked at each other and grinned even more broadly. After years of doing this sort of thing, they'd heard it all before. A couple of them chuckled a little too loudly.

"You laugh at me? You laugh at my men? He who laughs at the skills of my men will find there is little to laugh about!"

Captain Thomas thought about that one for a second, then nodded. "Quite." Then he turned to his team. "Well, that about wraps it up guys. I'll miss you all but I'm getting too old for this sort of thing. The powers that be have insisted I man a desk from now on. Good luck, people, and may your Gods go with you."

Thomas stepped off the rear ramp of the Rotodyne, his last mission as a SEAL operator successfully completed. It was time to hand over to a new generation and it was time he spent some time with his family. His eldest boy was two years away from being old enough to join up and he'd made his choice very clear already. Jeff Junior wanted to be a SEAL just like his old man. It was good to establish a dynasty. A very good feeling indeed.

F11F-3 Tiger Deva-One*, 14,000 feet over the Indian Ocean.*

"Deva-One, enemy contacts closing on you fast. Altitude plus angels six, bearing two-seven-five."

Lieutenant Sonlai Mart craned his head around. The warning from the AEW bird was that the enemy aircraft were six thousand feet above him and on relative 275. Then, he squinted as he realized that meant they were coming straight out of the sun. Now was not the time to let the situation develop. "All Deva aircraft, max throttle. We have bandits in the woods." Then he swung his nose up in an arcing turn, hoping to force the enemy fighters, they had to be fighters, into leaving the protective glare of the sun. His wing man followed him; the other pair of fighters turned a split second later.

"Deva-One! Break! Break-break-break! They're closing fast!" The controller's voice in the AEW bird was panicking. "They're sitting right on top of you!"

Mart stared into the glare of the sun and saw them. Three black spots, danced in the brilliant light, scything down towards his formation. Three against four, but the Chipanese aircraft had the advantage of position and speed.

"All Deva aircraft. Buster. Say again Buster."

He rammed the throttles forward to full emergency power, feeling the thump in his back as the afterburner cut in. Behind him, the three black dots had suddenly sprouted long white trails that arched down towards the four Tigers. Missiles, that left no doubt about it even if there never really had been any. These were enemy fighters. How they'd suddenly appeared this far out from any known enemy base was a mystery that would have to be explained later. Even as Mart realized that something important had changed, he was racking his fighter around in the tightest turn that the web of energy, centrifugal force and gravity would allow. At the same time, he punched the decoy button, sending his own series of white trails out. These were tipped with the brilliant white glare of the infra-red deception flares.

His wingman and the other pair of fighters were doing the same. The violent maneuver and the flares worked twice but there were three missiles inbound and Mart's wingman was unlucky. The Chipanese missile exploded just under the rear of his fuselage, causing the whole tail section to fragment in an orange blossom. A split second later, there was another, much smaller explosion forward as the Tiger pilot ejected. Mart pulled up in a sharp wingover, knowing that without his wingman he was alone and vulnerable.

As his Tiger arced upwards, he saw the three light gray Chipanese fighters swarming over his second section, their dark gray rising sun insignia standing out in the brilliant glare of the sun. The lead F11F was already extending, a Chipanese fighter snapping in on his tail. Mart recognized it as a Fuzzy, the American code-name for the Chipanese Ohtori seaplane fighter. Then everything went crazy. The fighter, fired a pair of missiles from its overwing racks while the Tiger's wingman carved in behind him and fired a pair of Sidewinders. For a brief second the sky seemed full of infra-red homing missiles. Then both the Tiger and the Fuzzy vanished in the rolling-ball explosions of missile warheads and aircraft fuel tanks.

Mart completed his wingover, beneath him one of the two remaining Fuzzys was sweeping in on the Number Two section wingman, the 30mm cannon already thudding its shells out towards the dark gray and white Tiger. Mart swept down. His own Sidewinders wouldn't acquire, the angle and the aspect were both wrong, but his own 20mm cannon were crackling, the tracers streaming towards the Fuzzy. It broke away, black smoke streaming from its fuselage. Mart swept past and then climbed away again. By the time he made another wingover, both Chipanese fighters had vanished and all that seemed to be left in the sky were the two surviving Tigers.

“Deva-one, I’m in trouble here.” Deva-Four’s voice was shaky. “He got solid hits with his cannons. I have lights and the engine is running rough.”

“Deva-four, hold one.” Mart orbited under Deva-Four. He’d been hit right enough; the fuselage had gaping areas were the skin had been blown off. One of the flaps was hanging loose and the wing structure didn’t look too healthy. “You’ve taken two hits, one’s blown skin off your aft fuselage, your port wing is chewed up. We’ll abort and head back for the carrier.”

The two Tigers limped away, heading for the safe haven of the aircraft carrier to the south. As they did, their course was very carefully noted by the two surviving Fuzzys.

Sugu Bay, Southern Coast of Hainan Island

“It was the AEW aircraft. They saw us coming and warned the Tiger pilots.” It was a statement of fact, one that nobody disagreed with. The twelve pilots were gathered around a table in their new briefing room, one that still smelt of freshly-sawed timber and new paper. The table was the scene of the re-enactment of the ambush. Models of the Ohtoris and Tigers were being moved as each pilot remembered what he had done and how. One of the pilots still smelled slightly of seawater, he’d ejected from his stricken fighter and been picked up by a flying boat.

The same aircraft had also picked up a shot-down Indian pilot who was presently sitting comfortably, if somewhat damply, in an improvised brig. Orders from Naval Headquarters in Tokyo were very strict; all prisoners to be treated with respect and under no circumstances are they to be handed over to the Army. Nobody was naive enough to believe those orders had anything to do with the Hague Conventions. Controlling and confining this conflict so it could be prosecuted to conclusion meant the Navy had to present itself as being ‘the good guys’ to the world at large.

“Our tactics don’t work. Ito losing his Ohtori proved that.” One of the pilots spoke reflectively almost absently. Ito started to make an angry retort, but Toda stilled him by lifting his hand.

"Ito-san, this was your first combat. Mine also and the same for everybody else here. We all made mistakes. We could all have done much better and there is no shame in admitting that. There is shame in refusing to learn from our mistakes. There is even more shame in not transmitting those lessons to others so they will not repeat our mistakes. And Haba-san is quite right. Our tactics, such as they are, do not work.

"Look what happened this morning. We went in as three independent aircraft, each selecting his own target. Of course, we went for the flight leaders, that was right and proper. But as we went for them, their wingmen protected them. Not well enough but they did. As you went for the leader, his wingman snapped in behind you and shot you down. Too late to save his leader, yes; but he still got you because you were on your own and there was nobody to protect your tail. So our tactics are wrong." Toda lapsed into silence and stared at the models on the table.

One of the other pilots cleared his throat. "We fly as sections of three. Suppose we were to assign the junior pilot in each three-plane section as the guard and the two most senior pilots as the attackers? The two most senior pilots engage the enemy while the guard picks off any Indian wingmen who try to interfere? Will this work?"

There was a mixed mumble from around the table. The junior pilots were immediately being very negative, they saw themselves being relegated to the sidelines while those who were already more senior would have all the chances to gain glory. The older pilots were more divided. The idea of fighting as a unit of three aircraft was new to them, it ran against their inculcated code of single combat. Yet, the evidence in front of them was clear. The leader/wingman concept did work. Could it be the code they were all trained to accept without thinking was wrong?

Toda stretched his back and looked at another chart on the wall, one that had a series of overlays. One marked the range of the F11Fs based on the Indian carrier. That was a limitation; the F11F was notoriously short-ranged. Another was the radar horizons from various Japanese-held land masses. A third showed SIGINT and

ELINT data; yet a fourth was the flight path of radar coverage from various over-sea flights including this morning's sweep.

All put together, they defined the area in which the Indian carrier had to be operating. There was a final piece of data, a brilliant red line, the course for home taken by the two surviving Tigers. That lead right through the "possible" area for the carrier. It wasn't definitive, a long way from it, but it was a start in narrowing down the carrier's location and operating pattern.

"We'll try it." His voice cut through the discussion. "First flight, you will reorganize as suggested, two most senior pilots designated as attackers, the most junior as the guard to protect them. Second flight will remain as it is. When third and fourth flights arrive later today, we will do the same with them, third reorganize, fourth stays as it is. We will compare the two systems and see which works best."

He stopped abruptly as an NCO knocked on the door and entered. "Lieutenant Commander, Sir, the Base Commander wants to see you in his office immediately."

A few minutes later, Toda knocked on the door of the prefabricated building that was used as the base Commander's office and entered. The Commander was bolt-upright behind his desk, facing two men in military uniform that was devoid of any rank or unit insignia. Neither of the men were military. They lacked the bearing that was hammered into military personnel. That and their uniforms identified them as clearly as any unit insignia would have done. They were Kempeitai. The temperature in the room appeared to be chilled but despite that, Toda started to sweat.

The younger of the two Kempeitai men turned to his superior. "He's here, Sir."

"I suppose he wishes he wasn't. He doesn't look like a fool or a traitor, does he?"

"No, he doesn't. But then if they all did, we would have to find another line of work."

“True.” The older Kempeitai man looked at Toda quizzically. “Lieutenant Commander Endo, I regret to inform you that your commanding officer, Commander Matsuda Ken, has been arrested and charged with crimes against the Emperor and the Imperial Japanese Armed Forces.”

“Involved in a racket; stealing fuel from the Navy and selling it on the black market.” The younger Kempeitai man joined his senior in staring at Toda. “You know, Sir, I bet you he thought he could get away with it.”

“He might well have done, of course. We were lucky the case broke open when it did. Look at this one, trying to appear confused and innocent.”

“He isn’t very good at it, is he?”

“I was expecting him to do better. Still, he’s very young. Not much experience.”

“That is true, of course. If he had been an experienced man, he would have reported the irregularities he found to us instead of getting involved himself.”

“Running around, stuffing a gun in the mouth of a supply depot manager. Still, I suppose if he hadn’t done that, the manager wouldn’t have panicked the way he did.”

“And then he wouldn’t have acted so foolishly and given us the break we needed to wrap up the black market racket. Also, of course, he wouldn’t have got his fuel back.” The two Kempeitai men seemed quite oblivious to the presence of the two naval officers who were both standing rigidly to attention.

“That is true, of course, I suppose we should note that Toda didn’t use the situation to benefit himself. He acted to get the fuel needed to train his unit. I suppose that counts for something. He didn't take bribes the way his commander did.”

"Which is why Matsuda has now been reassigned to a position assisting Unit 731 with their research."

"And Toda's unit did well this morning. Two kills for one loss, acceptable for a unit that has never been in action before."

"Marginally acceptable, I suppose."

"More than marginal for a unit that had so much training to catch up on." The older Kempeitai man addressed the bewildered and apprehensive Toda directly. "You are to receive a temporary promotion to Commander. This is temporary you understand. You are now the commander of the Tainan Kokutai pending the appointment of a new commanding officer with adequate seniority. This section based here is now the First Section of the Tainan, not the Second. What was the First Section, and is now the Second, will remain in Japan and act as a training base, feeding you replacement pilots and aircraft as you need them."

The man smiled coldly and without humor. "The duty of the Kempeitai is to punish wrong thoughts and actions. Sometimes we are able to reward the right ones. Commander Toda, you have gained some influential friends with your actions. Also, some powerful enemies. From today, you may count us amongst those friends."

The two men left without any of the courtesies a Japanese would normally regard as essential. Toda glanced out the window and saw them walking away, exhibiting a complete disregard for the surroundings and people. Then, both Toda and the Base Commander looked at each other and exhaled.

"I think we're still alive." The Base Commander's voice was tentative and unsure of himself.

"I think so too. I shall come to a more positive conclusion in a few minutes." Toda felt blood returning to his extremities. It was time to return to normality, Toda felt as if he'd just left the cinema after watching a particularly realistic horror movie. "How goes our base construction?"

"Ahead of schedule, and with those two around, heaven be praised for that. Minor problems, two Seiku-Kais had to abort with engine trouble. One was carrying supplies, the other our water distillation and purification plant. Neither are critical; the SNLF have sent recon troops inland to search for fresh water supplies. How are your fighters?"

"One down, one's damaged and beached." The shot-up Ohtori had started to sink when it had landed so the pilot had popped the flotation bags built into the wings and the aircraft had been towed ashore. It would remain there until the *Nisshin* turned up and was able to repair her. Time, Toda thought, for his first act as Kokutai Commander. "Can your communications get me though to Kagoshima? I need to have two replacement aircraft ferried down immediately.

Oval Office, The White House, Washington D.C.

"The National Security Advisor, the Chief of the Joint Staff and the Director of Central Intelligence are here to see you Sir."

"Send them right in." It had been less than ten minutes since The Seer had called requesting an urgent meeting with the President. Nixon could guess what was coming, he'd been having nightmares all weekend about it. Sure enough, it was The Seer who started speaking as soon as the meeting was convened.

"Sir, over the weekend one of our SEAL teams picked up the subject we discussed in Colombia. He was retrieved safely to this country and he has revealed some additional information that requires immediate action. He has confirmed the information we received concerning the fact that his organization was paid with several tons of Afghan heroin for some services to be rendered. Those services have now been identified. Three groups, each of twelve Caliphate agents have been sent to South America. The Medellin Cartel was instructed to collect them from their entry point, transport them to the Mexican-American border and then smuggle them over. Having got them over, they were to be infiltrated into vulnerable border towns: San Diego, Nogales and El Paso.

“The subject believed that the people in question were saboteurs or simple spies. We believe that he was mislead on this point and that all 36 men have been infected with blackpox. We have confirmation for that, circumstantial but none the less convincing. One of the terms of the contract is that the persons being smuggled over the border must be delivered to their destination within ten days of being collected from their arrival point. This is, Sir, the incubation period for blackpox. Assuming they were infected just before arrival, they would have three or four days when the disease is at its most contagious, but before the symptoms became apparent, to spread infection as widely as possible. Thirty six Typhoid Marys loose in American cities.

“The people in question arrived in South America, we have the route details, four days ago. In other words, we have less than a week to find those people and kill or isolate them. And we have to do that without exposing our own people to the virus.”

Nixon frowned. “Seer, something doesn’t add up here. If these people are being brought North and they’re already infected with blackpox, won’t they infect the coyotes bringing them up?”

“That is correct Sir. They will. That’s probably one reason why they didn't give the full story. Those 36 persons will infect the Cartel people they contact. It’s a typical Caliphate double-cross. They’re hoping to start a major epidemic down south as well, and we must accept that they will probably succeed in doing just that. They probably hope that the entire Cartel will be wiped out by blackpox and that will cover their tracks. Once we explained the real situation to the subject, he opened up and told us everything he knew. Give the man some credit; he really does appear to care about the people who work for him.”

CJS thought for a second. “We have to seal the border and that means we’re going to have to operate down south ourselves. We need to get ground recon teams into Mexico and get a tight air surveillance network set up.”

“Can’t we stop them at the border? Fences, minefields, that sort of thing?” Nixon’s voice was steady but the imminence of the threat had shaken him. “Just how bad is this attack? Worst case.”

CJS shook his head. “A single line of defense like that won’t hack it Sir. They never do. Fences and minefields are only of use if they’re kept under observation and covered by fire. Even then, they’re a single line and that can always be evaded or penetrated. Even if we did go that way, we just don't have the manpower to guard that border to the required standard. Even if we mobilized to Second World War standards, we don’t.

“We must rely on a defense in depth. Keep a deep swathe of the border region under surveillance and use mobile recon teams to ambush and detain illegal traffic. A lot of that we can do with what we’ve got. We can use SAC strategic recon training missions for a lot of the surveillance. SOCOM’s AC-133s can do a lot more. We can use air-transportable units and Marine Force Recon elements for the ambush role. We’ll be driving a coach and horses through Mexican sovereignty, but that can’t be helped.”

“That’s all very good but it won’t plug the weakest point on the whole frontier.” The Seer’s voice was thoughtful, remote even. “El Paso. The city’s right on the border; effectively it forms a single urban unit with the Mexican city, Ciudad Juarez, the other side. The border itself is crazy there. It runs down streets, through houses. There’s a factory there than has a wedge shaped triangle of its floor space in Mexico and the rest of its machinery in the US of A. Don’t ask me how we’ll secure that border. The only chance we have is to find and stop the Coyotes before they get to the city.

“As to how bad it is, given that we’ll be dealing with first generation infectees and the remarkable mortality of blackpox, AMRIID estimate that we could be looking at a million dead by the time the plague burns itself out.”

“A million!” Nixon was horrified. “That’s almost as many as we lost in Russia.”

"There are some good bits of news. Thanks to the SEALS we're one step ahead of the game; we know what to look for and where. Thanks to the French, we have samples of the infective agent and are well on the way to developing a vaccine. I hate to have to say it but we owe the French for this one."

"I have no doubt they'll trade on that to the max." Nixon's voice was suspicious and resentful.

"No doubt, they wouldn't be the French if they didn't." The Seer checked his pad. As usual Lillith had provided a quick digest of the news that morning. "By the way, three more of their Communales have been hit and their Air Force hit every Caliphate air base in range of Algeria this morning. Did a good job too, took down most of the aircraft there. They lost nine Super-Mysteres and three Mirage VFs to anti-aircraft fire. In addition, they're moving more fighters in to provide air cover. Problem for them is that they're stripping the Metropolitan French Air Force to do it. That leaves the south of France wide open."

"We can pay off then. Send some of our fighters to cover the area. NORAD can detach a couple of squadrons."

CJS shook his head. "The French won't have it. They don't like us and don't want us there. Anyway, our fighters are designed to operate within a systematic air defense network. The French have one but its incompatible with our systems. Our fighters won't do them any good. SAC has a squadron of F-108s and an RB-58C detachment at Aviano in Italy. They could run interference but that's it."

DCI chipped in while CJS was thinking. "The Brits are in tight with the French. We could hit up a deal with them. Their systems are compatible with the French defense net, they could shift some of their interceptors down to cover Southern France. We could offer to cover the costs involved, plus a reasonable percentage of course. The French wouldn't have to know 'officially' that we were bankrolling the deployment."

“Talk to the Brits. Sound them out on it. If they’re willing, do it.” Nixon thought again. “That leaves one question. If the attack on us materializes, if the information we’ve been given proves correct, if we link the Caliphate to the attack, how do we reply?”

It was a rhetorical question and everybody in the room knew it. All three visitors said the same thing, almost as a rehearsed chorus. “They burn.”

CHAPTER EIGHT
HARASSING

Conference Room, Naval Base Sugu Bay, Southern Coast of Hainan Island

Compared with the elaborate facilities of the Imperial Navy Headquarters in Tokyo, this "conference room" was a joke. A roughly-constructed timber building surrounded by earth berms to protect it against air attack, it was barely more sophisticated than a peasant's hut. The conference table was crudely-sanded fresh-cut timber resting on trestles and the seats were packing cases. The displays on the walls were paper maps stuck with pins and crayoned markings, not the sophisticated electronic displays boasted by Tokyo. The whole facility looked as if it had been thrown together using whatever had been left over from more essential projects and assembled by whoever it was who had nothing better to do. It looked that way because that's what it was and there was nowhere else Admiral Koga would rather have been.

"And what is the score so far, Toda-San?"

"As of noon today, we count eleven Tigers and two Skyhawks shot down. Of course we do not know how many of their aircraft crashed while landing; some went back to their base badly damaged. The battle this morning was particularly interesting, we think it was an armed reconnaissance mission looking for this base.

Four bombed-up Skyhawks escorted by four Tigers. That's where we got the two Skyhawks and three Tigers. If our count is correct, we have shot down almost a third of the carrier's fighter strength already."

"And it has cost us?"

"So far, Sir, it has cost us thirteen Ohtoris, including three that sank after landing. That's the problem with seaplane fighters, Sir, one that nobody thought of. A badly-damaged landplane can touch down on a runway and be repaired but a damaged seaplane sinks. In addition, we have four more aircraft on *Nisshin* being repaired." The *Nisshin* had arrived last night and her base facilities had been badly needed.

"So you have lost half your unit in exchange for a third of the enemy?" Koga's voice was not pleased.

"Not really Sir. We have lost only five pilots. The rest were rescued by our flying boats. Sir, the Americans were right all along. It's critical we save the pilots who have been shot down."

Koga's eyebrow lifted disbelievingly. *If a pilot got shot down, he was what the Americans so charmingly called a loser and wasn't worth saving. In fact, a real warrior would choose to go down with his aircraft rather than eject and put up with the shame of being rescued.*

"Sir, I know its against everything we've been taught, but it's the best way. We've seen it often here. All the aircraft that have been lost or had to abort from damage were pilots on their first or second missions. Get them through their first few battles and their loss rate drops greatly while their kill rate climbs. If we rescue a pilot shot down on his first or second mission, he lives long enough to start scoring on his later missions."

Koga snorted. *It wasn't the Japanese way but if it worked, perhaps it should be?* "What else have you changed Commander Toda?"

"The new system we have Sir, the group out here flying missions while the other half stays in Japan and trains replacements, it's good. That's why we've lost half our original number of aircraft yet can still have twenty ready for missions. I believe we should even start rotating pilots. We should get some of the most experienced back to Japan to teach what they've learned out here while the new recruits can get some experience under their belts.

"And, Sir, we have much to teach, so much of our doctrine just didn't work. We lost aircraft unnecessarily because of that. Our old-style, three-plane formations just didn't work. We've re-organized as three sections of four with each section having two two-Ohtori elements. We tried an intermediate step but it wasn't as effective. Two two-plane sections per flight, with each section having a shooter and a wingman to guard his tail. That's the way to do it. I've ordered the group back home to train all the new pilots to fly that way. Sir, the combat out here is the first real air war we've fought since the late 1930s, everything is different now."

Koga stared at the reports again. "You think we will win out here?"

"Sir, Yes Sir! We can replace our losses, the Indian carrier cannot. We started off, 24 against an estimated 36, now its 24 against 25. If they've lost planes trying to land on the carrier, we may already have numerical superiority. Soon, the Shukas can resume their raids and we can drive the enemy out of the Pescadores."

"The Indians are the opposition Toda-san." Koga's voice was distant. "The army is the enemy."

"Sir. And there is something else. We've been plotting opposition flights back by radar and observation. Every time there's an engagement. If I may draw your attention to this map, Sir. The pink area is where the opposition carrier might be sailing and the thick red lines are where the opposition aircraft have been flying. Sir, those lines concentrate on a small area, out here." Toda tapped the map. It wasn't really a small area but it was an improvement over the huge area shaded pink. "If we can get submarines into this area, we may well score. I originally thought that we couldn't hurt the carrier, just run it out of aircraft. But if we can pin it down, the submarines might hurt it."

The Submarine Commander nodded once, very sharply. "Our outspoken young pilot is right. We have our six submarines down here and I can order two more in. With eight submarines in that area, hunting down that carrier is possible."

Koga still sounded doubtful. "The Germans never had much success against the American carriers with their submarines."

"They sank *Enterprise,* Sir, and hurt *Boxer* and *Kearsarge*. But the Americans had the whole of the Atlantic to play in. They stayed far out to sea, selected a target and ran in at night, Then they stayed for a day or two only and were away again before submarines could catch up. Also, they were surrounded by destroyers and there were specialized ASW groups to intercept any submarines that did try to interfere. And look at where the American carriers were hit. *Enterprise* leaving New York. *Boxer* and *Kearsarge* off the Churchill naval base. Where their area to maneuver was limited and their screens were weak. Now, it's the Indian carrier that has a weak screen and is operating from a restricted area. She's doing the same maneuvers that gave the German submarines shots at American carriers. We can get her, Admiral, thanks to our young friend, we have a chance." The Submarine Commander settled back, his little mustache bristling at the thought of one of his submarines getting a carrier.

"And how is the surface squadron?"

Admiral Nashima tore his eyes from the map. "One rocket cruiser, one light cruiser, two Sawari missile destroyers, two Type B and two Type C destroyers. We are still integrating the reinforcements with the survivors of the previous squadron." Nashima's skin crawled slightly at the thought of that defeat. Admiral Kurita had been relieved of his command and had retired. It wasn't enough; not for turning back just as the battle had been won. "We can support an invasion but that's all. If we fight another division of the Flying Squadron, if it fights the way Admiral Dahm fought, we will lose."

“So, we are agreed? We carry on the campaign of air attrition against the Indian carrier and try to refine its position so a submarine can have a shot at it. We will prepare to land a Special Naval Landing Force on the Southern Pescadores, screened by the South China Sea Squadron but not start that operation until the carrier has been left ineffective, we have achieved air superiority and the Indian bases have been heavily bombed. I will also advise you that diplomatic moves have started in order to persuade the Indians to leave our Islands before the recovery invasion is launched. If you, Fighters, and you, Submarines, score greater success, those diplomatic moves stand a much greater chance of becoming reality. We will meet again in a week. Here, of course”

Koga looked around. It felt good to be in an operational headquarters, surrounded by the men doing the fighting. Even if the inevitable result was the final eclipse of the surface fleet he had grown up in.

Desert, South of Nogales, Mexico.

The truck was a six-wheeled AEC, the British built vehicle that was almost a standard in South America. The American trucks were great on good roads, but the British-built AECs had it all over them when the roads were as bad and neglected as this one. The truck had been on the road for three days now, stopping only to refuel from the drums of diesel lashed to the back and to change drivers. There were three crew in the cab which made it crowded but the other alternative was to drive twelve-hour shifts.

Perhaps the crowded cab was why the three men there didn’t feel so well. They were feverish, headachy and starting to itch. The latter was probably the lack of washing water of course. The twelve strangers in the back of the truck looked worse though; they seemed to be really ill. Probably the heat disagreed with them, but wasn’t where they came from hot? Perhaps it was the strangeness. The drivers had heard that people from the Caliphate didn’t travel much. These one’s seemed to like it though; they’d kept wanting to get out and meet the people in the local villages and had been really upset when they hadn’t been allowed to.

"Bridge out ahead." The youngest of the three called out the warning. The road led onto a rickety bridge, part stone, part wood; the ramp blocked by black-and-yellow striped warning signs. Unsafe Bridge it said, Closed. The alternative was more than thirty kilometers back and it lead through a major crossing checkpoint, one they were under strict orders to avoid. The bridge looked solid enough. Perhaps some busybody trying to justify their existence?

"We'll go through, take it carefully. If the bridge is bad, the arroyo doesn't look too rough." The truck started up again and edged towards the signs; it's diesel engine seemingly silenced by the desert around them. That's what made the machine gun fire so shocking. The sound of ripping paper or a chain running over rocks. A frantic hammering that tore up the desert silence and sprayed the road surface into a dust cloud. Almost by instinct, the truck driver floored the throttle, attempting to run through the burst of gunfire that was intended to stop them. It was the worst and last mistake he'd ever make. The next burst of gunfire, 90 rounds in less than three seconds, ripped into the truck cab. It didn't just kill all three men there, the high-velocity .276 bullets left them shattered and unrecognizable.

High on the hill overlooking the road, the Marine Force Recon team watched the truck with its shattered cab swerve out of control and plow off the road, turning over as it did so. There was silence for a few seconds, broken only by the creaking and grinding sound of crunched metal and settling dust. Then the back of the truck seemed to open. Some figures staggered out, three, four, perhaps five? The dust made it hard to tell. According to the briefing, there should be twelve in there.

"Stay where you are. Do not attempt to move. If you attempt to run away you will be killed." The voice over the loudhailer was a Marine, the language was Arabic. The figures by the truck froze for a few seconds and then one of them started to run. He didn't get far, the M-81 machine gun roared a quick burst and the figure was swallowed up in his own private dust cloud. When it cleared, the figure was on the ground, shredded by the burst. The sight seemed to stimulate the others, they started to run, spreading out from the wrecked truck.

"Damn." First Sergeant Esteban Tomas cursed and took careful aim. There was a stutter of shots, neither a volley nor a roar of automatic fire, just the careful patter from men taking their time to make sure their shots struck home. The range was long, two hundred yards or more, but the runners went down. Tomas nodded with satisfaction, there was no substitute for a proper rifle and a proper rifle round. It had taken time to convince people that the .27-59 was a real rifle cartridge but it had made it eventually.

The .27-59 was based on the .30-54, a more compact version of the old .30-06 and it had been bottlenecked to take the bullet designed for the .276 Pederson cartridge. The result was a very high velocity rifle round that tumbled and broke up in its victims. The military rifle world was divided between those who had gone to the intermediate-power rounds like the Russian 7.62x39 or the Anglo-Australian 7x43mm and those who had stuck with full-power rifle cartridges. Neither would admit the other knew what it was doing. The U.S. was in the full-power round group and that was just fine by Tomas.

"Scoopnet, this is Angler. We have intercepted the fish school at the fishing ground. They tried to make a break for it and they ain't standing no more. Catch is gutted, repeat, catch is gutted."

"Acknowledged Angler. What is your range from the fish school?"

"Two hundred yards, maybe a touch more."

"Good. Angler under no circumstances approach the school. Say again under no circumstances approach the fish school. Please acknowledge long form."

Tomas raised his eyebrows. He hadn't had to do that since boot camp. "Scoopnet, this is Angler. I acknowledge receiving the order not to approach the fish school. I understand this order and will comply. Over."

"Thank you Angler. You have no idea how important that is. We will be with you in five minutes. Out."

It took a little longer than five minutes before the weird whistling noise of the Rotodyne could be heard. It was one of the later versions, a Kaman-built Samaritan; a flying ambulance complete with a white paint job, green stripe down its fuselage and red crosses on the rear and wings. High, very high overhead, a four engined aircraft was starting to orbit the scene; an AC-133 Slayer known to the people on the ground as "Scoopnet." Although Tomas didn't know it, the aircraft was *Buffy*, an old friend of his.

The Samaritan transitioned from horizontal flight to vertical. Its two jets changed from propulsion units to gas generators for the tip jets built into the Rotodyne's rotor. As it did, the strange whistling picked up in volume and started to drown out the jets. A lot of people complained about the noise of the Rotodynes, but noise level measurements always showed that they generated less noise in absolute terms than a commuter train. It was the pitch of the noise that annoyed people and then only those who never used the intercity passenger service they offered. For everybody else, an aircraft that travelled with the speed of a jet airliner yet flew from the top floor of a multi-story parking lot was worth a little noise.

On the ground, the Samaritan's tail ramp dropped and figures got out, figures in white suits that looked for all the world like spacemen. Tomas had the insane thought that if anybody else was watching, they'd assume the world was being invaded. The figures went from body to body, collecting them and putting them in bright orange body bags. Through his binoculars, Tomas could see the glaring yellow word **BIOHAZARD** and the symbols that went with it. Before each bag was carried back to the Samaritan, it was thoroughly sprayed with something.

By the time all the bodies had been collected, the men in the isolation suits were obviously tiring, yet they too were thoroughly sprayed before being allowed back into the Samaritan. Then, more figures climbed out and started spraying the ground, coating it with a gushing stream of liquid. Even from their hilltop, the marines could smell the gasoline. Finally, its work done, the Rotodyne took off and Tomas couldn't resist it any longer.

"Scoopnet, what the devil is going on?"

"Devil is just about right Angler. We're talking a serious biohazard here. Trawler is going straight back to an isolation unit and won't be out for weeks. Now, get your heads down, its barbecue time."

As Scoopnet orbited overhead, a section of four jet fighters screamed low over the bridge. Almost without thinking about it, Tomas recognized them; F-110E Specters. He saw the black canisters wobbling clear from their fuselage and wing hardpoints, watched them arching down to saturate the area of the crashed truck with napalm. He only just managed to cover his face in time, for the heat waves off the orange-black fireballs was ferocious and raised blisters on the unprotected skin of his hands. *Air-dropped napalm and ground-sprayed gasoline, talk about a belt and braces approach to the problem. Just what sort of biohazard was it that needed such treatment?* For a brief second, he almost called Scoopnet and asked, then decided that the question would make him look foolish at best. Even so, he had to bite his tongue when the radio bleeped again.

"Angler, this is Scoopnet. Proceed to the village ten klicks south of your position. Observe but do not contact. Repeat do not contact, evade all local inhabitants. Observe and report any kind of sickness in that village."

"Acknowledged Scoopnet, observe and evade, do not contact but report all signs of sickness. Out." Tomas looked around at his men who were watching the dying inferno where the truck had once been. "Get ready to move out people, we have a village to watch."

As the Marine unit moved out, Tomas wondered what would happen if the village he was assigned to watch did start to develop an outbreak of serious sickness. Looking back at the blackened circle of ground and the word "biohazard" still echoing in his mind, he had an unpleasant theory about that which he intended to keep to himself.

Seer's Office, National Security Council Building, Washington D.C.

Lillith punched the telephone number for the White House and waited while the automated system connected her. "Hello,

Nammie? Lillith. Word from the Boss for your boss. One down, two to go.

Flight Deck, INS Viraat*, South China Sea*

By Indian Navy standards, Lieutenant Sonlai Mart supposed this was 'the big one.' By American standards he knew it was the 'so-tiny-it-needs-a-powerful-microscope-to-see-it one,' but the Indian Navy wasn't SAC and this was the biggest air strike they had ever launched. Sixteen Tigers were lined up on the deck, each with a full load of 20mm ammunition and four Sidewinders under their wings. Behind them were the Skyhawks, sixteen of them, each hauling seven 1,000 pound bombs. Ever since the Chimp Fuzzies had arrived, the Indian Navy had been searching for their base. Now, by a combination of observation and electronic intelligence, they had found it. A place called Sugu Bay on the southern coast of Hainan Island.

The strike was leaving *Viraat* with the bare minimum for her own defense. She'd started with 36 Tigers but six had been shot down and two more had crashed on landing. This strike just left her with twelve for combat air patrol and six Skyhawks for strike. It should have been eight but the Fuzzies had got two of them. Still, the Chimp Navy wasn't going anywhere and if they tried, the cruiser *Punjab* was in the screen and still had her missiles. After what one of *Mysore's* Sagarikas had done to that Chimp cruiser, they wouldn't be taking her lightly.

Mart shifted angrily in his seat. All the world was saying that the Indian Navy had lost that battle but they hadn't; they'd stopped the Chimp squadron cold and sent it running for home with its tail between its legs. The problem was, everybody had seen the crippled Indian ships being towed in, their dead lined on the decks ready for their funeral rites. Nobody had seen the Chimp cripples or their cruisers and destroyers now on the bottom of the South China Sea.

The catapult crew were waving him forward so Mart edged his Tiger up to the catapult and heard the scraping sounds underneath as the wire bridle was attached. The Tiger was an old aircraft and still needed the bridles, Mart had heard the new Hindustan Hornet would have the catapult gear built into its nosewheel. If the Navy ever saw them; the Hornet was still nothing more than lines on paper at the moment. Much like India's new carriers, they too, were just lines on paper.

It was a low-level ride out, it had to be. One reason was to avoid enemy radar as long as possible, to give the enemy fighters based at Sugu Bay as little time as possible to react. They had two powerful radars there at least. Those gave them good area coverage, but it was those radars that had given the final clue to the base location. The other reason was combat experience. The Fuzzy was faster than the Tiger; it accelerated better, could climb faster and it could turn tighter, at first anyway. Only, its big delta wings bled energy off fast in a turning match at low altitude where the drag from the thicker air was more of a factor. So, low down, the Tiger would have the advantage as the fight continued and the Fuzzys would be wallowing as their energy bled off and wasn't regenerated. This fight would be a long one; not the hit-and-run skirmishes of the last few days. The Tigers had to keep the Fuzzys away from the Skyhawks for as long as they could. The Fuzzies would know the strike was aimed at their base and they had to stop it if they were to have a home to return to. Yes, it would be a long fight today.

Mart's thoughts were interrupted by a sudden squawk from his radar warning receiver. It was a new addition; a British set called Sky Guardian mounted in the tail. To many of the pilots, it had been another unnecessary instrument to watch but this time it was worth its keep. The display was simple. A single light indicated an I-band radar and a bar pointing towards the forward left octant. There was nothing out there though. A submarine? Submarines often had I-band air search radars. The bar turned into a blip on the outer edge of the display. That didn't mean it was a long way away, it meant that it wasn't a threat. If it had been closer in, it would have been a search radar that was tracking his aircraft. Closer still and it would indicate a fire control radar tracking him. A dot close to the center would have been a radar homing missile locked in on his aircraft. This was just a search radar, scanning routinely; as if that couldn't be dangerous enough.

"Deva-One, we have enemy aircraft climbing to meet you, range 75 nautical dead ahead. Enemy count estimated twenty bandits. Aircraft climbing fast, be aware, the Fuzzies are coming up."

"All aircraft buster. We have friends. Ashra, Kali and Deva sections follow me. Lashmi section stay with the friends to stop leakers."

Mart was grim. With 20 bandits coming up, the escorting fighters would be badly outnumbered. If the worst came to the worst, some of the Skyhawks could jettison their bombs and help protect the rest. Of course, if they did that, they'd effectively be lost as bombers although any that survived could still do strafing runs. He'd had to split his fighters though. If he'd taken them all out to intercept the Fuzzies, they'd just have blasted straight past him and the bombers would have been unprotected.

Mart activated his own radar and was rewarded instantly with the appearance of the enemy formation ahead of him. The low flight had done part of its work, the Fuzzies had been late taking off and they were approaching head on, a slight altitude advantage but not much. If it hadn't been for that chance radar contact, the Indian formation would have been a lot closer and the advantage would have been with them.

Mart took his eyes off the scope and scanned the sky where the enemy had to be. Those who thought a pilot's white silk scarf was an affection had never tried this. A few minutes frantically twisting around looking for the enemy aircraft would soon leave his neck raw and bleeding but for the smooth slipperiness of that silk. There, far ahead and a little above him, he saw a flash of light, *sun reflecting of a cockpit perhaps? Whatever it was, there they were.*

"Bandits, 11 o'clock, angels estimated plus one. Coming in fast."

Mart pushed his Tiger over into a shallow dive. It was counter-intuitive. The rational thing to do was to try and climb to meet the incoming Fuzzies, but they already had the height advantage. By pushing the Tiger into a shallow dive, Mart was building up energy and that was what he needed to avoid the threat that was coming. Ahead of him. The Fuzzies had nosed over into a shallow dive themselves, closing the range fast. They had to be running at full power themselves, probably had been since take-off. The Fuzzy was even shorter-legged than the Tiger; they had to blast though the Indian fighters and get to the Skyhawks behind before they ran low on fuel.

There it was! The leading edge of the Fuzzy group suddenly exploded in white smoke. They'd been tracking the Tigers on their radars and they opened the battle by playing the best card they had. Their missiles were heavy and clumsy compared with the neat little Sidewinder, a lot of missile for very little oomph as Raytheon scornfully described it. But, the Alkali missile had one thing the Sidewinder lacked; the ability to home in on a target from its frontal arcs. They weren't very accurate that way but it could be done. Sidewinders had to be fired from the rear arc of the target. Also, the overwing mounts on the Fuzzies were reputed to cause parasitic drag, slowing the aircraft down and limiting performance. So, the enemy had fired them all off in one great salvo, hoping to swamp the group of Tigers coming up to intercept. That meant about 40 Alkalis were on their way in. A lot for twelve aircraft to dodge. The one thing though was that the Chimps hadn't aimed their missiles individually, they'd just let fly at the Indian formation and let the missiles decide who to aim for.

Now was the time to translate energy into agility. As the salvo of Chimp missiles closed, Mart hauled the nose of his Tiger up sharply into a barrel role, salvoing off his flares as he did so. The missiles couldn't cope with the sudden change, not all of them anyway. More were deflected by the cascading flares sprayed behind the rolling Tigers. Mart saw one Tiger explode as it was hit by two of the Alkali missiles. There was no hope of the pilot getting out of that one. Another Tiger didn't make its roll fast enough and it was surrounded by bursts as at least three missiles exploded around it. *Two down?* Mart didn't know. The Fuzzy and Tiger formations were closing at an aggregate of 1,700mph and there just wasn't time to look.

As he came out of his barrel roll, he was, at last, slightly above the Chimp formation. A light gray Fuzzy swept in front of him. Almost by instinct, without consciously making the decision, he thumbed the firing button for his cannon. Four streams of tracer licked out towards the Chimp seaplane fighter. He didn't even see the results of that though because he was racking his Tiger around, trying to get onto the tails of the Fuzzies before they plowed through his formation. Another light gray shape in front of him. The one he'd just shot at? Or another one? He didn't know and didn't care. The annunciator tone in his ears was warbling then changed to a constant pitch. His Sidewinders were locked on and he fired both outboard missiles. One failed to guide, it just flew straight off and disappeared into the sky. The other curved around and exploded just under the Fuzzy's tail. The aircraft went into a flat spin; this low down, there was no way the pilot was going to pull out.

The sky was full of shapes. Some familiar: Tigers, Fuzzys, Alkalis, Sidewinders, mixed up in wild profusion as the two formations merged. Some of the shapes were unfamiliar: explosions, the flowers of parachutes, a spinning mass where a Tiger and a Fuzzy had collided and the pair were heading for the sea, their wreckage at once locked together and shedding fragments as they died. Mart swerved again; in this wild furball, flying straight and level was suicide. Another light gray shape; two more Sidewinders squeezed off as the tone turned constant.

He didn't see whether they hit or not for he had to turn to avoid a Fuzzy closing in on him, its big 30mm cannon flashing. Those thirties were deadly, it only took a couple of shells to put a fighter down. Then an annoying thought struck Mart, *the fighter he'd just used his last two Sidewinders on, it had been light gray hadn't it? Not the dark gray used by the Indian Navy?*

The Fuzzies were in front of them now, extending the range as they dived away and closed on the Skyhawks underneath. Now Mart could afford a quick count. There were ten Fuzzies in front of him and he could see seven Tigers. His fighters had scored ten for five. Even as he watched, the Fuzzies fired their missile salvoes again and the effect on the four Tigers flying close escort was disastrous. Three exploded on the spot, some hit by multiple missiles, and the last swept away, trailing streams of black smoke. The ten Fuzzies were through and they were heading straight for the Skyhawks below. A hundred miles per hour faster than the Tigers, they had made it past the fighters. Now, the bombers were going to have to take their lumps.

In the lead Skyhawk, Commander Suresh Nanda saw the Chimp fighters break through the fighter screen and dive on his bombers. The Skyhawk formations started to disperse, spreading out so that they wouldn't be taken out in single blows. It was a battle of time now, the longer the Chimp fighters took to chase down each individual Skyhawk, to fix it and shoot it from the sky, the fewer aircraft they could bring down. So, the longer each individual Skyhawk survived, the more would get through.

Nanda saw the Chimp Fuzzies swinging around to come onto the Skyhawk's tails. He swerved, swerved again, then thumped the flare release as he saw the Chimp fighter behind him fire its two remaining missiles. The decoys worked; the books had said the Alkali was easily decoyed and it was true.

The 30mm cannon shells could not be deflected so easily. They were streaking past his cockpit, first one side, then the other, as he frantically jinked around and dodged the big shells. Loaded with bombs, his Skyhawk was jinking majestically and that wasn't the way to jink. Beside him, another Skyhawk was already trailing black smoke from its wing roots. As he watched, the wings themselves folded up and the Skyhawk just fell out of the sky. More black smoke, more explosions, still jinking frantically. Then it suddenly seemed to him that something was missing. At first he thought it could be his aircraft, that it had exploded under him but it was nothing so dramatic. Just the balls of light flying past his cockpit had gone. The fighters had given up? Or run out of ammunition? It was rumored the seaplane fighters were low on both fuel and ammunition. One of the penalties of being a fighter that had to float.

Through the defenses? No hope of that. Nanda's radar warning receiver was already screaming its warning. The dots showing the threats lined in front of him and touching the center of the display. Surface to air missiles, already on their way up. Now was the time for chaff; the flares had done their work and it was time for the aluminum foil to do their share. If the intelligence reports on Chimp SAM units were correct, there were 27 missiles down there, ready to be fired in waves of three. How many waves could the launchers get off before the bombers were within their minimum range? The thick white trails of the missiles were already rising from the ground; the threat was obvious but in launching, the batteries had revealed their positions.

Lieutenant Paromita Shastri's section had been assigned flak suppression. His Skyhawks were carrying Bullpups rather than thousand pound bombs on their wing racks. Three of his four Skyhawks had survived and their Bullpups streaked out towards the battery positions. One Skyhawk took a direct hit from a Guild missile and vanished in a black ball. Its Bullpups went ballistic into the sea, but the other pair of Skyhawks sent their missiles into battery positions. One of the red threat dots vanished as the radar truck exploded. Then the remaining pair of Shastri's section were racing across the harbor. One didn't make it; a shoulder-fired missile from the base area hit its tail and it staggered for a few second before plowing into the hillside. The survivor swept over the missile battery positions, dumped his retarded 1,000 pound bombs and vanished over the ridgeline, safe at last.

Lieutenant Alam Srinivas's section had the priority target, the big seaplane tender anchored in the harbor. That ship was the depot ship for the whole enemy squadron; take it out and the base would be crippled. He also had three of his four Skyhawks left as they made their run for the seaplane carrier. The Guild missiles took out one of his aircraft. The other pair made good drops, their bombs fell in neat sticks across the target. The seaplane carrier vanished behind the white eruptions of near misses and the red-black balls of at least three direct hits. As Srinivas made it over the ridge he saw the seaplane carrier was burning aft and already starting to settle by the stern.

Lieutenant Prem Shantiar Jha's section was assigned to the maintenance area. His section had take the worst of the battering, he had the only Skyhawk left of his four. Fighters had hit the other pair and a Guild had destroyed a third. On his own, Jha saw a set of quays with five seaplane fighters anchored next to them. That had to be the maintenance area, it had to be. He opened up with his pair of wing-mounted 20mm cannon, the orange-red tracers floated out, into the anchored fighters. Then the red pip of his continuously-computed impact point bomb sight started to cross the area and he salvoed his thousand pounders into it, the bombs dropped clear and their tail fins spread to slow them and get them clear of the aircraft that had dropped them.

Even so, the lurch from the blast was much worse than Jha had expected. Only when the controls on his Skyhawk started to freeze that he realized it had been more than just blast. Anti-aircraft fire, either guns or a shoulder-fired missile had hit him and his hydraulics were gone. It had taken just a second for the controls to freeze completely and it took even less for Jha to realize the game was up. He reached over his head and pulled the eject lever, his seat blasted him clear of the crippled Skyhawk just before it turned over and crashed.

That left Commander Nanda's section. Miraculously, all four aircraft had survived - so far - and he, as Commander, had the hardest job. Try and find the ammunition and fuel dumps and hit those. His Skyhawk was lurching as it was hit. *Mostly small arms* fire he guessed. He still fired off the last of his chaff and flares. Then, half buried in a gully and surrounded by berms, he saw the great black sausages filled with fuel. He altered course slightly, watching one Skyhawk stream black smoke and tighten its turn until it spun into the sea below. Then his CPIP started to approach the dumps and he released his bombs over the facility below.

Clear of the target area, Nanda looked around. Six Skyhawks had survived the run over the base. Jha's section had vanished completely, the others were sorely battered. At least two of the survivors were trailing smoke and/or fuel. Time to go home, there was no need to worry now; it had become an unwritten rule of this strange war that wasn't a war at all. Once a battle was over, nobody tried to chase down the crippled survivors limping home. Nanda, like all the Indian pilots, regarded that as being unsporting. The Chimps probably had their own reasons; against the warrior's code or something. He could see the pyre of black smoke rising from where the Sugu Bay naval base lay tucked in the hills. The Skyhawks had paid heavily but they'd done their job. How well? There was no way of knowing.

Farmhouse south of San Diego, Mexican side of the border

Humberto didn't like this job and he didn't like the people he was dealing with. His orders were to take them over the border, or, in this case under it, but that was it. He would be heartily glad when the job was over. They were, without a doubt, the most unpleasant people he had ever had to deal with. To make matters worse, they were quite obviously sick and getting worse., The final touch being that he and his men had undoubtedly caught whatever it was they were suffering from. It was inevitable, he supposed; the long truck drive up across Mexico had put him in constant touch with the passengers in the back. Whatever they had, it was likely he had. With luck, he would be rid of it as soon as he was rid of them.

That would be soon. He was leading them under the border in a purpose-built tunnel; tall enough for a man to stand in, wide enough for him to walk comfortably. Concrete-lined so it stayed dry, with battery-powered lights so those using it could walk safely along its length. Humberto had designed it himself and his men had built it, a project that had taken them almost a year. The tunnel was almost a mile long. It started at a disused garage on the Mexican side of the border and ended in a small country store the American side.

Like most Coyotes, Humberto was a self-employed contractor. He accepted jobs from the cartels when they were offered and ran his own groups of illegals to America when they weren't. His tunnel meant that Humberto got paid top dollar for his services. That was fair for, in his way, Humberto was an honest man. When he agreed to take a party of illegals across the border, that's what he did; all the way across and he made sure when he left them they knew what to do and where to go. Few of their jobs were legal, Humberto was no fool and knew that crossing the border legally was so easy that all the legitimate jobs were filled by legals. So the jobs his clients were going to were illegal. Still, they'd paid him honest money to be taken to those jobs and Humberto was an honest man. He made sure they got there, alive and well.

In the disused garage almost a mile behind him, men in white suits had closed in on the entrance to his tunnel. They'd found it quickly enough. That wasn't surprising since they'd been told where to look by a man who preferred to spend his life sentence playing golf in a minimum-security Federal "correctional institute" to playing survival in the general population of a maximum security penitentiary. Only, the men in white suits didn't open the tunnel. They were welding the entrance shut, piling heavy timbers on top of it and securing everything down. Others were placing thermite bombs in the truck that had brought the people down in the tunnel and setting others around the old garage. These were people who knew how to burn things down properly.

In the tunnel, Humberto and one of his men had reached the steps up to the American end of the smuggling route. Humberto sent his man up first to open the manhole cover, then frowned as he reported the hatch was jammed. Shut tight; it wouldn't move. Suddenly, Humberto noted the hatch was different. It had a wide pipe built through it. Something was wrong, terribly wrong. As if to confirm that impression, he heard a roar the ground shook and dust rained down from the concrete lining.

Outside the tunnel was a SAC emergency deployment refueling tanker, one of the ones used to pump fuel into a B-70 Valkyrie when it was operating off an Interstate Highway Emergency airstrip. It could blast thousand of gallons of fuel a minute into an aircraft's tanks. Here, its capacity and pumping power were being used to the max. The hose joining the tank to the manhole cover bulged and flexed with the sheer volume of fuel pouring down it. The needles in the pump controls were all far into the red, but that didn't matter. The limits were set by what the aircraft fuel tanks could stand, not what the pumps could deliver. The object of the game was to get as much raw gasoline into that tunnel as quickly as possible. This time, the red lines were a challenge, not a warning.

Inside the tunnel, the effects were catastrophic. The fuel didn't pour into the tunnel, it hit the bottom with the force of a hydraulic ram. Gasoline cracked the concrete and bounced down the passageway. Humberto's man was killed outright by the sheer force of the liquid column that broke his neck. Behind him, Humberto's legs were also broken by the force and he was blinded by the spraying gasoline. Further down, the illegals he was bringing over panicked at the sight and ran. No good; the tidal wave of gasoline overtook them and spread down the tunnel. The wave lost force as it did so but by then it didn't matter.

Above them, the fuelling tanker had emptied and was driving away. An Air Force Engineer walked over to the manhole cover and dropped a small four pound thermite incendiary down the hole where the fuelling hose had connected. Then he ran. As fast as he could, for the thermite charge had a time delay and he wanted to be a long way off when it ignited. He was still running when the ground behind him erupted in a long, snake-like column of smoke and dust.

Inside the tunnel, the effects were instantaneous. A fuel-air explosion ripped down the length of the tunnel, killing everybody and everything inside it. It didn't just kill them, it incinerated them leaving only a fine charcoal dust. Although he never knew it, Humberto got his reward for being an honest man, after his fashion. He died instantly, incinerated so fast his nerves never had a chance to tell the body about pain. That saved him from the days of agony dying of blackpox and was a reward for honesty worth appreciating.

At the Mexican end, the explosion was the sign for the garage to be blown, adding its fires to the inferno. Then began the long, hard and unpleasant job of backtracking the truck's trip across Mexico and finding anybody who had been infected by its lethal cargo

The Oval Office, The White House, Washington D.C.

"And so Mister President, on behalf of the mothers of America I must ask that you institute a speed limit of 25 miles per hour on all roads in America, regardless of whether they are Federal, State or county funded."

LBJ had called it "meeting Miss Whole Milk." What Richard Milhous Nixon called it was unprintable. Whatever the President called it, the job was the same. Meeting with people who represented organizations, hearing what they had to say and then finding ways to forget about it as quickly as possible. Sitting behind and to one side of him, Naamah found herself detesting the woman who was wasting their time.

She was the President of the Women's Road Safety League, an organization that had just over a thousand members, eighty percent of whom were over 65 years old and ninety three percent of whom had pet cats. This woman even looked like a cat; the same round face, puffy cheeks and vacuous smile. Naamah disliked cats. Her train of thought was broken by her intercom phone bleeping. She answered it and quickly took down the message.

"My apologies ma'am, Mister President, a very urgent message." She handed him the note, a simple comment, 'two down, one to go.'

"Thank you Naamah. That's most gratifying. Now, Mrs. Salamon, I'm sorry to say the 25 miles per hour speed limit you suggest is quite impossible, the economic consequences would be a disaster and. . . . ."

"But Mister President, do you know how many children are killed on our roads every year? Won't somebody please think about the children, Mister President. Look into my heart. . . ."

Naamah leaned forward and spoke confidentially. "Mister President, I do know a good Aztec priest. . . . .

Flight Deck, INS Viraat, *South China Sea*

Eighteen Tigers and twelve Skyhawks left. Almost half the airgroup was gone and some of the survivors were too badly damaged to fly. Still, the seaplane base had been given a good pounding and that meant the threat should diminish now. The effectiveness of those seaplane fighters had been a nasty shock; they were something nobody else had taken seriously. Still, with their tender sunk and their base hammered, they wouldn't be around for some time. That would give *Viraat* time to repair the damaged aircraft down in her hangar deck. She could still cover the Army troops on Pattle Island; that was the important thing.

Mart's train of thought was wiped out by the roar of two Fairey Defenders taking off. In addition to her fixed-wing aircraft, *Viraat* carried four ASW and four AEW Rotodynes. They were being used hard, providing air and surface cover for the carrier group. Even with the birds on the destroyers and frigates, it was a hard job keeping full 24-hour coverage. The truth was, the squadron simply wasn't big enough to do the job. They needed two carriers and double the screen; the Indian Navy just didn't have the front-line ships.

If that was so, then why are we sticking our neck out like this? Mart's skin crawled at the thought. He'd voted for the Hindu Nationalist Party last election and was now wishing he hadn't. This whole operation was turning out to be one bite more than the Indian Navy could chew. It had all sounded so simple; establish a presence on the Island, stay put and the Americans would force a cease-fire-in-place rather than have a war. Only it hadn't worked like that. The Americans had washed their hands of the whole business and forced the Teas and Ozwalds into doing the same. So now, the Indian Navy was carrying the load by itself. Still, despite it's mauled air group, *Viraat* was still the trump card. As long as they had *Viraat* the game was still afoot.

Control Room, HIJMS I-531 Shinohara*, South China Sea*

"Sonar trace Sir! Multiple screws bearing two-three-five. We got them!"

The *Shinohara* was drifting, trimmed so she was in balance with the surrounding water, neither rising nor diving. Just drifting, doing her best to emulate a hole in the ocean. Captain Aki Hento had noted the course and speed of the aircraft formation his navigation radar had spotted that morning, projected it back and moved his boat to a calculated intercept position. Trying to catch a fast-moving surface combat group in a diesel-electric submarine was almost futile. The nukes could manage it but a diesel-electric didn't have the speed or the underwater endurance. Mobile minefields; that was what the nuclear submarine drivers called diesel-electrics.

Well, that was what Aki had done. He'd moved his submarine to a calculated position and hoped that the Indian carrier group would run into him. It was the fifth time he'd tried it and four times he'd failed. There were seven other diesel-electric boats in the area and they'd all tried at least as often. Was it too much to ask that, after nearly fifty attempts, the gods would smile on them and one of the submarines would be in the right place at the right time?

"Range 23,000 meters Sir, speed estimated 22 knots. Course, it's hard to say, they're zigzagging. Mean is, one-three-five. They're coming our way."

Aki grunted and looked at the plot. The line representing the Indian group was approaching them all right but it would cut across ahead. Minimum range would be about nine thousand meters. Well, that was acceptable. The *Shinohara* had four 61 centimeter torpedo tubes, but what to load them with? Homing torpedoes were all very well but they had reduced range, speed and warload compared with the unguided weapons. The unguided torpedoes had a lower probability of a hit but a much bigger warhead, and they were faster and longer-ranged. Homing torpedoes could be decoyed; unguided ones could not. Unguided torpedoes could be evaded; homing ones could not. Which to choose? Aki snapped his fingers. "Load unguided torpedoes. All four tubes."

"Unguided torpedoes?" the First Officer's question was a tiny inflection noticed only by Aki and the officer himself.

"Unguided. We've got one shot at this and we've got to make it a good one. If we use guided torpedoes, we can only fire one at a time. This way, we can fire a spread of four so we've a better chance. And the heavy warheads on the straight-runners will really hurt when we do hit."

The plot fed the course of the Indian formation into the fire control system. It compared the course, speed and range, calculated the optimum firing position and fed the appropriate data to the torpedoes. The outer doors to the tubes slid open, immersing the torpedoes in water ready for launch. Then, at the moment calculated by the fire control system, the torpedo engines started up and the four torpedoes swam out. Their gyros gave each a slightly different course. Hopefully one, or more, would end up in the Indian carrier.

ASW Combat Direction Center, INS Vindhyagiri, *South China Sea*

"Torpedo Warning Red, Red, RED! High-revving HE in the water Sir! Bearing oh-four-five relative. Say again Oh-four-five relative. Estimated speed, 65 knots. Sir, they're Chimp 61 centimeter torpedoes."

"Target, what's the target? And why didn't we hear a launch transient?"

"Wait One, Oh my God, Sir, target is *Viraat*. Spread of four eels, probably unguided. They must have used a swim-out launch Sir. Time to impact three minutes.

"*Viraat.* Flash warning. Four heavyweight torpedoes approaching relative oh-four-five targeted on you. Evade NOW!" As he put the intercom down, Captain Andahal reflected that it wasn't often that a lowly frigate commander got to give orders to an Admiral. "Weaps, get our Rotodyne off now. Full autonomous ASW load; if she hasn't got it already, you're court-martialed. Engines power down to fifty percent. Ops, stream our VDS unit. Set for 150 feet. Comms, alert *Arnagiri* tell her to get her Rotodyne up, stream VDS, set for.... Number One, what's the inversion layer here."

"Don't know Sir, we'll toss a bathygraph buoy and find out."

"Good answer. *Arnagiri* to stream for 350 feet." It was lucky, *Vindhyagiri* was the designated ASW command ship in the case of an ASW contact. The destroyer *Ganges* was the designated AAW command ship.

"Rotodyne on its way Sir. Code sign Deeta-Three. Full autonomous ASW load. Julie, Jezebel, dipping sonar, MAD, six Crocodiles, four depth charges including one Mark Ten. No nukes. Say again. No nukes." The Weapons Officer paused. "May I live now, Sir?"

A chuckle ran around the CDC. A nervous chuckle, not a humorous one. It was cut off abruptly by the ship's internal communication system wheeping. "Starboard lookout here, Sir.

Viraat is making an emergency turn now, really swinging her bows around she is too. And two Rotodynes coming over in a great hurry. Really anxious they are, Sir."

"Deeta-one and Deeta-two calling Sir. Requesting orders."

"Backtrack those torpedoes, try to get an approximate fix. Then send all four Rotodynes to that point. They're to start a hunt there, fanning out from that point. Where are those torpedoes?"

"Just crossing *Viraat* now Sir. First one is clear, second, third. Oh damn."

Ops didn't need to say anything. The sound of the explosion was clearly audible though the hull. *Viraat* had evaded three torpedoes but the fourth had got her. In vengeance, four ASW Rotodynes and two frigates were converging on the estimated position of the submarine that had fired the torpedoes.

Control Room, HIJMS I-531 Shinohara, *South China Sea*

The seconds had ticked slowly by. The five minutes to the first torpedo intersection had come and gone, then the second and the third. Aki was just about to admit his gamble had failed when a dull rumble echoed through the submarine. The bridge erupted into brief cheers. They'd scored, the Indian carrier must have turned to evade the torpedoes but failed to get out of the way of the last one. Now, she was, at the very least, badly hurt.

"Take her down. The layer is at 100 meters, get us below it, then rig for silent running and we'll try to creep out of this."

Fairey Defender ASW.3 Deeta-Two *South China Sea."*

The Rotodyne was hovering; its dipping sonar streamed into the sea underneath it. The Rotodyne was almost the perfect anti-submarine craft. It had the speed of the fixed-wing aircraft, the hovering ability of a helicopter and its size gave it a capable sensor suite as well as a formidable warload.

"Nothing, Izzy, Nothing at all." The sonar operator watched his traces. "I thought I picked up a trace of something but it vanished again."

"If it's a diesel-electric, there'll be sod-all to pick up. Not on passive anyway. We'll have to set up for a Jezebel search."

ASW Combat Direction Center, INS Vindhyagiri*, South China Sea*

"Deeta-Two is setting up for a Julie drop now. Deeta-One, Three and Four are setting up Jezebel lines around the estimated launch point." This was something a helicopter couldn't even begin to emulate, the sheer speed with which the Rotodynes could move to new positions and deploy their Jezebel sonobuoys. "Dropping now."

The rumble of the Julie charges could be heard over the passive sonars. If there was a diesel-electric out there, the sound would reflect off her and be picked up on the Jezebel sonobuoys as well, with luck, as the Variable Depth Sonar fish now being streamed by the two frigates. The computers would isolate the sound signature of the reflections from the original explosions and give the contact. In theory, anyway. In reality, nothing.

"Dead loss, there's nothing out there."

"There has to be. Those torpedoes didn't come from outer space. The target must have gone below the layer, Tell Deeta-Three to drop a Julie pattern set for 360 feet. Deeta-One, Two and Four to listen using dipping sonar, set for 360 also."

"Message from *Viraat* Sir. She's dead in the water. Torpedo hit forward, front 100 feet of the flight deck is destroyed, both catapults gone. Back is broken about sixty feet aft of the bow, what's holding the bows on remains unknown at this time. Serious hangar deck, flight deck and forward accommodation spaces fires. All under control. Flooding serious, ship listing 20 degrees to port, flooding perimeter established. Ship is not in peril of sinking at this time"

"They said that about *Shiloh*."

"There she is Sir!" Deeta-Three had dropped her Julie pattern and the VDS fish had picked up the echoes. They were fuzzy, indistinct contacts that only cleared slightly when the data from the dipping sonars on the Rotodynes was added. "She's further out that we thought. Her torpedoes must have been running for at least a couple of minutes before we picked them up." A brief pause while the comms system squawked. "All Deeta craft are repositioning around the new position. Deeta-Four will be doing the Julie drop."

It took a minute or more for the Rotodynes to winch up their sonars, barely as much for them to move to their new position and another for their sonars to redeploy. Deeta-Four dropped her Julie charges about a hundred yards off the estimated position of the enemy submarine. The results were almost instantaneous; a bright red, sharp contact on all three dipping sonars and the two VDS fish. Almost immediately there was a roar as the two frigates each fired a pair of Ikaras at the estimated position. The lack of delay was hardly happenstance. Both ships had their Weapons Officers with their finger on the "fire" button, waiting for the fire control system to feed the coordinates to the launchers.

The Ikaras arced upwards and glided towards the target position. The Crocodile torpedoes separated at the pre-determined moment. They hit the water, then started their long spiral downwards, sinking at 30 feet per second. Their homing systems were set to active for an ASW hunt. They pinged, hunting for the submarine they had been built to kill.

Control Room, HIJMS I-531 Shinohara*, South China Sea*

The sharp crack of the Julie explosions was clearly different from the usual rumble of explosions and it left Aki with no room for doubt. The hunt was closing in on him, fast. The last set had been beneath him so the Indians had worked out that he'd dived through the layer. Against the Ozwalds, he'd have had a chance; their towed arrays would have been ineffective against a diesel-electric target this far down. The Indian frigates had variable depth sonars. VDS had less range but they could stream them a long way down. If they were dropping charges below the layer, it was a certainty they were streaming their VDS fish below it as well.

Almost to confirm his thoughts, a new sound was added to the symphony being played for him. The sharp, high-frequency ping of a torpedo homing sonar. Or, to be more precise, the sharp pings of four of them. A complete pattern, probably the Ikaras on the frigates. There was a terrible temptation to run up above the layer and see what it was that hunted him. Two frigates certainly, but what else?

"Four Crocs, Sir. They're all around us!"

That was it. The silently-creeping away game was over. To dodge the torpedoes, they had to go to maximum speed. "Emergency speed. Make 22 knots, course 335." Flat out and between the two torpedoes that were the least threat. Force the others into a tail chase. A lot of their fuel had been used in diving down, they couldn't do a chase for long. Aki snapped his fingers as the *Shinohara* surged under his feet. She was one of the fastest diesel-electric submarines in the world, a direct descendent of the I-201 class.

The German Type XXI had gained all the publicity but those who really knew submarines realized that the I-201 was by far the more advanced design. Now, the *Shinohara* would need all the speed she could give but giving it would run her batteries flat in less than 45 minutes.

"Two torpedoes acquired, Sir. The other pair have missed us."

"Fire decoys, full port rudder." A series of bubbling decoys popped out of the launch tubes under the *Shinohara's* bridge. At the same time, the submarine swerved hard, leaving a knuckle in the water. "Battery charge status?"

"Seventy percent Sir." *Make that 30 minutes*, Aki thought grimly. *Just what the blazes is up there hunting me?*

ASW Combat Direction Center, INS Vindhyagiri, *South China Sea*

"Whoa, look at it move. That spooked it!"

"*Ganges* and *Godavari* Sir. They have Ikaras up on their forward rails. They're holding Jab-Is on their aft rails, just in case."

"Right, we have a solid fix now, no need for Julie. Get those coordinates over to *Ganges* and *Godavari*. All ships fire." *Eight Ikaras around the fleeing submarine, that should settle her hash.*

Control Room, HIJMS I-531 Shinohara*, South China Sea*

"Torpedoes decoyed Sir, they took the bait."

And forced us to move so fast even a deaf man in an American concert could hear us. Aki ran the permutations through his mind. The Indians must know his position now, they had to. They'd be plastering his position with torpedoes any second now. "Where's the bottom?"

"150 meters."

"Get us down there. We'll sit there, with luck their torpedoes won't pick us up."

Shinohara lanced downwards. As her depthfinding sonar got disturbingly close to a zero reading. Aki pulled her out of the dive and settled her on the bottom. The bump and groan was only just in time for a barrage of eight torpedoes burst through the inversion layer and they started their hunt. Started and failed. Their high frequency sonars failed to pick up the submarine sitting on the bottom. The explosions as they ran out of fuel and self-detonated were far away. Aki breathed a sigh of relief but only a little one because he'd just played his last card.

Fairey Defender ASW.3 Deeta-Two *South China Sea.*

"Eight torpedoes and every one missed. She bottomed, had to. That leaves it up to us. Izzy, bring her around. Tell *Vindhyagiri* we propose going in with depth charges."

"*Vindhyagiri* confirms. Says to use all the Mark IVs first then wait for results before dropping the Mark Xs. All Deeta craft to make Mark IV drop."

The Rotodyne winched up its sonar; it wasn't really needed now that the two frigates were close enough to have accurate surveillance. The data came up on the ASCAC built into the Rotodyne's command center. Anti-Submarine Command Action Center, the equipment that meant a Defender could carry on its hunt without surface ships in support. ASW technology had come a long way since the convoy battles of 1944-46.

The data received from the frigates showed the probable location of the Chimp submarine. Now the four Rotodynes would drop their depth charges around that location. See what came up, so to speak.

Control Room, HIJMS I-531 Shinohara*, South China Sea*

The explosions were close, but not deadly so. Aki had spun *Shinohara* around as she'd dived for the bottom. He guessed the Indians would try to project his position so he'd done something out of the ordinary. It looked like it had worked. Smashed crockery and blown light bulbs nothing more.

ASW Combat Direction Center, INS Vindhyagiri, *South China Sea*

"First salvo of depth charges down." Weaps wished for a moment he had an Australian frigate with him. They carried a Limbo launcher, a three-barreled mortar that was ideally suited to this situation. It was a giant bear's paw that smashed everything over a wide area. *Just blow everything up, that was positively Septic in its subtlety. Indian frigates were too sophisticated for their own good sometimes.*

"Sir, we've got something!" The ship's computers had extracted something from the maze of explosions. They'd picked up reflections from the hull of the target. Perhaps they weren't too sophisticated after all. It was a hazy, imprecise contact but better than nothing. Closer than they'd expected. The sub driver must have done a U-turn as he'd dived for the bottom. *Smart guy, it was going to be a pity to kill him.* "All Deeta craft, on position transmitted, Mark X drop."

Fairey Defender ASW.3 Deeta-Two *South China Sea."*

"Here we go." The attack pattern was laid out. All four Mark X one-ton depth charges were going down, surrounding the position located by the first attack. The Mark X, the most powerful depth charge in the world, one that was rated as effective as a whole 14-charge pattern of normal depth bombs. That would avenge *Viraat*

Control Room, HIJMS I-531 Shinohara, *South China Sea*

The explosions were deadly, devastating. Water sprayed inside the hull through ruptured pipes, valves were blown open, electronic systems shorted out in cascades of sparks, the crew were hurled against bulkheads. "Captain, engine room. Sir, the battery compartment is flooding. Chlorine gas is entering the compartment.

It was all over. Aki gave his last orders. "Get out of there. Blow emergency tanks, make for the surface. Abandon ship."

Fairey Defender ASW.3 "Deeta-Two" South China Sea."

"Look at her go!" Deeta-Two had plotted the submarine suddenly detach from the seabed and claw for the surface. She made it. Her bows soared into the air as she broke surface, her metal skin looked as if a gang of demented trolls had been pounding on her with war-hammers. The sonar operator reflected that he'd been playing Dungeons and Dragons too much before realizing that it was a reasonable description of what had happened to the submarine. Then, the Rotodyne rocked as 4.5 inch shells passed perilously near to her. Down below, the submarine was surrounded by shell splashes. The ASCAC operator looked quickly down; the submarine was settling fast by the stern and men were pouring off her into the sea.

"Cease fire, repeat cease fire. They're abandoning ship down there, she gone, she's finished." Suddenly, now that she was dying, the enemy submarine had ceased to be an 'it' and had returned to being a 'she.' "Cease Fire."

"Acknowledged. All ships, all Deeta craft. Cease fire. Repeat Cease Fire. Stand by to pick up survivors."

Deeta-Two swept over the sinking submarine surrounded by the survivors struggling in the water. In the cockpit, Izzy lined up carefully and punched the button releasing two large cylinders from their bay behind the cockpit. Below him, Captain Aki thought they were bombs until they hit the water and expanded into rubber life rafts. Already his men were swimming over to them. The Rotodynes swung past again, dropping more rafts and Aki made for one, to be hauled on board by his men. Across the sea, two Indian frigates were already closing in, their 35mm Boer guns trained on the rafts. *Reasonable,* Aki thought, *the Japanese didn't have a good reputation for surrendering*. But this was different, it wasn't a war, this was an incident. Then he looked around. It had taken two destroyers, two frigates and four Rotodynes to get him. *Some incident!*

On Highway A-19, South of Ciudad Juarez, Mexico

The divided highway that lead into Ciudad Juarez was one of the best roads in Mexico. Well-built, well-designed and carefully maintained, it was smooth and fast. So much so that it was up to the standard of I-25, the great ten-lane Interstate that headed north from the American city of El Paso. In fact, the standard of A-19 was so good, it was so much above the usual standard of Mexican roads, few people noticed the engineers had made a mistake. In the long sweeping curve that lead into the final run up to Ciudad Juarez, they'd got the camber of the curve wrong. It wasn't very much wrong, only a slight miscalculation. If people had kept better statistics in Mexico, and if Mexican drivers were better, then perhaps somebody would have realized that the prolonged curve had an unusually high frequency of accidents caused by people drifting out of their lane. But, nobody kept those statistics and the fault went unnoticed.

This time around, the curve wasn't the only problem. Highway A-19 was a six lane road, three in each direction and this was where the signposts started for the junction with I-25 at the border. Like most long haul Interstates, I-25 had four carriageways; two in each direction. The left-hand carriageways contained two high-speed, limited access lanes. Trucks, vans and local, short-haul traffic weren't allowed on that carriageway. They had to use the three-lane right-hand carriageway, the local access road where the speed limit was 90mph, not 120 and where traffic from the towns and cities first entered the Interstate. That was the problem. There was no access to either Ciudad Juarez or El Paso from the limited access lane; the white truck had to use the right hand carriageway, even if it had qualified to use the left hand one. And that meant the driver had to make a lane change, if he was to get onto the extreme right hand lane of A-19.

The driver of the white truck was the third factor involved. Miguel Garcia was not a well man. He was running a high fever and he had a blinding headache. To make matters worse, his skin was crawling with the sensation of thousands of ants digging into him. He'd been driving resting his head against the side of the truck. The truth of the matter was, he wasn't seeing very well. As a result, neither he nor his companion, who was feeling worse if anything, saw the first signpost warning them to get into the proper lane. They missed the second one as well. They spotted the final one very late and they had to make a very sharp, very sudden lane change to get lined up for the local access carriageway. When they finally did so, they were right at the point where the error in road design was at its worst.

Garcia had to make that turn because only from the extreme right hand lane could he make the turn onto the feeder road leading into Ciudad Juarez. If he missed it, there was no other exit before the Mexican-US border. With twelve illegal immigrants in the back of his truck, an inspection by the US border guards was the last thing he wanted. Something was up; there were rumors that the Americans had troops on the border and there were dark whispers of the dreaded SEALs being loose in Mexico again. So he made the turn but, in his illness, he forgot to signal as he did so.

The faulty camber on the road turned his lane change into a disaster. It snatched at his truck and turned a sharp curve into a lurching wrench that cut off the 32-tonner big rig behind him. The driver of that big rig was good, one of the best on the road. That didn't help anybody or anything. His rig was too heavy to stop quickly enough; the faulty camber of the road stopped him evading one way and the other would have sent him down the embankment. He could only sit and watch as the small truck swerved across the road and listen to the sound of crunching metal as his right-hand fender caught the truck just above the back wheel, flipping it out of control and spinning it across what was left of the road into the side.

The truck flipped over as it crossed the hard shoulder, bounced off an emergency telephone pole, destroying the system in the process, and cartwheeled down the embankment. As it did so, the lightweight structure of its rear disintegrated, throwing wreckage and bodies all over the crash site.

Five cars behind the crash site, Police Officer Sidona saw the truck crash off the road and roll down the bank. He'd seen the truck swerve and was already preparing to give chase when it all happened. Priorities had changed though; changed in an instant. The big rig was already coming to a halt as fast as it could. Sidona guessed that his job would be to give first aid to the wounded truck crew and perhaps get a statement form the big rig driver, not hand out the ticket for reckless endangerment that he had planned. Pulling his Ford onto the hard shoulder, he started on the slope down to the wreck. His mind noted the still-turning front wheels and then, almost negligently counted the bodies strewn around. *There were HOW MANY*?"

Then, he remembered the alert that had come through, a bulletin to all police patrols on A-19. 'If you see a truck with a large number of passengers, report and detain. *DO NOT APPROACH.*' How they were supposed to do that was never explained. This time, the problem had been solved for him. The truck had stopped itself. Now, the next problem, isolate the truck. Already cars had stopped and people were getting out of them to help the wounded down below. The big rig driver was already walking back. They must not approach the wreck. Sidona didn't know why but those were orders and such odd orders must have a reason. There was a bull-horn in his police cruiser and he used it.

"STAY WHERE YOU ARE. DO NOT APPROACH THE CRASH!"

Most of them stopped but a few either didn't hear, the words didn't register or they decided to ignore them. Well, the police cruiser had an answer for that as well. In clips by the driver's seat was a PPS-45, a Russian sub-machine gun the Mexican Police had purchased for issue to its patrol officers. In the wilds of Mexico, instant firepower was sometimes the only way to stay alive and the steel-cored Tokarev Magnums fired by the PPS-45 would rip through any vehicle he wanted to stop. A burst fired into the air stopped the remaining would-be helpers just as efficiently.

Except one. A woman stayed on her way down. Sidona sighed, took careful aim and fired another short burst, spraying her with dirt from the impact points a meter or so in front of her feet. That stopped her. She turned and made her way towards him, every gram of her bearing rigid with fury.

Deal with her later. Sidona spoke quickly into his radio. "Kilo one-six here. We have a truck crash on the A-19 curve again. This one has many wounded, I think it is the one we were told to watch for. I have isolated the scene. Please send assistance."

By the time he'd finished the woman had reached him, her skin tight with rage. "I am a nurse. There are people down there who need help. They may die if they do not get it. How dare you stop me! How dare you shoot at me."

"Senora if I had shot at you, you would now be dead. We have strict orders. In crashes such as this, with trucks and other vehicles carrying many passengers, nobody is to approach the scene until proper help arrives. Why we have these orders I do not know. But they are strict orders and offer no room for argument." That wasn't strictly true but Sidona had a bad feeling about this whole business.

The nurse didn't seem to care about his orders. She was still red-faced with sheer anger. "Who are you to deprive the sick of care?"

That did it. One did not speak to police officers that way in Mexico. Sidona grabbed his black book with his free hand and waved it in her face, shouting as he did. "I am a police officer and you will do as you are told. If not I will arrest you and you will spend the time between now and the time you go to jail laying on the road in handcuffs. Do you understand me?"

The woman stepped back. Sidona wasn't sure whether it was his words, his mirrored sunglasses or the submachine gun in his left hand that had scared her more. But she backed off and turned to look down at the wreck.

In the distance, Sidona actually saw the Kaman rotodyne take off from the heliport at El Paso over the border. *The Americans were involved?* It made the short hop, circled the area then landed down by the wreckage. Men in white suits got out and started picking up the people down below. One of the men laying on the ground did something, moved threateningly perhaps. It was too far away to see but some shots rang out and the man didn't move any more. Then his body was picked up and bagged. Sidona raged inside, as far as he knew he had just seen cold-blooded murder committed in front of him and he was powerless to do anything about the casual contempt for his country's laws.

His reflections were interrupted by the nurse who was equally appalled at what she was seeing although for very different reasons. "Those are biological isolation suits." The nurse's voice was small, frightened. "Why would they use those?"

She was apologetic as well as frightened and Sidona was a gentleman in the best sense of the word. "I do not know, Senora. It must have something to do with the orders we received. I am sorry I frightened you but when we get strange orders it is always best to obey them and find out the reasons later."

"Officer, has anybody been down to the wreck site?"

Sidona turned around in shock. A man had appeared behind him, in a strange gray camouflage uniform that seemed to slide away from his eyes every time he tried to look at it. Without being told, he guessed this was one of the mysterious SEALs who did strange things in his country and then vanished as silently as they had arrived. Sidona bitterly resented the men who made free with his country's law on his patch but there was nothing he could do about it.

"No. I kept everybody away, at least sixty meters."

The SEAL nodded. "Officer . . . . Sidona. You have saved many lives today."

Behind him, Mexican police had taken over the traffic direction and were slowly clearing the jam that had built up around the accident scene. Sidona hardly noted the road of the rotodyne taking off but he did note the wave of heat as the wrecked truck and everything around it was burned. He got back into his police cruiser, returned the PPS-45 to its clip and started the engine. Instead of moving off, he looked at the intense fire burning where the truck had been. That alone told him that something very important had happened. He just didn't know what.

The Oval Office, The White House, Washington D.C.

"Mister President, Thank you for seeing me so quickly."

Nixon looked up at his visitor. "Seer, please tell me you have brought good news."

"I have indeed Sir. Three down, none to go. We got the lot. Not that we're dropping our guard but it does look like we dodged the bullet on this one."

Nixon's relief was palpable. "So it didn't have our name on it then."

"Sorry Sir?"

"The bullet we dodged. It didn't have our name written on it."

"Sir, on a battlefield, the one bullet with my name on it never worried me. It was the thousands marked 'to whom it may concern' that scared me. Still, it does look like this particular threat is contained."

CHAPTER NINE
FORMING UP

SAC Headquarters, Offutt Air Force Base, Nebraska.

"The border intercept plans worked then." General Myers sounded as relieved as he felt; the attack could have bypassed all of the defenses America had so laboriously built up against attack. His feelings transmitted through the elaborate conference facility that linked him with Washington.

At the other end of that link, the Seer hesitated. "Sir, we lucked out, I mean we really lucked out. The last group of plague carriers weren't intercepted by us, their truck crashed about six miles short of Ciudad Juarez. A local cop was on the scene and he isolated the crash site and prevented anybody entering or leaving. We flew in a delousing team and picked up the bodies then sanitized the site. Pure chance, if that truck hadn't crashed, the plague carriers would be crossing from Ciudad Juarez to El Paso tonight."

President Nixon shuddered at the thought, he'd read the reports on blackpox and his mind's eye saw himself being flayed alive by the disease while his body bled out. "Have AMRIID come back with a link on the disease?"

"We have a preliminary report, yes. AMRIID and CDC will be confirming as soon as the tests are done but their initial finding is that the infectious agent in the bodies and prisoners we recovered is the same as that in the samples sent to us by the French. They have to confirm whether it is first-generation the same as used in Algeria. If it is, then we have proof positive, smoking gun evidence that this was a Caliphate attack. The really good news is that they are developing a broad-band vaccine that will immunize people against this disease and offer some protection against other smallpox variants."

"Then start to generate the attack plan. Generate two, a Big One that takes out the whole Caliphate, and a Little One that destroys their biological and chemical infrastructure."

General Myers did a double take at that; he'd assumed the response would be to wipe the Caliphate from the map. "Sir?"

"Two plans General. I want to have options. I want to make the decisions."

"Sir. There's something else." The Seer was as surprised as SAC HQ at Nixon's demand but there were more important things to deal with. "We dodged the bullet on this one because the Caliphate screwed up badly. This whole thing went off half-charged because they didn't understand the people they were dealing with. The Medellin people's plans crossed them too badly. They'll learn, we may face this again, sooner than we would like. We have a plan, called Project Lifeboat, to deal with this possibility. It exploits our space program. . . ."

"I don't like the space program. Its expensive and its a Democrat Party boondoggle. Just gets them free publicity. I want to close it down."

"We can't do that, Sir. I mean we literally can't. Our surveillance and future attack capabilities all use manned space facilities. We'd be stripping away most of our technology lead over the rest of the world. We need space stations and they provide a backbone for the another program, one that involves putting a core of people and everything we know in an easily-isolatable environment. Sir, you need to attend briefings on what we need to do and why. In the meantime, we need to get information on the Caliphate industrial capacity so we can prepare your alternate plans.

"How will we be doing that?"

"Partly observation from space, but mostly we'll be reactivating an old spy ring we used once."

Top Floor, Bank de Commerce et Industrie, Geneva, Switzerland.

Branwen bumped the door open with her hip before maneuvering the trolley carrying the food through and putting it next to Loki's desk. A man was in the office with Loki, an old-looking man with a graying mustache and keen, deadly eyes.

"Henry! I haven't seen you for a couple of years. Since the Grand Teton business."

"Hi, Branwen. Yeah, its been too long. And much too long since I was last here. '46 wasn't it?"

"'46 indeed. A very good year." Loki's face clouded for a moment as he remembered the year that came afterwards. And all of his people who'd died with the German cities they'd lived in. "Smoked herring, Henry, try some. 1946, those were good times. Remember Hartzleff?"

"Hartzleff. Yes indeed. Big man, from Bavaria. What was he, six-six? At least? He used to boast he was the German counter-intelligence man here because he was tall enough to see over the Alps. Remember his face when he stepped into an elevator and found you'd removed the bolts that held the floor in place?"

Loki burst out laughing and shook his head affectionately. "I really felt bad about that. Anyway, you didn't fly all the way over here on a Superstream just to discuss old times. What can we do for you?"

"Some more of this herring would be great. Never tried this before."

"You wouldn't. The Seer destroyed the herring fisheries." Branwen cleared her throat. Loki looked embarrassed for a second.

"Sorry, I shouldn't have said that. Question stands though, what can we do for you."

You know very well what we want Henry thought. *You told us you had it after all. But you want The Seer to ask you for it.* He glanced at Branwen and the two shared a moment's empathy. This stupid feud between Loki and the Seer was wearing on the people around them. "You told us that you'd collated information on Swedish exports of machinery and chemical production equipment to the Caliphate?"

Loki munched on some herring and toast. "Yes indeed. Have some beer. It's good Swiss beer. We started to collect it as a result of our futures trading activities and we didn't like how it fitted together. So we collated some more and we liked that even less." He pulled out a file and handed it over. A ring binder, three inches thick and bursting. "Look at those products, capabilities and locations."

Henry McCarty looked down the list and shook his head. "Loki. I'm a pistolman, not a scientist. This is all double Dutch to me. Ammonia is something our maids use to clean the kitchen. This means nothing to me."

"I got one of our chemists here to put it together and Isambard looked at the engineering side. The report's in there. Just an example though. This facility here at Salman Pak. It produces ammonium nitrate, urea fertilizer, pharmaceuticals and baby milk. Or so it says." Henry's face was still confused. "Those products just don't fit together Henry. It's ohhh, like trying to carry a shotgun in your hat band. Ammonia, urea and nitrates are dirty, agricultural industries. Filth, pollution, you name it. Pharmas and so on need clean surroundings, sterile clean. These plants aren't what they are supposed to be. They're biological warfare plants. Baby milk is a great culture medium for bioweapons. And given what's happening in Algeria right now. . . ."

Henry nodded. *And what nearly happened in Mexico* he thought but carefully didn't say. "So by checking where the suspect plants fitted together, you've listed the Caliphate biowarfare plants?"

"That's right. The Swedes are about the only people who will sell advanced chemical processing facilities to the Caliphate. So that's the list and we think its all of them. So tell The Seer that's where blackpox is coming from."

Prime Minister's Palace, New Delhi, India.

"Suddenly, it doesn't seem to matter too much, does it?"

Prime Minister Atal Bihari Vajpayee shook his head, then hesitated and decided to clarify the matter. "You are correct, John. Our little squabble out here seems very insignificant now."

Australian Prime Minister John Barry Gardinier, JBG to his friends, of whom Prime Minister Vajpayee was not one, leaned back in his seat and looked out of the window, east towards where America sat in the darkness of its night. When dawn reached the country nobody doubted that SAC's fleet of bombers would be taking off and heading towards the Caliphate. Nobody doubted that at all. The crews were being briefed, the aircraft were being prepared, the bombs and mines were being winched up into the cavernous bellies of the Stratofortresses and Valkyries. Across the world, people were watching and holding their breath, knowing what was to come. There was no doubt, none at all. The Americans were furious and when they got that angry, countries vanished.

First there had been the announcement that the new strain of smallpox, the terrifying disease named blackpox had been identified as coming from the Caliphate. That it had been identified as an air- and surface delivered biological warfare agent and that a number of disease carriers, plague rats the Americans had called them had been killed or captured trying to enter the United States. They had been infected with the same strain of blackpox, exactly the same strain, and that meant they had to have been infected from the same mass cultures.

Then, at 18:00 Eastern Standard Time, President Nixon had made an address to the nation, explaining what had happened and how the attack on the US border cities had been averted. He'd made it clear that the attack had been traced back to the Caliphate and that the appropriate action would be taken. Then there had been silence.

The Caliphate had made a statement a little later, accusing the world of Islamophobia, denying their involvement and claiming they too had been hit by the disease. They had claimed it was a French plot, a conspiracy to incriminate Moslems and goad the Americans into attacking Caliphate territory. The Americans had remained silent.

A few hours later, the Caliphate had released another statement, a tirade of hatred directed at the United States and describing the plague rats and the Caliphate subjects who'd died of blackpox as martyrs. The Americans had remained silent.

"Perhaps, the Caliphate will fold, rather than be bombed. They did last time." JBG looked around, almost defensively. "They might."

"Last time, the Americans gave them an ultimatum, a way out, something they could accept. They haven't made that mistake this time." The Ambassador delicately licked a last morsel of cheesecake off her fork, then returned it and the small plate to the credenza in one corner of the office. "This time the Americans have said nothing. That means they consider there is nothing left to say. Or rather, there is, but their bombers will say it for them."

"Why are they waiting then? If not to give the Caliphate a last chance to surrender?"

The Ambassador looked at the buffet arranged in one corner of the room and succumbed to temptation. She collected another slice of cheesecake and resumed her seat. "They'll want to brief the crews. They've probably been refining their attack plan and selecting targets. They'll want the aircraft to arrive over their targets at what they consider to be the best time. Many of their bombers are based in the north eastern states, Maine, Massachusetts, New York, and it's winter up there. We can check the weather reports but they're probably waiting for the best time to take off." She turned her attention to the slice of cheesecake, carefully selected an area where the white chocolate frosting covered the jellied raspberries and speared it with her fork.

"Are they going to destroy the whole country?" Vajpayee's voice trembled despite himself. "They can't, they couldn't, surely?"

JBG seized the opportunity while the Ambassador was savoring her cheesecake. "They could, they can, but they won't. They'll destroy the industrial facilities and economic resources but they won't wipe the country from the map, not like they did with Germany. The Caliphate is too big. If they wiped it out completely, they'd drag the whole world down."

The Ambassador's tongue darted delicately out and licked a tiny crumb from her upper lip. Her eyes were expressionless, unblinking, and combined with the gesture made her look like a strange, exotically poisonous snake. "That would not stop them. But the Americans are a practical people. They have a list of all the suspect facilities in the Satrapies of Iraq and Iran, and in Saudi Arabia. Those facilities are gone.

"There are major air defense installations, in Bahrain and Qatar, those they will obliterate. They will mine the Straits of Hormuz, with nuclear mines of course, and cripple the Caliphate that way. But no, they will not destroy the whole country. President Nixon does not want to start his presidency with quite so many deaths."

The room relaxed slightly. JBG seized the moment again, earning him a sideways glance from the Ambassador. "Which brings us to the main point of our meeting. The fighting in the South China Sea. It may be minor in comparison with what lies ahead for the Caliphate but it is serious none the less. It may even be that the Chipanese will seize this opportunity to spread the conflict while the Americans are distracted."

Vajpayee shook his head. "We have not achieved all we hoped but we have done well. We won a naval battle despite what the public thinks and we have our troops holding Pattle Island. We hold the upper hand still."

"You do now, yes." The Ambassador's voice was urgent. "But that is a declining asset. With your carrier torpedoed and out of the battle, you have no air cover in that area. The Chipanese have their seaplane fighters, Lord, how we underestimated them, and they have their Harry bombers. Soon, they will have air superiority and they will wear down your ships and your troops. You have the upper hand now, certainly. That means you must get the best deal you can. Now."

"There is a deal on offer? I did not know this."

"The Chipanese Legation in Washington has transmitted an offer to us, to Australia and to Thailand, for onward transmission to you. It is long but it comes down to this. If India withdraws its troops and recognizes Japanese sovereignty over the Southern Pescadores, not least by using that name from now on, the Chipanese Government will give India fishing rights in the area, 30 percent of the gas and oil exploration rights and they will allow you to put one weather station and one fisherman's refuge on one of the smaller islands of the group - provided they are civilian manned of course. It's a fair offer, Mister Prime Minister; it's a very fair offer and delay will only jeopardize it."

"But we still have a naval presence and our troops on Pattle."

"For how much longer? So far the honors are tilting your way, I agree. You have lost a destroyer, two frigates and an old transport. You have a carrier, a cruiser and three destroyers badly damaged. The Chipanese have lost a cruiser and five destroyers with a seaplane carrier, two cruisers and two more destroyers crippled. This is a very finite time though. Tonight, perhaps tomorrow night, the Chipanese will get to work. Their Harry bombers will start to pick off the anti-aircraft systems on Pattle. Their submarines and bombers will start hunting your surface ships. As your losses climb, the deal on offer will fade. I urge you to accept the deal offered now. You will not get a better one."

"If you and the Australians had supported us as our treaty demands we would not be in this position. What use is a treaty that is not there when we need it? Perhaps we should reconsider the worth of this treaty."

"The Americans made it clear they would be seriously displeased with any attempt by us to support you with military assets. To do so would be to widen the conflict and they will not have that. To quote their National Security Advisor, 'We cannot prevent all wars but we can make sure that they stay little ones.' Instead, we have acted as brokers and won you an honest deal."

Vajpayee nodded, reluctantly but none the less firmly. "Very well. Please advise the Chipanese Government that their offer is acceptable as a basis for negotiations."

The Ambassador stood up. "Prime Minister, I am pleased to hear that. I will inform the Chipanese Embassy in my country immediately." She turned to leave the room but Vajpayee's voice stopped her.

"Madam Ambassador, I'm afraid I don't know your name?"

Her smile was bright, in stark contrast to the gathering gloom over the impending American strike on the Caliphate. "Very few people do."

The Military Command Center, Dezful, Iran Satrapy, The Caliphate.

By preference, Morteza Farzaneh was a historian. That was a hard and unforgiving choice for a society where history and theology were so tightly intermixed that the former was almost entirely a matter determined by the latter. Only, things were changing. For the first few years of its turbulent existence, the Caliphate had been governed by the Ruling Council, a group of theologians who drew their inspiration wholly from their interpretation of the Koran. As long as they had succeeded, their antiquated beliefs and anachronistic ideas had been accepted. '*The Mandate of Heaven*' thought Farzaneh, reflecting on an old Chinese concept that he was supposed to know nothing about. The idea that success meant approval from the gods while failure meant the gods were displeased. Enough failure and the ‘Mandate of Heaven’ was deemed to have been withdrawn and the legitimacy of the government was forfeit.

And the failures had come. First the idiotic fracas in the Mediterranean where the Caliphate had ended up on the wrong end of the American sledgehammer. They’d provoked the Americans for no reason and then been forced to back down. In the process, their failure had brought about penalties far beyond those demanded by the Americans. The strength and power of the Ruling Council had not laid in its religious appeal. In the fractious and disunited Caliphate, there were many schisms and sects that interpreted the Koran any way they wished. The strength of the council had been the troops they commanded; a core of hardened professional soldiers brought by Model. Those troops, loyal only to the Ruling Council had been the tool the Council had used to control its enemies. In the aftermath of the Mediterranean incident, those troops had gone.

They had left behind the ‘Guardians of the Faith’ the remains of the Einsatzgruppen who had converted to Islam. They had been the weapon the Council had used against the schisms and sects whose beliefs varied too far from those that the Council considered acceptable. Now, the ‘Guardians of the Faith’ had gone too. Despite their fanatical belief in their new religion, their habits and customs had been all to westernized. In the end, they had become too much of a danger. On June, 15, 1968, there had been a second “Auspicious Incident” and they had been purged. Fanatical they may have been but 15 salvoes of artillery fire pumped into their quarters had ended them.

Then there had been Algeria. It had seemed so easy, a country already torn apart by civil war, surely it was ripe for absorption? But Algeria had fought back; bad enough by itself, but they had fought back and won. The Muslims in Algeria had allied with the infidel French against the Caliphate and destroyed the claims of the Council to be the unified voice of Islam. With that news, the Ruling Council had lost its weight. It had become a walking corpse, awaiting only its death certificate.

That was coming, Farzaneh knew it. He had known it the moment the plans for this assault on the Americans had been raised.

The Council had seized on it as revenge for the Mediterranean disaster and added in their reprisal for Algeria's temerity in daring to resist them. When the possibility of an American counter-stroke was raised, it had been dismissed. Allah, they had said airily, would not permit it to succeed. And their plans had gone ahead.

In the silent circles of technologists and administrators, the professionals at running countries who had kept their heads down while the Ruling Council had passed its decrees and postured, that decision had been met with relief. The Mandate of Heaven was already in grave doubt, another blow would prove it had been withdrawn completely. The Ruling Council wouldn't fall, but it would be reduced to impotence. Then, the Caliphate could be rebuilt, to run as a country should be run. The American bombers would be the midwives that would bring about that rebirth.

Residential Apartment, Georgetown, Washington D.C.

Raven paused for a quick last look, using the polished steel of the elevator door as a mirror, then took a deep breath. It was time and she didn't want to be late. Anyway she was committed now so she went over to the apartment, and hesitated once more by checking the number against the paper she'd used to take down his address. Already, she was feeling out of place and had an urgent desire to leave. She'd got her best clothes out for this date, at least she supposed it was a date. A new blue-and-white check shirt from Kmart and a pair of new jeans. She'd indulged herself and bought a pair of Levis, instead of the store brand. Even though she hadn't seen anybody staring at her, she'd still imagined people's eyes on her back and the comments 'what's *she* doing here?'

That was strange, the door was open. She'd been expecting to have to wait outside if he wasn't in. She pushed it, and stepped inside, then stopped dead. A blonde woman was inside, sorting papers out on the table. After a quick second of stunned surprise, Raven's face tightened with anger and she turned to leave. A voice stopped her.

"Oh, hi Raven. You here to see The Seer?"

"I was, yes. But don't worry, I'll get out of your way." Her voice dripped acid and she turned to leave again.

"No need, I'll be finished here in a moment. I'm just dropping some papers from the Department of Defense off for him to read before tomorrow. We have met, haven't we? I'm Inanna."

"Yes, we have." Raven's voice was sharp and hard. Inanna smiled gently in response.

"Don't worry, I won't spoil your date. He won't read this lot until tonight and he's a fast study. Where're you two going."

Raven couldn't hold her anger in the face of that genial smile. It sort of shriveled up inside her, leaving a void where it had previously flared. "I don't know. I hope it's nowhere dressy." Then she crumpled a little, her fears got the better of her, and her voice was tiny. "These are the best clothes I have."

Inanna looked down at the tailored, Italian designer silk suit she was wearing, and a burst of understanding opened her eyes. Raven was alone and probably frightened. She, almost certainly, had never been part of the Washington social scene and the poor girl had scared herself stiff. Not of the scene itself; but of doing something wrong and making herself look foolish. And, she probably thought Inanna was the Seer's partner and the Seer was planning to cheat on her. Time for some reassurance.

"Raven, how did you get here?"

"Gusoyn drove me. The Seer asked him to bring me over."

"Is he still down there?"

"I think so. He said he had to wait for somebody."

"That's me, then. Look, we've got a few minutes and Gusoyn's a nice guy, he won't mind waiting."

"He is so nice. So why does he just drive people around?"

“Gusoyn? He likes it. And don’t let the apparent position fool you. Gusoyn’s one of the most important people around here. Think about it. Where do people talk business in this town? In their limos. And who else is in the limo? A driver. So the drivers know everything that’s going on and Gusoyn, being one of them, hears it all and passes it through. Don’t worry Raven, we’re all set up here, you’ve been around for, what, three years? You’ll get the hang of how things work. First though let’s clear something up. I’m not the Seer’s partner right now, haven’t been for a year or so.”

“What about Igrat? She and the Seer seem very close.” Having had her first set of suspicions dispelled, Raven seemed almost grimly determined to find something else to be upset over.

“They should be close, she’s his daughter. Adopted, but still his daughter. Anyway, look, my visit here is purely business, nothing personal. Yours, I guess, is purely personal, nothing business, and good for you, I’m cheering you on. When Gusoyn gets me home, I’ll be going off to a show with Tom.”

“Tommy Blood?”

“No, Tom Lynch, my current partner. So don’t worry, you haven’t stumbled into anything and you’re not cheating on anybody. Now, you’re worried about where you two will be going?”

Raven nodded.

“Don’t be. The Seer has his faults, the Gods know that, and even they have probably lost count of them, but he’s always at least two jumps ahead of the game. If he asked you out, he knows the sort of place you’ll be comfortable in and since he knows how you dress, I wish I look that good by the way, he’ll have fixed up something appropriate. He’ll never put you in a position where you’re out of place or ill at ease.

“Look, being with him is a strain, you’ll find that out. He’s always ahead of you and its really wearing being with somebody who knows what you’ll do before you do. On the other hand that makes him predictable.” Inanna giggled for a second. “Want to know a secret? Us chicks put bets on what he'll do in various circumstances. Let's see."

Inanna stared at Raven for a second. "He knows you, he knows you have a limited wardrobe, and also that you're traveling on a tight budget so you can't buy a new outfit for the date. Given known food preferences, my guess is Bugaboo Creek."

"What on earth is a Bugaboo Creek?" Raven was awed, hearing America's National Security Advisor spoken about with such familiarity. After three years, she still couldn't quite get used to the idea that people in Washington were humans who had a life outside the Government. Or that she, a Shoshone, was associating with them. The Grand Teton affair had brought them together and that had led by strange and peculiar paths to the Seer and his group getting involved in the problems that afflicted her people. And that had led to the plan to build casinos on Indian tribal land and the creation of a highly successful television series. The way things were happening left her bewildered.

"Steak and ribs restaurant, up-market but casual, not pretentious. Modeled on a Canadian hunting lodge and they make a thing of having really odd, well I suppose 'discussion objects' is the best way to describe them, around. Like talking beavers hiding in whisky kegs. You'll see. Want to take me up on it?"

Raven shook her head.

"Pity, I could use some pocket change. Raven, we've all had time to get used to his funny little ways, you haven't. He's as cold as they come, completely ruthless, self-absorbed and self-confident to a fault. So that takes a lot of adapting to, and you'll have to do it because he won't change. But, then adapting is something we've all had to get used to. I guess you probably don't have that problem, you're lucky enough to have a background you fit into without problems. We can't.

"Show you what I mean, I'm blonde right? Once there was a time when all I had to do was this." Inanna shook her head and her waist-length hair shimmered in waves "and bat my baby blue eyes

–

and men would fall into my arms. In the late '40s and way into the '50s I had to dye it brown. Being a blonde back then wasn't popular. Especially in Boston and the Irish areas of New York, when the word was spreading about what the Germans were doing in Ireland. More than a few girls who looked a little too German for their own good ended up having a bucket of hot road tar and a sack of feathers poured over their heads.

"We've always had to watch that sort of thing and every time we've moved we've had to learn new customs and new rules of behavior. Do that often enough and we forget who we originally were. Acculturated is the official word for it. You've no idea how much we all envy you. You know who you are, we've forgotten. The Seer's never changed though. Once Loki accused him of moving armies and countries around like some giant game of chess and caring nothing about the people who suffered as a result. Lot of truth in that too, enough to hurt. He's isolated himself from the consequences of what his decisions mean for the people who get in the way. And all of that means he needs a partner to keep him in touch with the rest of the human race. He hasn't got one at the moment and that's why I said I'll be cheering you on. Just remember, all of us chicks, we're on your side, we're here for you to talk to if you need it. And that ding was the elevator. More later as the saying goes."

The Seer walked in, tossing a briefcase to one side and flipping his hat on top of it, showing no sign of picking up on the tension still in the air. "Got the papers, Inanna honey? We're still doing the backsweep on the intercepts. Had some hits, not as many as we'd feared."

"Got them here boss. I'll be on my way."

"Right, enjoy yourself. Raven, how does Bugaboo Creek grab you for dinner? It's a steak place just down US1"

Behind his back Inanna punched her fist in the air and made a money-rubbing gesture with her fingers. Without turning around, the Seer carried on smoothly "You been placing bets on me again Inanna? Watch this one, Raven. When the new Casino's open up, she'll be your first customer."

"Love you too, Boss. Be seeing you. Have a good evening Raven."

"Thanks for bringing the stuff over honey, Gusoyn's downstairs waiting for you. Sorry about this Raven, I meant to be here earlier but things are pretty grim. Worse than you can imagine. Everything all right?"

"It just shook me to find Inanna here, I didn't know what to think. When I came in, it looked like she owned the place."

"I'm pretty sure she does. I'd have to check with Lillith, she keeps all our records, but I'm pretty sure this one's hers. We all own bits of property scattered around and we all use them as convenient. We've got a beautiful old house down at Jamestown in Virginia you'll love."

"Oh no, I was darned rude to her at first."

"She won't mind. Bet you she just ignored it and kept on talking. Inanna is one of those people who just lets things like that slide off her back. Before we go, two little bits of business. One is, we've got the blackpox vaccine ready. First batches anyway. As soon as it's in full production, we'll divert some to you and the rest of your people along the border. You're right in the firing line if there is another cross-border incident and if we leave things to the system, you'll be at the end of the queue for vaccines."

"That's new. The white man giving us a cure for smallpox."

"Oh, you don't believe that old myth do you?"

"Seer, those epidemics decimated our people."

"I know and I know a lot about General Amherst. Not a pleasant man at all, if I didn't know better I'd think he was the reason brother-sister marriages got a bad name. Anyway, we'll fight over that some other time. The other thing is, I have to go to Cuba soon, on business. Want to come? We can disguise it as a research trip into running Casinos, with the first of yours opening soon, you'll need some personal observation of what's involved."

Raven's eyes lit up. "That would be wonderful. I'd love it."

"Good, I'll have Lillith arrange for you to have your own rooms in the hotel. Not sure which one yet. Probably the Havana Tropicana."

There was a brief pause while Raven looked down and made up her mind. Like it or not, she and her friends were being absorbed by the Seer's circle. It was inevitable she supposed. They were a tiny group of people that had spent their time within the Indian society of the reservations, isolated from the world at large. Now, they weren't alone any more, they were part of something much, much larger. But being absorbed like that they would be losing their identity?

After all, they were different from these people. They were accepted by the population they came from, they didn't live in the shadows the way The Seer and his people did. Would they have to give up its daylight and live in the shadows also? Then Raven realized something. The Seer and his close friends, his extended family, were an identifiable entity within the larger American group. The impact of Inanna's words sank home. She and her friends had as much to offer the Seer's circle as they were as liable to receive. The Seer and all his people had no real home or society, they just went along with whatever they had to. Suddenly Raven realized that Inanna had been telling the truth when she'd said she envied her. The stability of a known and established culture where they were accepted was a gift they'd value.

"Raven, I'm running late, I've got to change. Can I be discourteous and leave you for a few minutes? Perhaps you could check the news channel weather broadcast for me? The streets are clear so we could take my car, but if its going to snow again, I'd rather grab a cab."

"Of course." The Seer vanished into another room while Raven turned the television on. She was lucky, she just caught the end of the weather forecast. Clear, cold but no snow. "No snow, we'll be fine."

"That's great. We won't put the top down though." Raven snorted at the idea of driving in a convertible with the roof down in mid-winter. She could probably stand it but she guessed the Seer's pampered ears would fall off. Behind her, there was a thump as a door closed and she turned around. The Seer had changed out of his suit and was in casual clothes. He walked over to drawer, took out a stainless steel Colt M1911 and chambered a round.

"You carry, Raven?"

She shook her head. "Off the reservation, we're not allowed to carry weapons Whites are probably afraid we'll go on the warpath or something."

The Seer said something under his breath. "Another bloody stupid thing to fix. Meanwhile we can get you sorted out." He picked up the telephone and dialed a number. A couple of seconds later, the person on the other end had probably picked up. "Lillith, not disturbing you am I honey. . . . . . Good. Look, can you fix up a concealed carry permit for Raven? Federal ones, we don't want her to worry about state lines. Better sort them out for Menewa, Five Elks and the others as well. Yeah, that'll do fine. Thanks honey." He turned to Raven. "You'll have a Federal concealed carry permit in a week. Let you carry anywhere, any time. Ask Henry and he'll give you some lessons in practical pistol craft."

"Thanks Seer." Raven wasn't actually sure she was grateful and she guessed that Menewa wouldn't carry a gun even if he was allowed to. "Hey what's this on the news?" The on-the-hour broadcast was starting.

"*Tonight, the situation around the world continues to deteriorate as the new smallpox epidemic continues to spread. The disease is reportedly known as blackpox to distinguish it from the less deadly variants. The first cases were reported in Algeria and that continues to be the main center of infection. More border Algerian villages have reportedly started to suffer from the disease and there are some suggestions that one or more of the larger towns have been infected. More worrying though, is the news that cases of blackpox have been reported from Colombia and Mexico. We now speak to our Washington correspondent. Stan?"*

"Well Barbara, word here tonight is that we now have definite proof that blackpox is a Caliphate-inspired biological weapons attack. There are rumors that the United States was attacked as well as French Algeria but the attack was thwarted and that the infections in South America are just by-products of that failed attack."

"The United States was attacked. Does that mean we're at war?"

"One might think so but there's no sign of it here. The Pentagon, the NSC Building, the White House, they're all quiet with just the usual night shift at work. Whatever the United States plans to do, there's no sign that they're doing it now."

The Seer laughed "One thing about Washington you can guarantee, honey, is that Stan Mather will always get it wrong. It never occurred to him that when there's a crisis and nothing seems to be happening, the reason why is that the decisions have all been made, all the plans are ready and everybody might as well get a good night's sleep."

"We are going to war?"

"We surely are. Tomorrow, the President gives the word and we go. How hungry are you?"

Raven blinked, disorientated by the sudden change of direction. "Very."

"Good, me too. Let's go."

"Uhh, Seer, I've got a small cabin on our reservation. It's nothing much, not much more than a single room but may I share it with the rest of you, add it too the pot of properties? I doubt if you'd want to live on a reservation but. . . ."

"Don't bet on it. Henry will jump at the chance. He hates living in motels when he's out west. Quick question, its real cold out there, you got a heavy coat?"

Raven gestured downwards and the Seer glanced. It was heavily padded but polyester, cheap. It wouldn't keep out the biting winds of a Washington street. He walked over to a cupboard and looked inside. Raven held her breath. *He wasn't going to give her a fur was he?* Nothing could be less appropriate for the reservation and having it would cause words to be spoken behind her back. About what she'd done to get it. She might be ghost-touched but a reservation was a small place with vicious tongues ready to wag. Then she breathed out. He'd got a heavy, fleece-lined leather jacket from a cupboard, something that would pass unnoticed back home.

"Genuine, military cold-weather gear. Russian-designed SAC-issue no less. Available in military surplus stores at way less than the cost Uncle Sam paid. This doesn't come from there of course but nobody else need know that."

Inanna had been right, he was always two jumps ahead. Raven smiled to herself as she made a decision. The Seer wouldn't find out yet but there would be no need for Lillith to book her rooms for herself. "Are you sure we should be going out with a crisis going down?"

"Nothing else to do, honey. Eat, drink and be merry; for tomorrow we're going to start a nuclear war."

CHAPTER TEN
CHARGE!

State Department Communiqué

The United States of America will be conducting military operations against the Caliphate effective as of 08:00 February 25th, 1973. Any attempt to interfere with or otherwise impede those operations will be considered an act of war against the United States of America and treated accordingly.

National Oceanographic and Atmospheric Administration Notice to Mariners.

The United States of America draws your attention to the fact that the Strait of Hormuz will be permanently closed to all shipping effective as of 08:00 February 25th, 1973. Mariners attempting to transit the Strait of Hormuz after that time will do so at their own risk.

P6M-4 Seamaster Tigerfish *Approaching the Strait of Hormuz*

She was finally doing what she was designed to do. Lieutenant Commander George Dixon settled back in his seat as *Tigerfish* dropped down to her penetration altitude and started her run towards the Strait up ahead. Unlike SAC's ferocious arsenal, the Navy's P6M flying boats were intended for low-altitude penetration missions, laying mines and hitting coastal installations. They'd rarely done that; most of their time had been spent inserting SEALs or picking them up after they'd done their deeds ashore. Sometimes they'd run electronic intelligence missions, sometimes air-sea rescue or few other unglamorous runs. Never before had they done the job they were supposed to.

As a result, the flying boats were seen as something of a backwater in the Navy, a posting that held very few prospects for promotion. Flying off the carriers or serving on the missile cruisers, that was another matter. Those career paths lead to the top. But the flying boats didn't and even the need to maintain the force was being questioned. After all, what did they offer that SAC did not? This mission was intended, in part, to answer that question. Neither the B-52s over 50,000 feet up, nor the B-70s 30,000 feet higher couldn't lay mines.

The briefing a few hours earlier had been explicit, the American strike aimed at the Caliphate was intended to do two things. One was to shatter the Caliphate's ability to produce biological weapons by destroying the industrial complexes suspected of making them. The other was to limit the Caliphate's access to the foreign currency it needed to buy replacement industrial equipment. The Caliphate's industrial ability was limited at best, they were barely capable of building crude automobiles and low-performance aircraft. Precision machinery was way beyond them and machine tools were in such short supply that nobody was prepared to supply them without massive comprensation. So the Caliphate had to import what it needed and the money it needed to buy them was gained through sales of oil. Those oil exports ran, mostly, through the Straits up ahead. So those Straits were about to be closed.

Of course, the primary customer for the Caliphate's oil was Chipan and removing that oil from the market would hurt Chipan's economy. Hurt it badly; from an American point of view that was no regrettable thing. To get around the problem, Chipan would either have to buy Russian oil, helping to strengthen America's ally in the process or Indonesian oil, helping to strengthen the Triple Alliance and put an end to the idiotic but lethal fighting going on in the South China Sea. If Chipan built pipelines in the Caliphate to bypass the blocked Strait, that would use financial and industrial resources that would otherwise have gone to strengthen Chipan's military forces. No matter which way one cut it, the Seamasters were executing a vital mission. One that SAC, for all its power, could not.

"Target up ahead." Lieutenant James Wicks, *Tigerfish's* copilot, confirmed the course plot. The whole point of this mission, the whole reason for assigning it to the Seamasters, was to lay the mines in the flying boat's belly accurately. This was a precision mission after all.

"*Tigershark* confirms. Any hostile air activity?"

"A lot of radars lit up Sir." That was Lieutenant (jg) Joseph Ridgeway in the back, the Seamaster's defensive systems operator. "A lot of air surveillance radars, we're even picking up the big ones on Bahrein. But no fighters."

"Ducting, this area's notorious for it. We must be picking up every radar in the region. Bahrein won't be on the air for long. The Vigilantes will see to that."

"Mines ready to drop, Sir." Lieutenant (jg) Arnold Becker, the fourth crew member, cut in. There were fifteen rising mines in *Tigerfish's* belly. Each was a marvel of engineering; a circular sonar array built around the outer casing and a series of thrusters. The array would pick up the sound of a ship and determine its range, then rotate so that an underwater rocket would be fired at the contact. At 200 knots, the target would have no chance of escaping and an 1,200 pound rocket hitting at that speed didn't really need a warhead to destroy its victim. The rocket still had a warhead of course, just to make sure.

Tigerfish wasn't carrying nuclear mines. The rising mines were intended for the outer ring of the minefield. Other Seamasters were carrying the nuclear mines for the center of the field. Still, the Russian-made rising mines were deadly enough. The Russians had always been good at mine warfare.

"Tell *Tigershark, Tiger Ray* and *Tigersnake* to get ready to drop in one minute from synchronization signal - now."

The four P6M-4s changed course slightly, now heading parallel down the Strait. *Still no opposition*, Dixon thought gratefully, *this was where enemy fighters could really cause nausea*. Still, with all the F9U-5 Crusaders and F4H-4 Phantoms in the area, any Caliphate fighter that showed its face would have a very short life. Not that their lives were scheduled to be much longer if they stayed on the ground. The Vigilantes with their nuclear weapons were going to see to that.

Dixon glanced quickly sideways. Frank Collins's *Tigershark* and James Simkin's *Tiger Ray* were in position. Charles Carlson's *Tigersnake* was on the outside of the turn and had dropped back slightly. As he'd watched, Dixon had seen him pull back into place. Two of Carlson's four crewman, Miller and White were newbies, they'd only joined Tiger Flight a few days before. No problem, they were learning their trade well.

A loud ding almost drowned by the rattle as the watertight rotating bomb door in *Tigerfish's* belly opened up and the fifteen mines started their falls towards the sea. The American assault on the Caliphate had started.

Chipanese ULCC Aikoku Maru, *Approaching the Strait of Hormuz.*

"Ahoy, Imperial Japanese Merchant Ship, this is United States Warship 174 calling on the international hailing band. We have an urgent amendment to your charts. Request permission to come on board and deliver new charts to you, courtesy of the United States Navy."

The nuclear-powered cruiser was sleek and gray in the sea a few hundred meters off the *Aikoku Maru's* port beam. "174, what ship is that." Captain Tan's voice was interested rather than urgent. First Officer Chao needed the practice more than anything else. While the Captain focused his binoculars on the cruiser, he heard Chao thumbing through the pages of his naval reference book. Tan shook his head slowly, no matter how much Britain had declined since they'd collapsed in 1940, they still produced the naval reference book every warship in the world used.

"*USS John C Stens* Sir. Improved Long Beach class. Will we let them board?"

"Of course. Make in reply 'Thank you for your concern. Welcome on board.' Have some whisky and fresh sushi sent up to the bridge."

Tan returned to watching the cruiser. The two twin Terrier missile launchers forward and the twin Talos launcher aft were all loaded. No way of telling from here, but Tan was prepared to bet that all six missiles were nuclear tipped. They were trained fore and aft though, as were the four eight-round boxes for Sea Falcon missiles on the corners of the superstructure's main deck. Tan was under no illusions about his importance, if the Americans wanted to sink him they'd use one of those. The 0.25 kiloton warhead on a Sea Falcon would do for his tanker quite nicely. Then he looked aft. There was activity on the flight deck. That was the difference between the original Long Beach class and the improved version. 8,000 tonnes of displacement and a hangar that could hold four to six Kaman Seaking Rotodynes. One of those hulking brutes was on the flight deck at the moment, dwarfing the little SH-2 Seasprite helicopter that was being readied. *Why do the Americans prefix all their naval equipment with the word Sea?* Tan asked himself. *To remind the crew they weren't on land perhaps.*

The Seasprite took off and made the short hop over to the *Aikoku Maru*. The pilot didn't bother to climb much; the flight was too short. The helicopter had hardly begun to fly when it turned and landed on the cleared pad set on the tanker's stern. Two figures climbed out and hurried up to the bridge. Fortunately for First Officer Chao, the refreshments the Captain had ordered arrived on the bridge before they did.

"Permission to enter the bridge Captain?" One of the Americans spoke carefully in Japanese. Obviously a rote-learned phrase.

"Permission granted Commander. . . ." Tan spoke in English, the international language of the sea.

"Alexander, William Alexander. Sir, the Strait of Hormuz is closed for the indefinite future."

Commander Alexander's voice was interrupted by a sonic boom followed by the sound of jet engines. Overhead, four dark blue A3J-5 Vigilante bombers were heading north. "Military operations in progress require us to seal off the Gulf. I have new charts for you sir, they show the danger areas."

He handed the charts over. The new minefields were marked with the deadly black-and-yellow trefoil. Nuclear mines. Tan shook slightly.

"Commander, may I offer you some refreshments while I study these? A drink, perhaps? I know your ships are dry, we do not suffer from that problem. And the sushi is freshly made."

"Thank you sir." Alexander and his assistant picked up pieces of sushi. Raw fish, well it wasn't in the American diet but this was a ticklish matter and courtesy was everything.

"Commander Alexander, you know that 80 percent of Japan's oil is carried through that Strait?"

"Indeed I do sir. But I am advised that the Caliphate blackpox attacks make our action essential."

"Blackpox." Tan thought of the film he'd seen of the victims dying of the disease. Horrible. "Very well Commander, I will order my ship to hove-to and radio Tokyo for instructions. You are contacting the other tankers heading this way?"

"Indeed I am Sir. It will be a busy day for my ship." The bridge was lit suddenly by a flash. In the far distance, four mushroom clouds were forming. "That was the main Caliphate air base this side of the Straits. It is going to be a busy day for many, many people." The thunder of the laydowns was muted by distance. Somewhere a lot of people had just died. “Thank you for your courtesy and consideration in these difficult times, Captain.”

Kozlowski Air Force Base, Limehouse, Maine

“It’s quite a sight General, quite a sight.” General van der Camp looked at the lines of silvery-blue bombers on the taxiways, the heat from their engines causing the blood-red rising sun to ripple and distort in the last fleeting shreds of pre-dawn darkness. “Your boy’s number 17.”

General (retd) Bob Dedmon swung his binoculars down the line in front of the control tower. There she was, *Texan Lady II*. Idly, he wondered if his *Texan Lady*, sitting in her enclosure at the end of Bomber Row knew that a Valkyrie bearing her name was going to war. The nose art was the same; only now it was in muted grays against the anti-optical paintwork of the bomber’s airframe. “Fly high Robbie, fly high.” The words were barely audible but the next ones weren’t.

“It looks the same as it did back then, Rex, bombers are different of course but it looks the same. Only, back then, we all thought that if we did our job right, The Big One would mean we’d never have to do this again. I guess we were wrong.”

Rex van der Camp shook his head. “We’ve had almost-peace for a quarter of a century. No major wars between nations at all. And look at the fuss down in the South China Sea, both sides keeping it limited to a small area and fighting like real gentlemen. Both scared spitless that if the fighting spreads or they don’t stick to the rules, we’ll end it with the sledgehammer. If it wasn’t for you guys in the ‘36s back in ‘47, that would have spread to the whole Far East by now.”

Dedmon watched his son taxi his B-70 forward. “By the way, Rex, thank’s for letting my boy carry the name on. Guess it messed up the naming traditions.”

“Nah, about a quarter of the birds carry non-Valkyrie names from older aircraft, usually the one’s flown by the next generation.

Have you noticed how SAC's getting to be a family affair? Anyway, there's no way this command will get between a crew and their chosen name for their bird."

"Any word back from the lead elements?"

"Some. Navy's at work mining the Strait and blasting coastal defense positions around the Gulf. Last we heard, *Maine* and *Ohio* were hitting the air defense bases at the north end of the Gulf. Bahrain's already down we know that, four Vigilantes took it down, total of eight 100 kiloton Mark 61s."

Neither man said anything but after a small island like Bahrain had been hit like that, there wouldn't be anything or anybody left. An entire community wiped out for the sin of sharing an island with a very large strategic air search radar and the long-range SAMs that went with it.

"That's about a quarter of the Navy's laydowns to date. Last we heard, they'd lost seven planes, four Viggies, two F9Us and a P6M. Just like the old days Bob, the Navy's kicking the door in for us again."

"Hope it doesn't have the same cost." Dedmon's mind went back to the sight of *Shiloh* burning twenty five years earlier. "You seen the display we've got on *Shiloh* down at the museum?"

"Sure have. Great model, who built it? Newport News?"

"Bunch of kids believe it or not. Local high school. Made it their term project, NAVSEA looked it over and said that it was better than any shipyard model they'd ever seen. They're rolling. Still holding 15 second intervals I see."

The windows in the control tower shook as the first of the 100th Bomb Group's B-70Cs hurtled down the runway and rotated, heading upwards for the safety of the stratosphere. Even as its main wheels lifted from the runway, the second in the formation was accelerating down the runway while the third was just starting to move. One aircraft lifting off every 15 seconds. In less than twelve minutes all the 100th Group's 45 B-70Cs would be on their way to targets in Iran Satrapy, the Caliphate. The Group's 30 remaining B-70As would be sitting this one out, a decision that had caused some measure of discontent. Still, they might have their role to play if the Caliphate didn't get the message. Any sign of a fight or counterstrikes and they'd go in, along with the lumbering B-52s.

Cockpit, B-70C Sigrun *100th Heavy Bomb Group, Runway Oh-Nine-Oh, Kozlowski Air Force Base, Limehouse, Maine*

"Cockpit checks complete. Mission equipment operational?"

"Twelve Frisbees, four AIM-47s, eight AGM-76s in the front bay. Two 550 kiloton Mark 43s and auxiliary fuel cells in the rear bay. Onboard diagnostics confirm all safed but operational."

"Confirm, all weapons safe. All crew prepare for take off."

Sigrun rolled forward; rolling fast since one of the B-70s little quirks was that she was uncontrollable if taxied too slowly. O'Seven counted three joins in the concrete sheets that made up the taxiway before making the U-turn onto the runway. The cockpit was so far in front of the nose wheels that maneuvering on the ground was a highly skilled artform. Then, *Sigrun* came to a shuddering stop. O'Seven reflected that North American still hadn't quite got the brakes sorted out. Then he stood on the brake pedals. "All engines full power!"

Jim Hook rammed the throttles forward, causing the six J-93 engines to spool up to maximum power. As they did, the view out of the cockpit changed from sky to runway as the aircraft's tail rose and the nose dipped. Then, *Sigrun* was sliding forward on her locked wheels, *time to go before the tires blew*. O'Seven let off the brakes and *Sigrun* bounded forward, her nose porpoising wildly as she picked up speed. Hook hated this bit; the motion of the cockpit, so far ahead of the nosewheels made him seasick. Then, as *Sigrun* started to rotate, the motion ceased and she was airborne, her undercarriage retracting as she headed skywards, climbing at 27,500 feet per minute.

“IAS five-sixty-five. Nose visor rising.” Ahead of the crew, the Valkyrie’s nose was elevating into its triple-sonic position. Technically, the aircraft could fly triple-sonic with its nose down but it cut range and speed. Those weren’t the main problem though; fly triple-sonic like that and the heat from the windshield would make looking out of it like staring into an oven. Heat was the one constant, ever-present factor in flying the Valkyrie. “We’ll level off at 75,000 feet and cruising speed Mach 3.15. That’ll take us out to Gibraltar and over the Mediterranean. We’ll refuel over the Aegean then go to 3.25 for the flight over Syria and Iraq Satrapies and to 3.4 and 80,000 feet for the final runs on the biofacilities at Kushk e Nosrat and Qom in Iran.”

“This is for real, isn’t it. We’re not playing this time.” *Sigrun’s* voice was apprehensive, a little frightened even.

“That’s right *Sigrun*, this time we’re going in for real. All the way to the Caliphate. Two hours flight time to Gibraltar, an hour and a half to Feet Dry and 30 minutes to get to target. Four hours total. Then we either return home or if we’ve got damage, divert to a base in Russia. Your MiG friends are waiting to escort you in if that happens.”

“We didn’t get the jackpot though. *Texan Lady II* drew those.” John Henty was disappointed, he’d hoped *Sigrun* would get the two targets close to Tehran.

“You surprised? Robbie Dedmon’s old man was in the control tower watching us go. Anyway, they’d make sure a *Texan Lady* got the capital targets again. We’ve got the big bangs though. Her Mark 43s are dialed back to 100 kilotons.”

“Tehran. There will be a lot of people down there.” *Sigrun’s* voice was sad. “Even with her weapons dialed back.”

“Look at it this way *Sigrun*. If we take away their ability to make bioweapons and hurt them badly enough so they don’t try again, think of all the people, our people, who won’t die of blackpox.”

"I know. It's still sad."

War Room, Underneath the White House. Washington DC

"God rest ye merry gentlemen
Let nothing you dismay,
If things don't work out quite right
The Valkyries are on their way."

The Seer reflected that if Messalina had been singing, the melody would have been perfect, the verse would have scanned properly and the accompaniment would have been a joy to hear. Naamah, on the other hand, had the singing voice of an unoiled cement mixer running a load of gravel. That wasn't what had made President Nixon wince though.

"Naamah, this is no time for levity."

"Quite right Mister President." General Thomas Power gave the impression he was speaking to a room full of new recruits. "We don't blow people *up*. Most people think our nuclear weapons kill by blast, fire and radiation when in fact it's the *fall* to the bottom of the crater that kills them."

A ripple of laughter ran around the war-room it was an old joke but a goodie that got played on every newcomer. Nixon was about to respond when the door slid open again. Lillith entered with a series of files. She winced and limped slightly, it had been a busy morning and the bitter February cold was biting into the damaged joints in her feet. Power noted her discomfort and quietly slid a chair behind her, seating her. The gesture was deliberately unobtrusive. If it had been noted it would have spoiled the image he so carefully constructed, but it won him a dazzling smile of thanks from Lillith.

Despite the care, Nixon did notice and it put the graveyard humor that had been floating around the war room into context. These were grim times; laughing at them was a way of accommodating their gravity. He wondered, briefly, what sort of jokes had been floating around the war room twenty five years earlier, while The Big One destroyed Germany. "Talking about radiation, isn't there a danger we'll have another Great Famine?"

"We learned a lot from The Big One, Mister President. There, we planned many, most, of the air bursts too low. We're doing it differently now. We're dropping about the same number of devices as we did in The Big One, the Navy are doing 60 laydowns, the Valkyries 115 and the Russians 25. That's 200 total, but the total yield is more than eight times greater. The attack's scattered though, its across a much larger area than The Big One. The targets in Iran Satrapy, the ones we've assigned to the 100th, they're mostly in remote, barren areas. That doesn't apply to the ones the 35th are going after in Iraq Satrapy, some of those are close to major urban areas."

"Close to major urban areas. That'll mean a lot of civilians, did we have to hit those?"

"Mister President, if we gave a target a miss today because its surrounded by civilians, this time next week, every strategic target will be the center of a mass of them. I believe it should be our announced policy that military targets placed in civilian areas will be given high priority, not exempted from attack.

"Be that as it may, the devices we're using are far more efficient than the ones we used back in '47. They were horribly inefficient, about eight percent, they blew most of their fissile all over the place. That was a big contributor to The Great Famine. It was low-level heavy metal poisoning as much as any other factor, although there were a lot of other factors. The devices we're using today, fusion-fission weapons, some of them are over 90 percent efficient. For all that though, yes, there will be some radiation problems. That's why we waited, the wind's from the North East, it'll direct the plumes south west over Caliphate territory."

"Anyway, Mister President." Power spoke thoughtfully. "As far as radiation is concerned, you know, it's never been proved to me that two heads aren't better than one."

Nixon's jaw dropped at that but before he could say anything Naamah cut smoothly in. "But General, suppose one head wanted to vote Republican and the other Democrat? Who would the hand obey?'

Admiral Stanley had been speaking on one of the banks of phones. Now he looked up from his desk. "You know, my dear, I had a Senior Chief once who could have answered that one very easily. Probably recommended the use of a guillotine. Ras Anuras has gone. Cost us two A3Js and an F9U but the missile complex, radars and fighter base are all history.

"The Caliphate fighters are coming up at last, they've learned that if they stay on the ground, they die on the ground. According to Dickie Armstrong on *Ohio* it's like clubbing baby seals out there. Lot of Irenes, a few Brandis. They're like an elevator according to his CAG, going up, going down. We've pretty well cleaned out the Gulf, One target left, a long-range missile base just outside Riyadh. Once that's gone, the carriers will recover their planes and pull out. Navy's done, its up to the Valkyries."

On the situation display maps, the red lines representing 100 Valkyries from the 100th and 35th Bomb Groups were streaking across the Atlantic.

Cockpit, B-70C Shield Maiden *35th Bomb Group, 77,000 feet over the Atlantic*

"Outer skin temperature has stabilized at 624 degrees. All systems nominal. Hydraulics all in order." The last was critical, the B-70 had a temperamental hydraulic system that wasn't entirely debugged yet. The real problem was that the hydraulic fluid was at the temperature of the oil in a deep fat fryer. If the system leaked, the secondary damage could be very serious. Captain Mike Yates leaned forward in his seat and put a color snapshot into a clip in front of him. It was of a girl with a caramel-colored skin and black hair braided into cornrows then swept back into a bun. Beside him, his copilot grinned.

"She said yes then, Mike?"

“Last night. She said what clinched it was she’d heard how I’d been besieged by Natashas in Russia and anybody who could keep turning them down like that had to be serious.”

“Yeah, what happened there? It seemed like they were coming in from all over. There were rumors one of the fighter regiments was flying them in towards the end.”

“I suspect a foul plot. Anyway, Sellie reckoned that resistance like that deserved its reward.”

Bill Cobb hesitated for a second, this was a sensitive area. “And your folks? How did they take it when you told them?”

“About Sellie being black? Pops didn't care too much, he just said we’d have to expect problems from others but we wouldn’t get any from him. Momma threw a fit, burst into tears and stormed out the room. Pops just said ‘See what I mean’ and ignored her.” Yates was pensive for a moment. “Odd that, I expected it to be the other way round. Momma always acted so enlightened and tolerant. Guess when it was all right in the abstract but not when it came home.”

“Set a date yet?”

“First Sunday in April. Sellie wants to be married in her home town, placed called Brandon in Maryland. So she’s getting all that fixed up.”

Around the cockpit, the crew made private notes of the time and place. A SAC wedding meant they had to make arrangements as well. One was a fly-past; another the traditional archway of swords. The rest would have to do with the stag party. That could turn out to be almost as destructive as the mission they were on now.

“We’re coming up on Gibraltar now.” A little less than 15 miles below them, the perfect curve of Algeciras Bay was passing underneath, the long finger of the Gibraltar fortress sticking out. It was a measure of how fast *Shield Maiden* was eating distance that the sight was quickly lost behind them and the Valkyrie had crossed from the Atlantic to the Mediterranean.

"I suppose that means I'm going to have to get you back home now, doesn't it?" *Shield Maiden's* voice was amused, slightly mocking.

Defensive Area Simone, French Algeria/Caliphate Border

The continuous thunder sounded like an artillery barrage. To the uninitiated anyway. The battle-hardened would realize the thunder was neither inbound nor outbound; it came from high overhead. It wasn't a thunderstorm though. The continuous barrage of booms came from the dozens of thin white threads, high, high in the sky overhead.

After a night in which the world had held its breath, the American bombers were on the move. General Marcel Bigeard looked up at the thin contrails with the first shred of hope for weeks in his heart. Morale in Algeria had plummeted as the blackpox took hold. Who could lay blame for that? To go to sleep every night, not knowing whether a fine, invisible, untouchable mist would descend and condemn to a dreadful lingering death.

"Look boys. Overhead. It's the American bombers on their way to the Caliphate." The troops around him looked up and cheered at the sight. Nearby other troops stopped when they heard the noise and then joined in, the first time in many, many, years French troops had cheered Americans. Bigeard heard the cheering spread down the defenses of the border line. To make his day even better, he had heard that a vaccine against blackpox had been tested and was on its way.

Then, Bigeard's thoughts were interrupted by a private who'd grabbed his sleeve. A gesture that would have been unthinkable in the old French Army but one which the paras viewed as being perfectly normal.

"Look General, there's more of them up there." And there were indeed, accompanied by another rolling barrage of supersonic bangs. Once it had been thought that if aircraft flew high enough, the booms would be attenuated by the time they hit the ground. The B-70 had proved otherwise and a 250,000 kilogram aircraft made a very solid sonic boom.

Then another sound interrupted the cheers, music played over the loudspeakers that were emplaced every few hundred meters down the defense line. Bigeard grinned broadly as he recognized the tune, one not so often heard in a Europe where things German were still despised. It was Wagner's *Ride of the Valkyries*.

The Military Command Center, Dezful, Iran Satrapy, The Caliphate.

Morteza Farzaneh looked at the radar displays with fascination. The inbound American bombers were already visible, up high and coming in fast, they could be seen a long way away. That didn't worry the Americans; they actually wanted their aircraft to be seen approaching, to give the intended victim a last chance to back down and save themselves from destruction.

That wasn't why he found the sight so interesting. It was the historian in Farzaneh that was rapt. Looking at the plan, it was an exact replica of The Big One, the nuclear strike that had destroyed Germany. Two separate groups of bombers. A northern formation aimed at targets in the north and east, a southern formation heading for targets in the south and west. Going by reports and information from sources in America, it was even the same groups responsible. In The Big One, the northern formation had been the Third Air Division; in this strike, it was the 100th Bomb Group that had once been part of the Third. The southern formation in The Big One had been the First Air Division; here it was the 35th Bomb Group, a unit that had then been part of the First. Idly, Farzaneh wondered if representatives of the Fourth and Fifth Air Divisions would be following up with conventional bombs as they had so many years before.

Of course, the resemblance wasn't deliberate, it was simply that a good plan worked and tended to get reused. The Air Divisions in SAC had long gone, discarded as an unnecessary command layer. And there would be no conventional bombing. Then it had been necessary because targets were in countries occupied by Germany, not by Germany itself. The atomic bombs had been reserved for the German homeland. Today, all the targets were in the homeland; all the targets would be receiving nuclear weapons. Farzaneh wondered if the Americans realized how big a favor they were doing the Caliphate.

MiG-25 Pchela Gray-447 For Illena Karenina *Over Iran Satrapy, The Caliphate*

They were the Gray Wolves, streaking ahead of the formation of bombers behind them. Their task described as "free chase." The orders were simple; hunt down Caliphate fighters and shoot them from the sky and they had the absolute freedom to do whatever was needed. Over the Rodina, fighters operated under strict ground control; steered to their targets by instructions from the ground that would not be disobeyed. Here, though, over hostile territory, the rules were different. It was "free chase," kill the enemy and do whatever it took to achieve that objective. It was a fighter pilot's dream.

Yet, there were restrictions, even in a free chase. The Russian aircraft were coming down from the north; the Americans were coming in from the west. Their F-108s would be first, doing a free chase all their own. They were followed by the RB-58s who would take on and destroy the ground-based defenses. The B-70s would be behind them, running in towards the targets that lay deep in the heart of the Caliphate. Following behind the B-70s were what the American liaison officer had described as "a thundering herd of B-52s." Just as the priest, who had lead the Regiment in prayers before take-off, had described it, they were all 'doing God's work.' Still, even doing God's work, there was still a risk with two air forces form two countries conducting air operations over the same piece of airspace and at the same time while fighting enemy defenses. The previous night had been a frantic effort to ensure that both Russian and American Air Force's Identification, Friend or Foe systems were synchronized and shared the same codes.

The MiG-25s had another job as well. The Americans were far from home; if any of their aircraft were damaged, the Russians were to find them, and escort them to an emergency landing at a number of designated airfields close to the border. If the worst happened, if any of the aircraft, Russian or American, went down, there were SEAL teams and their Russian equivalent, Spetznaz groups, ready to go in and rescue the crews. But, all that lay in the future. For now, the watchword was "Free Chase."

The targets richly deserved their fate. The Russian Air Force was using the American onslaught to settle a few scores of their own, scores that ran deep and wide and justified a terrible vengeance. A few months earlier, a group of Chechen terrorists, ones who were demanding an independent state of Chechnya in Southern Russia had seized a school on the first day of the new academic year. They'd gone through the motions of making demands and opening negotiations but they hadn't been sincere. At the first excuse, they'd opened fire on the children and their parents, killing hundreds. They'd ***killed the children!!*** Even the thought of that hideously depraved act made Major Ivan Josevich Peterenko's muscles jerk in fury. He honestly couldn't imagine a loathsome or more despicable crime and the violence of his reaction made his *Illena* lurch in the air.

"Problems Major?" His wingman was on the radio. The MiG-25 was new and still riddled with teething problems. One of them was a dislike for sudden, violent interruptions to the airflow over the wings. Peterenko breathed deeply in an effort to cool down. There was no need to risk his aircraft; much better to get revenge for the atrocity. Well, facilitate revenge. The act itself would be performed by the Tu-22s flying some tens of kilometers behind. Their nuclear-tipped stand-off missiles would erase the training bases the terrorists had come from; wipe them from the face of the earth. All the Gray Wolves had to do was clear the way in.

"No Georgi. All is well." Peterenko broke for a second as the "All Seeing Eye" far behind them radioed in the warning. "But we have customers coming up. Four of them, all hostile. High rate of climb, probably Irenes or Brandis. May be Elles. Bearing oh-three-two, range fifty kilometers. Weapons are free."

Let it be Elles, Peterenko thought. *Nobody had shot any of those down yet.* Technically, the Elle was a Japanese Army improvement over the J12K-5 Irene. The Army had wanted a bigger, longer-ranged radar which would take up all of the nose so they'd had to move the air intakes back to the wing roots. The problem was that wing root intakes feeding two engines stacked vertically was an airflow nightmare so they'd switched the engines to the more traditional horizontal pair. That had caused structural problems with the wings so they'd had to move those from the mid-fuselage to a low-mounted position. That had meant redesigning the tail, so the Elle ended up bearing no relationship at all to its purported ancestor. All of which proved that if one started off with a lousy design, fiddling with it wasn't going to help much. But the Elle was reputed to be a far superior aircraft to the much-derided Irene.

"I have them on radar. Four contacts, spread right out." Peterenko grunted; even the Caffs learned eventually. Bunching aircraft tightly together might have worked thirty years ago but now it was just an invitation to slaughter by the American's nuclear-tipped air-to-air missiles. Everybody spread out these days. This gave the Pchela a problem. The scan cone on its radar was quite narrow since Russian designers preferred high power down a tight beam to gain range and enough power to burn through jamming. The price was a narrow field of view. Still, the Gray Wolves had height and speed over the enemy aircraft. They were still climbing from their airbase. Look-down, Shoot-down the Americans called it.

"I have target on the extreme right, you take extreme left Georgi. R40Ts locked on, radar homing."

"Locked and ready to fire."

"Take them!"

Gray-447 fired its pair of radar homing R40T missiles followed a split second later by Gray-441. Below them, the formation of Caliphate fighters suddenly split apart. The four aircraft divided into two loose pairs that curved away from each other, putting space between them and the incoming missiles. Peterenko grunted; obviously the aircraft had radar warning receivers. That was new. Usually the Chimps exported aircraft that were stripped down to the bare essentials. Either they'd had a change of policy or the Caffs had woken up to the fact that what appeared to be more than a "bare essential" was vital for survival. Or perhaps they'd realized that a martyred fighter pilot wasn't really very much use. Whatever.

The R-40s were following the curves made by the enemy fighters but they were having already difficulty matching the steadily-tightening turns when the enemy fighters barrel-rolled, taking them around the incoming missiles. The R-40s, designed to engage Frank and Geoff heavy bombers, couldn't begin to match the maneuver. Peterenko watched helplessly as all four streaked through the enemy fighter formation without scoring a hit. The two R-40s under his wings were both heatseeking variants and his MiG-25 didn't have a gun. That left him with just the four R-60 missiles on his belly racks; two radar homing, two heat seekers. They'd have to do. He flipped the armament select switch to the R-60 radar homers and heard the immensely satisfying bleeping of the annunciator telling him they were locked on.

By now he had a visual on the four Caliphate fighters, twin engines, solid nose, low set delta wing. He'd lucked out, they were the new Elles. With only a little luck, he'd be the first to kill one. The lurch as his radar homing R-60s fired was nothing like the kick of the big R-40s. For a moment he thought they were dead drops but the white curling trails in front of him proved otherwise. The R-60 was a new concept of air-to-air missile, designed to replace guns, and featured a very short minimum range, high-G turns and low weight. Quite the reverse of the big R-40 and its American cousin, the AIM-47. It was also new and it too had more than its share of teething problems. This time, though, luck was on Peterenko's side. Both missiles worked perfectly. The Caliphate pilot tried the barrel role again but he was out of energy and the missiles had the agility to counter the maneuver. He couldn't see whether one or both missiles hit; the explosions merged into a rolling ball as the Elle disintegrated in mid air.

Time to go up. His *Illena* could outclimb anything the Caliphate could get its hands on; sheer raw engine power saw to that. *Illena's* engines may not have too long a life compared with the American jets but they had the edge where power output was concerned. *Illena* soared skywards, leaving the Elles behind, then rolled at the top of her climb before heading down again. The maneuver, named after the German ace Immelman although most Russian pilots tried to forget that, put the two surviving Caliphate fighters ahead of her, and their twin engine exhausts were an inviting target. The two heat-seeking R-60s were locked on and Peterenko let fly with both. Only one streaked away, the other malfunctioned. The one that had launched guided perfectly and exploded in the Elle's port engine. Peterenko poured on the power again, and swept up into another climbing turn.

And, as he did so, he felt a tremendous thump directly under his seat. Peterenko looked around the cockpit displays and saw no warning lights. A brief flare of relief was quickly squashed by the realization that he couldn't see anything else either. Every electrical display in the cockpit was dead. The mechanical instruments were still working. One of them told Peterenko that his engines were running at 10,000 rpm, a rather ominous figure since the fans were supposed to explode at 8,700. The control column was frozen stiff and he had to use both hands to shift it. It was definitely time to go home. Fortunately, that last Immelmann had pointed his nose in the right direction.

For some reason, Peterenko couldn't quite work out why, his Tumansky engines kept running. They were screaming in protest at the abuse but running nevertheless. He tried to dive but the movement on the control column started a reaction that tried to drag him forward. This was bad; he was already crossing the border and ejecting was an option but if he could bring the aircraft in, he would. He was the first fighter pilot to kill an Elle, he didn't want to cap it by being the first fighter pilot killed by one. He tried working the controls and made an interesting discovery. The whole of the left side of the cockpit was dead and the controls that routed there were frozen but the right hand side was more operational. Some of the bits there still worked and using them Peterenko started a slow descent. By the time he had reached his home base, he'd managed to get enough control to bring his *Illena* in. Of course, doing so with jammed controls and no instruments was going to be interesting.

Emergency system to lower the undercarriage. That was good in theory but the problem was, there was no way to tell if it was down. Peterenko banked towards the sun, hoping the shadow would tell him what he needed to know. It worked, sort of. The undercarriage was down but whether it was locked was another matter. He brought *Illena* around in a wide curve, towards the runway, and put the MiG-25 firmly down. As the aircraft came to a halt and the ground rescue crews surrounded him, he tried to rise but couldn't. He hadn't realized his legs had been hit by fragments before.

Three hours later, Peterenko left the base aid station, limping on his bandaged legs. Gray 441 had filled in the missing pieces. The second aircraft he'd hit hadn't gone down after the R-60 hit. It had lost an engine but kept flying and, as Peterenko had passed, had put a burst of 30mm cannon fire into his fuselage. Gray-441 had killed the other Elle, then escorted Peterenko clear while another MiG-25 element took over the escort role. And the terrorist training camp had died under the lash of two 750 kiloton airbursts. As the Americans often said 'Nothing succeeds like excess.'

Peterenko pushed open the doors of the mess, his stomach growling. The mess sergeant looked at him without even the slightest trace of sympathy. "Sorry, Sir. You're too late for lunch. You'll have to wait for afternoon tea."

RB-58G Xiomara *Over Syria Satrapy, The Caliphate*

"Tell me again, why we are doing this? What exactly was wrong with my nice warm hangar at Andrews?"

Brigadier-General Kozlowski was amused by the slightly wary questions. "You were bored stiff at Andrews and you know it. Anyway, you're the G-model lead ship and what better opportunity to test the new gear out?"

"Anyway *Xioey*, we missed out on the Jaffo attack so we haven't doled out any payback for *Marisol* yet. And that means, we're out here hunting SAM sites while the Rapiers take care of the fighters." Eddie Korrina listened to the suppressed snort over the intercom system. Even after flying *Xiomara* for six years, he'd never worked out whether she was jealous of *Marisol's* near-legendary status.

"Speaking of SAM sites, Xav, what have we got? How's the new gear working?"

Back in the Bear's Den, Xavier Dravar was scanning the new displays that had been installed. The RB-58G had the reconnaissance end of the B-70's DAMS and provided an almost real-time defense electronic intelligence assessment to the bombers flying behind. In theory, it was simple. The RB-58G would collect the information on the defenses threatening a specific ingress route for the Valkyries and relay it back to the bombers, supplying them with the locations of the enemy missile and anti-aircraft positions and the electronic intelligence data needed to jam and spoof the enemy radars. All of that was downloaded in the Valkyrie's DAMS computers and used to update the situation display the bomber crew used to penetrate the defenses.

Easy to say, not easy to do. It was an old story, one that had plagued the B-70 since its inception. The computer memory and processing power available weren't up to the tasks demanded of them. Originally, there was to have been a specialized version of the B-70, the RS-70 that would have filled the role, but it had been delayed even more than the Valkyrie. The RB-58 had been radically upgraded and modified with new engines and electronics as an interim solution. The resulting RB-58F had worked so well the RS-70 had been canceled. *Xiomara* had the equipment needed for the DAMS recon role installed as a test-bed for the definitive RB-58G. The only problem was that the RB-58 configuration with its underbelly pod was incompatible with the Pyewacket anti-missile system.

The computer data transfer limits remained. Instead of relaying everything back, the RB-58G crews would have to make value judgments on what the bombers behind them really needed and ration the data flow accordingly. In a very real sense, that made Dravar effectively a fifth member of the Valkyrie crews behind them.

"Threat display is quiet at this time. Syria's clear, after Jaffo the Caffs shifted most of their stuff back from the coast. *Xioey's* got a good point Mike, how come we suddenly got re-attached to the 305th? Or, more to the point, who did you blackmail?" It really was a good question. Dravar and Korrina had just made Colonels and were immersed in the schools needed to fully understand the new equipment they were being given when they'd been hauled out of academia and found themselves sitting in their familiar seats aboard *Xiomara*. They'd known Kozlowski would be taking command of the 305th when his Pentagon tour was done and that they'd be the senior offensive and defensive systems experts when the group re-equipped with the RB-58G but this had been completely unexpected. "Forget that, we have life. Search radars just come on. Long-range search, no launch signatures."

"That sounds unpleasantly familiar." Korrina was scanning the frequencies of the radars that had just lit up.

"We're OK up here, 74,500 and cruising at Mach 2.8. We're in the envelopes of Guidelines and Guilds but we'll get plenty of warning if they fire. Xav, warm up a couple of AGM-76s just in case though."

"Mike, got a read on the new radars. They're playing games down there. I count at least four decoy sets around the primary search sets and there's three of those. From the fix, they're in an equilateral triangle, about ten - fifteen miles per side with landline connection. They're rippling the transmissions between the three sets, sort of rotating quick bursts around the triangle and using the decoys to mask the pattern. These guys are a lot better than they were six years ago."

"And that's supposed to make me comfortable?" *Xiomara's* voice in the intercom was indignant.

"Don't sweat it. We can handle this. I'm relaying the data back to the Valks. They need to know this pattern."

"Hey guys." Dravar's voice had just picked up urgency. "We have a lock-on from the ground. Probably Guilds. Want to take them out Eddie?"

"Hold it guys. We need to know what's coming up before we treat them to an instant sunrise. You sure it's Guilds Xav?"

"Think so, no. Hold that, we've got continuous wave tracking. Must be Gainfuls. Recommend we take them down."

"Do it, as soon as you've got the fire control locked."

The rotary launcher in *Xiomara's* belly pod whirred and a nuclear-tipped AGM-76 slid into firing position. Dravar was already triangulating on the enemy missile battery and the data was being relayed to the waiting missile. Then, there was a lurch as the missile fired and it streaked off, angling down towards its target. Almost at the same time, *Xiomara's* radar picked up four missiles leaving the area where the search radars had been detected. It wasn't a contest. The AGM-76s were accelerating downwards, picking up speed all the time. The four Gainfuls were fighting gravity in the steep climb towards the bomber high overhead. In this sort of contest, the aircraft at the top of the gravity well always held the advantage and the AGM-76 initiated before the Gainfuls had even climbed half way towards their target.

Kozlowski hadn't taken any chances, as soon as the missile was on the way, he pulled a wingover, blew chaff and anti-optical flare/smoke decoys. Dravar had started to pour white noise energy into the frequencies used by the Caliphate missile battery. The white flash and kidney-pounding shockwave told *Xiomara's* crew that their precautions hadn't been necessary. The enemy missile launchers were now little more than slag on the desert sands. Where they had been was now a shadow on Korrina's radar screen, an artifact of the burst of random electronic emissions that were a by-product of nuclear explosions. Korrina selected a pre-determined pulse repetition factor, amplitude modulation and jitter factor for the ASG-18 and cut in the filters. The shadow magically cleared as the radar set rejected all the transmissions except those with the specified values.

The site where the missile battery had been was silent. No transmissions, no sign of activity. That information too would be sent back to the Valkyries, where it would be noted along with the caution that quiet and apparently dead didn't mean that the site really was dead - although after having 81 kilotons initiated over their heads, survival probably wasn't too probable.

"Well *Xioey,* you aren't a virgin any more. Scratch one SAM site guys. Xav, any more life after that little excitement?"

"Getting reports from *Witchy Woman* that they've taken down a Gammon site a bit south of here. Apparently it came up at the same time as the one we just fried. We've got nothing else yet. That'll change when we get over Iraq. Intel is that the air defense system in the Tigris-Euphrates triangle is pretty dense.

Kozlowski thought for a second. The usual arrangement was three Gammon batteries surrounded by a hexagon of six Guideline or Gainful positions. A single launcher of each type out here in the middle of nowhere didn't smell right. "I don't like this people, there should be more out here than just these. Xav, hang our ears out really careful and let the Valks know what we're doing." Kozlowski thought some more. *Suppose the missile battery they'd just taken down was the northern tip of the hexagon and the Gammon was the northern tip of the interior triangle? That would mean the main strength of the SAM belt lay further south. On the direct route from Damascus to Baghdad. Interesting.* There'd been rumors and reports of low-level fighting between the various satrapies that made up the Caliphate. The installation of air defense systems between the satrapies suggested that the fighting was anything but low-level.

"Xav, tell *California Girl* that there's probably the rest of this nest in front of her. There's got to be a reason for that defense site stuck out here. If there isn't then the internal tensions in the Caliphate must be a lot worse than we realized. We'll nose around a little, see what we can find.

War Room, Underneath the White House. Washington DC

The red lines marking the progress of the attack formations had now reached the westernmost parts of the Caliphate. The leading elements, the RB-58 strategic reconnaissance elements and the F-108 fighters were already deep inside enemy territory, ferreting out the hostile defenses and neutralizing those that could threaten the bombers following behind. The speed of advance of the Valkyries had slowed briefly while the aircraft refueled over the Aegean, now it was picking up again as they started to penetrate hostile airspace.

"Message coming in from the Recon Rats, Mister President. General Kozlowski's *Xiomara* has detected an anomalous defense area inside Syrian territory. It's nothing we'd mapped, so he's taken command of an effort to find out what gives there. Four RB-58s are exploring it now. If they find what looks like a target, we'll take it down."

"Exploring it?" President Nixon's voice was confused and slightly resentful. He was realizing just how little he knew about the forces he commanded and the capabilities they had. That knowledge was making him suspicious, causing him to speculate how much more there was that he just didn't know. And did that mean that people were keeping the information from him?

"Reconnaissance by fire, Mister President." General Power's voice showed no such doubts or suspicions. He'd been President LeMay's protégé and he'd inherited LeMay's manner of absolute dedication to the mission. "They fly over an area and shoot at anything suspicious. Anything that shoots back also gets hammered."

"With nuclear weapons." Nixon's voice had doubt added to confusion and resentment.

"Only little ones" The Seer's voice was slightly distracted, he was looking down through the force roster, arranging for a B-70 to be retargeted on the newly discovered complex - if there was a complex there that deserved to be taken down. He had a feeling there would be.

"I've been meaning to talk to you about that Seer." Power spoke sternly, reproof evident in his manner. "The whole point about nuclear weapons is that they cause a very large explosion. We've had scientists at work for thirty years trying to cause bigger explosions. Deliberately scaling them back seems almost treasonous to me."

"A nuclear event isn't technically an explosion, General. That's why we call them initiations. However, we don't want to do more damage than we have to. We like to have a range of yields available so we can match weapon to target. That way we can try to reduce collateral damage as much as possible." Everybody in the room knew that 'collateral damage' meant people killed because they had the misfortune to live too close to a target. Like the population of Bahrain.

"Permit me to disagree with you Seer. I've always believed that if there's one enemy left and two of us, we've won."

"But General, we'd have to hope that our survivors are one man and one woman." Naamah's comment cut off the snort of outrage from Nixon. She knew very well that Power's blustering attitude was a deliberate construct that allowed others to play 'good cop' to his 'bad cop'. It was a game that LBJ had played very, very well. Nixon had a long way to go before he could step into those shoes.

"My dear, I feel quite convinced that you would be one of the survivors. And in that case I can but hope that I would be the other."

Naamah was about to respond to the gallantry when another message cut into the room. A communications technician read it out. "*Xiomara* Mister President, Sirs. Large industrial complex, some of it apparently underground, in the center of the defense area. *Xiomara* reports that it has the characteristics of a nuclear research and production facility."

"Oh well, that can go then." Nixon jumped in to take the decision. "What have we got that can do it? And why wasn't this one on the original target list?"

"No problem, Mister President, we have almost an embarrassment of destructive riches out there. We'd anticipated we'd find additional pressing targets as we penetrated the airspace so we made accommodation for the probability. As to why we hadn't spotted it, no coverage of a large area is ever complete. We're bound to miss things. Doesn't matter, we can retarget our bombers right up to the instant they make their laydowns. We have two Valkyries carrying a pair of B-87 Skybolts each still over the Mediterranean. We can order *Xiomara* to relay the coordinates through and we can drop a Skybolt on that complex. Probably two to be sure, if the target really is underground, it might take two to wipe it out."

"What's a B-87's warhead?"

"One megaton. These will be the biggest devices we're using in this assault. We brought them along in case of a buried target."

"*Xiomara* is reporting emissions from Gammon missile batteries." That caused a few eyebrows to be raised around the room. Gammon was a new system, a high-altitude SAM with a serious anti-missile capability.

"Interesting. We got word from the Russians that they're running into Elles up north. It seems like the Chipanese are selling their latest kit now. What do you think Tommy, still use Skybolts or divert a bomber?"

Power thought for a second. "Ballistic missiles, even air-launched ones, are only suited to a low-threat environment, so my first thought is to say send a bomber, Seer. But, I like the idea of a big warhead on that buried complex. Also, let's see how well Gammon works. I'd say toss a couple of B-87s and if they get shot down, divert a Valkyrie."

"Sounds fair to me. Mister President?" Nixon nodded. "Tommy, could you send orders to *Skuld* asking her to launch on coordinates from *Xiomara,* please?"

Cockpit, B-70D Skuld *100th Heavy Bomb Group, 77,000 feet over the Eastern Mediterranean*

"Do you think they put us in back-up because I'm Navy?" Lieutenant-Commander Paul Flower was, in his opinion, justifiably aggrieved. He'd been given this exchange tour of duty with SAC to learn about heavy bombers and to give SAC's aloof bomber crews some insight into the world of fighters. Now, *Skuld* had been assigned to back-up, waiting to be assigned targets of opportunity.

"They don't think like that. We got back up because there are only four B-70s in the 100th that are Skybolt-equipped and two of them don't have DAMS. So that left us and *Hrist*. If its any consolation, since we'll be going in behind the main wave, we've got more offensive and fewer defensive weapons on board so we get to blow up more things." Captain Kevin Madrick grinned at the last thought.

"Spoken like a true SAC-man. What did your old man say about you joining the Air Force?"

"When I asked him what he'd say if I joined the Navy, his reply was 'Before or after I break your legs with a baseball bat?' So I joined the Air Force instead. He never forgave the Navy after it blamed him for *Shiloh* going down. Bitter about it to the day he died. Newport News invited him to the christening of the new *Shiloh* but he wouldn't even reply."

"Kevin, target information and orders coming in. B-87 coordinates from one of the RB-58s, orders to fire from the War Room. Both Skybolts. After impact, we're to penetrate the target area and do a gravity drop if anything's left, we'll have an RB-58G and a -58F in support."

"Thanks, Mack. Get the data typed in and the 'Bolts warmed up. Paul, calculate ideal course and launch point. Make sure there isn't an island under us when we fire, we don't want a 'Bolt dropping on dry land if there's a failure. You know just how unreliable these 'Bolts are."

"Computed, swing to course oh-eight-eight, fire in one minute five seconds."

"Roger that. Missiles ready and armed?"

"Check."

"On course, approaching fire point in five - four - three - two - one - GO!"

Skuld lurched as the two externally-mounted Skybolts detached, their motors igniting with separation, then streaked ahead of *Skuld*. As soon as they were clear of the bomber, they curved upwards, starting the long ballistic arc that should end in the newly-discovered target in Syria.

"Wow, look at them go!"

"They're OK, I suppose, if one likes that sort of thing. Time we followed them in to do the job properly."

RB-58G Xiomara *Over Syria Satrapy, The Caliphate*

"Clear of impact area." That was one of the advantages of high-speed aircraft; they could clear a danger zone fast. Kozlowski eased off *Xiomara's* throttles slightly and started a gentle turn. The aircraft's flash screens were down and the crew had their anti-flash visors in place. If the missiles got through, this was going to be a major event.

"Skybolts on the way in. They should be on the way down now." Korrina was tracking the two Skybolts arcing through the air on his radar. Normally, he knew the Gammon battery on the ground would be doing the same with its target acquisition radar but that set and its bunker had just met with a multi-kiloton accident. The missile crews would be working to get an intercept solution with their fire control radars. That took time and they didn't really have it. "Gammons firing now. Targeted on Skybolts."

"Good." *Xiomara* sounded relieved. The Gammon was a long-range, high-altitude interceptor missile; one that could present a threat to an RB-58 and possibly even a B-70.

"Two missiles airborne - heading upwards. Two more firing now."

"Shoot-shoot-look-shoot-shoot." That was the standard for conventionally-tipped anti-missile missiles. Isolate the target, fire a pair of missiles at it, look to see what the situation was and fire another pair. Kozlowski assumed these Gammons had conventional warheads; the ones grouped around Chipanese cities were like their American cousins, nuclear-tipped. Intelligence was that Chipan hadn't exported nuclear weapons to the Caliphate. He guessed that the complex presently behind them, had been designed to rectify that.

Korrina watched the tracks of the missiles converge and vanish as the missiles made the intercepts. "First pair of Gammons missed, Mike, they exploded at the end of their runs. Conventional explosions. Second pair...... they got one of the Skybolts." The missile track downwards veered sharply away from its projected track. In his mind's eye Korrina could see the crippled Skybolt tumbling through the air, its fragile skin shredding as aerodynamic forces tore it apart. Its partner though still lanced downwards. Another pair of Gammons were on their way up but they were too late. Far too late. "Hold on guys!"

Even through the flash screens and visors, the glare from the one megaton surface burst lit up the inside of *Xiomara's* cockpit, reducing Kozlowski's vision to floating red and green shadows. He blinked and shook his head, helped by the slam of the airborne shockwave that threw *Xiomara* sideways. Instinctively he grabbed the controls and corrected the savage yaw. "Eddie, as soon as the screen clears, check for damage. *Skuld* is coming in behind for another laydown if its needed."

"On it, Mike." Korrina was trying to clear his vision as well. The target area was covered with the usual electronic shadow that would last anything up to a minute or more but that was no more than a minor annoyance. Korrina tagged his radar transmissions and flipped in the filters, causing the shadow to vanish just as magically as ever. Where the complex had been was a giant crater, the ground still heaving with the reflected after-shocks of the surface burst. The whole complex had gone - or had it? Korrina looked at the image again. The way the ravine curved, north of the crater......

"Mike, it looks like the 'Bolt hit about 2,500 yards south east of the planned impact point." *Xiomara* snorted contemptuously over the intercom. A bomber crew who missed their target by that much would be in trouble. "If *Skuld's* got B-61s on board, the target could use one. Suggest they set for the whole 500 kilotons, ground burst, and target seven miles north of the Skybolt point of impact."

"Roger, I'll relay that through."

War Room, Underneath the White House. Washington DC

"Mister President, sirs, one Skybolt downed by Gammons, the other got through. It's rated as a near-miss. *Skuld* is going in to get a possible northern extension of the complex with a B-61 ground burst dialed up to the max."

"That's my boys." General Power's voice was affectionate. "Don't do things by halves."

"Ground bursts? I thought we weren't going to be using those. What about radiation? Fall-out?"

"We had none in our original plan Mister President. They're only of use in handling deep-buried targets. These two are going to cause a plume, the winds aren't strong so it will be a short, fattish one. The worst of it will be within Caliphate territory. Fortunately, no rivers flow through the area into the Mediterranean so we won't get the contamination that ruined the North Sea and Baltic. The Nile is the nearest river we have to worry about and that's right on the edge of the projected plume."

The Seer stared at the map for a few seconds. "The Gulf, that's a different matter. Most of the 35th's targets in Iraq Satrapy are on the Tigris and Euphrates, they empty into the Gulf. Still, the initiations are all high airbursts, the problems shouldn't be too bad. Anyway, offering the Caliphate the opportunity of catching self-frying fish can't be all bad."

Nixon wasn't listening. "The Nile? What about the International Zone! All the scientists there, they're right in the path of the plume. Nobody told me about this. Why wasn't I told the radiation plume would stretch all the way down there?"

"We warned the South African government that the prevailing winds meant there was a danger from fall-out plumes so they got all the people there under cover. Some, I believe, are sheltering in the Pyramids. Nice to know those things are finally going to be of use to somebody."

"I'll tell her you said that." Naamah's voice was pitched way down, just loud enough for The Seer to hear.

It didn't matter, Nixon wasn't listening. "Anyway, if ballistic missiles are so useless, why do we have Skybolt? Why not just drop bombs from the start?"

"The idea, Mister President, is to equip the bombers with the widest possible range of attack modes. So we have developed long, medium and short-range cruise missiles that fly at high, medium or low altitudes. We have developed long- and short-range ballistic missiles that can be fired from our bombers. That way, the enemy have no idea what any individual bomber can throw at them until it does it.

"The big problem with ballistic missiles is their vulnerability, they come in on a fixed trajectory and that makes them very easy to hit. Skybolt is air-launched so it has almost infinitely variable launch points. That means it's much less predictable. Even that, as we've just seen, isn't enough to offset the basic vulnerability of the missile. However, it does mean that the presence of Valkyries and Stratofortresses forces the defense to be on their guard against a ballistic or stand-off cruise missile attack. Just another factor that loads the dice in favor of the bombers."

The Seer broke off again to look at the developing situation map. As he did so, Power cut in. "For all that Mister President, free-fall gravity bombs are still our preferred delivery means. They're light compared with missiles and much more accurate. A whole load more reliable as well."

Nixon nodded, his lips pursed. "Gentlemen, its obvious I need to know much more about this area. Naamah, after this affair is over, arrange for General Power and the NSC staff to set up a series of briefings for me, on the types of weapon we have and why we have them. Seer, please find out what the facility we have just destroyed was. Perhaps the people who we contacted in Switzerland can help on that."

RB-58G Xiomara *Over Iraq Satrapy, The Caliphate*

The improvised attack on the Syrian complex had drastically cut the lead *Xiomara* had over the B-70s following behind her. The days when the RB-58 had a speed advantage over the pure bombers were dying fast. The B-70 was actually faster than the Hustler and that meant the time lost over Syria couldn't be restored. Also, four of *Xiomara's* AGM-76s had been fired. That, combined with decreasing fuel levels, was causing Kozlowski concern.

The primary target he had to deal with was still ahead, the huge industrial complex of Salman Pak, south of Baghdad. It was heavily defended due to the concentration of high-value targets within it. He had been briefed to expect modern SAMs and fighters. Still, if necessary, he could divert to bases in Russia to rearm and refuel.

Slower than the B-70 she might be, but *Xiomara* still chewing up the distance that lay in front of her. The Middle East might look big on a map but cruising at Mach 2.7 made perceptions shrink a lot. It hadn't been this way with *Marisol*, for all her supersonic dash capability, the RB-58C had cruised at subsonic speeds. *Xiomara* was a true supersonic bird. The comparison made Kozlowski feel guilty, as if he was somehow betraying his first love. Mentally he apologized to *Marisol's* ghost and transferred his attention to the navigation display. It was only a small repeater screen, the main display was in the cockpit behind him but it showed the first edges of the defensive concentrations around the Iraqi industrial facilities.

As if to confirm that the secondary display was telling him the truth, a message came through from behind him. "Mike, multiple transmissions ahead. Search radars, both 3-D and 2-D, target acquisition and fire control. Also airborne search radars, large numbers of them. If what we can see is correct, there are defensive systems all over the place. This is going to be interesting."

"Thanks Xav. Open communications to the Valkyries, let them know what we detect and what we blow up. Right people, here we go. Time to earn the big bucks the government pays us."

CHAPTER ELEVEN
MELEE

The Military Command Center, Dezful, Iran Satrapy, The Caliphate.

The attack was developing exactly as Morteza Farzaneh had predicted. The two larger formations of bombers were running in to hit north-east and south-west, in this case Iran and Iraq satrapies respectively. Ahead of them, the strategic reconnaissance bombers dismantled the defense systems while the fighters carved a path through the defending interceptors. It was like watching a very well-performed ballet, although watching such things was not permitted in the Caliphate. Not officially, anyway. Unofficially, many things had been saved from the prying eyes of the religious zealots.

The Americans were indeed very predictable. Farzaneh had predicted what had happened to date and now he was prepared to predict what was about to happen. The Satrapy of Iraq had gone its own way in setting up its defenses. They'd concentrated their industry into a few complexes and stacked their defenses around them. Missiles were massed around each target with fighters between them. They'd boasted that they could bleed the Americans to death but Fazaneh didn't believe it would be the Americans who would do the dying. They'd spent almost of a quarter of a century honing their skills for just that sort of attack.

By Caliphate standards, Iraq Satrapy had used the rich man's defense. Iran hadn't been able to afford that level of missile procurement so their facilities were spread out and camouflaged. They would lose many of them, but some might escape.

Once again, Farzaneh looked at his map. The destruction of the Gulf hadn't been expected but it wasn't really consequential. The Caliphate could do without oil revenues for a few years. Those revenues were used to purchase military equipment. If they weren't there, that equipment would have to be built in-country. It wouldn't matter that much, the truth was that the Caliphate didn't need that much military power and if it stopped provoking people it would need less. What was important that being thrown on its own resources would mean more industrial development. Such development would transfer yet more power away from the useless theocrats in the Ruling Council and towards the surviving technicians and bureaucrats who were slowly rebuilding an industrialized society.

One thing disturbed him. There was a small knot of aircraft over an industrial site in Syria Satrapy. Farzaneh looked it up – it was supposed to be just a concrete plant. *But the Americans had dumped two of their biggest warheads on it, using surface bursts. That was the way they treated buried targets. So what had they spotted there? And come to thing of it, why was a concrete plant defended by Syria's scattered handful of missiles?* There was something not right there and Farzaneh guessed that plant was a whole lot more than it appeared to be.

Concrete production. A uranium extraction facility looked like a concrete plant, a little bit anyway. But why would Syria want uranium? There was only one answer to that, they were trying to build nuclear weapons. The Caliphate didn't have nuclear weapons or the facilities to build them, so the Ruling Council had declared them blasphemous. They'd forbidden the nuclear research they couldn't undertake anyway. But did Syria have a nuclear program and if so why?

Farzaneh sighed. The Caliphate was such a disordered and chaotic structure that almost anything could be going on. And probably was.

Cockpit, B-70C Spear Lady *35th Heavy Bomb Group, 77,800 feet over Iraq Satrapy*

"*Belle Ringer* is calling in, Dennis. Reporting running into heavy defenses around Salman Pak. Engaging Gammon and Ganef missiles. They're sending as much data as they can back to us. Even without the data link, we're getting the data back on emitter locations in almost real time. We're downloading the data into DAMS as fast as we get it. *Belle Ringer* is also reporting a lot of decoys and false emitters down there that are making things a lot harder. The Caffs are using their kit well. Burst transmissions from the search radars, buried in the signals from the decoys. The fire control radars don't switch on until the last minute, doesn't give the ladies much time to react."

"Any air-to-air reported?" Major Dennis Novak absorbed the information coming in from Lieutenant Benjamin Savitz in the co-pilot's seat. The Caliphate opposition was a lot heavier that had been expected and their technical skills had improved dramatically over the last six years.

"None at the moment. Not in our sector anyway. The Navy have reported heavy fighter opposition down south and the Russians up North but none in the middle. Looks like they might have cleared the air for their SAMs. The Navy reported mostly older types, Irenes and Brandis, but the Russians have run into Elles and Faiths. Had some trouble with both types, we're getting reports of some fighters down and others damaged. The Russians are getting through to their targets though."

Novak nodded thoughtfully. Clearing the air for the SAMs was logical; filling the air with friendly fighters would just confuse the tactical picture and give the American bombers more targets. There were a very few fighters that had a marginal capability to engage a B-70; the Elles and Faiths weren't in that category. The Russian bombers were much slower and lower flying than the racing Valkyries and Novak suspected the Russian fighters, mostly designed as defensive interceptors, weren't too good at combat against hostile fighters. So the Caffs had pitched their fighters against the Russians and the Navy and would try and stop the Valkyries with SAMs. Which raised the obvious question.

"What does the DAMS picture look like?"

"Like the ladies said, it's oscillating. I'll put a picture on the mini-screen forward for you. The Caffs are flipping from search radar to search radar and from target acquisition set to set. The stuff coming back from the ladies is helping us filter out the decoys and dummies but it's still confused. The long-range search sets are picking us up, there's no doubt about that. But then they probably saw us hundreds of miles back. Won't do them much good."

Lieutenant Charles Andrews looked again at his DAMS display. The display was constantly shifting as the radars on the ground switched on and off. The Caliphate air defense people really had learned a lot, none of the radars remained on the air long enough to allow an anti-radar missile to home in on them. At least that was what their crews had been taught. Savitz looked at the repeater screen for the DAMS display. Already bright green dots were appearing on the black background, the position of the emitters being detected by the electronic surveillance systems on the RB-58s in front of them and the B-70s own electronic warfare systems. Then it was being stored in the memories of the systems and compared with the known and developing threat libraries. Slowly, the decoys were identified and filtered out.

In the defensive systems position at the rear of the flight deck, Andrews had the full version of the display and could see the patterns being formed by those emitters. Once the RB-58G became standard, a whole mass of electronic data would be coming back instead of the bare information on position and activity that was sent by the F-models. Still, what was coming back was good enough for the moment. The defenses were being mapped out and that map was growing in detail and accuracy by the minute. Briefly, Andrews wondered just how hard the RB-58 crews were having to work for this information. Their Hustlers would be twisting and turning in the defense zone, dodging missiles while identifying and destroying the defenses. *Belle Ringer's* crew had sounded casual and relaxed but that fooled nobody.

Already, the picture was stabilizing as the decoy emitters were identified and filtered out, just leaving the genuine fire control sets. It was easy to tell the difference. The decoys were omnidirectional while the fire control sets produced a thin beam that was locked onto the intended target. Of course, determining which was which meant getting that beam locked on to the aircraft making the investigation. That added a level of urgency to the task. Not only had the RB-58s got to map out the defenses and erode their capability, they had to do so in time to help the B-70s following behind them, closing in at 37.5 miles per minute.

"190 miles to target." Savitz gave the read-out, *just a touch more than five minutes to weapons release*. They would be hitting the outer edge of the air defense zone within a few seconds. Had they been flying B-52s, they would already have been just within reach of the Caliphate Gammon, depending, of course on exactly which version Chipan had sold them. The early Gammons were limited to 81 miles range and 66,000 feet altitude. That made them close-but-no-cigar for the racing B-70s, but put the B-52s squarely in their sights. The later Gammons had a 160 mile range and could reach up to 116,000 feet, well above the maximum ceiling of the B-70.

"Data dump coming in!" Andrews whistled. Racing to catch up but still far behind them, *Xiomara* was the only RB-58G in the formation. She had been on-site for a Gammon launch and her ESM systems had recorded the signatures of the Caliphate electronic gear. Now, it was being relayed forward. As if by magic, more than three quarters of the contacts vanished from the display as the new data allowed the decoys to be filtered out. That was the good news; the bad part was what Novak needed to know right now.

"Dennis, *Xiomara* reports the Gammons did a ballistic missile interception, shot down a Skybolt." That meant late-model Gammons, the earlier versions didn't have that capability. As if on cue, another emitter cut in, one that had remained quiet as the RB-58s had passed overhead. Andrews guessed that the missile fire control crews had kept everything shut down, relying on the input from the other radars in the defense zone. The American bombers weren't the only people who could relay data.

It wasn't as easy as that, of course. The Gammon, like all missiles, used most of its energy climbing so the actual radius the missile could cover was dramatically reduced. In fact, even the Gammon had a maximum range of only fifty miles up here. The catch was that it had a minimum range of 32.5 miles. This left an intercept zone that was a donut only 18 miles wide. *Spear Lady* could cross it in less than 30 seconds. Nevertheless, the ground radar crews had timed their light-up to perfection. The green donut was in front of the B-70, a bit to the left but well placed for a shot. Or, as the Caliphate obviously preferred, six shots. That was the number of Gammon missiles that were being fired at the approaching bomber.

Up in the pilot's seat, Novak responded instantly to the threat warning. He pulled *Spear Lady* into a tight right turn, swinging away from the missile site, hoping to force the missiles into a stern chase that it had to lose. On paper, the Gammon had a 300 feet per second speed advantage over a B-70. In a stern chase that was far too little for an intercept. Unfortunately the enemy radars had opened up far too late for *Spear Lady* to complete that turn. The missiles were still coming in although at a steadily increasing angle off the nose.

This is where other factors cut in. Missiles were a compromise. They had to be small and light enough to have the agility to make an intercept yet the demands of range and altitude meant they had to carry large amounts of fuel. The contradiction was solved by giving Gammon four large boosters. However these prevented the missile maneuvering at all until they fell away. By that time, the missile was out of the relatively dense air lower down and was entering the thin stratospheric air. There, the small control surfaces of the missiles were virtually ineffective compared with the much larger surfaces of the bombers. As a result, the maneuverability of the missile was severely constrained even after the intercept stage was free to change its course. A missile that could pull 20 or 30 gee lower down would be lucky if it could manage five percent of that up here. Very lucky indeed.

The net effect was that *Spear Lady* was out-turning the Gammon missiles aimed at her. Even while they made the attempt, Andrews was using his electronic warfare equipment to intercept the pulses from the ground-based fire control units. A simple counter would have been to pour electronic energy into the frequencies, drowning them out with white noise. Barrage jamming was too simple for what Andrews wished to achieve. Instead, his deception jammer was re-transmitting the received pulses, amplified and subtly distorted, with the severity of the distortion increasing steadily. The result was that the apparent course seen by the guidance radars was steadily diverging from *Spear Lady's* real track. Andrews was attempting two distinct tasks, one was to mask the turn *Spear Lady* was making so that the incoming missiles wouldn't try to match it even if they could. The other was to position those missiles perfectly for a Frisbee shot at any that looked like they were coming too close.

As it happened, it wasn't necessary. Deception jamming caused the inbound missiles to chase after the wrong track, turning away from the bomber rather than towards it. Combined with their inability to match *Spear Lady's* turn at this altitude, they passed aft of the bomber. A long, long way aft. They missed by more than 7 miles, so far that their explosions didn't even shake the B-70. *Spear Lady* said nothing but a disdainful sniff could be clearly heard throughout the cockpit. The crew took a second to grin at each other. There were times when words weren't needed.

"Conventional warhead. It wouldn't have mattered though. We were outside the lethal radius of the Gammon nuke." A few seconds later, a flash of brilliant light illuminated the cockpit. An RB-58F had seen the launch and dived in to eliminate the battery with one of its AGM-76s. Andrews continued deadpan, as if nothing had happened. "We were outside the radius of that one as well. And if we weren't, I'd have had very strong words to say with the 305th."

"Three minutes to weapons release." Savitz was splitting his attention between the radar mapping display and the view through *Spear Lady's* raised visor. Ahead of him, the huge Salman Pak industrial complex was covered by a fine yellowish fog, the emissions from its dozens of chemical factories. Savitz remembered the briefings, the complex was more than forty miles long and fifteen wide, bridging the gap between the Tigris and the Euphrates. A solid mass of petrochemical and chemical industry plants, ammonia, urea, sulphur, phosphates, cryogenic gas, vinyl acetate, dioctyl phthalate, propylene, acetic acid, chlorine - and the targets for today's exercise, plants that were coyly described as "pharmaceuticals," "antibiotics," "insecticides" and "pest control." The plants that were the home of blackpox and who knew what else.

Eight Valkyries were targeted on Salman Pak. They would release twelve weapons, varying in yield between 50 and 150 kilotons. The formation had four weapons in reserve in case of unexpected targets or the defenses getting lucky. Another formation was hitting a second massive complex around Samarra; a third would be dropping on a smaller, more compact group around some place called Didiwanyah. Then a strange thought passed through Savitz's mind "Just what the hell is dioctyl phthalate?"

"Lord knows. You'll have to ask the brainiacs when we get back." Captain Tony Simeral, the offensive systems operator squeezed off an AGM-76 at a Ganef battery fire control radar. On paper, Ganef was effective to about 90,000 feet, making it much more marginal than the late model Gammons. The catch was that it was a much more energetic missile. It climbed faster and was more agile. At this altitude, its maximum engagement range was a mere 5 miles and its minimum was 4.3. The threat zone was a tiny 3,500 feet wide and that was far too small to be worried about. Simeral blew the battery apart with a 25 kiloton warhead anyway, more as a matter of principle than anything else. Then he reset for his bomb drop, feeling the slight vibration as the bomb bay door slid forward into its closed position and the aft bay door followed it to open the way for the two Mark 61s in the rear.

"Nav attack system running now." *Spear Lady* was on course and had the radar picture of the target loaded into her computer. She would calculate the release point for herself and, unless a member of the crew over-rode her decision, she would release the first device herself. Then, she would make a slight turn and search for the radar picture of the second drop point. Unless something went very wrong, there was no need for the humans to touch the release system at all.

"Releasing now." The slight lurch was hardly noticeable, lost in the continuous bouncing from the initiations all over the target area. Some weapons aimed at destroying the complex; others the fire-storm deaths of the missiles that had been installed to protect it. There was a slight tilt as *Spear Lady* changed course then another ripple-like feeling as the second warhead dropped. “Right, that’s it. Let’s go home.”

War Room, Underneath the White House. Washington DC

“The 35th are hitting their targets now.” The report coming in had a ring of triumph about it. “First indications are good laydowns.”

“Opposition?” Power and the Seer spoke simultaneously, then grinned at each other. For their different reasons, both needed the answer to that question quickly.

“Reports of heavy missile opposition, Gammon-Bs and Ganefs. Three RB-58s are reporting damage and heading for divert bases in Russia. The Valkyries got in and out clean.”

“The 35th done good.” Power made the comment with an approval that would have made the crews in question sigh with relief.

“They had the easy job.” The Seer was still speaking distantly for his mind was elsewhere, computing the strategic implications of the news coming in. “They had three relatively concentrated target areas. The ones in Iran Satrapy are dispersed all over the place.”

“More reports Mister President, Sirs, one RB-58 was lost, hit by a Gammon and blew up in mid-air. No survivors. The 305th are reporting that the Caliphate are firing Galosh missile interceptors at the bombers. No luck with them of course.”

“Boot’s on the other foot now.” Nixon tried to equal the graveyard humor that was running around the war-room and was rewarded by a chuckle at the pun. “I gather the missile interceptors are no good against bombers?”

“None at all, Mister President. They’re designed to intercept targets that are coming in along a predictable ballistic course. They stress range and speed at the expense of agility, real easy for a manned bomber to duck.”

“Dumb Caffs.” Nixon’s voice was scornful.

“With the greatest respect, Mister President, it’s a tradition of the war-room not to use abusive nicknames for countries.” Naamah spoke quietly, as always making sure her principal had the information he needed to work effectively. Power heard the remark and spoke equally quietly.

“That’s so Mister President. When one is reducing their country to a smoking radioactive ruin, being rude about them also is, well, tacky.”

Nixon nodded. He could see the point although personally he preferred the more vulgar epithets. “Heavy opposition, one RB-58 down, three damaged. Please tell me our defenses will do better.”

“Against B-70 type bombers, probably not. The defense has been playing catch-up for thirty years and has never quite made it. They tend to have the answer to the previous generation of bombers about three or four years after they start to be replaced. Our fighters would do a lot better than the types used by the Caliphate but the latest Hercs won’t do much better than the Gammons or Ganefs used today. Mind you, both would do well against B-52 type targets. If we’d been using BUFFs against these complexes, I’d guess we’d be looking at twenty, perhaps twenty five percent losses. The BUFF’s a grand old Lady sir, but her day is passing quickly. We need the B-70s.”

Nixon absorbed the information. “Shouldn’t we speed up replacing the B-52s then?”

Again, it was The Seer that answered. “Sir, North American is turning out Valkyries at eight aircraft a month. That’s a multi-year procurement that has another six years to run.” He flipped over some pages on his clip-board. “We have about 300 B-70s of varying types on the roster at the moment. Technically four groups have formed and four more are forming, but none of them is anywhere near up to strength yet. The B-70 hasn’t been an easy program Sir. If you like, we can arrange a visit to North American and they’ll brief you on its development and take you up in one. It’s way late and we need it fast. Stepping up production would be nice but it's not the right answer. Anyway, we can do what we are doing here, use the Valkyries and Hustlers to batter down the defenses and clear the path in for the B-52s."

Once again, Nixon realized how little he understood about the forces he now commanded. It all seemed so easy from the outside. Whenever he thought he understood a bit, it turned out that it was merely a gateway into a world that was even more complex and obscure. He'd thought SAC was the invincible guarantor of America's safety. Now he was learning that invincibility was an illusion; the product of skill, courage and very careful planning. The tools were shiny; the finest the most advanced technology in the world could provide. In the end they were still tools and what really mattered was the ability of the tool-user. Just the way it always had.

RB-58F Vicious Vixen*, Heading Towards The Caspian Sea.*

"Fuel leaks increasing, we're losing power on number three now. We're losing altitude as well now." *Vicious Vixen* had left dodging a Ganef a little late and had been raked by fragments from the warhead. They'd taken out one engine, damaged another, smashed up the underbelly pod and knocked a lot of the electronics out. They'd been luckier than *Antoinette.* She'd taken a direct hit from another Ganef and gone from an aircraft to a fireball and shattered metal in less than a blink of an eye.

"Fighters closing. No IFF." The trace was clearly visible on the radar display in The Bear's Den. The lack of IFF was ominous, but *Vicious Vixen* was so shot up that the system probably wasn't working. Still, if it was enemy fighters, they were an easy kill. The formations were closing at well over 70 miles per minute. They'd soon know one way or the other.

"American RB-58. This is Gray-972. First Guards Fighter Division. We will be with you soon. Please don't shoot the pianist, he is doing his best."

"Gray-972, this is *Vicious Vixen,* we have severe on-board damage and are losing fuel. We estimate radius no more than 500 miles."

"Understood *Vixen.* We can see you now. Follow us, we have an airfield ready to receive you."

The appearance was sudden, the aircraft seeming to materialize out of nowhere. *Vicious Vixen's* crew were painfully aware of just how blinded their aircraft had become. Two MiG-25s formed up on either side of the crippled Hustler. Four more were ranging around her to prevent enemy fighters from coming in close.

"It's good to see you, 972. Thank God you made it."

"Yes, to thank God would be a good idea I think." The Russian pilot's voice was serious. "After you have landed, I will show you where the base chapel is located."

Cockpit, B-70C Sigrun *100th Heavy Bomb Group, 82,500 feet over Iran Satrapy*

This time, the target set was different. The 35th had hit three concentrated complexes. Big certainly, heavily defended undoubtedly; the loss of *Antoinette* and *Dejah Thoris* had shown that. But they were well defined and their size had made them unmissable. Over Persia, the bombers were trying to locate small targets, scattered across the maps, buried in the vast expanse of the Iranian back-country.

Quickly picking up the experience learned in the assault on the Iraqi biological warfare complexes, the RB-58s had changed tactics. Previously, they had gone for the target acquisition radars and the missile batteries themselves. The long range search radars had been left to a later date. Because the B-70's radar signature was so huge it had been assumed they'd been seen coming from so far away that taking down the long range radars was superfluous. That judgment had been wrong and two RB-58Fs had paid the cost of that mistake. Three more were heading north for Russia, leaving trails of smoke and fragments of structure behind them.

“Another data dump coming in.” Henty spoke quickly, trying to get the word out before the new data started to modify the tactical displays. *Xiomara* was still crossing Iraq, well behind the Valkyries of the 100th Bomb Group but she was picking up more data all the time. The new electronic signals characteristics were downloading into *Sigrun's* DAMS system. A number of the decoys vanished as they were isolated and filtered out.

“Any threats?” C.J. O'Seven wasn't too concerned. Information suggested that the Iranian heavy defenses were around the big cities, particularly those that had religious significance. In any case, they hadn't run into any really serious defensive firepower yet. The Guilds and Guidelines they'd run into to date weren't a factor this high up. Guideline would only be a problem if they flew directly over the launch battery and had held a straight enough course to allow that crossing to be predicted several minutes in advance. They didn't do that. All the bombers were making random changes of heading to render their flight paths as unpredictable as possible.

“None, nothing to worry us about anyway. *Texan Lady II* reports that the defenses up Tehran way are firing Guidelines off unguided, like giant Fourth of July fireworks. Straight up in barrages. Wonder what happens when they run out of oomph and head down again?”

“I guess there must be enough of a horizontal vector to take them clear of the launch site of that's what you're thinking. Wouldn't surprise me though if a lot of the damage on the ground gets caused by missiles coming down. Remember the Staten Island Ferry?”

There was a sound of sucking teeth in the cockpit at the memory of one of the more embarrassing incidents of the Second World War. German Type XXID U-boats had got into the habit of firing Fi-103 buzz-bombs at American coastal cities, usually New York and Washington. Responding to public outrage at the attacks, the New York National Guard had tried mounting some 40mm guns at key points around the city.

One of the batteries had been sited on Governor's Island. One foggy day, just the sort of day the German submarines loved for their attacks, the radar had picked up an inbound. Things had gone wrong; procedures had been ignored. In their desire to show how effective the defense was, the gunners had engaged it. They'd shot it down all right; the only problem had been it was a B-25H returning from coastal patrol. The fact that it was moving at barely half the speed of a Fi-103 and was flying only a couple of hundred feet up hadn't registered. Nor had the fact that there had been no alert called. Even worse, the barrage of 40mm gunfire had raked the Staten Island Ferry, killing more than sixty people. That had made it the worst single air-raid casualty toll on the American mainland.

"Didn't some lawyer try to sue the Army over that?" Hook didn't like lawyers.

"Uh-huh, went all the way to the Supreme Court if I remember. Any airborne signatures? Or reports?"

"*Brunnhilde* reported a couple of Irenes trying to climb up. They topped out at 60,000 and squeezed off a couple of missiles. No threat and she sent them a return package. Got one and the other scuttled for home with its tailfeathers singed. They don't pack up close like they used to."

"Guys, doesn't this strike you as odd? The 35th and their 305th detachment stuck their heads into a hornet's nest, had to fight their way in and lost birds doing it. Up here, we've hit nothing of any consequence, yet this is supposed to be Caliphate heartland. Something's wrong here people."

"Suits me." James Fitzroy was scanning his offensive weapons suite, trying to match the radar images to the ground targets assigned to *Sigrun*. "I've got enough problems here."

"Radar pictures no good? Which one? Kushk e Nosrat or Qom?"

"Both. The pictures seem OK, they were obtained from one of the Lacrosse satellites. They're a bit out of date that's all. That means it's matching them up that's the problem. There's been changes down there since the pictures were taken."

"Can't be that much, surely. Guys, Hamadan's just gone off the air." The green dot and shadow of the huge Hamadan long range surveillance radar had suddenly vanished. A few seconds later, there was a slight thump as the residual shockwave from the explosion rocked *Sigrun*.

"It's not just changes, they're using decoys down there to distort the ground radar image. Looks like reflectors and radar mats. Can't get an absolute match."

"Hey the lake down there looks familiar." *Sigrun's* voice sounded slightly conceited.

"Got it!" Fitzroy all but cheered, the lake had been the key. "We're about 30 miles north of where we should be. I suggest we swing south, loop around and hit Kushk e Nosrat from the east, then do an S-turn and do the laydown on Qom halfway through."

"Good move, we're getting too close to Tehran for comfort." O'Seven swung *Sigrun* south away from the target set around the capital of Iran Satrapy. At this speed, *Sigrun's* turning circle was a little over 38 miles across. That wasn't bad for an aircraft that big and that fast but still enough to require a certain level of forethought in plotting maneuvers.

"We've got company."

"Hostile?"

"Not according to IFF. From course and speed, I think they're F-108s." There was a prolonged pause, then Henty made a small grunt. "I see it, there's four aircraft coming up from Mahadan. From the rate of climb I'd say Irenes or possibly Faiths. Our little friends are firing now." Henty saw his radar screen blossom with electronic noise and he thumbed the filters on, wiping it clear instantly.

"They've gone, the little friends are climbing away They can't have done the airfield that much good."

"Is it in AGM-76 range?"

“Not yet, another minute, minute and a half. Want to take it out?” Fitzroy sounded ghoulishly hopeful.

“Might as well, we’ve still got all our ground pounders on board. These airfields are big, better give it two. Did the little friends get all the fighters?”

“Think so, Seejay. They squeezed off four missiles to do it. You know, nobody clumps up any more; why do we still carry nuclear air-to-airs?”

“To make a point I guess. Mess with us and nukes are the first thing we throw back. AGM-76s locked in Fizzy?”

“Sure, approaching optimum now.” Underneath *Sigrun*, the forward bomb bay door slid backwards, exposing the tactical missiles in the bay. AGM-76s on the sides, AIM-47s in the middle. “Weapons dialed at 81 kilotons, full yield. Launching. . . . . . now.”

There was hardly a jolt as the two AGM-76s dropped away and streaked off, down towards Mahadan airfield. O’Seven changed course slightly, curving away from the target. No need to get closer than one had to. A few seconds later the cockpit lit up with the familiar brilliant light followed by *Sigrun* rocking with the blast.

“Rest in pieces, Mahadan” Hook was checking airspeed and course. “OK to acquire Fizzy?”

“Target acquired. We’ve got the coordinates and radar bomb-nav locked in. We’ll do this in two runs.”

Once again, the bomb-navigation system switched on and a Valkyrie was heading in, matching the radar images from the ground against the pictures in the navigation system memory. The two bomb bay doors slid forward, closing the forward bay and opening the one aft. Then, there was a slight lurch as the first of the gravity bombs detached and headed down for its target.

“Almost takes the fun out of things, the bomb-nav system.” Fitzroy sounded almost bored. In a strange, perverse way he found himself wishing they were back in the old days when a real, honest-to-goodness bombardier would aim the device and release it. Then the cockpit lit up with the brilliant white flash and *Sigrun* lurched heavily before her long nose dipped as the blast flipped her tail up. She lost almost 3,000 feet before O'Seven brought her back under control, then swung her around to start the attack run on Qom to the south.

"How was the laydown?"

"On target, I'd say around 250 feet north."

"You must have got my initial navigation point wrong then." *Sigrun* sounded aggrieved.

"I'll try and do better on the next run." Fitzroy promised soothingly. There was no reply but a slightly skeptical grunt could be heard on the intercom. "Speaking of such things, we locked in yet Seejay?"

"In theory, we're on course for Qom. Matched up the radar maps yet?"

"Got a lock, the distortions aren't so bad this side. Guess the Caffs must have thought we'd do a straight run in from the west. Setting up the run now."

Off to the left, the mushroom cloud from their first drop was still twisting skywards, darkening as it cooled. The crew felt *Sigrun* making tiny course changes as she lined up on her target, ready for her second and final laydown. She was lurching frequently as the blast from the other drops started to reach her. Then, the familiar shake as the second bomb dropped clear.

"Right, that's it guys. Let's go home. The surgery has been successful."

"But the patient died." *Sigrun* still sounded sad. "Why did they go and make us do it?"

War Room, Underneath the White House. Washington DC

"That's it. We're done." Power's voice was triumphant. "My boys are coming home."

"Did they hit the targets?" Nixon was half-afraid of the answer. He'd thought he would enjoy the sight of SAC at work, removing the threat of blackpox; that wasn't how he felt now. The fate of Bahrain was beginning to weigh upon him. The island had a population of over 600,000, once. Now it was wiped clean and that was only the start. The strike had the horrible fascination of a train wreck; impossible to watch, impossible to tear one's eyes from it.

"Yes Sir. Although the bombers had a job finding some of the targets. Several of them had to make repeated runs before they had a lock accurate enough for the laydowns. We're lucky there was no serious opposition, I guess the Caliphate must have thrown their best fighters against the Russians."

"You know, that's really odd." The Seer's voice was reflective.

"How so, Seer? They didn't stand a chance against the Valkyries so they sent them where they were better matched, against the forces where they might gain some success. Sounds a reasonable military decision to me."

"That's not what I mean. Look at the different styles that we can see here. The Mediterranean Satrapies, underdeveloped, pastoral even. Except for that complex we found in Syria, of course. We still don't really know what it was. Iraq, industrialized, all the stuff grouped into giant complexes around the big cities. Heavily defended by missile batteries, well-operated ones too, but missiles none the less. Fighters conspicuous by their absence. They'd set their facilities up, ringed them with defenses and tried their best. They took a pounding and a lot of collateral casualties, even areas that didn't have the target complexes around them had defense installations we took out to clear the way in for the bombers.

"Now look at Iran. Defenses grouped around the cities yes, but the industrial infrastructure we wanted was scattered all over the place. Defenses were fairly minimal, certainly nothing to cause our bombers much concern, and what there were concentrated on fighters, not bombers. It's a totally different way of fighting, it's as if they purposely sacrificed defensive power in an attempt to disperse and hide their infrastructure. Nations just don't do that, Tommy. It's as if every state in our Union had its own defense policy and its own way of doing things. Which, I suppose, if Thomas Jefferson had had his way is where we would be now. But nations just don't do that. Oh, our National Guard units reflect regional differences certainly, one needs only compare the Bayou Militia and the Massachusetts Minutemen to see that, they've got totally different characters but they're both F-106C groups and they both fight more or less the same way.

"And another thing. Notice how none of the satrapies came to assist any of the others? That's really strange, we got pretty well no opposition when we overflew satrapies on the way in, not until we shot up that complex in Syria at any rate. No real defense in depth at all. It's as if the other Satrapies simply didn't care."

"What are you getting at, Seer? Nixon sounded impatient.

"Mister President, we've always known we don't understand the Caliphate, how it makes decisions, how its ruled or anything else. We know it has a ruling council, they pretty much surrendered to us once, but that's it. It's internal structure, both social and political, we know nothing about. We know that there are many different religious sects inside Islam, how those are accommodated by their system we just don't know. Because of our space-based assets and Open Skies, we can put our finger on any tangible asset they have and say, 'that is where it is, this is what it is'. But what they think, how they think. . ."

"If they think." Power's voice cut in dryly.

"Oh, they think Tommy. The way the Iraqi missile crews fought back shows that. They stuck to their sites right to the end. Or at least we're pretty sure they did. We don't know how many didn't of course. But the ones that fought, they held fire until the bombers were right on top of them. 'Whites of their eyes' and all that. Anyway, as I was saying, we don't understand what or how they think. For that we need human intelligence assets and we just don't have any. We've got better human intelligence on Chipan than on the Caliphate. It's telling the best on-the-ground data we have on the Caliphate comes from Geneva, not Tehran or Kabul or Baghdad. The most important thing about today may not have been the damage we've inflicted but the graphic illustration of how little we understand about the entity that is now very obviously our prime enemy."

Nixon had started slightly at the names of Caliphate cities, as if he was reading them from a tombstone. "Any idea of losses?"

"Two RB-58Fs down, three more are landing in Russia with severe damage. The Russians are holding their crews for ransom."

"WHAT!" Nixon was furious. "I thought they were supposed to be allies."

"They are, Mister President." The Seer thought he'd better explain before Nixon had a stroke. "It's an old military custom. When aircraft land at the wrong base, the parent unit has to pay a ransom to get them back." The Seer looked at his clipboard and shuffled some papers. "I believe the Russian First Guards Fighter Division are asking for a Sammy and Sherry concert."

"They want a Sammy and Sherry concert?" Nixon's temper was subsiding as quickly as it had flashed up. "No accounting for taste I suppose. But I didn't mean our casualties, what about the people on the other end?"

"We estimate around 200,000 military casualties, mostly the crews of the air defense installations and about 1.4 million others. After Bahrain, Iraq's been the worst hit, the industrial complexes were clustered around big cities. By the time its all over, probably a total of more than two million. That'll rise in the aftermath of course."

"Dear God." Nixon was stunned. "Nobody told me. . . ."

"Sir, how many people do you think are dying in Algeria from blackpox? The latest extrapolation from the French is that the death toll there could hit at least 10 percent of the population. That's over 1.4 million dead there alone. And we're getting blackpox outbreaks all over the place. We know that blackpox has washed back into the Caliphate but how widespread it is, guess what, we don't know.

"Sure, we dodged the bullet but a lot of places haven't. Colombia and Mexico have outbreaks and we can't make vaccines fast enough to prevent them spreading. If it hadn't been for that French doctor right at the start of this thing, we'd be even further behind the curve. You know Sir, for the length of time this war has lasted, it's certainly the bloodiest in human history. And I very much doubt if that'll be understood out there. In a few years time, people will write this off as a minor affair, a bump in their otherwise tranquil worlds.

"And that's why we need Lifeboat Mister President. This was a half-baked plan, carried out using minimal resources and with very limited success. We lucked out. We got very lucky in fact, and they tried to be too clever. Also, they got carried away. They used a disease that was painfully obviously not natural. So we knew what was going on and we were able to offset the worst of it. And still, almost four million people will have died.

"One day, they're going to cut loose with those things and we won't be lucky and they won't mess up. The Good Lord only knows what the death toll will be then. We have to have a secure place to go to, somewhere enough people can shelter so they - and all of us through them - can survive. There's only one place for that Mister President, up there."

The Seer pointed skywards. "We're running against the clock Sir, and we don't know when the alarm bells will ring again."

Military Command Center, Dezful, Iran Satrapy, The Caliphate.

The American bombers had gone, mostly westward but a few heading north to Russia. The carrier planes had gone from the south, the Russian bombers from the north. The storm had passed, leaving destruction and chaos in its wake but it had passed. There was evidence of that not so far away. The airfield at Vahdati was a ruin; destroyed as thoroughly as the missile batteries that surrounded it. But this complex, buried deep underground had survived.

Briefly, Morteza Farzaneh wondered if the Ruling Council in their sumptuous palace near Teheran had survived. There had been strikes up there; at least two targets had been taken out. There was still no word on what had been destroyed and what had survived. Not that it mattered very much; that bunch of posturing fools counted for very little.

Farzaneh looked again at the plots of the bombers that had struck the targets in Iran and Iraq. The patterns were very striking. Over Iraq, the bombers had flown straight to their targets, fought their way in and destroyed them. The defenses the Satrap of Iraq had erected had proved of little value. They had shot down two bombers. That would become two hundred for public consumption in the Caliphate, but that hadn't stopped the assault. Over Iran it had been different. Farzaneh looked at the tracks, saw the bombers circling, looking for their targets. They'd had problems finding them although they'd managed it in the end.

An elegant concept had been born in Frazaneh's mind as he had watched them hunt. The Americans could destroy anything they wanted, their bombers could punch though any defense that could be mounted and the destruction they wrought was terrible beyond belief. *Yet, they couldn't destroy what they couldn't find.* They couldn't send their bombers if they didn't know there was anything to send them against.

There were times when differences were valuable and this had been one of them. Sometimes, Farzaneh wished that the Caliphate really was the great monolithic block that its enemies believed. Reality was that it was a very loose aggregation of virtually independent states whose allegiance to the greater whole was dubious to say the least. This whole affair had kicked off because of that. The satrapies competed for power and influence two ways. Internally they directly conflicted with each other. Externally they tried to spread the Caliphate as far as they could. Each extra territory they brought in added to their own power and prestige. The Council was where they fought out their political battles, where the influence they had tried to gain was put to the test and proved or lost. Iraq had started the whole affair by its attempts to expand into Algeria. Then, when that attack had been defeated, they'd developed this plan to save the situation.

There was a gentle knock on the steel door. Doctor Abdolali Shamsae, better known as Doctor Germ entered. His arms were loaded with files.

"Doctor. How bad?" Farzaneh looked over at his visitor. *Not too gloomy. There is hope.*

"The facilities in Iraq have gone, all of them. The Americans destroyed them all. Here in Iran, there are some survivors. A few the Americans missed, some others they didn't know were there. Not enough to restart what we had. We have lost all the cultures, the equipment, almost everything. But we didn't lose the people. We have evacuated most of the researchers in time and got them to safety. We still have the cadre of skills we need. We cannot restart what we had but we can rebuild from new. Those few hours delay, that was priceless."

"Then start again. Only this time, no more great complexes, no more installations that can be seen from hundreds of miles away. Build the plants small, hide them away. In villages, in isolated farms. No more plants built of imported equipment. If we cannot build it ourselves then we will do without."

"Iraq will not like that."

"Iraq does not matter anymore. It was their insistence on launching this attack now that brought this down on our heads. The Council warned them against it but they ignored those warnings. They will have little influence now."

"Does that matter?" Shamsae almost laughed.

"Not really." And that was true.

No, the Caliphate had to introduce a new policy. They would have to fly under the radar, keep their biological programs hidden, low-key, out of sight. Industrial development would have to go the same way, dispersed, low-key, hidden. And undefended. Defenses just marked out a place where there was something worth destroying. It would be down to the Ruling Council to find the theological justification for the new policy. And they would, if they knew what was good for them. The days of a theocratic Caliphate had just ended.

Chittagong House, New Delhi, India

"It is an inspiring thing to see a democracy at work." The King's Personal Ambassador-Plenipotentiary leaned back in her seat, allowing herself a small and entirely genuine sigh of satisfaction. Sir Eric Haohoa attributed it to the excellence of their evening dinner. His domestic staff had really done him proud and he was quietly pleased that his old friend had been properly entertained. He was, however, slightly mistaken on one point. The sigh of satisfaction was only partly due to the superb food. The rest was because, in the Ambassador's own unspoken words, she loved it when a plan came together.

The Indian political crisis had been headline news right up to the time the Americans made their announcement of the origins of the blackpox epidemic that was threatening to tear across the world. They'd also announced that their bombers would be destroying the source of that plague. That pushed the Indian crisis to the bottom of the innermost page. In every newspaper in the world except *The Hindu* and the other Indian nationals. There, the crisis into which the BJP Government had plunged was still on the front page. While the world held its breath and the American bombers had crossed the Atlantic to burn out the plague pits, the Indian government had made a brave and unique decision.

When the Congress Party had presented its motion of 'No Confidence in the present government,' the Indian Parliament had announced that the debate would be shown, live, on television.

Cynics suggested that this had been an attempt to delay the debate by opening the doors for "technical difficulties" but they had quickly gone quiet and red-faced.

Despite the technical difficulties and the unique problems in broadcasting from the Indian parliament building, the television network had managed to put it together. The sound wasn't good and the visuals were poorly-constructed but they'd done it. Now that the American bombers were back home, the debate was on every television in India. The Indian political crisis was working its way back towards the front page.

"This should be interesting, Madam Ambassador. The next speaker is the Minister for Foreign Affairs, a BJP stalwart. His defense of the government will be critical. If he drops the ball here, the vote could go badly."

"The BJP could lose Sir Eric?"

Sir Eric thought for a second. "I don't think so, not unless something startling happens. But with a no confidence motion. Its not so much whether the Government wins but how well they win. If their own supporters hold solid, then the Government really does win and all is well for them. But if a significant number of their members vote for the opposition, then their authority is fatally weakened and they will fall eventually. In that sense, yes, the BJP could indeed lose." He turned the sound on the television up slightly.

"My friends, fellow members of Parliament, let us review the events of the last few weeks. We had a claim to the Paracel Islands that we attempted to exert. We did so on our own, without the assistance of our allies, as an example of India's growing strength and position as a regional power in the world. We successfully occupied those islands and raised our flag over them. Despite enemy air attacks our gallant troops held on. When the enemy fleet tried to intervene, our gallant seamen in their Indian-designed and Indian-built ships took them on, head to head. It was a terrible and costly battle. Many of our brave men lost their lives as they laid their ships alongside the enemy and fought them to the last round of ammunition. The great hero Admiral Kanali Dahm died on the bridge of his cruiser, leading his fleet to victory. Who of us, watching his funeral but a few days ago did not have tears in his eyes as we paid our respects to the man who brought so much honor to India?

"And then my friends, our pilots fought on, defeating the Chipanese enemy in the air. Our ships fought on, sinking enemy submarines. Our troops on land fought on, shooting down the enemy aircraft that attacked them. Yes, my friends our gallant men fought on. But who, I ask you, did not fight on? ***Why, our Government did not fight on!*** Yes, I see you are as shocked as I! Despite all the sacrifices made by our Army, our Navy and our Air Force, our Government threw away the fruits of their struggle. They have agreed to withdraw from our islands. They have even agreed to the Chipanese name of the Southern Pescadores as a sign of our defeat. Our defeat my friends. Not a defeat suffered on the battlefield but one suffered here, at home, by a government that has lost its nerve. The deed is done. The peace agreement. . . . . No, let us give it its proper name, our surrender, is signed and being an honorable nation we cannot go back on our word. But we can think what we wish about those who gave that word.

"What have we won for the sacrifice of so many ships and men? A shelter on one island and some fish! ***Some fish!*** If Prime Minister Atal Bihari Vajpayee likes fish so much I have a gift for him." The Foreign Minister paused dramatically, reached into his pocket and brought out a small paper packet. He laid it on the podium in front of him.

"I am sorry it is such a small fish but it was caught only a few hours ago by a lady who is one of my constituents. A lady whose eldest son died on board the Indian Naval Ship *Ghurka* in the Battle of the South China Sea. But perhaps a small fish is appropriate for I have so little confidence in the government of Prime Minister Atal Bihari Vajpayee that I no longer wish to be part of it."

There was a gasp around the gathered Parliament as the Foreign Minister stepped away from his podium and ostentatiously took his seat with the Congress Party rather than his own.

"Sir Eric, I am not that familiar with Parliamentary procedures. In my country, votes of no confidence in the government tend to be much more emphatic and involve the use of tanks. But, to me, that did not sound like a defense of Government Policy."

"No my dear." It was a mark of how surprised Sir Eric was that he forgot to use the customary title for his guest. "That wasn't a defense. That was something startling happening."

"Will the Government survive, my friend?"

Sir Eric absorbed the familiar address with pleasure. Then he thought for a few seconds. "No, not from a speech like that, not from one of its own ministers. It's not just a blow; it's the death-stroke. The BJP will split, probably three ways. One part will stick with the Prime Minister. One part will condemn him for giving up. The third will condemn him forever starting this mad venture. The Congress Party will vote in a block of course. The smaller parties will split evenly. When the vote is taken, the BJP will lose and lose heavily. If it hadn't been for that speech, it would have hung together but not now. My dear, you have just seen a very public political assassination."

"How much will this affect you Sir Eric? I know the Cabinet Secretary is a part of the Civil Service and not affected by changes in ruling party but how much practical effect will this have?"

"Well, Madam. . . . ."

"Sir Eric, we have known each other long enough I think. My name is Suriyothai Bhirombhakdi na Sukhothai. The 'na Sukhothai' part is just a courtesy. It means I am distantly related to the Royal Family." The Ambassador carefully refrained from saying which Royal Family. "And we very rarely use our family names. So please call me Suriyothai when we are having a pleasant evening like this."

"Thank you Suriyothai. In answer to your question, this will mean everything will be very much back to usual. The rule of the BJP, relatively brief as it has been, will be seen as a gamble. Could

India stand alone and ignore its allies or does it need the alliance structure that the Congress Party had constructed?

"Had the Paracel operation succeeded, the BJP would have made its point and we would have seen India progressively turn its back on the Triple Alliance and attempt to stand on its own. But the Paracel Operation was a disaster and we have been defeated. The BJP Hindu nationalist position has been discredited and they have lost public respect. Their hold on power was tenuous at best. In the election to come they will be defeated.

"The Congress Party has always been internationalist in outlook, I suppose their origins as a socialist movement is at the root of that. No matter what the reason, they favor international alliances and multi-national organizations. As a result, when they win the next election, as I am sure they will now, the Triple Alliance will be safe."

The Ambassador leaned back once more, watching the minor speakers making their plays for and against the BJP government. Her political antennae, honed by more years of experience than Sir Eric would believe possible, were telling her that it was all over. The Foreign Secretary's ringing denunciation of Prime Minister Atal Bihari Vajpayee and the BJP had been decisive. As she had guessed it would be although she had been delighted to have Sir Eric's confirmation of that fact.

"What will become of him, Sir Eric?"

"The Prime Minister? Stick a fork in him, he's done. He won't survive as leader of the BJP, not now. There'll be a new leadership election and a new party leader. So even if the BJP did manage to win the coming election, their old policies will be gone."

"I meant the Foreign Minister. Such a brave gesture to stand against his own party like that."

"Brave, but politically very foolish. His chances of further high office have just vanished. If he stays in the BJP, he'll spend the rest of his parliamentary career on the back benches. They will never trust him again. If he joins the Congress Party, they won't trust him either. They'll always see him as BJP at heart. So, he's finished there as well. It's a pity, he was indeed a brave man to do what we have just seen."

Sir Eric thought for a second. "Mind you, it could be argued that he had little to lose. It is fairly well agreed that he'd reached about as high as he was going to go. His faction of the BJP is weak and has little influence. He only gained the Foreign Office because he was seen as a reliable supporter of the Prime Minister. It's always been pretty much accepted that he would be eased out soon and start the long decline downwards. Perhaps he thought it was better to go out with a bang than a whimper. If that was his logic, he's certainly achieved that aim."

On television, the debate had ended. Long lines of figures rose and headed out to the lobbies. In the rows of seats, the party whips converged on those who seemed undecided or their own members who appeared to be wavering. The minutes ticked by in silence as the members voted and returned to their seats. Then, there was a boom as the Speaker struck his staff on the floor.

"In the matter of the motion 'This House has no confidence in the administration of Prime Minister Atal Bihari Vajpayee' the votes of the Lok Sabha, the People's Assembly, are as follows. Aye, two hundred and eighty one. Nay, two hundred and sixty four. I therefore declare that having a majority of seventeen, the Ayes have it. The Motion stands."

Vajpayee rose to his feet. "I accept the verdict of the Lok Sabha. The Government resigns, and a writ for a new election will be moved immediately."

The BJP Party Government had fallen. The Ambassador without giving any external sign of the reaction, sighed with relief. The Seer's words still echoed in her mind. 'Anyway, your opposition here isn't Chipan, its India. Who else's actions have put you into an impossible position? They've gone ahead and dropped you in it with a vengeance. So they're the opposition here that has to be thwarted.' The American help had been absolutely crucial, if it had not been for their offhand comment 'That gives you the perfect excuse to refuse to join the conflict because if you try, the Chipanese won't take your Air Force out, we will,' the conflict would have spread.

Nobody in their right mind, nobody who had even a vestigial level of intelligence, would believe that the comment was intended as a serious threat. But the very fact that it had been made had given her the excuse to keep Thailand and Australia out of the conflict. And, by doing so, had allowed her to maneuver Vajpayee into the militarily-inevitable but politically-suicidal step of accepting the ceasefire offered by Chipan. Even the timing of the American assault on the Caliphate had been critical. The desperate hours spent waiting while the American bombers had taken off and crossed the Atlantic had created the gloomy atmosphere of desperation that had been instrumental in making Vajpayee fold.

Only one piece of the puzzle had remained; a fuse to set the explosion off. The Foreign Minister had provided that. A man honorable enough to place his country above his party, highly-placed enough to carry political weight and intelligent enough to understand that, no matter what he did, he had reached the peak of his career and would go no higher. And practical enough to accept the inducements that had been dangled in front of him. A secure, post-political career that would still give him work that would benefit his country, put wealth into his hands and secure his family's future. His political career might be over but his business career was just starting and it would be very remunerative. A few well-placed contracts would see to that.

"A successful political assassination indeed Sir Eric."

"Indeed so my dear. And one that means I will never again doubt the wealth of Thailand."

The Ambassador grinned in response to the gentle, friendly gibe. She should have remembered that the Indian Cabinet Secretary's duties also included supervision of the country's intelligence services.

CHAPTER TWELVE
EXPLOITING

Inaguchi 2-chome, Himori, Tokyo, Japan

Getting to come home in a staff car was compensation, in part at least. Commander Toda Endo got out of the back seat, squared his shoulders and adopted the impassive expression expected of an Imperial officer. Behind him, his driver quietly closed the car door and pulled away. He hadn't been thanked for his services nor did he expect to be. Thanks would have been regarded as a gentle rebuke; he was supposed to fulfill his functions without being seen or noticed. To be thanked would have meant he had been seen and noticed.

Toda walked towards his home. As he approached, the Chinese maid opened the gate for him. Most Japanese officer's families had a maid these days, brought in from China for the purpose. *It is a generous gesture*, Toda thought *for the war in China has left many widows and many children without parents, providing them with work is an example of the kindness of the new rulers of China*. Something uneasy stirred in his mind at that, a thought that quietly slipped away as he tried to get hold of it.

His family were waiting in the small garden that lay between his home, the street and the rest of the world. His wife was formally dressed in Kimono and Obi to honor his return from the war. His children, wore their best and were waiting quietly beside their mother.

Then, when he was inside the gate, his wife bowed deeply and his children knelt on the grass, his little daughter was helped by a hand placed gently but firmly on her back. Toda returned the bow gravely, allowing no trace of expression to touch his face. Behind them, the maid closed the wooden gate and the children could wait no longer. They ran over to their father, seizing his legs and burying their faces in his uniform. His daughter was crying; his son wanted to but had fought back the tears and tried to equal his father's stoicism. Toda looked proudly down on him. He was young for such an effort; even making the attempt was praiseworthy. To succeed was a mark that showed great promise of distinction.

"Welcome home. Welcome back." His wife was also crying now, the tears ruining her elaborate make-up. It didn't matter. She reached out, gently, tentatively, touching the brand-new badges of rank on his shoulder. "Commander?"

"Commander, Hanaka-chan. My new rank was made permanent today." Then the fighter pilot in Toda burst through. "Seven kills! Five Tigers, two Skyhawks! And the Tainan Kokutai is mine!" Then the matter that was clouding his mind took over again. Instead of speaking further, he slipped his arm around his wife's waist, feeling the soft, firm luxury of the silk kimono. He had missed his Hanaka so much.

"Our evening meal is ready." Together, they went back to their dining room; a simple place whose clean austerity pleased Toda's eyes after the frenetic improvisations of Naval Base Sugu Bay. There, she served his meal as befitted a wife whose husband had returned with honor from a war. Beautiful rice, snow white and steamed to perfection. His favorite smoked eel, thinly sliced just so, and dressed with his favorite sauce. Fresh shrimp served with more of that beautiful rice.

Toda told his family how their Indian prisoners had eaten rice, seasoned with strong spices and mixed with other things. They shuddered at the barbarity of people who would ruin the delicate flavor of fine rice that way. While he ate, his wife kept his sake bowl filled. He wouldn't know but she had spent a whole day hunting for his favorite sake so that his homecoming would be perfect. And, underneath it all, she knew that something was troubling him.

After the family had eaten and the children had gone to bed, Toda and his wife walked quietly in their garden, enjoying the peace and quiet, barely disturbed by the sound of the traffic beyond the walls.

"You will be staying for a while?" The question was gentle.

"The Tainan will be based not far from here. We are to be equipped with a new fighter, the N6M Tsurugi. Hanaka-chan, it is beautiful. Twin engines, Mach 3, and we can fly high enough to intercept the American bombers at last." Had Toda Hanaka been American, she would have made a barbed comment about boys with their toys, but she was not. She was a well-brought up Japanese wife and she remained quiet, just thinking the comment instead. "It will be for us to bring it into service.. But. . . . . ."

His wife said nothing still but gently squeezed his arm. He hesitated for a second then plunged on.

"Hanaka-chan. I am thinking of resigning my commission. I made my report, all the lessons we learned from the weeks out in Sugu Bay. Everything we learned fighting the Indians, what worked, what did not. Everything that my men lost their lives to learn. To fly in fours, protecting each other, not alone each seeking single combat. To keep half the unit back here, out of combat so they can train replacements. To send the veterans back so they can teach the cadets. Everything we learned I reported, and they," Toda's hand sweep indicated who he meant by 'they,' "have accepted nothing. Nothing! We might as well not have gone to war. We might as well not have won. Everything will be forgotten and next time around, it will have to be learned again."

Once again his wife squeezed his arm gently. He stared upwards. "Why is it we hang on to the old ways when we can see they do not work. What is the point of fighting to improve things if nobody will listen to our lessons?"

They went quietly back into their home. *At least*, Toda thought, *I survived.*

Next morning, the car was waiting for him again. His driver opened the rear door for him and he slid in. The seat was already occupied by somebody Toda recognized. The older of the two Kempeitai men who had visited the naval base at Sugu. Before he could react his partner, the younger man, slid into the seat as well.

"He's thinking of resigning his commission." The older man spoke sadly to the younger.

"I suppose he thinks he's wasting his time because the Admirals didn't follow his recommendations."

"As if Admirals would obey the orders of a newly-frocked Commander."

"And now he's sulking."

"And thinking of resigning as well. What is the Navy coming to?"

"I don't know. What are we to do with him?"

"A good question. Commander, what shall we do with you?" Toda was goggling at the interchange. *I havn't decided to resign yet and already the Kempeitai know? How?* "He's got no ideas on that score either. Or perhaps he thinks he'd be better off keeping quiet."

"Another bad idea."

"Commander Toda, your recommendations have been heard. And, yes, ignored. But we counsel patience. The Admirals did not act on them because who could reasonably expect Admirals to turn over the habit of a lifetime on the word of a young commander? But wait, and you will see that step by step, all that you have learned will come to pass. You have the Tainan Kokutai now. You can train it in your image, with your ideas. When your Tainan pilots outfight and outmaneuver all others in training exercises, other units will copy you. When enough do, all that you have learned, every recommendation that you have made will become standard. Others will take the credit but the work will be yours."

"He never listened to us, did he?"

"I think you are right. Did you listen to us Commander, when we told you that you had gained important friends? We know where these ideas came from. By the way, Commander, you may be interested to know that the orders to scrap the six remaining aircraft carriers have been signed. The money saved by doing so will be invested in the seaplane fighter units. More fuel for training, more flying hours, more ammunition to practice with. In a few months, the seaplane fighters and the flying boats will be our naval sea-based air arm just as the Navy's long range bombers and the B10N theater attackers will be the naval land-based air arm. The days of the surface fleet have gone. Now we will concentrate on the air and under the sea. Your Tainan will lead the way in that change Commander."

The two Kempeitai men got out of the car and walked across the road without looking around, ignoring the traffic that swerved to avoid them. Then, they vanished into the crowd. Toda thought for a second then told his driver to wait. They had the time needed for a quick decision. Inside his gate, his wife was still kneeling, waiting for the sound of her husband's car leaving before carrying on with her daily routine. He went over to her and lifted her up by an elbow. "Hanaka-chan. I have made up my mind. I will be staying with the Navy." He stepped back, bowed briefly and left. Behind him, his wife smiled with contentment.

B10N-1 Shuka Kiku-san*, Pattle Island, Southern Pescadores, South China Sea*

The runway was short but *Kiku-san* had come in with her wings fully forward and her nose held high. A short landing, on an extemporized crushed-rock runway. Few heavy, high performance aircraft could have managed it. *Kiku-San* had and she was now parked in a revetment at one end of the field. Behind her, *Shurayukihime* was landing. Captain Genda Minoru watched her come in. *Shurayukihime* was named after a famous female assassin of the Meiji era, one who had single-handedly wiped out the corrupt leadership of an entire province. There were whispers that she still lived, watching those who ruled her province, ready to slay any that slipped back into the ways of corruption. Pure superstition of course.

This was a forward base only. Four B10N-1s from the Mihoro Kokutai would be based here, rotated out from the primary base back on the mainland. From here, they could dominate the South China Sea, sweeping out to intercept the ships that brought in supplies for the Viet Minh. If there were any of course. Everybody knew where the supplies really came from but engaging that source of supply meant taking on the Americans. That would be brave but very foolish.

The noise of *Shurayukihime's* engines died down as she was parked in her revetment. The airbase was well laid-out. Genda had to give the Indians credit for that; from their point of view he supposed it was a pity they'd never got to use it. The big Arrows and TSR-2s couldn't operate from here; they were American-style aircraft that needed long concrete runways, but their little Gnats could. There had still been some fears that the Indians wouldn't accept they'd lost, especially after their government had collapsed as a result. So the Shukas had flown down in fighter-bomber configuration, bombs in their bellies but Tanto missiles hanging under their wings. The air-to-air capability of the Shuka was still one of its little secrets. It hadn't been needed. The Indians were keeping their word. They were pulling back.

Out in the bay, one of the H13K flying boats was pumping fuel to the camouflaged rubber bladders. Engineers were already around them, building walls of sand and chipped rock to protect the precious fuel from attack. Others were repairing damage and clearing wreckage from what had once been the Indian base. Overhead, the Ohtoris of the Mitsuko Kokutai were circling. They'd replaced the battered but victorious Tainan Kokutai at the Sugu Bay base but that facility was already being dismantled and moved to Pattle Island. In a war of islands, the big flying boats were worth their weight in gold. Soon Naval Base Sugu Bay would be gone and the seagulls could have their home back.

Admiral Tanaka was also watching the bombers land. "Captain Genda? Welcome to Naval Base Pattle Island."

"Sir, thank you sir. We are established then."

"We are indeed. The first Lajatang batteries are in place. The remainder and the anti-ship missiles will be here as soon as they can be removed from Sugu Bay. The first fighters are here and a seaplane tender is also on its way from Japan. You have heard, approval to build two more has been received?"

"Sir! It is great news." And so it was indeed. The two new seaplane tenders were the largest ships ordered for the Japanese Navy in many years.

"You may not have heard this yet, but Nakajima have been ordered to step up production of the B10N. The Mihoro will be up to strength by the end of the year. Even if other groups have to be stripped to achieve that." Tanaka looked out across the bay again, to where a pair of wrecked Indian ships disfigured the smooth waters. One was a burned-out wreck; the other less mauled but hard aground. "They will make good targets for your training missions."

"They fought well, Sir, much better than we believed. When we did our first strike, the men on the ground were firing back with their rifles, even as the bombs fell upon them."

"But they didn't have lead-computing sights on their rifles did they?" Both men burst out laughing. The tale of the old Model 99 7.7mm rifle was notorious, held up to every engineer as an example of how not to do things. Not a bad rifle in itself but ridiculously over-complicated. It had been fitted with a dust cover on the bolt, a built-in monopod and, most notoriously of all, a lead-computing anti-aircraft mechanism built into the rear sight. Only two metal bars certainly but a total of six parts that had no earthly use. It had taken the capture of Russian-made PPSH-41 and SKS rifles from the Chinese to show the Japanese engineers the reality of weapons engineering. Both weapons had been copied and now armed Army units.

"Captain." The Admiral stopped laughing. "When the two remaining aircraft have landed, equip two with reconnaissance pods in their bellies and start flying sweeps across the South China Sea. High altitude, area surveillance. We've got this base, we'd better start using it."

Pilot's Mess. Dromodevo Fighter Base, Moscow, Russia.

"You are walking down the street carrying your Kalashnikov when suddenly there is a loud scream and a German lunatic runs at you from one corner waving an ax. Them there is another scream and a Finnish lunatic runs at you from another corner also waving an ax. You have plenty of ammunition but which do you shoot first?"

"The German?" Captain George Tarrant guessed.

"That's right my friend. Business always comes before pleasure!" There was a roar of laughter around the mess as the punchline came out. Still, Tarrant had one of his own.

"How do you tell the difference between a dead rat and a dead Finn lying in the roadway?"

"I don't know my friend, how?"

"There'll be skid marks in front of the rat." Another gale of laughter swept the room and Tarrant got a clap on the back that nearly dislocated his shoulders. The Russians hated the Germans with an intense passion, yet one that was mixed with grudging respect for their military skill. Their hatred for the Finns was mixed with nothing but contempt. That had come out in the Russo-Finnish peace treaty of 1949. It had been savage almost beyond belief; it had left Finland gravely reduced in territory, disarmed and paying a reparations bill that would impoverish them beyond the end of the century.

"How are the repairs on *Vicious Vixen* going?" The RB-58F had been patched up quickly down south then flown up to Sheremetevo for further repairs. After they had been completed, she would be flown back to Convair for a complete rebuild and conversion to RB-58G standard.

“Very well. We have three Tiger Teams here working on her and the other two damaged birds, and three C-150s full of spare parts. And the stage show for your concerts.” This time a loud cheer split the air around the Mess. The USO had come up trumps. They’d organized not one but three concerts for the Russian fighter groups. It never did any harm to be known as people who paid their debts unstintingly. Which brought up another matter.

“Any word about what’s happening in the Caliphate Ivan?”

Major Ivan Josevich Peterenko shook his head. “Both our assets and yours can detect nothing. Your SR-71s did reconnaissance runs over the targets and brought back the post-strike images. We destroyed them all but were they all that was there to be destroyed? I think not and missing what we have will come back to haunt us one day. Their radars are down, their surviving fighters are grounded. I think they do nothing that might bring down a follow-up attack on them. That is unusually wise of them. We even sent an Ilyushin electronics bird over the border to smell around and they did nothing.:

“Perhaps this bombing taught them something that they failed to learn from Yaffo?”

“Perhaps. We hope so. But if our attacks have stopped just another atrocity like Beslan. . . .” There was a grim silence around the Mess now, memories of Beslan damping the party spirit. To a nation that had nearly been wiped out, that had lost a huge percentage of its young men and a much smaller, but still terrifying, proportion of its young women, children were a sacred trust. Even now, a quarter of a century after the war had ended, Russian was a country of the very old and the very young with a yawning gap between. Children were safe in Russia; everybody looked out for them, everybody protected them. So the massacre at Beslan had seared deep into the national soul. That debt had been paid, unstintingly, with nuclear fire. The memory of the mushroom clouds rising over those responsible brought cheer back to the party.

“Still, my friends, we have done what we can and the rest can wait. Now, where is that wretched bar maid with the vodka.”

Peterenko shook his head with shame and grief. "That a guest in Russia should have an empty glass in his hand. . . ."

Saint Joseph's Church, Naperville, Illinois, USA

"Brothers and sisters, we are gathered together here in both grief and celebration. Grief that our beloved sister Jane Cooper has been taken from us but also a celebration of her life that brought so much joy to all who knew her and contributed so much to our community.

"Of Jane herself, every person here has memories of her kindness and generosity. When sickness struck a family, it was Jane who was first to offer help. It was to Jane that we all turned when any one of us needed comfort or advice. Jane never turned the needy away from her door and never denied those who were in serious want. When her own time came and she started her battle with cancer, who does not remember her courage and steadfastness? And, when the time came that she realized this was a battle she could not win, who cannot fail to have been impressed by her quiet dignity as she made her final arrangements for the inevitable?

"Beyond Jane herself we have her family, her husband James, who has been left without the support of his loving wife, who was his best friend for so many years. Yet, he is not left alone for Jane gave him five fine children. Four of them are here today, two sons, two daughters, with children of their own. A decent, honorable, upstanding family, a credit to our community and to Jane itself who had the satisfaction of seeing her first grandchildren before she was called home. Let us never forget the child who is not here today, in body at least although his spirit surely looks down upon us. I speak, of course, of her eldest son, William Cooper, who, at the age of 19, sacrificed his life, fighting for his country, in the snows of Russia."

There was a brief silence as the congregation looked at the wreaths in the church. One had two flags, the Russian tricolor and the other the Stars and Stripes, crossed together. Brought by the local chapter of the Russian-American Friendship League. There was a representative of that League in the congregation and some of

William Cooper's old comrades from the 84th Infantry had turned up as well.

"We can comfort ourselves with the knowledge that Jane is now reunited with her oldest son and both now enjoy the rewards of a life well-spent. Yet, Jane's family extended far beyond her own. In a way, we can all claim to be part of her family. Jane spent so much of her time teaching the children of this community, opening their eyes to the new world she herself had found in her own love of dance. She brought history to life with her stories of the Prohibition era, putting faces and characters to the names that would otherwise be just words on the pages of a book. The rest of us remember her 'other' stories of those years." A gentle ripple of laughter spread around the congregation for, after the children had gone to bed, Jane Cooper had told racier tales, ones that drew from her own days as a dancer in one of Chicago's more notorious night-clubs. Privately, not a few members of the congregation wondered what the glittering showgirl called Jane Andrews had seen in the staid, unexciting car salesman James Cooper.

"And so, we must indeed mix our grief at losing Jane with a celebration of all the gifts she brought to our community and gratitude for the time that she was able to spend with us. So, may I ask you to join together in Hymn number. . . . . ."

After the service, the Pastor stood with James Cooper beside the door talking quietly with the members of the congregation as they paid their last respects and left. One couple was unusual enough to stop them, a man who appeared to be in his late 50s with a bushy mustache that already showed the whitening of age, was accompanied by a younger woman, late 30s at most, with stunning red hair.

"My condolences, Mister Cooper." The man spoke slowly and gravely. "William always spoke of his mother with great love. Her spirit helped us all out there, even though most of us had never met her. Her kindness and warmth somehow shone through to us from William."

"You knew my son in Russia?" James Cooper's voice nearly cracked.

"He was a tower of strength Sir. One of those men everybody in the unit turned to for support. I never got a chance to say good-bye myself, with everything that happened. So, when we were in Chicago on Government business and I saw the notice, I just had to come."

Cooper picked his ears up on the words "Government business". Then he looked at the woman a little more closely. "Excuse me ma'am, aren't you Naamah Sammale? The President's Executive Assistant? I saw your picture on the news after the Senate Steps Shooting."

"That's right Sir." Naamah spoke carefully, mentally noting that this was going to be a growing problem, one The Seer needed to think about. *Just how long could they stay in the shadows with television spotlights around?* "We felt privileged to come. Your Jane sounded like a wonderful person."

"She was. Thank you both for coming, with everything that's been happening, we're honored that you came."

They bobbed at eachother and moved on. Behind them, unnoticed by either party, one of the other guests apparently started speaking to his thumb.

"Gunman and Deadeyes are out. Be advised, there's a friend here as well." Ever since the Senate Steps Shooting, Naamah had had a Secret Service bodyguard, one who knew the significance of the words 'Persons of Special Interest.' "He's moving in on our subjects." Her bodyguard watched the other Secret Service Agent approach his charge.

"Miss Sammale. Didn't expect to see you here."

"Agent Delgado. We didn't expect to see you either. We thought you would be in Cuba or something."

"No such luck. I thought the same though, I assumed you would be in Cuba with the rest of the party from the NSC. Did you know Janey?"

"No, but I knew her son in the Army. So this was my chance to pay my respects." Henry McCarty's voice was still slow and grave. Delgado marked that little piece of information down. That was one of the characteristics of the 'Persons of Special Interest' that drove the Secret Service mad. Try and find out anything about their backgrounds and the paper trail ended up going in circles. Frustrating.

"The Delgados have been friends of the family for decades. Way back when, when Janey was still dancing in the clubs, there was a ruckus one night. My gramps was there with a couple of associates, Sean Mahoney and James O'Hare. O'Hare wasn't a bad sort according to Gramps but Mahoney was a really nasty piece of work. He got way out of line started throwing his weight around and was about to work Janey over with a set of brass knuckles.

"Gramps was about to put a stop to it when some crazy old coot with a howitzer straight out of the Wild West came running down from the entrance hall, blazing away like there was no tomorrow. Bullets all over the place according to Gramps, could have gone anywhere but one killed Mahoney dead on the spot, which wasn't a loss, and another blew a hole in O'Hare which killed him a week later. Gramps pulled Janey out of the line of fire but caught a shot doing it. Lost his right arm and that meant he missed the St. Valentines Day Massacre so he got religion. Did it properly, got ordained and everything. He was the pastor here for a while. Anyway, he kept in touch with Janey and the families stayed close. Still are."

Henry shook his head. "Amazing story. They must have been lively times back then. Anybody ever find what happened to the old guy?"

"Ran out, never seen again. Not alive anyway. There was a November Witch blowing and those storms are killers. His body was found frozen in an alley a few days later. Frank Nitti sprung for the funeral, he owned the night club. So the old guy got put away properly. He was the club doorman or something. Anyway, Capone himself turned up, guess he kind of respected the man who blew away three of the opposition with a museum piece. Janey cried really bad about the whole thing, she really liked the old guy. Guess he was kind of a father to her, her own old man was a piece of, well, he's dead now. Leave it unsaid. You going straight back to Washington?"

"We are Agent Delgado. We've got a Superstream waiting for us, want a supersonic ride back?"

"That'd be great Ma'am. I'd love it." *And*, thought Delgado, *maybe a chance to learn something more about the mysterious 'Persons of Special Interest'*.

Peterson Household, Alexandria, Virginia, USA

Judith Peterson heard her husband close the front door and hugged herself in delight. The delivery man had brought the package that afternoon and it was sitting on the kitchen table unopened.

"Darling, it's here. . ."

David Peterson's eyes lit up. He barely stopped to kiss his wife as he headed for the securely-wrapped package on the table. The outer package of cardboard and tape surrendered quickly to reveal a black plastic case. Peterson released the catches on the side and lifted the lid. Inside was a violin-case shaped wooden box, highly polished with a brass nameplate on the top. It read 'Auto Ordnance Corporation Of America.' Peterson was almost holding his breath as he opened the locks.

Inside was a 1921 model Thompson sub-machine gun, its dark, blued metal contrasting beautifully with the polished walnut stock and twin pistol grips. There were three magazines in the case; a 30-round stick, a 50-round drum and a 100 round drum. Also inside was a copy of "The Gun That Made The Twenties Roar" signed by Meyer Lansky himself. The gun rested in the purple velvet of its case, its finned barrel sat in the cutout. It gave real meaning to the phrase that a thing of beauty was a joy forever. It was a special edition weapon, one that could only be purchased in Cuba. Its quality put the cheaper versions on sale in the States to shame.

"Oh Dave, its beautiful. You're are not going to take that with you if the town call out the militia are you?"

Her husband shook his head, his eyes still glued on the Thompson. "I could though, nothing would happen to it. After all, its Constitutionally protected."

He and his wife looked at each other and burst out laughing. When the New York assault on the Second Amendment had come before the Supreme Court, the Justices had finally spelled out exactly what the Amendment said. They'd started by confirming that the right to keep and bear arms was an individual right. After all, in the other nine amendments that made up the Bill of Rights "the people" referred to individuals not collectives. There was no reason to presume that the Second was any different. They'd gone on to define "arms" as any weapon that could be carried and used by a single person.

So far, so good. The counsel for the National Rifle Association was beaming happily. Then, the Justices had gone on to state that the first phrase of the Amendment meant that its purpose was to provide a body of armed citizens from whom a local authority could raise a militia to act in service of that community. So, they had opined, the Amendment specifically protected only those weapons that were militarily useful. Revolvers, pistols, manual-action, semi-automatic and automatic rifles, sub-machine guns and light machine guns were all constitutionally protected. Authorities could only regulate or prohibit weapons that had no military use. And that, the Justices averred, meant weapons that were only suited for sporting or hunting purposes. The counsel for the NRA abruptly stopped smiling. His lifetime gravy train had just ended.

They had ended up by pointing out that under the 14th Amendment, the States or other local administrations couldn't abridge the rights granted under the Second. With a certain flourish, they'd ended up by stating that given this interpretation, all Federal, State and Local firearms regulations, including the National Firearms Act of 1934, were unconstitutional and were set aside with immediate effect unless it could be shown they complied with the Justice's ruling. Having dropped that bombshell, the Justices retired, leaving the entire courtroom stunned into silence. Years later, the Chief Justice had been interviewed on television and it had been proposed that the Court's ruling owed much to the Justices feeling that they couldn't please everybody so they might as well upset everybody. The Chief Justice had replied "I couldn't possibly comment."

David Peterson picked the Thompson up, checked that the chamber was clear and peered down the sights. "I can't wait to get this to the range."

"You'll have to Dave. We lost twice as much money as we expected in Cuba and the way that thing will eat ammunition, we can't buy enough until we hit the end of the month. Unless of course. . . ."

"I don't want us borrowing money from your friends." Peterson's voice was slightly petulant, his desire to flaunt his new Thompson down at the range conflicting with his reluctance to take advantage of his wife's strange background.

"We wouldn't be. Look, Dave, Nefertiti's circle has two sets of funds, I've told you this. Each of us has their own and we all kick in from our earnings into a common pool. I've been doing that since. . . for years." Judith stopped herself from going further. "That money is invested and it is a common pool. For anybody who needs it. I can ask Lillith what my share would be and we can draw a little out. Pay it back later if we wish. If not, well, it's our money. They've just invested it for us. Very well too. Those investments made us all a fortune."

Peterson sighed. "I know, I tell you what, we'll wait for the end of the month and go down to the range together. I've got to take this apart and clean it out anyway. Its probably coated with cosmoline inside. That'll take a week or two."

"OK then." Judith wagged her finger at him. "But don't you dare scratch the finish!"

Parliament House, Canberra ACT, Australia

"The election results are in Madam Ambassador. Congress Party two hundred and ninety five seats, the BJP two hundred and forty, the rest divided between the small parties. Indira Gandhi is the Prime Minister again. I must admit to a great sense of relief."

Australian Prime Minister John Barry Gardinier relaxed and looked at his guest. What had seemed like a hair-brained scheme had come off. Vajpayee had been a disaster as a Prime Minister but it had never occurred to him that he could be toppled. Then again, things had worked out just right, everything had come together in just the right way to make it possible.

"We were very fortunate JBG. Very fortunate indeed. If the *Viraat* hadn't been hit when she was, it would have been much more difficult to persuade him to accept that peace offer. And the Americans preparing to go in as they were, it meant the right atmosphere of fear and worry helped him make the decision. Just as the relief when the bombers were home and we knew it was all over helped the debate in the house. Yes, everything worked out very well for us."

"It would concern me if things were that finely balanced again."

"We must make sure that it never happens. We were lucky this time, the Americans made sure the fighting remained local and that worked for us. We cannot be sure this will be the case again. Our alliance must be made stronger, more certain. A defensive alliance has worked well to date. That is certain but we are outgrowing that."

"A Federation, Madam Ambassador? That is a long step to take and I do not think it will be accepted. We still have our links with the Commonwealth. They may not be of real value now but they are of great sentimental import. I do not think the people here will tolerate them being discarded."

"A Federation? No, I think not; not in this generation or the one after it. Perhaps, in the fullness of time it may come. I was thinking of ways to lock us closer together so that it would be more difficult for a situation like this to happen again."

"More joint programs perhaps? Like Alliance Aviation?"

"I was thinking of something more fundamental than that. The blackpox plague has made me consider our future more deeply. The disease is burning out. It is not infectious enough to spread quickly and it is so lethal that its bearers die before they can infect too many others. Also, our doctors are telling us that it is suffering from regression, that it is becoming less lethal with every generation and is reverting to smallpox. Will we be so lucky next time a man-made plague strikes? Perhaps we need to think on ways of preserving ourselves from such attacks, a way of establishing refuges. Places where a core of our people can hide so that we can survive through them."

"That seems an overly dramatic response Madam?"

"JBG, have you seen film of the victims of blackpox dying? But, we do not need to establish the program as just a refuge. It can do scientific research as well, with a last refuge against disease as its ultimate purpose. I was thinking, under the sea. Undersea habitats that can be used to explore the ocean deeps and even to farm them. And then, if disease, if plague strikes again, the people who live in those habitats will be safe."

"That sounds a practical idea. One we can sell I think. And we must watch the Caliphate very carefully from now on."

The Ambassador stared out of the window and for a second, JBG thought he saw her eyes glow red. But, it had just been a trick of the evening light. "JBG, have you ever watched a forest fire? The main fire is bright and it races from treetop to treetop, with a great display of flame and much roaring. The firemen pay attention to that fire and fight it bravely. But there is a second fire, one that burns low and quietly, spreading slowly in the undergrowth. The firemen do not see it for they are watching the noisy roaring fire above them. Only when it is too late do they realize that the fire in the undergrowth has spread behind them and they have been trapped. JBG, let us not be so consumed with vigilance over the Caliphate that we lose sight of the other threats around us. The world's largest Moslem nations are not even part of the Caliphate. They are part of the Triple Alliance."

VC-144F Queen of Biloxi*, Dillinger International Airport, Havana, Cuba.*

"Lillith, what does our bottom line for FY72 look like?"

"For the Hudson River Institute? What do you want it to look like?"

"The real one, for our eyes only."

Lillith closed her eyes for a second. "We made a few millions, HRI lost money on running the NSC, of course. We have to eat the cost of the services we provide to people like us worldwide. On the other hand, we make money on the other Government administration contracts we have and there's a worthwhile overlap that more than covers the NSC losses. All in all, we're pretty healthy. Why do you ask?"

"I was just thinking, it would be nice to have a Superstream III of our own. Save us borrowing an Air Force VC-144 whenever we want to go places. Especially ones where we don't want too much publicity. The only other option is going on one of those." He gestured out the window at one of the big two-deck 747s unloading at the airport terminal.

"He wants a supersonic business jet." Tom Lynch grinned patiently. "Don't recommend it, Seer. It's much cheaper to get the Air Force to fly us and charge the cost against our administration contracts. Anyway, civilian Superstreams don't hold their value. They're expensive to buy, horribly costly to run and the resale market is tiny. Guys who bought Superstream Is and IIs have a job giving them away. They're ostentatious consumption and status symbols. Who wants a second-hand status symbol?"

"Doesn't that mean we could pick one up at bargain basement cost?"

"It does, Seer, but you don't want to." Lynch leaned back, enjoying the luxury seating. *The VC-144 sure beat the 747 for comfort.* "The running cost is even higher. Anyway, the whole RB-

58 and Superstream line is running down now that Convair have delivered the last RB-58s. All they've got left on that program now is rebuilding the remaining C/D models to G standard and updating the Fs to Gs. They've been trying to sell the civilian Superstreams to make up the slack but they haven't had much luck. Looks like the F-116 is all they have at the moment."

"And North American are doing well with their airliner. The Machliners and Sonic Clippers will be in service in a couple of years, they'll give us the supersonic travel capability we want."

"That you want." Inanna spoke dryly and winked at Raven.

"And if we don't want to ride commercial, the XC-170 prototype is flying as well. VC-170s will be replacing the VC-144s by the middle of the decade. How you getting on honey? You like flying supersonic?" The Seer directed the remark at Raven who was still staring out the window at the airport rolling past the executive jet as it taxied to the VIP section of the airport.

"I've never flown anywhere before. Is it always like this?"

"Err, no." Lillith hid her amusement carefully. "Those big people haulers out there are flying cattle cars. Small, uncomfortable seats, not much room. The only food comes in plastic packages, its expensive and it doesn't taste any different from the wrapping. That's why we try not to use them. So, how do you get to Washington?"

"Greyhound bus." Sometimes we drive but mostly get the bus. It's not so bad, the People Haulers sound just like them."

"Raven, honey, tell Menewa and the rest, they're on the Government payroll now. Or on our payroll which comes to the same thing. The Government hires us and we hired you. That means you get perks, one of which is using Air Force or Navy aircraft, if they're available, which they mostly are. If you want a ride, see Lillith, she'll talk to Air Bridge Command headquarters at Andrews and see what's available. You'd be surprised how often a plane with spare capacity is going somewhere you want. You might get stuck on a C-141 or a

C-150 but even a C-137 is better than the bus. And if you're thumbing a ride on a plane that's going that way anyway, its probably cheaper. Anyway, none of you should be short of cash now. If you are, let us know, we've got funds set aside for that sort of problem."

"We don't want charity Seer, we've had enough of it." Raven's voice was sharper than she'd intended. She was still painfully aware she bought her clothes from KMart.

"It's not charity Raven, its an investment. And a safety precaution." Lillith spoke matter-of-factly, just as she did when she was making financial reports. "When people run out of money is when they do stupid things, and get caught doing them. So, our reserve funds are an insurance policy. If one of our people is in financial difficulties, we tide them over and they refund the money later. So, if you or any of our friends have problems, let us know. It's what we're here for."

Raven shook her head. "It's not that. Its just there is so much to do. We've all got responsibilities back on the reservations. Old habits die hard as well. We've survived so long with minimal resources that its hard to break away. What was that?" The VC-144 had lurched sharply.

"Just coming to a halt, we'll be out of here in a couple of minutes. Our bags are in the belly pod, I guess the boys down there will look after them. I guess, to them, a diplomatic party is almost as important as a private plane full of high rollers."

By the time the party had disembarked, the VC-144s belly pod had been opened and their bags unloaded into the two limousines that were parked under the wings. The ubiquitous "boys" were waiting to usher their guests in. As they passed, Lillith slipped them tips that they managed to make vanish without any obvious effort.

"We're taking youse guys to the Tropicana Hotel?" It was, just barely, a question. Normally a diplomatic party would stay in the national embassy but the US didn't have an Embassy in Cuba. Very few people did. The exact national status of the Cuban "Government" was nebulous to say the least. Privately, The Seer believed the real reason why so few governments recognized the gangsters running Cuba as a legitimate administration was that it would make comparisons between the conduct of gangsters and diplomats all too easy. So, diplomatic parties stayed in the Tropicana. It was, after all, where Meyer Lansky lived.

"The Tropicana, yes."

"Right. Youse guys'll have to be patient. Shifts're changing at the casinos and the roads will be blocked. We'll take you round the back way, miss the worst of it, but it's still a bad time for the ride. The Boulevard's eight miles long now, growing each year. Two more Casinos due to open end of the year, The Steppes and The Riviera."

"Who owns them if it isn't an indelicate question?" In the back of the car, Lillith's ears pricked open. The question was in the casual voice The Seer used when he was onto something.

"Not those two. The Steppes is owned by MGM, film guys. The Riviera's a consortium, the Hilton group and one of the airlines. Think its TWA, might be wrong there. Guess the Families have an interest in both, wouldn't know that." The wiseguy finished the phrase with a definite hint of 'and I wouldn't tell you if I did.'

"Sounds healthy." The Seer looked around the limousine. "What do you think of the new Packards?"

"Good for us, nice engine. Not too well put together though, but are any of them these days? Not my kind of wheels though. Whad'ya drive?"

"Chevvy Camaro Super Sport. Convertible. It's in dock at the moment, it doesn't like Washington winters."

"Nice. I've ordered a new Cord. Reckon it'll give Chevvy and Ford a run for their money?"

In the back, Lillith and Raven glanced at each other and raised their eyebrows as The Seer and their driver drifted off into a long and involved debate over automobiles. Privately, Lillith wondered if there was anywhere else in the world where a limo driver would be talking cars with the head of a diplomatic delegation. Probably not, she concluded. Cuba was unique.

The Tropicana reception staff was well-briefed. The luggage was already on its way up; the reception desk had their keys ready. "Sir, Ma'am. Room 1410." The receptionist gave their key to The Seer and Raven held her breath. This was a little surprise she and Lillith had set up and she wanted to see how The Seer would react. There was fear mixed with anticipation, she was afraid he would be shocked, reject her. Instead, he grinned broadly and took it. "We'd better have one each I think. We'll probably be on different schedules most of the day."

At that point Raven remembered Inanna's words. 'He's always ahead of you and its really wearing being with somebody who knows what you'll do before you do.' She finally saw what Inanna had meant. It was disappointing to realize that her surprise had been anticipated. Then, she saw Lillith smiling and guessed that Lillith had known their little joke would be welcomed. Lillith wouldn't have let her go through with it if it wouldn't be.

"Ohhh, look Mom, she's from The Nations." They were crossing the reception area when the little boy's voice cut through the gentle background murmur.

"Johnny, don't point, its rude. . . . . Johnny, come back here."

A split second later Raven felt a tug on her sleeve. "Ma'am, do you know Brave Eagle?"

She looked down at the face staring up at her, then settled a little on her heels to drop closer to his height. "I'm afraid not. Brave Eagle is Oneida and I'm Shoshone. But I know some men on our reservation who are just like him."

"I'm sorry, Ma'am, but Johnny loves Warpath. Refused to miss an episode, even when he had measles." The boy's mother was embarrassed at the disturbance and was smiling apologetically at Raven and The Seer. Her embarrassment grew even more obvious when she suddenly realized who The Seer was. But, she seemed a genuinely nice woman and The Seer decided it was time to let her off the hook.

"No problem ma'am. No problem at all. Have a good holiday." Then, the Seer and Raven stepped into a lift and the doors slid shut behind them.

"Two years, not bad." The Seer was grinning broadly. Raven looked confused. "Two years ago he'd have called you a squaw or a redskin. And his mother would have been frightened of you. Now, you're from 'The Nations' and she's embarrassed because inconveniencing you is impolite. All because of a successful television program. Attitudes are changing at last Raven, we're making headway."

The Presidential Suite, Tropicana Hotel, Havana, Cuba

"Do you want a drink, Seer?" Meyer Lansky opened the liquor cabinet and surveyed the array of bottles within. "What can I get you?"

"Whisky please, The McCallan if you've got it. Straight."

"25 year old McCallan coming up. And I'm glad you drink it like a civilized man. One of the boys tried to put ginger ale into it so we put him into the bay. Wearing cement boots."

The Seer wasn't sure whether Lansky was joking or not. He watched the President of Cuba pour a generous mixture of the whisky into a glass, then take an unopened bottle of Johnny Walker Swing, crack the seal and pour out a measure for himself. Into a glass that came out a sealed plastic bag.

"I guess that flame head of yours will tell me that nobody can stop a skilled poisoner?" Lansky grinned at his guest. "Yeah, we'd noticed how people who cause really serious trouble get sick when she's around. Don't worry, we noticed because we're all crooks, nobody else made that connection. She's right too, nobody can stop a poisoner.

"When we were kids, Charlie Luciano, Bennie Siegel and I had a run in with a guy called Johnnie. He was shorting us on deals and that wasn't done. If you wanna be a successful crook you gotta be honest with them you work for. Otherwise they get mad and turn you in. So we took him out to the swamps threw him out and used him for target practice as he made a run for it. Three of us hit him four times. Anyway, he made it out of sight and got to the emergency ward. He swore outta charge so we had to finish him. Arranged for his wife to get a juiced-up chicken. She never knew it came from us so she took it in for him. He ate some, got real, real sick and guessed he better keep his mouth shut. His wife never guessed, she sued the hospital for giving him food poisoning." Lansky sighed. "Life was simple back then."

"Running a country isn't what you thought is it?"

Lansky shook his head. "Sounds so easy. When we was on the mainland, we always said how come these guys in Washington act so crazy? We had all the answers. You know Bennie Siegel put a contract out on Adolf Hitler? And Himmler? Only Mussolini talked him out of it. Seemed so easy to do things our way. Only it ain't. Curious on something, Seer. How come you here? I was expecting State Department, some nobody telling us they're dropping the boom. How did NSC get into this?"

"Meyer, Cuba isn't a political problem. State deals with external relations, we've honestly no idea what Cuba is. You and your associates, you've broken every diplomatic rule in the book. If it's any consolation, anytime anybody writes a political science textbook in the future, each chapter is going to have to end 'Cuba under Mob rule was, of course, the exception to the above.'

"So if State comes here, that's an admission that Cuba is an external entity. At the moment, nobody is sure of that. You're pretty much immune from external pressure now because nobody knows whether we think you're part of the US of A or not. Nobody is going to take the chance of messing with us directly.

"As for lowering the boom on you, that isn't going to happen. It's politically impossible, no way are we going to invade America's favorite playground unless everything hits the fan. Cuba isn't a political problem, it's a security problem, a national security problem and that's why we're here. Cuba's wide open, you've got no defenses, nothing. If somebody like the Caliphate tries a bioassault on you, there's nothing you can do to stop it and the volume of traffic from here to the mainland means we'd catch it as well. You've seen those people-haulers at Dillinger International? Any one of them could carry plague rats."

"Yet defenseless-us saved your asses, Seer. Would you have stopped the plague rats without us?"

"No, we lucked out. That's another reason why we're here. Just how do you plan to stop plague rats getting in here?"

"You said we got no defenses; well, that ain't true Seer. We talk to the mobs in Europe, the Corsicans, the Mafia in Italy, the Russian Obshina. We give them a skim from the take, they watch our back. Not a big skim, but Cuba produces so much money, a small percentage is a lot of hard cash. Risk free for them, and we're useful other ways. So we watch, we hear what goes on. Its not much, but its better than nothing and money's a powerful weapon. From now on, we hear anything that makes us worried, you get to hear it as well. And if your Navy wants to patrol our waters, what can we do to stop you?"

Lansky finished his drink and poured another, topping up his guest's glass in the process. "We can talk more about that later. Got another question for you. Your Shoshone girlfriend is hitting our casinos already, gambling a little, watching and learning a lot. For setting up their own we assume. Not that the prospect worries us, much. Cuba's an experience, more than just casinos. If anything, the Indian ones will give more people a taste for gambling.

"Anyway, so what's up with NSC and the Indians? How come you're helping them out? That ain't national security and don't tell me its because of your comare back in 1410. What you playing at?"

"Pure national security, Meyer. The Indian reservations sit on the biggest reserves of strategic materials in the continental United States. It's in our national interest to have free access to them. Moving in on them the old-fashioned way, we catch all kinds of nausea. So, we set the Indians up so they can stand on their own feet, make them rich, de-emphasize the reservations and we end up getting our strategic materials without any fuss. And since we're righting a wrong in the process, one that should never have been committed and has been a stain on our national honor ever since, we even look good doing it. Sound common sense?"

Lansky nodded. It was his old maxim: never wave guns when you can negotiate a deal. "You seen this, Seer?" He walked to the huge bay windows overlooking the Golden Boulevard. Night had fallen and the glare of the neon and floodlights turned the darkness into a dazzling cascade of multi-colored jewels on black velvet.

"When we came here, Cuba was a cess pit, a nothing. Poor people living in a rich land and getting ground into the dirt by a bunch of foreign big shots who never came here and didn't give a damn about them. Now look at it. We may have broken every one of your rules, but we've brought more wealth here in fifteen years than anybody else has in a century. And we've shared it out too. Not because we're good guys but because its the smart thing to do.

"You really think we've done so badly Seer? We've given birth to a new country here, perhaps this is how people want to live. Everybody here knows who his local boss is. If they have a beef, they see him direct about it. If the sidewalk has holes, he fills them in, If somebody is disturbing the tranquility, he reasons with them. He kicks some of his income upstairs to his superior and he lives on what's left. The button man lives in his block. Everybody there knows where to find him, they know where he eats, where he has coffee, the neighborhood women know his wife and comare and can take their special problems to them. A smart button man listens to his people because that keeps things quiet and keeps the money flowing in.

"If a button man is good - if his neighborhood is quiet and the people in it are happy and he kicks up his share to his superior, he gets moved to a bigger and/or more prosperous block where he earns more and kicks more upstairs. If he doesn't make the grade, he'll get pushed down, sent back to the mainland or (if he's caused trouble) he vanishes. If he continues to do well, eventually he gets Made and will have several Soldiers and associates reporting to him. And so it goes; he can either advance, stay in place or sink, all determined by his ability.

"The families have areas of the cities which are theirs to run. If there is a dispute between two people it goes to the next level management who have a Sit-Down. The superior listens to both parties and makes a judgement. And don't get me wrong Seer, when a Captain makes a decision it's a "this is like it is - capiche?" judgement. Nobody's going to argue it. Right at the top is the Commission and wouldn't you like to know who they are? Well, I'll tell you because they all live here. It's the heads of the five New York families plus the major non-New York people. They're the top of the tree and everybody's kick backs eventually end up with them. That so different from income tax, Seer?"

"Look, that sounds good on paper Meyer but the system works because there are huge amounts of money flowing in at all levels and this funds everything. Everybody involved has got to know that if the money stops, the system with all its luxury and freedom will fall apart. Just how long is this place going to last before somebody decided to grab the pot while the going is good?"

"You tell me, you're the Seer, the great strategist. They say you can see into the future. Well, Mister Strategist, how much of a future does our Cuba have?"

The Seer leaned back, his eyes defocused as the strands of possibilities played in his mind. "A lot depends on you Meyer, you're holding this place together. What happens when you die? Anybody going to step into your shoes? If nobody does, there's going to be a power struggle over who takes your place. The various families will end up fighting over the prize and the place will tear itself apart.

"Then we'll have to invade and stabilize the place our way with Uncle Sam's Misguided Children. Oh, it may hang together as long as the present Commission survives but how long will that be? Will their replacements see things the same way? Meyer, what you've got here is pretty unstable unless you've got a succession set up. My guess is that you have, in part at least. You're training successors in your image, the scrupulously honest crook who's a member of nothing but trusted by everybody.

"The question is if you've got time to get a successor trained and accepted. That's something only the gods can answer. Even allowing for that, I guess your Cuba, Mob-run Cuba, isn't going to survive. It has another 15 years at a minimum, twenty five at a max. Might make thirty but it's going to be hard.

"Meyer, you're not giving birth to a new country here; at best your midwifing it. Look around, the process has already started. MGM and TWA are moving in with hotel-Casinos of their own. They're better at running businesses than you are, they'll make more money at them than you will. In time, they'll buy into the ones you own. You'll sell because you'll make more money from your share than you did from when you owned it all.

"Eventually, you'll all be minority shareowners here and the Casinos will be owned by legitimate business. They'll want laws. Settling a dispute by sending 'the boys' around to give somebody the elbow won't cut it any more. As much as everything you have here seems to work, the bureaucracy needed for civic functions is hard to come by. You're buying it at the moment but as this place grows, so will demands for things like education, water purity, sewage disposal and so on. The problem is the lack of people qualified to run large scale services like water, power, healthcare and who are willing to work under the "sleeping with fishes" method of management. Particularly as it would have to be exercised at all levels of the organization. The only way out will be paying large sums for the professional expertise and that's going to cut the profit margins by a fair deal.

"And your Mob is already changing. How many of your lower rank guys are Italian and how many Cuban? Those Cubans will work their way up and the Mob here will become more Cuban than anything else. They'll become legitimate. The families will become political parties, the Commission will become the government. It's a fast-forward repeat of what's always happened. The biggest, toughest, smartest criminals and warlords seize power, become the government, then they give themselves fancy titles and pretend they never were anything other than the ruling class.

"What matters now is how you stamp them. You train them to do things your way, Meyer, Cuba has a good chance of stabilizing. In twenty five or thirty years, people will look back on these days with nostalgia, they'll say how much better things were when the Mob ran everything. There'll be real crime then, because there always is. You've already got the first elements of an island-wide police force. People will point to today and ask why things ever changed. But they won't really want to go back.

"So my recommendation to our government is that we hold the ring for you. We'll make it known that Cuba really is under our protection, we'll do what we can to back up your own security arrangements. Meyer, whatever happens here, keep it peaceful, keep it civilized and we'll leave things to work their own way out. If there's gun battles in the streets and our citizens are in mortal danger as a result, we'll send in the Marines.

"So, the future is very much up to you Meyer. You're in a unique position in more ways than you know. It's very rare for a single person to hold the keys to how a country develops. You get your succession set up, you get the Commission to accept that they won't be the power here forever, that the seeds sown in Cuba will outgrow them and what you're helping build here will last."

Lansky nodded. "I'm a professional gambler Seer, I always have been. And I know how to calculate odds. I'm betting we can pull it off, that a rich, stable Cuba will grow out of this. Want to drink to that?" The two men touched their glasses and looked down at the blazing mass of lights that marked Havana's Golden Boulevard. The Boulevard lead somewhere; where to was something only time would tell.

EPILOGUE

Tea Room, Raffles Hotel, Singapore

"Want me to be mother, ducks?" Nell sat forward slightly and lifted the "Chinese" willow pattern teapot. She didn't get much of a chance to act as hostess at a traditional tea party and was making every moment of this one count.

"If you would please Nell." She smiled and filled The Seer's cup with China tea. Any good hostess knew her guest's preferences and Nell was a very good hostess indeed. She'd learned the art living in Pall Mall and the skills had never left her. "How's your principal doing in there?"

'There' was the conference room where the final parts of the South Sea Islands agreement were being hammered out. The American presence was a formality, as was that of Thailand and Australia. The three nations were 'observers' only. The real negotiations were between Indian and Japan. Thailand and Australia had some interests in the final settlement but the presence of the new Secretary of State, William P. Rogers, was purely a courtesy. As Nixon had remarked in Cabinet, sending the Secretary of State to remind everybody to play nice was cheaper than keeping bombers circling the conference room.

As Roger's Executive Assistant, Nell had made sure her principal had everything he needed to hand. But, he hadn't needed much help, just the patience to sit there and look sinister.

"Pretty well. He commended everybody on making peace so promptly and on repatriating the prisoners of war in good health. Said the United States had noted that both sides were treating the wounded in an honorable and decent manner. Then he kept quiet. Did very well indeed." Nell delicately offered a tray of finger sandwiches around. She'd very carefully specified the fillings and made sure the crusts had been trimmed in the approved manner.

The Seer took one and nibbled it. A fish spread and cucumber. "You know people, this reminds me of Avebury. Those were good days back then." He sighed and finished his sandwich.

"Ladies, Gentlemen, please excuse my temerity in interrupting you but I would like to pay my respects to the Executive Assistant to the Secretary of State. My name is Lal Krishna Advani, I am the new leader of the BJP in India."

"Welcome Sir. India or China?" Nell smiled gently at her new guest. Most depictions of her had her speaking with a cockney accent. In fact, her accent was Oxford English. Advani smiled when he heard it.

"India please. With a little milk but no sugar."

Nell poured on his tea. As she did so, The Seer took the chance to introduce himself. "Please take a seat Sir. I believe congratulations are in order. I hear you have replaced Atal Bihari Vajpayee as the leader of the BJP?"

"I have that honor although I am not so sure that congratulations are entirely merited. Being the new party leader means I have much to do to reassemble our party. Between them Jaswant Singh and Mister Vajpayee have split the BJP badly. It is my decision to steer a middle path, avoiding the excess nationalism of the previous government while pursuing a less centralized and more liberal economic policy than Congress. Between ourselves though, I fear though that we will not have a chance of regaining power for some years. I fear that I will carry the burden of rebuilding the party but my successor will gain the rewards. Mister Vajpayee was. . . . . ." Advani stopped, searching for the proper English phrase.

"A dozy great pillock?" Nell offered demurely.

Advani grinned with delight. "Yes, that's it. That's exactly it. That is the description I was searching for." He sighed slightly. "English is such an expressive language sometimes; what would we do without it?"

Nell offered around the silver tray containing the little iced sponge cakes, each with a spot of cream on top, under the icing. "It's so hard to get real cream cakes in America. Most of them have a horrible artificial cream. Sir, if you visit our country, I advise that you avoid them, they are a sad disappointment." She took one of the little cakes herself and bit into it. To her delight, the cream was real and fresh. The Raffles was living up to its reputation.

Advani exchanged a few more pleasantries before taking his leave. The Raffles staff refilled the teapots, one of the waiters appearing with a small tray carrying finger-pieces of cheesecake. Nell raised an eyebrow at the delivery.

"Ma'am, the Ambassador-Plenipotentiary from Thailand was asking after your party and is on her way here now. Raspberry and white chocolate cheesecake is her favorite delicacy. So the staff thought you should be prepared."

Sure enough, the Ambassador appeared almost immediately and sat down with a cup of China tea and the first of a series of pieces of the cheesecake. "Your Secretary of State is doing well, Seer; he is conveying just the right air of genial menace. But I think it is unnecessary. The agreements are all very much as we originally contemplated."

"Good to hear Snake. On both counts. This was an avoidable incident, one we could all have done without."

The Ambassador blinked at the implied criticism. "It's easy for you Seer, America is the undisputed world hegemon and you maintain that position by decisively smacking down any who would challenge that position. You have very few allies so maintaining the alliances you do have is easy. But what would you do if Russia suddenly started going off and attempting some adventures of its own. It could happen, you know."

"It could. It's not likely at this time but its certainly a possibility." The Seer looked pensive for a few seconds. "It is a good point, one we'll have to address. That's the weakness with any alliance system. Governments don't have permanent friends, they have permanent interests."

"And ours are more permanent than most." Lillith's quip came out mixed with sponge cake.

"That is so, but it makes little difference here. At the moment, Russian and American interests are so closely aligned that the present close alliance is almost inevitable. Russia is a military power certainly, a very strong one, but its immense manpower losses in the War mean it's also very vulnerable. Our firepower offsets that and in exchange we get the bases to project that firepower. Our money is helping to fund Russian economic recovery but that money is dependent on an economy supported by access to Siberian Oil. Yet, that oil is only easily recoverable because of our technology. We and the Russians are linked into a lockstep and it'll be at least two generations before that situation changes. By then our security and economic interests are likely to be so tightly integrated that we couldn't disentangle them even if we wanted to."

"Which is very good for you but it doesn't apply to us. The Triple Alliance is based on our national objectives certainly but the degree of convergence is much less. The trouble in Indonesia is a good example of that. There, we are in direct conflict with both of our partners and them with us. The Indonesian authorities themselves are not much help in keeping things on a low key. They have never forgiven the Australians for making off with their largely-Christian easternmost islands and turning them into a Australian protectorate. The Indians have their interests also. Bali for example is mostly

Hindu and is a de-facto Indian protectorate. That means each of us is likely to wander off in their own direction at regular intervals."

"Then you're going to have to find ways of binding the components of your alliance together. Come on Snake, you've had enough practice at this sort of thing."

"I know. That is what I wanted to talk to you about. The Australian Government and our own have decided to make a start building undersea colonies. To try and recover the mineral reserves on the seabed and exploit offshore oil and gas reserves. The undersea world is barely explored; we know little of it. Who knows what treasures we will find down there? The economic rewards will be great and the joint effort will help to bind the alliance together more closely. The project will be of the greatest value from many points of view. In some ways, it could almost be described as a lifeboat." The Seer looked up sharply at the last word but the Ambassador carried on, apparently without noticing. "We need expertise though, in offshore deep water work, like oil drilling from surface rigs. Is there a way this can be arranged?"

"Probably. The simplest way is to start genuine offshore drilling rigs by selling exploration rights with a caveat that any production facilities must employ local labor. We can take it from there. There are any number of companies who would be interested in getting in on the ground floor of a project that large. "

"Beware boss, strangers approaching." Lillith's voice was quiet but urgent. Two Japanese were approaching, an older man, obviously the senior of the pair and a younger. They strode through the tearoom, ignoring everybody in their path. The other clients scattered before them. *Ignoring was probably the wrong word,* Lillith reflected. *That meant being conscious of the other's existence. These two gave no sign that they were aware of the presence of the other occupants. That badged them as firmly as their insignia-less uniforms. They were Kempeitai.*

"His Excellency the Foreign Minister has asked us to convey to your Secretary of State the appreciation of our Government for your assistance in bringing this unfortunate affair to a close and wishes to arrange for a meeting with him so that we can, perhaps, resolve some of the issues that have divided our two countries." The older of the two men spoke in a monotone.

"I will advise Secretary Rogers of your kind words and he will, I am sure, make a point of seeing you at the earliest possible opportunity."

The two Japanese nodded sharply in acknowledgment, then prepared to leave but as they did so, their eyes flicked over the assembled group with surprise that only just stopped short of amazement. Then they turned on their heels and left.

In their wake, the tea party also stared at each other, dumbfounded by the light that was flickering in the backs of their minds. The strange sensation that they experienced when meeting others of their kind. A familiar, almost welcome, feeling yet one that was utterly unexpected. They knew that the two men from the Kempeitai had the same feeling and had been equally stunned. Were they even aware there were others like them?

"Both of them?" The Seer asked quietly.

The Ambassador, Lillith and Nell exchanged glances and nodded. "No doubt about it ducks. Both of them."

"Now that," said The Seer, "is a complication."

THE END

998438

Printed in Great Britain by
Amazon.co.uk, Ltd.,
Marston Gate.